"An enchanting literary debut – I couldn't put it down!"
Lavie Tidhar, World Fantasy Award-winning author of
A Man Lies Dreaming *and* Central Station

"*Under the Pendulum Sun* is a weird, ingenious, and ravishing story of the Fae and the outsiders driven to discover their secrets, told with a heady melange of disturbing beauty and enticing dangers."
Kate Elliott, author of the Court of Fives series

"Hauntingly beautiful and masterfully told. This looks like the start of a brilliant career."
Keith Yatsuhashi, author of Kokoro

"An evocative, claustrophobic Gothic novel with strikingly creepy set-pieces, which repeatedly dislocates its reader's and characters' worldview in a forceful examination of faith and the power of stories."
Aliette de Bodard, Nebula, Locus and BSFA Award-winning author of The House of Shattered Wings

"Jeannette Ng's imagery is breathtaking, her setting dark and delightful, and her use of theology is pure genius. Like some sinister elf, *Under the Pendulum Sun* will steal your imagination and never give it back."
N S Dolkart, author of Among the Fallen

JEANNETTE NG

UNDER THE PENDULUM SUN

A Novel of the Fae

ANGRY
ROBOT

ANGRY ROBOT
An imprint of Watkins Media Ltd

Unit 11, Shepperton House
89 Shepperton Road
London N1 3DF
UK

angryrobotbooks.com
twitter.com/angryrobotbooks
A sin like salt

An Angry Robot paperback original 2017

Set in Meridien and Modern No 20
Cover by John Coulthart

ISBN 978 0 85766 727 4
EBook ISBN 978 0 85766 728 1

Printed and bound in the United Kingdom by TJ International.

9 8 7 6 5 4 3 2

To the fictions of our childhood,
I add this apocrypha.

PART ONE
Gethsemane

Chapter 1

The Quiet in the Port

Great and ancient empires, Mahomedan and Heathen, have received a shock by the prowess of British arms, nerved and strengthened by GOD, which has broken down strong, and hitherto invulnerable barriers; and so a way has been opened for His blessed Gospel to pass from here to the remotest bounds of reality.

Thus, Palestine is now accessible; and Englishmen may travel freely through the length and breadth of the Holy Land. The enlarged, and still enlarging, boundaries of our dominions in India, open new fields of labour for the Lord's servants. China, its forbidding gates forced open by war, calls out to the faithful.

But it is the Faelands that arrest our attention. Arcadia's vast unknown, which has been for many ages closed against us and the Divine Word, is at last made clear and knowable. And, as Britain has had the high and singular honour, in the wonderful providence of GOD, the Lord of Hosts, of breaking down that barrier, it is but apposite that she should have the honour of being the first to carry in the balm of the blessed Gospel.

Rev William E Matheson, "Appeal on Behalf of Arcadia", NEWS OF THE WORLD, 5th December 1843

My brother and I grew up dreaming of new worlds.

Our father had owned a paltry library of books and a subscription to the most fashionable periodicals, all of which we gleefully devoured. We would linger by the gate, impatient for the post that would bring new sustenance for our hungry imaginations. Bored of waiting, we told each other stories of what *could* be. I remember my brother, Laon, finding one of our tin soldiers at the bottom of his pocket. The red paint was barely worn and it looked up at me with a long-suffering expression. I snatched it from Laon's hand, declaring it the Duke of Wellington, and ran off claiming that the two of us would adventure together. Like Lord Byron or Marco Polo.

We invented whole new worlds for our soldiers to explore: Gaaldine, Exina, Alcona, Zamorna. From our father's books we learnt of pilgrims and missionaries and explorers, and so we wrote of grand journeys, long and winding. As we read of the discovery of the Americas, of the distant Orient, and of strange Arcadia we added similar places to our ever more intricate maps. We mimicked the newspapers and periodicals we read, writing new ones for our tin soldiers. In the tiniest, tiniest writing, we detailed their exploits, the politics of their parliaments, and the scandals of their socialites.

But for all our stories, our imaginations were small and provincial. For the talk of tropics and deserts, our childish fictions filled them with the same oaks and aspens that grew in our garden. We built on their landscape, exotic buildings that were just our little   whitewashed church in Birdforth in disguise. We rained down on strange soil the same Yorkshire rain as that which drenched our skins and drove us inside, peeling off our clothes, housebound by the weather and desperate for diversion.

As such, I could never have imagined Arcadia.

I was familiar with all the tales, mind. The first explorers had spun overwrought stories upon their return: *Until I laid eyes upon the Faelands, I was blind, and now I see. I have never seen colour, nor grandeur, nor wonder, until I saw the shores of Arcadia.* Later travellers were more prosaic, but still offered no adequate description. There were few maps and fewer landscapes available, and almost all of them had been denounced by one explorer or another as fraudulent.

For all the many contradictory theories I had read on the relationship between our world and that of the fae, I was no more enlightened. It was said to be underground, but not. It overlaid our own, but not. It was another place, but not.

All I do know was this: Our ship, *The Quiet*, sailed in circles on the North Sea for six whole weeks. On the dawn of the first day of the seventh week, my wavering compass informed me that we were heading straight back towards smog-shrouded London.

Nervously, I clutched my compass. My brother had given it to me before he left for Arcadia to become a missionary. He was among the first to be tasked to bring the Word of God to the Fair Folk. He had been there three years now and had been nothing but terse in his correspondence. I tried to swallow the worry that consumed me, but it knotted around my heart.

That was when I caught my first glimpse of the Faelands.

Impossibly white cliffs rose from the white sea foam. For a moment my mind feared it to be Dover, that I had simply returned to those mundane cliffs of chalk and stone, that no foreign land awaited me.

Yet those cliffs were too white, too stark. They could not be Dover.

Behind them I expected the rolling hills of home. But instead the landscape was jagged and jutting knife-sharp from the sea. It seemed cobbled together, each part eerily familiar but set against something other. I recognised the leering profile of a hill, the knuckle-like crest of a mountain. Yet as wind and wave shifted the shapes, it all seemed different again and my strained eyes watered.

The Quiet glided gull-like into a wide, wide river. Unfamiliar structures sprawled against the green grey mass of the land in arching, crumbling lines. Squinting, I made out the spined turrets, barbed roofs and oddly leaning walls. For a moment I thought the town to be an endless dragon coiled around the edge of the harbour, huffing smoke from its distended nostrils. It shimmered, the shingled roofs seeming scale-like, and then it *shifted*.

I blinked, and buildings were back to where I remembered them. There was no dragon made of shifting structures. Just a town of crowded streets.

The ship heaved under our feet like an unruly stallion. A shout broke out among the sailors in words I didn't understand. They started busying. As they clambered up and down the ratlines and hauled rope this way and that, they muttered invocations under their breath. I wanted to chide them for their superstition but we were sailing to Arcadia and none of it made any sense.

I tried to stay out of the way as the sailors blasphemously crossed themselves in the name of salt, sea and soil.

An unnatural wind curled around the sail, whipping it back and forth. It fluttered full and then deflated with each breath of the wind. *The Quiet* became anything but as the timber groaned. The cabin boy flung his arms around the prow and cooed at it.

It was a long while before the ship was tamed and brought to shore.

And then I was simply there, stepping unsteadily from the ship into the shamble of a docks. Twisting streets full of seeming people reminded me of crowded London.

The ground was a shock to my feet, and I staggered. My carpet bag and trunk joined me on the docks. I fumbled for my documents and scanned the milling crowd for my guide. I tried not to notice the oddities of each figure – the strange colours and the wings and the horns. There would be time aplenty for the wonder of Arcadia once my bags had been unpacked and I had found my brother.

"Miss Catherine Helstone, I presume? The missionary's sister?"

With an upturned nose, round chin and soft, brown eyes, the woman I turned to meet was perhaps one of the least ethereal people I'd ever met. She was shorter than me. But as her skirts hung long and limp, without a murmur of wave or curve, her figure seemed tall and lank. She dressed in sombre, mortal colours, her gown being a muddy shade of navy blue and her shawl more grey than white.

A smile spread across her freckled cheeks as I nodded.

"I thought I recognised you," she said. "You look just like your brother."

"I do?" Though Laon and I shared the same dark hair and strong nose, few remarked on our resemblance. Features that were handsome on a man were becoming on a woman's frame.

"I'm Ariel Davenport, as I'm sure you know. Your guide."

"I am very pleased to finally meet you," I said. We had exchanged a handful of letters through the Missionary Society in preparation of my journey.

She shook my hand vigorously between her two clasped ones and swooped in two sharp kisses. Her smile getting wider, she added, "Though I'm not the real one."

"I'm... I'm not sure I follow."

"I'm not the real Ariel Davenport, you see." There was an unpleasant edge to her laugh; it was a touch too brittle. "I'm her changeling."

"Her changeling?" Many of the intermediaries between the fae and humans were said to be changelings. One of Captain

Cook's botanists was said to have learnt of their fae origins upon arrival to Arcadia and was conscripted to their cause. Despite such accounts, changelings never seemed quite real to me. But then, given how sheltered I had been, the French were never quite real. "So you were raised as her–"

Ariel Davenport gave an exasperated sigh and rolled her eyes at my ignorance. "She was a human child, I was a fairy-made simulacrum of a human child. We traded places. I grew up there and she grew up here."

"What became of her?" I asked.

"That's not for me to tell." She gave me a disarmingly lopsided smile and in an impeccably proper accent, added, "And it's hardly polite to ask."

"I- I'm sorry," I stuttered. I dropped my gaze. Our nanny, Tessie, used to keep a pair of steel scissors by our beds to ward off faerie abductors. In restlessness and boredom, I once said to Laon that we should close the scissors, so that they no longer formed the sign of the cross, and invite in the fae. He was horrified. And so I never suggested it again.

"Regardless, now I'm here again. Because I'm useful to them and I understand you humans," said Miss Davenport. "Speaking of which, I am most remiss in my duties. I should hardly keep you talking here all day." She waved for an expectant-looking porter to hoist up my trunk onto his shoulders. His sallow skin glinted green as it caught the sunlight.

Miss Davenport hummed tunelessly as she led our way to the rounded carriage. I tried not to stare at the flaring gills of the porter as he heaved my trunk and bags onto the carriage. He lashed them with rope to a wizened stem that jutted from the middle of the roof.

"How far to Gethsemane?" I asked, an ominous shudder passing through me as I said the name.

"That what the missionary called the shambles?" said the coachman.

"Yes, I believe so," I said. "It is where Reverend Laon Helstone resides. Though I believe his predecessor did the naming."

The coachman grunted, turning his attention from me.

"You've not answered me," I pressed. Perhaps it was simply that Laon's predecessor was overly enamoured with winning the martyr's crown. After all, what other reason has one to name a building after the garden in which Christ spent his final hours before his Crucifixion? "How far to Gethsemane?"

He tutted to himself, the space between his brows folding like an accordion. "Two revelations and an epiphany? No, there has to be a shortcut... Two painful memories and a daydr–"

"Sixteen miles," interrupted Miss Davenport. "It is sixteen miles away. We'll arrive well before dark."

I nodded uncertainly.

"He says that for the tourists," she added, glaring at the muttering coachman.

As I alighted, a cacophony of bells chimed midday.

Hand still resting on the carriage door, I turned and looked up. My breath caught, heart bursting with expectation. I had read so much of the pendulum sun of the Faelands. Foolishly, I half-expected to see it waver in the sky before rushing east again, like my own pendant did in my experimenting hands when I was trying to comprehend the very idea.

It did not, of course.

The sun was significantly larger than the one that had been a constant of my life. But it seemed otherwise the same, stinging my eyes as I squinted at it.

"It doesn't move *that* fast," said Miss Davenport. "You won't see much by just looking up. Even at midday."

I looked back down, white spots swimming in my eyes from

the brightness. I pressed my own cold fingers to my closed eyes. I knew I wouldn't see anything, of course. Arcadian days were as long as earthly ones.

Still, the temptation had been too much.

"Sorry. I should know better," I murmured, shuffling into the carriage and sitting myself on the dappled upholstery. I even knew that I was at the very edges of the Faelands and that many of the oddities of the sun's pendulum-like trajectory would not be discernible here.

"Your brother also did that when he first got here," she said.

I smiled. For all the distance that had come between us, I felt closer to him again.

Laon and I were inseparable from the second I returned from the Clergy Daughters' School after the death of our sister, Agnes. I was seven and a half when I was bidden to press my lips on the cold, dead skin of her corpse. I tried not to think of the coffin laid out on the table. Of how the corpse seemed like a stranger wearing my sister's clothes, of how hollow the promise of other worlds seemed then. I laced my own fingers, not thinking of the warm hands of my brother holding mine when we stood watching the soil swallow up the coffin.

"It's not very far, Gethsemane," said Miss Davenport, interrupting my reverie. "But it's outside of Sesame, you know, the port town. Not many people go beyond the borders of that. Almost all the other missionaries we've had set up in Sesame or one of the other ports. Things are rather more earthly there, you know. Though perhaps it doesn't matter. You do not seem alarmed by the carriage."

I glanced about the bare, woody interior of the carriage and calfskin upholstery, which was scored by a disconcerting pattern of scrape marks.

"The seats are a little lumpy?" I ventured, resetting myself on the stubborn cushion.

"Ah, yes. The fabric is.... We are but borrowing the skin from the cows."

"What?" I was understandably incredulous.

"It's my fault, really," she said, sheepishly, scratching her upturned nose. "The artisans had no idea what a carriage was so I had to describe it to them. I did so incorrectly, or rather in ways that weren't correctly understood. I try not to make that sort of mistake, but I was in a hurry and old fishbrains out there has a very specific mind. And more used to making animals. Point is that I forgot to mention that the cow was dead when you made seats out of their skin, so here we–"

"How is he?" I interrupted. I almost dared not ask. The thought clasped a cold hand around my throat. The allegedly living upholstery under me roiled; the carriage rumbled and I felt sick to the core. I had kept my worries in check for a very, very long time and now, and seeing the possibility of a reprieve, it was all the harder to endure. "Laon. My brother... the Reverend, I mean."

Miss Davenport shrugged. "I don't really know how to answer that. He's as I've always known him. Alive and healthy, I suppose, you care about that." She frowned, her high forehead furrowing.

"I- Yes, I do. Very much." My fingers hurting with how hard I was holding myself, I forced myself to loosen my hands. I would be seeing him soon enough.

"Why! Pleasantries are a lot harder than I remember them to be." Miss Davenport giggled behind her glove, a piercing twitter of a noise. "He's very well. Better than the mission, truth be told. Which I probably shouldn't say, but it's not easy to be a missionary around these parts. He's conducting services no one comes to, begging to gain access to the rest of the Faelands and asking them questions about their–" She cleared her throat and continued in a deep, ponderous tone, "cosmological and metaphysical importance."

I attempted a laugh, but faltered. "That doesn't sound like him."

"That is rather the point," she retorted. "That's where the humour comes from."

After a silence, Miss Davenport filled the empty space of the carriage with amiable, effortless chatter. She described to me the properties of the pendulum sun and the fish moon. Much of what she said was familiar to me from my reading, but it was good to be distracted by her voice. Too long have I spent alone with my own thoughts aboard *The Quiet*.

I found myself staring and studying her mannerisms more than her words, trying to detect her fae origins. At first glance she seemed as human as me with that scatter of freckles and lopsided smile. Still, she had that awkwardness I heard rumoured of changelings, a certain deficiency in their simulation of humanity. Tessie once told me to stop my tantrum and to behave so as to prove myself not a changeling.

"You could look outside, if you want, Miss Helstone. The window does open."

After excessive fumbling, I unlatched the window and leaned out. Mist closed around the spiny sprawl that was Sesame, like layers of gauzy curtains. We were alone on the road as it stretched into dense fog. Frowning, I could make out the hunched canopies of bearded trees. Above us, a cloud-bruised sky was heavy with rain.

"The weather isn't always like this," said Miss Davenport. "But at least you'll feel at home. You could pretend that it's moors behind the fog. It'll chase away all those feelings of homesickness you feel."

"I'm not homesick."

"Not yet."

Her eyes darted to the window and she hesitated, her gregariousness stemmed by some unspoken emotion.

Studying her gloved hands, in a voice quite quiet and quite different to her earlier demeanour, she said, "I was raised in London. Spitalfields."

I waited, unwilling to intrude upon her vulnerability. I realised after a moment that I was holding my breath. I tried not to stare, but glancing over at the now silent Miss Davenport and her features, I noticed there was something odd about her, though if this was to do with something unsettled rather than unsettling about her aspect, I could not say.

She seemed to gather herself as she smoothed her skirts and disguised the brushing away of tears as the tucking of stray locks behind her ears.

"I'm not crying," she said, quietly. "I can't. This is just a force of habit."

"I've only been to London once," I said.

"It's rather splendid," she enthused, animation returning to her face. "There's no place quite like it. Even here. Sort of."

It was impossible to tell if the clouds burst open or if we drove into the storm, but at the first droplets of rain splattering into the carriage Miss Davenport urged me to close the window. The rain was sickeningly warm against my hand. Before I could marvel at the sheer strangeness of hot rain, a gasp of wind chilled the splashed raindrop.

Our vehicle slowed to a squelching walk, mired by the mud underfoot. Our coachman clambered from his seat on the roof to lead his horse by hand.

It was some hours before the rain lightened enough that I could again open the window to look out. An admittedly futile effort, given how my eyes failed utterly at penetrating the murky, roiling fog. Half curious, I clicked open the compass. I had expected to see its needle spinning indecisively but it pointed more or less ahead.

So there was *a* North.

The fog was a shroud, seeming to muffle everything beyond the ghoulishly yellow lamplight. There was a curious emptiness as many of the natural sounds of birds or the rustling of trees that I so often took for granted were simply absent. I told myself this was no different than any other isolating storm, that the silence was but a mundane illusion cast by the wind and rain tormenting the carriage.

Unearthly shadows shifted in the swirling eddies. Harsh lines pushed against the sky, implying severe cliffs and narrow valleys. Hulking shapes darted behind one another and I tried not to give them faces but, unbidden, my imagination began filling in the grey landscape before me. Half-remembered etchings from *The Voyages of Captain James Cook* and exotic phantasms from *Sketches of a New World* populated the space.

And so in the thick swirling eddies of the fog, I found ethereal sylph faces staring out at me and picked out gnome forms playing, imagining their gait like that of a strutting Lancashire moonie.

"There, you can see it now!" Miss Davenport's voice summoned me from my reverie as she pointed out my brother's home to me.

I blinked. At her voice, the fog parted like a curtain.

Laon had always referred to it in his few letters as his lodgings. Despite the name, I had not imagined anything particularly grandiose.

But the house defied such expectations as it coalesced from the sheets of rain before me. It was more castle than manor, a knot of spires and flying buttresses atop a jagged hill. Stone leaned against stone in a bizarre edifice, with nothing but scorn to the very concept of aesthetic consistency and structural purpose. Though silent and lonely, it was far too skeletal to be termed picturesque.

The vast edifice disappeared again behind dense fog and foliage.

"Gethsemane," I murmured.

The gatehouse was flanked by two angular towers of dark grey stone, overlooking what appeared to be an endless chasm.

We stopped. There was no whisper of footsteps, no voices, no sound but for a loud undrawing of heavy iron bolts. I saw how overgrown the walls were, veiled in moss and nightshade. At the rattling of chains the portcullis gave way and we progressed ever so slowly under it. Further gates creaked open and we were delivered into a courtyard.

When I finally stepped out of the carriage, I looked back to see the shattered outline of the embattled walls and I could not shake the sense of unease that welled up inside me.

Of all the places to grant him, why had the fae chosen this one?

CHAPTER 2
The Sister in the Tower

There may indeed be countless worlds revolving around countless suns, as Lady Cavendish described in her poems. These wandering worlds may indeed be hidden from us due to the brightness of their stars.

But Arcadia is not one of those worlds.

The Faelands do not possess a sun in the way we would understand a sun to be. The cycle of a sun rising from the east and setting in the west is a sight wholly alien to this place for it does not orbit a burning star.

If you would imagine a bright lantern hanging at the end of a long cord. Then imagine that it swings as a pendulum over a surface, bringing each part in turn into its light.

That surface is Arcadia and that lantern is their sun. Thus at the edges of the Faelands, the sun reaches the pinnacle of its upswing before falling back the way it came. The equilibrium position of the pendulum sun is near the centre of the Faelands, directly above the city of Pivot. There, it is almost never night, as the sun is always close enough to impart at least a hazy twilight of illumination.

Thus, periods of light and dark – I hesitate at using the word "day" – are very different along the length of the Faelands, depending on where under the swing of the pendulum sun one is. For those in the city of Pivot would experience two periods of light and relative darkness for every one experienced at the far reaches. Those in between would experience a long "day" followed by a short "day."

This makes the reckoning of days in Arcadia rather complex, to say the least. It has been proposed that regardless of periods of light and dark experienced by those beneath the pendulum sun, one should term one full oscillation a "day." Inconsistent adoption of this has only caused further confusion.

The Faelands do possess something approximating seasons. As their year progresses, the arc of the pendulum sun grows smaller, but the duration of the oscillation, as with any pendulum, is independent of the arc and thus remains constant. The edges of the Faelands thus have less heat and light, giving them a recognisable winter.

The sun is also, I am reliably told, literally a lantern.

Adriaen Huygens, On the Horological Nature of the Faelands Skies, as translated by Sir Thomas Rhymer & Coppelius Warner, 1839

A wide, maw-like arch and worn steps led me into the keep. A red door opened into darkness.

"We seem to have caught them rather unprepared," said Miss Davenport dryly as she strode over to the far side of the room and pulled open the thick dust-coloured drapes. A stark, surprising light pierced in, through the startled moths and dancing dust.

Partially panelled in dark woods and edged by lacy balconies, the foyer was a grand affair. Ornate pendants of painted wood dripped from the intersection of each arched rib, holding up the ceiling. The tight weave of the elegant curves reminded me of a birdcage.

Gloomy faced lords and ladies stared out at me from rows of portraits in mismatched frames. Though long-faced and vacant-eyed, they seemed so very human. Threadbare tapestries and faded carpets amassed from several lifetimes cloaked many of the surfaces.

This was a storied dwelling, its vast history written in a language I only half understood, though the seams of where ancient masonry met newer brickwork were visible even to my eyes. The patchwork of different styles alluded to a long succession of prior owners, each with their own eccentricities of taste. Each mark in the mortar, each old window placed into older walls, each revision and addition to the stone told of some greater past.

A short goblinoid being with speckled, silver birch skin introduced himself as Mr Benjamin Goodfellow. He bowed low and awkward.

"I- I was not expecting you so soon," he said haltingly, squinting at me through his wire-framed spectacles. "The Reverend is away."

"Laon is away?" I tried to suppress a flash of worry, remembering the letters I had received. "I thought–"

"Away-away," he said, nodding. "Very away. Away for so long. Back soon. And we does what we must. We does what we cans. Does and the doings. The tower room is always ready for guests." He paused in his mutterings, face crumbling in thought. "You are the sister, are you not?"

"I am," I said. "But where is Laon?"

"Away?" he said, voice lilting upwards.

"Do you not know where he is?"

"The tower room," he said resolutely. I was confused for a moment before I realised he had just ignored my question. "Yes, the sister in the tower. And the changeling in the green quarters. Yes, yes. That makes sense. I will lead you to it."

"Then I thank you for your pains, Mr Goodfellow."

"Mr Benjamin, if you please." His accent assumed the affectations of the Oxford voice. "Just as the Reverend named me."

Miss Davenport was by my side, curtsying at the creature. "Charmed, Mr Benjamin."

He brightened at her display and so I mirrored her action. Miss Davenport gave me a solicitous smile and wink, though I was not certain entirely what she meant by them.

"You should get settled, Miss Helstone," said Miss Davenport. "Or at least see your room. I'll pay the coachman, take care of the luggage and see you at dinner. I can't wait for dinner. I am very hungry."

Tucking my carpet bag under his arm, Mr Benjamin led the way to the tower room. He gave his history as we walked. He identified himself as a gnome, which I understood from Paracelsus to mean an elemental of the earth. He had been the first and only convert of the prior missionary in residence, Reverend Jacob Roche.

"The Reverend always said Mr Benjamin seemed the littlest of the biblical brothers," he said. "Little name for little gnome."

"Do you mean Roche or my brother?" I asked.

"The first but not the last."

There was also, apparently, a housekeeper somewhere in the castle, whom Mr Benjamin termed "the Salamander."

As we wound through the keep, I felt as though we were coiling back in time, through the layers of the castle's history. The comparatively modern foyer joined onto a corridor lined in dark flock paper that was the height of fashion just under a hundred years ago. The lush floral designs in dark green and gold gave way to tapestries hung over crisp walls and then finally a spiral staircase of worn, naked stone.

At the top of that tight twist was a single wooden door. Once unlocked, I stooped into the chamber.

"Here is room," announced Mr Benjamin brightly. "Use water, throw out of window after."

I thanked the gnome as he set down my carpet bag. He bowed ornately, dragging a gnarled hand into the ground as he did so.

As he turned to leave, he started as though remembering something important. In the most solemn tones he told me, "Almost almost forgot. Remember, no walking down the silver corridor when it's dark. No looking behind the emerald curtain. No staring portraits in the eye. No eating things without salt. And no trusting the Salamander."

And then he was gone, the door bolting shut before I could ask him how I might recognise the Salamander, what food he had thought I would be encountering or, rather more practically, when I could expect dinner.

The room was round. All the furniture, from wardrobe to bookcase to bureau, curved with the wall. A window had been cut into the thick, ancient stone, but very little light filtered in through the lattice of lead and glass. A number of cushions made the recess into a window seat. Slivers of light from the knife-thin arrow slits cut through the shadows of the room.

A narrow door with an oversized knocker stood opposite me. Three pairs of brass eyes looked out at me from the foliage-wreathed face that held the heavy ring in its mouth. It was green with age but for where the hand would rest on the ring. There the brass had been polished by wear to a gleaming brightness. It reminded me of a hagoday, the enormous knockers affixed on cathedral doors that used to grant sanctuary to any who touched them.

Wondering what part of the castle I was in and what purpose this round room could have served, I unlatched the door. It opened silently.

The rush of cold air engulfed me; colder hands clawed at my heart. Hands still gripping the knocker, I shrieked and threw myself backwards. I was glad that I had not unthinkingly stepped through.

The door led to nothing but thin air. Perhaps there had once been a balcony or even a bridge of sorts. For all of Mr Benjamin's warnings, he had not thought to warn me of this particular danger.

Heart still thundering, I bolted the door with shaking hands.

It was a moment before my breathing settled and I was able to stagger to my feet.

I poured myself some lukewarm water from a pitcher on the sideboard and washed myself in the basin. Finally, I could lick my lips and not taste a shadow of the sea.

The majority of my belongings were still downstairs. But my writing case was in the carpet bag and so was a change of clothes, which I made use of. The gown was not clean per se after my seven weeks on *The Quiet*. But it and my last clean chemise were still a welcome reprieve from my woollen travelling dress.

The wardrobe was latched shut with a pair of interlocking wooden hands. I approached it to throw my carpet bag inside, but it was not empty as I expected. My hands found buttery soft wool, rippling silk, and velvet as thick and luscious as ermine. As I examined the wealth of stiff dresses, a flurry of moths spiralled out from the depths.

Some of the long trailing dresses seemed to be as old as the castle, belonging in a world of tapestries and paladins and courtly romance. A few of them I recognised as being no more than sixty or so years old; I had cut up similar brocade gowns when I had briefly been a companion to Miss Lousia March. The gowns had mouldered in their attic for decades but as the fashion began to favour again thick, rich fabrics over light muslins, they had raided the splendour of the past. They were things of such impractical beauty and it had saddened me to tear them apart even if it was to remake them for new use.

Of the dresses, only one bore any resemblance to recent fashions and it was ivory in shade. Wide necked and layered in lace, it reminded me of the etchings of the queen's wedding dress and the subsequent efforts to imitate it in the seven years since.

Opening my writing case, I found the letter from the London Missionary Society. Sitting on the bed, I read it again, though I had already committed its contents to memory. The preamble was mostly concerned with assurances that for all the numerical success of the Catholics in other lands, it was but built on a rotten foundation of formalism and thus we should not envy their cause.

After a barbed allusion to the work of the Society for Missions to Africa and the East, Rev Joseph Hale echoed my concerns for my brother. After two years of near silence, I had written to the Society asking after Laon. The Reverend had few answers for me and though he never outright stated what he thought had happened in the Faelands, his worry was evident in his circling of the issue, apologising for not having sufficiently prepared Laon for his post and making dark reference to others who had perished.

It also included a request that I recover the journals and notes of the previous missionary, Rev Jacob Roche.

In youth, I had shared Laon's restlessness. University had only nourished and nurtured his ambitions, but education had stifled mine. I had been taught to tame my wild impulses and desires that had agitated me to pain. I had folded it with my soul and learnt to drink contentment like you would a poison. Drop by drop, day by day. Until it became tolerable.

Laon disdained tranquillity. He could not learn my glacial stillness, for all that I had tried to teach him. When I had just turned nineteen and had no position of my own, I watched as he chafed under the surplice of priesthood. His parishioners desired a mild-mannered curate, but he had the soul of a soldier, a statesman and an orator. He longed for all that lay beyond the petty concerns of his parish. He grew sullen and silent, withdrawing into himself.

It was a long winter, that year.

In spring, light had returned to Laon's eyes: He was to be a missionary.

I hated his epiphany. Selfishly, I had thought myself abandoned. I spared not a heartbeat for those that languished in the grim empires without word of the Redeemer. All I knew was that he would leave behind the scenes and skies of our shared childhood and, in seeking adventure beyond my reach, he would sever himself from me. Festering full of fear and envy, I took up a position as a lady's companion and later, a governess.

It wasn't until I opened his first letter home, all smelling of sugar and sulphur, that I discovered that he been sent to Arcadia. His letters were infrequent at best and spoke little of his life here. I had assumed he thought such details would agitate me and reawaken that buried wanderlust.

But my brother had apparently been just as worryingly terse to the mission society. After the extent of his silence became evident to me, I began planning my own journey. In a flurry of letters, I somehow managed to convince the London Missionary Society that though it may be unorthodox for an unmarried woman to travel abroad, I should follow my brother. I had never thought myself particularly persuasive in writing, but I must have been superlatively so for them buy my passage on *The Quiet*.

And so, here I was: clutching the compass he had left behind, knot tightening within my heart, under the light of a pendulum sun.

CHAPTER 3
The Sun on the Horizon

Scorn the food and shun the drink,
For faerie food and faerie tricks,
Will snare the tongue and trap the sick.
  Sprinkle salt from human lands
Sprinkle salt with human hands.
  Meat loves salt and salt loves meat,
I pray the lord my soul to keep.
So sprinkle salt, else restless sleep,
So sprinkle salt, else endless weep.

> Traditional folk rhyme, collected by J Ritson in
> FAIRY TALES AND FOLK SONGS, NOW FIRST COLLECTED,
> WITH TWO DISSERTATIONS ON PYGMIES AND ON FAIRIES

And every oblation of thy meat offering shalt thou season
with salt; neither shalt thou suffer the salt of the covenant of
thy God to be lacking from thy meat offering: with all thine
offerings thou shalt offer salt.

> LEVITICUS 2:13

The hazy light implied dusk when I awoke. I found a tray piled high with food by the door and a note informing me that the writer had found me asleep when they had tried to fetch me for dinner. The lettering stained my fingertips black. Squinting, I saw that the words had been scorched into the parchment rather than written with ink.

The rich scent of hare and juniper stew drew my attention back to the meal itself, reminding me how hungry I was. It was still steaming and the copper jug that held it was almost scalding to touch. A heap of breaded asparagus fenced in lightly charred mushrooms. Half a loaf of crusty bread sat in a basket. I sniffed at a small jug to discover it was full of blood, presumably hare, to go with the stew. Usually, though, it was stirred in before serving rather than after.

There was a salt shaker on the tray, but I found the grinder at the bottom of my carpet bag and ground salt onto a side plate. I threw the salt onto the stew, then upon the mushrooms, the asparagus and lastly, the bread. Hands pressed together, I murmured an *Amen*.

Some would dismiss this as superstition, but salt protected humans from the food of the Faelands. Captain Cook and his crew, the first British explorers to reach Arcadia, were said to have perished because of their misdealings with salt.

I thickened the stew with blood and started eating. I had missed such food on my weeks on *The Quiet* and it was a while before I saw that the mushrooms were an odd shade of purple in the middle.

It was then I noticed that the narrow door to empty air was unbolted. I frowned to myself, got up and bolted it tight. I had thought I had left it bolted shut after I had accidentally opened it.

A light rapping on the door signalled the entrance of Miss Davenport, who announced that we "simply must" watch the sunset from the roof. She had a bright, mischievous grin on her face and jangled a great ring of keys at me triumphantly.

"Oh, your dinner," she said, lingering by the great vat of uneaten stew on the tray. She breathed in deeply, entranced by the aroma. "Are you finished with that?"

I nodded.

"It's a little forward, I know, but may I?"

"If you want," I said, hesitantly. "I thought we were in a hurry…"

"You remembered to salt, didn't you?"

I nodded and watched her simply inhale my leftovers. She stopped short of licking the plate, drinking down the stew in large gulps and picking up the mushrooms with her hands. She mopped up the dregs of stew with bread.

Tucking the last sprig of asparagus into her mouth, she grinned at my appalled face. She brought a handkerchief to her lips with a dainty flourish. "I do apologise about my manners."

"It's quite alright," I said. Idly, I wondered if this would be the greatest affront to my sense of civilisation.

"Now, to the sunset," she beamed. "I ate quickly, so we shouldn't be too late. And sunsets last so long in Arcadia. No horizon, after all."

Throwing a shawl around myself, I eagerly followed her.

I had thought my room the highest in Gethsemane, but we ascended another flight of stairs and raised a trap door into an attic. Phantom relics of a bygone time rested under dust-laden sheets. Rolls of carpet and tapestry nestled against large trunks. I held the lantern as Miss Davenport struggled with the lock.

"When your brother returns, you should ask to stand atop the gatehouse at sunset," she said. "It is rather different there."

"How so?" I asked, trying to angle the lantern so that she

could better sort through her collection. Key after key scraped against the unyielding lock.

"Only he could really force the Salamander to give up that set of keys... Aha!" she exclaimed, as the key finally turned.

The door opened onto the parapets of what she had called the north tower, leaning into the innermost of the castle's curtain walls. There was a palpable chill in the air and I shrugged my shawl a little tighter around my shoulders.

The sky was awash with hazy greys, and beneath it, Arcadia was swaddled in mists and mystery. I could imagine fields and forests, but I did not think them true. A halo of golden light surrounded the pinpoint that was the sun, cast upon the clouds that enfolded it. It was now notably smaller than at midday and smaller than I had ever seen our earthly sun.

"What is Arcadia?" I muttered, half to myself. "How could this place truly be?"

There were no answers as we watched the sun recede further. There was no dramatic change in the light, as it did not set behind land or dip into the sea. It was far higher in the sky than it was at midday when it burned overhead.

"I asked myself that too," said Miss Davenport. "And you won't like the answers any more than I did."

"What do you mean–?"

"Nothing," she said quickly, glancing away.

I watched that strange, false light slowly dim and the darkness thicken upon the landscape. There have been some whose faith was challenged by the very discovery of Arcadia, a realm which the scriptures spoke barely of. Yet the Good Book made no reference to English shores. Our clouded hills and green mountains are no more false for that silence than the landscape before me. How could I limit an infinite God with finite words?

"And now the moon," said Miss Davenport.

My eyes followed her pointing and turned to where the

darkness had already fallen. The landscape seemed dark and hard, like charcoal, and the clouds were but a softer reflection of that harsh, brittle heap.

The moon was, at first, but a luminous shadow behind a mist, flashing for a moment before disappearing again behind the burnt-scone clouds.

Then suddenly, a bright silver shape swam out. Clouds clung to the arc of its gleaming fins, trailing thin wisps of seeming light.

I gasped in wonder, and rather secretly, chided my younger self for the limits of her imagination. More than being on the moors of home, more than standing on the docks of London, more than being lost on the North Sea, *this* reminded me of how limited my twenty-five years has been. All the restlessness that I thought I had buried alongside my sister, returned with a passion that left me breathless.

The moon was a fish.

Or rather, the moon dangled from a pole in front of a wide-jawed piscine. As it swam closer, I saw the light gleaming off its long, long teeth that curved from its lips. Its eyes bulged from its face, white, lidless and staring. Tail whipping back and forth, its scales shimmered, iridescent in its own light.

I cast my eyes to the limits of my vision, where unfocused sight made my eyes water. I hungered to know what lay beyond. A medieval heretic once wrote of standing on the encircling walls of the universe and shooting arrows ever outward. Would there not always be more walls and more arrows? There were more suns and more worlds than I could dream. My mind would always be more finite than that of God. And still, I wanted to behold greater, to become greater than my frail bones could hold. With each laboured breath I felt as though I would tear the papery skin that held the coals of my soul in check. Glimmering embers had lain hidden among those ashes, and now these alien climes had breathed upon them and nurtured new flame.

The moon grew hazy as it swam behind a cloud and the body of the fish was obscured from sight. For a moment, it seemed like an earthly moon, suspended in the air through divine Providence rather than a sea monster that dwelt not in the sea.

"We should go inside."

Miss Davenport's voice was a surprise. I turned to her, unclenching my fists and wincing at the painful imprint my fingernails had bitten into my palms. I had tensed without thought.

"It gets cold very quickly out here."

I nodded, and Miss Davenport led the way back into the keep. Casting a backward glance at the moon, I thought of Laon and the passions he had sought to burn and bury. I wondered what he had thought when he first saw the Arcadian moon, if it too stirred in him such restlessness and if he knew how to quench it.

It was written that in Arcadia, everything – even your eyes – would lie after dark and thus it was perhaps unsurprising that I would get lost the moment Miss Davenport left me. She had assured me that my room was at the end of the corridor, but somehow, without turning, the walls were no longer lined in portraits and instead were starkly whitewashed and draped with faded tapestries.

I retraced my steps but could not find the stairs that led into the attic, nor the gimlet-eyed portraits, nor the corridor of bare stone. I must have taken a wrong turn; corridors don't change for no reason.

A breeze from a loosely latched window danced over the back of my neck. My lantern jerked in my hand, and the glass door swung open. The flame within flickered. Panic welling up inside me, I fumbled to close the lantern.

My fingers slipped.

The lantern clattered to the floor, smashing against the stone and spilling wax and glass. The soft glow of the guttering wick extinguished. I was plunged into darkness.

The cold felt keener in the dark and I could hear my heart beating, steady but fierce. I glanced up to the inky blackness of the corridor, hoping to catch a glimpse of light to guide me. Seeing little, I closed my eyes, knowing I needed to adjust to the dark. Another snarl of cold air painted gooseflesh down my spine. Fear flickered in me. I drew a steadying breath and reminded myself that night would not last forever.

When I opened my eyes again, everything was still bathed in shadow. Resolving to simply wander until I found somewhere bright and recognisable, I walked forwards, hand trailing on the wall to guide me.

Ahead, I noticed a half-open door behind one of the tapestries. Imagining a glimmer of light, I ventured within.

I was in a study, of sorts. It had a bookcase and bureau. White sheets shrouded most of the furnishings, transforming them into childish phantoms.

Laon and I used to play games, scaring each other under the sheets. We had no words for what we felt then, but the very idea of ghosts both enthralled and repulsed us. We had buried so many in our youth. I still remember huddling against him, hooking our fingers together and promising under every token that we held sacred that if one of us were to die, we would come back and haunt the other.

The light scattered into glowing pinpoints of pale red. Squinting, I could just about make out the flutter of insectoid wings furling around each tiny glow as they settled again on the far side of the study. Fireflies.

The moon swam from behind a cloud and silver shone in through the window. The stained glass gave the light a shimmering, underwater quality. That light guided my gaze to a bureau.

Despite being half closed, frost-like dust clung to every item within it. The icicles of cobwebs dripped from the end of the birdlike claw of the letter opener, the edges of the half-open drawers, the mouth of the bottle of desiccated ink, the leaning pens.

Spindly, long-legged shadows flickered at the edge of my vision. Startled, I spun around, startling again the red fireflies, but there was nothing.

My eyes scanned the loose pages, each crowded with a scrawl. I traced a finger against the filigree of dust, squinting to make out the faded words. Easing myself into the creaking chair, I leafed through the spread of documents.

A shiver spidered up my spine.

I did not recognise the script as from any mundane language. It was angular, full of squares and dots. Many of the symbols were scratched out. Others appeared in lists. Others still curled around strange spirals, wide-eyed, coiling creatures and crude charcoal sketches of moths.

Then, a line of Latin: *In principio erat Verbum et Verbum erat apud Deum et Deus erat Verbum.*

It took me a moment to recognise it, having spent so long staring at the unknown symbols. I mouthed the words to myself.

In the beginning there was the Word and the Word was God and the Word was with God.

Not so much a translation as a memory of the line within my Bible.

Fleetingly, I wondered if these could be the missing diaries of Rev Jacob Roche, but why would he write these strange symbols? Rev Hale had warned me that I should not read them, but surely these ancient papers could not be those journals. Every stone in this castle alluded to a long history, surely it must have been one of its previous inhabitants?

Yet such assumptions rendered me no answers.

I smoothed open crumpled papers, each speckled with holes. My eyes followed each dot and flourish of their meaningless words. I sorted through page after page of arcane nonsense. As I leafed through, more and more pages were riddled with holes. Some were so fragmentary that they fell apart at my touch into a dusting of inky snowflakes.

Attempting gentleness, my hands trembled. I swallowed. Recognisable English words roamed on the edges of the broken pages, but few of them were informative.

My breath was heavy, though I did not know if it was excitement or the dust. The final layer in my excavation was a worn leatherbound notebook. Its gilded spine was cold to the touch. Coughing at the dust that swirled up as I turned the page, I read: *Translation of the Bible into Enochian.*

My brow furrowed. Enochian. I had heard that word before, but I could not recall where. It tugged at the edges of my memory.

A tuneless humming roused me from my excavation. Leaping to the conclusion that the owner of the voice would be able to help me, I called out.

"Hello? A little help, if you please, my lantern was broken–" I rolled up the scattered pages and bundled them into a writing case that rested against the bureau. I wanted to keep studying the pages.

The humming seemed to grow fainter. I latched shut the writing case and gathered up my skirts, stumbling towards the sound.

"Hello? Is there anyone there?"

There was a faint tinkling sound, somewhere between bells and laughter. I felt warmth flutter against my neck, like a candle going out.

Once out of the study, everything was but shades of shadow. Half blind and hand reaching out before me, I

followed. Making out the edge of a wall and the faint lines of
a silver mirror upon it, I felt around the corner.

My eyes stung.

After a moment of furious blinking, I saw that in the middle
of the floor there was a lit lantern. The bright, painful light
was itself a relief. Beside it was the arch that opened onto the
stairs of worn stone, the top of which was my room.

I spun around, trying to catch a glimpse of who could have
left it here, but I heard no footsteps.

I noticed a smudge of coal on my fingers when I put down
the lantern in my room and I wondered at who could have
left it for me.

CHAPTER 4

The Bird in the Cage

The deliberations of the Royal Society in 1767 and the beginning of 1768, seconded by the liberality of the government, produced a result highly interesting to our navigator, opening to his genius new and extensive spheres where he was destined to shine. At this period, and for some years before, the British government had the honour of instituting voyages of discovery very different from those early navigators. Expeditions of this kind were formally set on foot for the purpose of conquest, the acquisition of territory and of wealth. But now commenced a new era in the annals of navigation, when the voyages of discovery were undertaken for the interests of science; for acquiring a knowledge of the different seas, continents, and islands on the face of our globe; and for ameliorating the condition of the savage tribes that might be discovered.

From the triumph in observing the Transit of Venus over the sun's disc in June 1769 to his meticulous mapping of the South Sea, to his crossing of the Antarctic Circle and the further mapping of the Northwest Passage, Cook proved an unparalleled navigator and was celebrated throughout the Empire.

Yet still beyond the calculations and projections of any of these involved parties was the fourth and most fantastical voyage of our captain, when the greatest navigational mind became impossibly lost and thus impossibly discovered a different realm. Many have no doubt gotten lost on high seas and brought their ships to the coast of Arcadia but it is only Cook who could have realised that getting lost is intrinsic to journey.

Rev George Young, THE LIFE AND VOYAGES OF CAPTAIN JAMES COOK, DRAWN FROM HIS JOURNALS AND OTHER AUTHENTIC DOCUMENTS; AND COMPRISING MUCH ORIGINAL INFORMATION

I did not get lost again after that first night in Gethsemane.

Life at my brother's castle – strange as it still is to even think of it as such – settled into a rhythm, of sorts. Laon hadn't returned yet from whatever mysterious errand he was on and neither Mr Benjamin nor Miss Davenport were much help in working out where he had gone.

"He'll return when he returns," said Miss Davenport with half a shrug, pausing in her knitting.

"Doesn't he need to be here?" I said.

"I suppose he would run out of salt eventually," she said thoughtfully.

I suppressed the flutter of panic at the thought. Folktales warned of the claim Arcadia had on any who consumed its food, that one would be forever trapped under its unearthly sun. I pressed on: "I meant the mission. Doesn't he have a congregation?"

She laughed, an airy sound, breathier and more high pitched than her speaking voice. "Heavens, Miss Helstone. There isn't a congregation."

"I thought–"

"The Mission to Arcadia has, at present, met with little success. We urge you, dear reader, to open up your purses and pray harder so as to sway the soulless to turn their godless minds heavenward," she said, over-enunciating in the manner of mocking quotation.

"Miss Davenport!" I said, quite appalled. Though my weeks on *The Quiet* had taught me to hold my tongue at little blasphemies, Miss Davenport's teasing touched a raw nerve.

"Aside from Mr Benjamin, of course," she added. The wide, flat grin that spread over her face showed that she was clearly taking inappropriate pleasure at my distress. "That is one resounding success. Even if it isn't your brother's."

In that, she was indeed correct. Though the gnome proved to be an odd character, he had a fervour for the faith that was rivalled only by the ancients who hunched over their Bibles and loved nothing more than to snarl quotations at the curate whenever he saw fit to paraphrase.

Mr Benjamin grew no more or less disconcerting the more I knew him. He exuded a sense of earthy familiarity that made it hard to stare for too long, but his warmth felt genuine. He even offered a little of his past, speaking of his time as a miner of azote at the far reaches of Arcadia.

"It's very, very cold out there. The sun is too far to make light and so the azote and vital air form seas and mountains. We mine it and cart it back to Pivot."

"What *is* azote?"

"Air," he replied, oblivious to my incredulity. "The winds blow outwards, see? So it all congeals at sides. Solid wind and solid air. So we mined it and brought it back. But the Lady of Iron closed the mines." The gnome's features drooped despondently, but lifted as he said, "Then I came here."

His conversion he spoke of with but sparse detail, but he would sometimes allude to his companions from his miner days. It seemed that they had all come to speak to the prior Reverend together, but only Mr Benjamin stayed. He prided himself on being the mission's only convert and often came to me with odd questions.

"I was thinking, Miss Helstone," Mr Benjamin said. "Could I ask a question?"

"Yes?"

"So, Jesus Christ the Ever Anointed Son of God, Hallowed Be His Name..." His voice trailed off. He took off his spectacles and cleaned them nervously. "I mean to ask, Miss Helstone, the question is: Why does the parentage of the Holy Cuckold matter if he's the Holy Cuckold?"

"Pardon?" It took me a moment to realise he meant Joseph and before I could correct him, he rattled on.

"The Genealogy of Jesus is given twice in the book Mr Benjamin was given by the Reverend. By two of the writers... Their names be..." he paused, clicking his tongue, thinking. He scratched his jutting chin. "Luke and Matthew, yes, yes. That be. The two writers say Jesus is of David's line through Joseph, which is to say the Holy Cuckold. I recall this. Luke said: *And Jesus himself began to be about twenty years of age, being (as supposed) the son of Joseph, which was the son of Heli...* And Matthew wrote: *And Jacob begat Joseph the husband of Mary, of whom was born Jesus, who is called Christ.*" Mr Benjamin was panting, breathless at his barrage of words. "You see what I mean?"

"I do follow," I said. It was a question I had asked before, at Clergy Daughters' School. My palms stung for days afterwards as I was whipped for impertinence. I gritted my teeth through the pain as I wrote to Laon about it, my letters curling all wonky. Looking back, the pain and my injured sense of justice distracted me from the question. I never found an answer.

"So... so, why matters Joseph's parentage?"

"Well," I swallowed, mind blanking at the abruptness of the question. "That is a very interesting question."

The answers I had toyed with as a child started bickering in my mind like geese. Maybe Matthew and Luke were both mistaken and it was Mary who was related to David (but if they can be wrong about this one detail, what else might they be wrong about?). Maybe the fact that Joseph can be said to have adopted Jesus and he is thus of his house (but even then the two genealogies diverged significantly, which suggests one must be wrong). Maybe Matthew and Luke were reporting it for the benefit of those who thought the Messiah had to be from the House of David (and if so, how wrong is a falsehood told to support something true?).

I remembered Laon's letter back to me, filled with condolence and encouragement. His hand had been shaking too, though I knew it to have been from anger rather than pain.

My mind wandered back to the rose window at the Whitehead chapel, panelled to suggest the inside of a ship, a curving hull and arced wooden beams. It was dedicated to martyred missionaries. I had always thought that it was where Laon had his epiphany, though he never really said as much. That chapel's window, however, had nothing to do with missionaries. It depicted the lineage of Jesus, with David in the centre and each of the ancestors upon the petals of the rose, each name picked out in black – barely legible – gothic lettering. But its vivid splendour held no answers.

"Miss Helstone?"

Mr Benjamin looked up at me with his large brown eyes, expectant and trusting, like the sloping eyes of a dog.

He cocked his head to one side. Waiting.

"I... I think, I think you should ask Laon when he gets back."

"Very wise. I will ask the Reverend!" The gnome nodded his head and pottered off, seeming to accept my answer.

But I was not content. The question continued to haunt me. I wondered where my brother's books were; I knew he had a copy of Cruden's *Concordance*. But I had been unable to locate my brother's study, or any sort of house library – even the room in which I found those dusty documents.

I was left to scour my own Bible, turning back and forth between the pages of the Testaments. Before I had sufficient time to content myself with all the particulars of the two lineages of Joseph, did Mr Benjamin totter up to me with another theological quandary.

"Miss Helstone, is it possible to make restitution for sins one doesn't repent?

"Has the fig tree been forgiven by Jesus? Should we stop eating figs altogether or is it just that one tree that got cursed?

"If the Christ Our Lord was made wholly human in order to bear human sin, does that mean he must also have been wholly fae to bear our sins? Or is that the Covenant with the divine been extended to both fae and humans the way it encompasses more than simply Abraham's descendants?"

My brother's house became to me a place of questions without answers. Over time, the lineage of the Redeemer simply became one of the many questions that haunted my sleep.

Miss Davenport appeared each day to keep me company. For the first few days, I politely indulged her desire to sit in the solar and knit, making conversation about the idiosyncrasies of her gauge and teaching her how to turn a heel on a sock.

"It is good to make things with one's own hands sometimes," she had said. "Other methods simply don't have the same tactile satisfaction."

The yarn she had brought was ethereally light and frothed around the needles as I wound it round and round. Every clicking stitch I made was a step back to Yorkshire and the confinement of my previous positions. I remembered sitting with Miss Lousia March when I was her companion and after, for all my stated title of governess, I spent as much time darning socks as educating young minds.

The solar was bright. Had this been a mortal castle I would have guessed that the curved wall was evidence that it had been a chapel in the past, but this was no such thing. The thick stone was interrupted with stained glass windows that were obvious additions. One spiralled dark medieval colours, fragmenting the dust-dancing light into flecks of oxblood red. Another showed a knight battling a web of serpents. Given their diverse styles and shapes, the windows had probably been taken from another place and installed here by one of the castle's previous masters. I wondered who had lived here before Laon, before the Reverend Roche, and what they called it then.

"The windows here remind me a little of Ariel Davenport's home. In Spitalfields," she said. "It weren't stained glass, of course, but we had latticed windows all along the front of the house. So there could be enough light to weave. We had three looms to keep all our hands busy."

Perhaps it was simply out of a desire to avoid other subjects, but she often spoke of her past in the mortal world. Sometimes I thought it merely a distraction, but at others, it genuinely seemed as though she wanted more.

"What did you weave?" I asked, feeling provincial. Having grown up in the strange uncivilised little place that was Birdforth, Spitalfields and London itself was an unimaginable world away.

"Silk. Everyone was in the silk trade round those parts. The littles would quill it and pick it. I wanted so much to be useful. I begged and begged to be taught weaving early. I remember my arms being barely long enough to reach the end of the loom and I was learning how to weave."

"They must have been proud of you."

Miss Davenport gave a brief laugh. "Got me nothing but beatings. I was awful at it. Wasted so much good silk."

I smiled at her humour, but added gently, "I wasn't much

of a quick learner either."

"Ariel Davenport's father always talked about getting a fourth loom, but I was never good enough. The rooms were cold with all the windows, but it was always awash with light." Her eyes were no longer looking at me, but past me to the flock of dark birds on the stained glass. "We worked to the sound of birdsong. Our roof was lined with traps, you see."

"Traps?" I was confused.

"Weavers are good at making traps, I suppose. Nimble fingers and all that. Ariel Davenport's father liked to listen to birdsong whilst we worked."

"What did you do with all the birds?" I asked. I turned my knitting, and glancing over my completed stitches, my fingers counted their diaphanous flow.

"Sold them. Songbirds are worth a pretty penny, especially the pretty ones. Though I'd prize more one with a pretty voice. I assume the London gentry like to keep them about. We did, filled the house with song. We'd drop all arguments when the right bird sang."

"Sounds beautiful."

"I wasn't much good at weaving traps, but I could train the birds. We'd have one of ours call the others down. I thought their song loveliest then. When they're tricking their kin."

"You... You must have caught many birds then," I said, haltingly. I was no stranger to baiting traps (moles were a perpetual menace, after all), but I couldn't help but be reminded of the warnings in Captain Cook's memoirs, of how the fae were inherently a duplicitous race.

"I didn't like it much, but you can't really argue with beauty. They just sang best then." Ariel was lost to her memories and she heaved a sigh. She smoothed a hand over her knitting, fingers dwelling lovingly on each stitch. "Ariel Davenport's mother always wanted me to learn to braid pillow lace. Kept lying to me about it being simpler than weaving. And there's better money in selling lace, she always said. You'd never be hungry if you had a proper trade."

"I know that sentiment," I murmured. I gave a bitter smile, glancing down at my trade-less hands. A clergyman's daughter is genteel enough to be educated and accomplished, but never useful. Caught between the world of labour and that of letters, I had lamented my lack of employment under my brother's room. Those were long months of inactivity.

"I'd always retort that you can knit lace as well, which would earn me a cuff to the ears. You don't really knit silk, you know," said Miss Davenport. She held her knitting up to the light, squinting at the sun's weave through the intricate pattern. "I just don't have the hands for pillow lace. Too many bobbins."

"I wasn't ever taught lace-making."

"It involves a hundred bobbins. And a pillow. Because there's nothing more precious than partly made lace that it needs its own pillow." She gave a huff. "It's a horrid art."

"You must miss them all terribly."

"Sorry?" she said, confused and startled out of her memory.

"Your – I mean, Ariel Davenport's family. You must miss them."

"No, I don't. Not really," she said, shaking her head. "I do not miss them at all."

"But you speak of them often."

"It's good that you think I might miss them. I like that." Miss Davenport smiled weakly. "Not many here understand why I might miss them. Why I could miss them. The others, they're just not made that way. Much like my hands. I could try to make the shapes for lace-making, pass the threads over one another, and something like lace sometimes results. But it's not quite the same. Doesn't come naturally."

For all my restlessness, I was unable to leave the castle. I was beginning to regret not looking about the bustling port of my first day. Though the strange sights I had seen then fuelled my daydreams, they were fast fading into fantasy.

As consolation of sorts, Miss Davenport took me walking around the courtyard. She seemed to dislike the gardens. Miss Davenport explained that until Laon returned, the protections that bound the inhabitants of the Faelands to not harm him would not extend to me.

"Blood binds blood," she said, a little primly. "And blood knows blood. You can't expect mortal salt to do all the work. You need to keep yourself out of harm's way too."

I winced; Miss Davenport was developing a habit of reprimanding me for carelessness, all dark warnings and strange taboos.

"There's a geas that knows you."

"A *geas*?"

"A ban, though some call it fate. It keeps your brother and those of his blood safe. The Pale Queen has promised him that he and those of his blood would not die in these walls and it protects you because you're staying within them. They can't touch you here, no matter how much they want to. So you really shouldn't go wandering about out there by yourself, Miss Helstone."

"Who do you mean by *they*?" I stopped to turn and look directly at her, hoping to read something in her disconcertingly human eyes.

She gave a half shrug, avoiding my gaze. "Simply what is beyond the castle walls."

"Then what is beyond the walls?" I said, my voice rising in frustration. "What should I be afraid of?"

"I'm not sure I could, that is to say, should—"

"I saw faces," I said. At the crossing of her brows, I hurried an elaboration: "In the mist. The day I arrived. There were faces, figures in the mist."

"It was probably just your imagination running wild. You… you shouldn't be so curious," she said. "Remember what happened to the original missionary."

"No one's ever told me what happened to Roche."

She stopped herself, rolled the unspoken words over her tongue like a boiled sweet and swallowed. She cleared her throat and without a hint of sheepishness, said, "Best you don't know."

"I would rather know, Miss Davenport." I jutted out my chin stubbornly.

"That may be the case, Miss Helstone, and I may rather tell you, but I fear I cannot."

"You haven't even told me who Laon is petitioning or what you're hoping to achieve by keeping me here."

"Secrets keep you safe."

I wanted to argue with her, to press her further for the truth. But given how she was one of the only two people I knew in Arcadia, it seemed short-sighted to cross her.

We walked in silence for a while after that, a coldness settling between us despite the closeness of the pendulum sun.

It was Miss Davenport who spoke first. I looked at her, noting a disconcerting, deceptive humanity in her eyes. A smile wavered at her lips and she spoke quite gently, as though her words were actually a reconciliation. "Not all knowledge brings joy."

Miss Davenport reached a reassuring hand towards me and I took it. I nodded and offered her a smile, trying to bury my discontentment.

Eyes suddenly faraway, she added: "There are things I wish I didn't know."

With peace so recently restored, I allowed her that cryptic remark, though one day, I promised myself, I would have answers.

"You are a lot like your brother," said Miss Davenport. "He was also full of questions. He couldn't just accept the way things worked."

Laon had been particularly distant during his first days abroad.

"You seem very familiar with Laon," I said, and asked if she had similarly acted as his guide and companion.

"It was rather different with your brother," she said. She never called Laon by his name or even referred to him by title; he was always *your brother*. "Being a companion to a man is not exactly the same thing as being that to a woman."

I had the decency to blush, but for all my flustered feelings it wasn't until afterwards that I realised how opaque she was being. She had not actually answered my question. Surely any indigence was akin to a refutation.

When I reconsidered the impudence of my question, I came to realise that for all her outward appearance of humanity – she even took her food and drink with salt – I had never quite forgotten her to be fae. Thus I had entirely not considered her to be a woman.

Still, the imagination was a traitorous thing and, after that it took a force of will not to imagine her with my brother. Perhaps to goad me, she spoke more often of him – always, always in those terms, *your brother* – and yet these scraps, these glimpses of Laon did little to satiate my curiosity.

Whenever we sat together she would allude to him, holding up her knitting as though a veil between us as she spoke. She had thoroughly mastered the art of saying a multitude of words without any substance. In passing, she would tell me that my brother was careless on his first day, or that he had gotten lost in the blue wing, but such detail gave me no sense of his whole. I continued to worry about him and his curt letters, and my own harsh words at his decision to become a missionary echoed within me.

I could not now bear to articulate the hopes that I had when first setting foot on *The Quiet* at Dover, but I had not thought that I would be again sitting in a solar, needlework in my hands, empty conversation in my ears, waiting.

CHAPTER 5
The Changeling in the Chapel

Hymn 47. Trichinopoly. P. M. (7's & 6's, double.)

From Greenland's icy mountains,
From India's coral strand,
Where Afric's sunny fountains
Roll down their golden sand;
From many an ancient river,
From many a palmy plain,
They call us to deliver
Their land from error's chain.

In newly discover'd Elphane
Long shrouded from our sight
Where creatures strange 'n' profane
Have never known his light.
Salvation! Oh, Salvation!
The joyful sound proclaim
Till each remotest nation
Has learned Messiah's name.

What though the spicy breezes
Blow soft o'er Ceylon's isle;

Though ev'ry prospect pleases
And only man is vile;
In vain with lavish kindness
The gifts of God are strown;
The heathen in his blindness
Bows down to wood and stone.

Waft, waft, ye winds, His story,
And you, ye waters, roll,
Till like a sea of glory
It spreads from pole to pole;
Till o'er our ransomed nature
The lamb for sinners slain,
Redeemer, King, Creator,
In bliss returns to reign.

Collected by Rev John Sanford, PSALMS,
PARAPHRASES, AND HYMNS, ADAPTED TO THE
SERVICES OF THE CHURCH OF ENGLAND

It was Sunday, and after weeks of mumbled service from *The Quiet*'s captain, I longed to hear my brother's sermons again. He had a passion that surged under the measured cadence of his voice and, more than that, I had begun to miss his discordant singing.

I wandered into the dining room to find Mr Benjamin in his Sunday best, which constituted the addition of a large straw hat, a grubby handkerchief to his front pocket and a bright lilac fern to his lapel.

"Good morning, Miss Helstone." He bowed, sweeping off his hat. "I look forward to your sermon today. Will we be singing *Jerusalem* today? I do love that hymn."

"Pardon?"

"You will be speaking today?" His eyes seemed to widen with hope. "Yes?"

I shook my head, taken aback by his assumption.

"But a sister for a brother, is fair trade," he said. "And the brother has been away for so long. The chapel has been empty and–"

"How long has Laon been away?" Worry leapt in me. "You said he'd be back–"

"Long! Forever and a day!"

"That–"

"He'll be back. You have faith. We all believe he will be back." He gave a long sigh. "All the parishioners were excited because we had you. Thought we had a Helstone to spare."

"All the parishioners? I thought you were the only convert."

"Me is all. All is we. We is me." Mr Benjamin faded to a mumble, playing with variations of the words; he was easily delighted by wordplay.

"Well, I cannot give a sermon or conduct the service or sacraments. I'm afraid I am not a priest the way my brother is. I am not a priest." I was moved by his obvious need. I had always been a timid thing growing up, relying on Laon to speak for me, and thus I did not entirely believe my own voice when I said, "But I can pray with you."

For all the thoughts of adventure, I had not forgotten that his purpose here was that of a missionary and he – we, even – were here to turn whatever simulacrum of soul the fae possess to the service of the Lord Above.

It was a great work, though not one I imagined myself capable of being part of.

Yet here I was, being led by a gnome to the chapel in Arcadia.

"Chapel in the garden," he told me with a backwards glance. "Is where the Reverend Roche put it."

Walking behind Mr Benjamin, all I could think was that he

was even shorter than I had originally observed and that the soles of his bare feet were very dirty.

He led me through half a dozen dizzying corridors that seemed to all spiral in on each other until we reached a large courtyard.

Looking up, I saw a blue sky hemmed in by high stone walls. A great history of glaziery stared down at me, from small, stained windows to elaborately latticed contrivances.

A small brick chapel had been built leaning against the far wall of the courtyard. In shape it was squat and inelegant, not unlike my father's church at Birdforth. A bell tower had also been built against the corner of the courtyard, completely dwarfed by the surrounding walls.

"Is Miss Davenport joining us?" I asked. Remembering her tales of growing up in London, I had assumed her at least passingly devout. But now I could not recall a single mention of church.

Vigorously, he scratched his head. "Think not, though your brother used to wait."

"Then we should too."

He shrugged. "Changelings. Their fingers bend out and not in."

"Do you care to explain that?"

"Changelings just need to be not like their people. They need to be a little odd, not quite fit in. Is just their way of being made wrong. It's in her nature."

"That…" I swallowed. "That seems quite sad."

"No, no. Isn't in their nature to be."

I unlatched the double doors and pushed in.

I had expected the whitewashed severity that I had grown up with, where all the medieval excess had been purged by the Reformation and all that was left was a hollow shell of a building.

This was not my father's church.

A series of elaborate gothic bay windows looked into the chapel. Whomever built this place against the castle had not bothered to dismantle the windows that were originally set into that wall. The ornate stonework set the simple brick chapel to shame. Stone vines and stone rosettes framed each window. The faces and hands of the figures that crowded the surrounding panels had been worn away and their stories were unrecognisable to my eyes.

As I lit the candles and set them in their wooden holders, the light reflected against the thick, uneven crown glass. Each tiny pane of it in the lattice bulged in fishy scrutiny of us below.

Four rows of dusty pews faced an altar and a lectern.

"I ring the bell?" said Mr Benjamin.

I nodded.

I pulled out my handkerchief and, coughing at the dust, wiped down the pews.

A single bell sang out, clear and very loud. It was an earthly sound, very like that of the church at Birdforth. Though I knew it should raise up my thoughts to heaven, it merely reminded me how far away I was from home.

I struggled to imagine this church full of fae. I tried to fill it with all the strange faces and twisted forms I neglected to study on my first day at port and now felt as though I would never see again. I tried to imagine my brother by the altar, his curate's surplice always seeming too short on his tall frame. I remembered his smile.

My eyes stung from all the dust as I shook clean my handkerchief. I pushed the water from my eyes with the back of my hands.

I missed Laon. I used to tickle him in church to keep him awake. All too often, we'd giggle and bicker under our breaths until our father cast us a stern gaze from the pulpit and we'd silence. I'd keep holding his hand, though, as he needed my nails in his palm to not fall asleep.

"We start?" said Mr Benjamin, re-emerging.

"The bells call to the faithful," I said. "We should wait. If my brother waits, then we should wait."

Perhaps all missionaries thought that of their own place, that it was uniquely difficult in the challenges it presented the devout soul. Yet where else would hold inhabitants so familiar with the English mind yet alien to it? For all the weird and wonderful accounts of Captain Cook, I had no idea what to expect beyond the walls of this castle.

"What is beyond the castle?" I asked.

Mr Benjamin looked up from the hymnal he was clutching and drew together his wide brows. "Beyond?"

"Yes," I said. "I want to know what's outside. When I came in the carriage, I saw nothing but mist. And Miss Davenport tells me I shouldn't go out."

"You shouldn't go out."

"What is outside?"

"Not much, mot nuch." The gnome grinned to himself, causing the lines of his face to deepen as he noticed his verbal fumble created words that pleased his mouth. He savoured them like someone would sweets or chocolates. "Mot nuch, not much."

"That isn't much of an answer, Mr Benjamin," I chided.

He shrugged. "It's not much of a place."

I could not help but think on the missionary reports that I had studied in anticipation of this journey. How differently they had described the distant shores that teemed with savages and cannibals, each unenlightened race finally brought to the faith through the eloquence of the missionaries and the good work that they do. It was not simply a battle of words, however, as for many the cultivation of the hearth mirrored the cultivation of the heathen. The accounts described the world beyond as a wide, wild waste awaiting the seed of instruction so that sure word of Prophecy could grow.

I had always wondered at those wastes, if they truly were wilder than the blasted heaths of home.

When I was young and I walked on the moors with Laon, I could not imagine a wilder place, given over to nature. The biting chill in our faces and the mists hanging over the endless, treeless dales. We chased each other, through the rippling heather, through ruined farmhouses. We would pretend that we were the only people left alive in the world; there was such a loneliness under that infinite Yorkshire sky.

Yet even those seeming wastes were carefully cultivated. Heather, sapling trees and other plants were culled with fire so that they might be suitable for grouse and sheep.

I still remember seeing it for the first time: the sea-like fire engulfing the banks of heather. It was a rising tide – that consumed seemingly everything. I remember the blaze on my face as I clutched Laon's hand and explained as our nurse, Tessie, had explained to me that morning: *It is how things are done. The moors need to stay the moors. It's just like cutting your fingernails.*

For all that we may be surrendering that land to nature, we chose for the moors to be empty.

As such my mind simply could not imagine truly empty, unclaimed land and I wondered if the wild wastes that those genteel missionaries wrote back to us about were as carefully cultivated as our own. If someone was choosing it to be empty.

Still, none of the lessons taught by those faraway tales seemed relevant here.

We waited for an hour for Miss Davenport.

In that time, Mr Benjamin asked further questions that arose from his reading of the Testaments. His asked them most sombrely, though some I had to smile at. I had resolved to answer each of his questions with a referral to my brother, but the gnome's enthusiasm was infectious. He took a great interest in the importance of sacrifice and the significance of price – he explained that fae liked numbers and costs.

"It is as a debt paid in full by Christ with his death, his sacrifice. A debt to redeem the first sin," I said. "The transgression in the garden, the forbidden food."

"But it is human sin? Or is it the sin of all? Did we all fall or is it just Mankind?" Mr Benjamin had a habit of referring to Adam by the literal meaning of his name in Hebrew, Mankind.

"I would hold that it is shared, by she who first bit into the fruit, at least."

"It is dangerous eating forbidden foods." He frowned, nose wrinkling as he tried to remember. "This is in the Psalms, is it not? *Behold, I was shapen in iniquity; and in sin did my mother conceive me?*"

I nodded. "Yes, it's often cited in reference to original–"

"It is about fae. I think. Maybe. But we are made that way. So it is about us, yes?"

"I don't know." I was dreading his answers. "How... how are you made?"

"Like it says. They are true words."

From there he pressed me to explain more of ransom theology and original sin, but an aside soon had us talking of antediluvian monsters. Soon we were in a lively discussion about the Apocrypha and how an archbishop once decreed any who published the Bible must do so with the Apocrypha intact, else be imprisoned for one year.

"What's in them, this Apocrypha?"

"Wild stories," I said, only half remembering. "Some of the youth of Jesus and how he gave life to clay birds. Judith and Holofernes is Apocryphal, of course. And there's all the fallen angels and nephilim in the books of the watchers."

"It's the wild word weeds," said Mr Benjamin. "They spring up even if you pull them out. No place for them in gardens."

"Scotland's Bible Society thought so. They petitioned

the British and Foreign Bible Society to not print it. I still remember my father marching up and down his study about that."

"He was angry?"

"He was opinionated on the matter, but also torn. He no more wanted to teach us the Apocrypha than to uproot it entirely."

"Weeds happen. You can never pull them out completely. I'm a gardener, I should know." He nodded very sagely at that, and I could not help but laugh.

My various disagreements with Miss Davenport only made me all the more hesitant to share my discovery of the papers with her. It was thus a few days before I was able to study them in earnest.

I waited until the few hours of true night, when the fish moon swam from the dark clouds and its light reminded me of standing at the top of the coal cellar stairs in the dead of winter, gleaming black blocks of brittle coal beneath me. I opened the travelling case of papers and reverently took out each page. Carefully, I sorted through them, spreading them out on the threadbare carpet.

I allowed myself a moment to appreciate the beauty of a simple mystery before plunging in.

The papers varied greatly in size and shape and texture. Some had torn edges, some were crudely scissored and others caught the light as though they were pages torn from a gilt-edged book. Most of them were scrawled over in that arcane lettering.

Enochian.

The name was one I had encountered before, but I still could not quite recall where. Medieval gnostics perhaps? Or part of Nostradamus' speculations? My father didn't have a copy of the seer but one of his books did quote the mystic for purposes of refutation.

Then I came to the book I had found on my first night here. I flicked through it, noting that it was written over in several different hands and that the words jostled against each other for space.

> *...There is something they aren't telling me. I can feel it in my bones. The house they keep me in is wrong, everything is wrong. I should have known. They are duplicitous by nature, but more than that, I can tell that they are keeping secrets. Yet truth is their weapon. How can I make them tell me? I am full of fear, but also so very full of hope...*
>
> *...They barely speak our tongue, more a mockery of it. I cannot keep my salt close enough. The covenant will protect me...*
>
> *...I know now more than I thought I could and I thought I should. Things that should not be written down...*

I was then on the first page, which declared it the private journals of Rev Jacob Roche. The original missionary.

I snapped shut the book.

My heart was thundering. I should not be reading this. The Reverend Hale had warned I should not read the journals of the previous missionary. He was explicit in how I needed to find them and bring them back, untouched.

And yet.

My eyes followed as my fingers caressed the worn leather spine. He did not ask that I refrain from studying the bindings, after all.

It was bound in a very thin, papery leather. The candlelight exaggerated the rough rise and fall of the leather's texture, though it was hard to see the animal's exact scarring.

There were a series of half-moon scorch marks down the middle of the back cover, arranged in a slight curve.

Wondering, I placed the tips of my fingers against each of the marks. Under my thumb was the fifth half-moon mark, soot-black against the pale leather. Squinting, I could see the suggestion of whirled patterns in one of the half moons and indents at the arch of each.

As I turned the volume over and over in my hands, I reasoned that Rev Hale had asked me to not read them so that I would know to not tell him that I *had* read them. He couldn't possibly expect me to restrain my curiosity.

I knew so little of Arcadia and, after Miss Davenport's cryptic warnings about what happened to the previous missionary, I couldn't help but wonder if his journals could contain a clue.

Resolute, I set down the journal and turned attention again to the papers.

Translation of the Bible into Enochian.

That one line in the Queen's English was my key. Assuming this to be the work of a student of these strange glyphs, "Enochian", then the lines by the Latin could be but translations. This also made sense of the more repetitive, shakily written pages which had the air of someone practising their letters, like Laon and I used to do, filling page after page with our intertwined names.

I had a firm grounding in French and German, taught to me so that I may translate poetry and pursue other such genteel pastimes. My knowledge of Latin and Greek was rather paltry, borrowed, as it were, from Laon's books.

Still, I knew enough of Latin and translation to start comparing the verses. I didn't think it entirely possible to piece together an entire language through these fragments, but the recognition of a few repeated words seemed very much in my grasp.

There were more edges to maps than simply the physical. Though confined as I was to Gethsemane, my soul was singing in the excitement of exploration. I could not help but imagine myself now standing at one such border of our knowledge, staring into the shadowy abyss of mankind's ignorance.

It was, perhaps, a foolish thought. But I had been restless for days and both soul and mind needed more than simply bread to sustain them. Presented now with something more, I eagerly plunged into that darkness.

My fingers itched for something to note my observations. My haphazard guesses needed to be recorded to be made sense of and picked apart later. It was all too easy to leap to conclusions when one was clutching a dozen disparate pages. Experience has taught me the importance of being systematic about such things.

I glanced up from my work and noticed that the door to empty air was unbolted. I had assumed myself negligent or forgetful the first few times it had happened, but now suspicion was festering in me. I tried to pay no heed as I pulled the bolt firmly across the lock.

It was just a door. There was no need to be afraid.

Glancing down at the lock, I saw that it had little angular symbols etched into it. I brought the candle nearer and upon closer inspection they seemed similar to those in my papers. It might even be a word that I could translate. I smiled in anticipated triumph.

Vaguely remembering there to be writing implements at the bottom of the case, I opened it and felt around its base. There was, indeed, a bottle of ink and an archaic glass-nibbed pen. Noting there was more at the end of my fingers, I pulled from the case a small corner of paper, folded over in upon itself.

A loud, long wail came from the door to empty air.

I turned, startled.

It was just wind. I knew it to be just wind, wind strong enough to rattle the heavy door in its hinges. I heard it howl against the other towers of the castle and I heard a distant shutter clatter against its window.

Having dropped the folded page, I fumbled for it on the floor. The candle cast long shadows and my hands were chilled from groping about on the cold stone floor when I found it.

Unfolding it, I found a printed page. The scrawl down the side identified it as being from Meric Casaubon's *A True and Faithful Relation of What Passed for Many Years Between Dr John Dee and Some Spirits*. Though the gothic print was awkward to read, I began to understand in part the veiled history of Enochian.

I did not sleep much that night.

CHAPTER 6
The Mysteries of the Night

Just as the mind of man is moved by an ordered speech, and is easily persuaded in things that are true, so are the Creatures of God similarly stirred when they hear the words with which they were brought forth into the world. For nothing moves, that is not persuaded; neither can anything be persuaded that is unknown.

The Creatures of God understand you not; you are not of their Cities. You are become enemies, because you are separated from him that Governeth the City by ignorance.

Mankind in His Creation, being made an Innocent, was not made partaker of the Power and Spirit of God.

Not only did he know all things under His Creation and spoke of them properly, naming them as they were, he also partook of our presence and society, yea a speaker of the mysteries of God; yea, with God himself. Though he spoke in innocence, he had communed with the Almighty, and us, His good Angels. Thus was Adam exalted.

The Speech which I will teach you, it is not to be spoken of in any other thing, neither to be talked of with Man's imagination. For as this Work and Gift is of God, which is all power, so does He open it in a tongue of power, to the intent that the proportions may agree in themselves: for it is written:

Wisdom sitteth upon a Hill, and beholdeth the four Winds,
and girdeth herself together as the brightness of the morning,
which is visited with a few, and dwelleth alone as though she
were a Widow.

Thus you see the Necessity of this Tongue.

Meric Casaubon, A True and Faithful Relation of
What Passed for Many Years Between
Dr John Dee and Some Spirits, 1659

Mysteries had a way of keeping me awake, gnawing at the
edges of my mind until they crept into my dreams as a jumble
of nonsense. Sense eluded me as I tossed and turned. I chased
shadowed secrets down the serpentine corridors of Gethsemane.

When dawn filled my room with light, I awoke to ink-
stained hands and blotted pages. I had fallen asleep atop the
pile of spread papers.

Dried ink stung my eyes as I scrubbed sleep from them. I
stumbled to my feet.

Reflexively, my eyes darted to the door to empty air. I
moved to secure the door before my eyes even focused. It
was, however, as I had thought, and I firmly pulled the bolt
in place. It was probably loose. Even as I told myself that it
was just the wind shifting it in the night, a cold chill danced
up my spine.

I scrubbed my hands and face at the basin until my skin
was red instead of ink-black, my mind still entangled in
what I had learnt of Enochian, the divine tongue, named for
Enoch, the last man to know it. The pages made grand claims,
that this language of frail and angular marks was used by the
Almighty to create the world and then given to Adam so that
he might name all creatures and all things within the gardens.
The pages promised that within this language of angels lay all

sorts of secrets, that there was a power in the knowing of the first and truest names of all things.

My heart was thundering. I told myself it was just the shock of the cold water on my face.

I wondered at the intentions of the person – Reverend Roche? – trying to translate the Bible into Enochian. Perhaps they had thought it an act of restoration, that the Word of God needed to be in the language of God. Or perhaps there is more to it.

My eyes ached. I closed them and pressed my too-warm fingers against my lids.

At the edge of my mind, I wondered if this was an evangelical tool and if so, was it the true language of the fae? Was there truth in the old theory that the fae had been angels? Or was it simply that they remember it from the time of Adam?

I changed, fingers fumbling over the tiny cloth-bound buttons of my clothes. Questions tumbled through my mind, twisting into one another in endless, writing circles. I had made lists of unique symbols and began comparison of the words. None of it made sense, but it was progress of a sort. A foothold upon the cliff of unknowing.

More than ever, I missed Laon. I wanted to tell him about this, to press my forehead against his and whisper to him what I knew like old secrets shared in the dark under blankets and sheepskins.

I wondered what he would make of such revelations, if he would be dismissive of paper scraps found in a random room of his castle or if the questions would haunt his mind the way they haunted me. I wondered if he already knew of the contents of these pages and that was what was keeping him silent.

I had cried the day Laon began his lessons in Latin and I was left alone; he offered afterwards to teach it all to me and share his books. He promised then that we were the same and he would treat me as such even if others refused to see that.

Secrets have a way of making me feel lonely.

I tried to imagine his voice. I remembered the curve of his ears against my lips and the warmth of his hands in mine. We had not laced together our fingers for a very long time. He didn't even shake my hand before he left.

But this felt too big for susurrus words and cupped hands; I felt too big.

Had it really been so long ago that we were chasing each other on the moors and hiding among the ruined farmhouses?

I remembered how close Laon and I used to be and, all at once I realised that it may never be that way again. Had it been simply the physical distance of when I was sent to school? Yet I wrote to him every day, each moment catalogued for his eyes, and he wrote back just as faithfully. Was it after? Yet we exchanged letters even then, though work dictated that neither of us could be as diligent in our correspondence. And then, being without a position, I returned to him and found him–

It didn't matter. He was still my brother. Nothing could change that.

There was a knock on my door and I heard the voice of an enquiring Miss Davenport.

My panicked eyes darted over the documents still spread about the room.

"A moment, if you please!" I said, trying to keep my voice even as I gathered up the papers and hid them among my own. I pushed over the neat stack of books I had brought with me. They spilt across the writing desk and onto the floor with a heavy thud.

A low creak signalled Miss Davenport's intrusion. I tried to steady my hands and slow my rapid breathing.

"You weren't at breakfast," she said cheerfully, keeping the door open with her hip as she manoeuvred a large heavily laden tray into the room. The scent of sweet bacon and buttery toast wafted over. "So I thought I should bring it to you. I didn't think I should trust the Salamander to take care of you. Even if she is the housekeeper."

There was a soft clink as she put down the tray and danced over to my elbow.

"Whatever have you there?" asked Miss Davenport.

"P-primers," I said, slamming shut the writing case and latching it closed with too much finality. "I was organising them."

"Primers?" She stooped to pick up one of the books.

"I was given them by the Society."

Leafing open the volume, Miss Davenport haltingly read out its frontispiece. "*The... Child's Spelling... Primer, or... First Book for... Children...*"

"The Society wanted to put me to good use, I suppose."

She laughed, the mocking note unmistakable this time. It was as sharp as an untuned violin.

"I do have passing experience as a schoolmistress," I said, prickling.

"Had they assumed there would be surfeit of pagan children eager to learn?" she said, a wide grin stretching tightly over her teeth. "Grubby-kneed brownies and adorable little pixies all gathering around Miss Helstone asking to be taught the most noble English language?"

"I don't think I had any particular expectations."

"Oh, but surely you had wished to teach them whilst you all sat on mushrooms together and sipped nettle tea from buttercups." Laughing, she hooked her fingers around an imaginary teacup and mimed dainty drinking. "We would curtsy to you in our precious little daisy petal dresses and tip at you our caps made of rue. We would be ever so grateful for your bequeathing language to us..."

"I had expected to make the acquaintance of more than two fairies and roam further than my brother's home." I crossed my arms. "I had expected some answers."

At that, Miss Davenport stopped laughing quite abruptly. "You needn't–"

"I'm sorry–" I said reflexively, seeing her discomfort. It was too easy to see her as my gaoler.

"We should eat," announced Miss Davenport, cheer returning to her voice. "I am rather famished."

I nodded, eager to make peace between us. I helped her rearrange the furnishings of my round room to accommodate two to dine. She shook out a tablecloth over my trunk and unloaded the full extent of the breakfast tray onto it.

She gave a satisfied sigh as she pried open a row of boiled eggs. Glancing over at me, she pushed it under my nose and gave me the salt.

"Sprinkle for me," she said.

"Pardon?"

"Human hands and human lands," she said, referring to the folk rhyme. "Meat loves salt and salt loves meat, I pray the Lord my soul to keep." She added a sarcastic edge to the pronunciation of *soul*.

"Oh, of course," I said, sprinkling salt upon the opened eggs. She had been demanding that I do so during our meals together but I had not quite managed to ask her why. Enquiring about her changeling state always seemed a little intrusive for an acquaintance, especially given how she was shunning services. "What do you do when I'm not here?"

"Not eat."

"Oh," I said, softening. I wondered how long she must have starved when my brother was away. "Don't you–"

"Can you do me another?" she interrupted. "I am very hungry."

I nodded, complying with her request and adding salt to the fruit tarts, pound cake, butter and the pot of chocolate coffee. The strawberries gleamed green atop their lemon-yellow crust, but turned pink at the touch of salt. The pound cake seemed to heave a sigh and drooped in its plate with dense, moist weight.

"Have you news of my brother?" I asked, knowing the answer before I spoke. It was a question I asked her almost every day.

Miss Davenport shook her head. "I'm afraid not, he's still at... I'm not sure where. Inland. Where the court is."

"Court?" It was more than she had said before. I sipped the spiced chocolate before stirring in another spoonful of sugar. I was still not used to the tinge of salt in everything I consumed.

She squirmed under the directness of my gaze. "I don't really know. Faeland politics isn't simple."

"But you at least acknowledge that there is politics. Thus entities who are politic." I put down the chocolate and studied her expression closely, trusting that she'd flinch if I neared the truth. "A court implies a judge or monarch? Something or someone presiding. Thus all I'm really missing is a title..."

"Don't bait me for answers, I beg you."

"If you won't answer me that," I said, reasoning that fae were keen on bargains. "You could at least tell me how Roche did his work."

"What do you mean?"

"Proselytise," I said. "I know you can't tell me how he... how he earned his crown of martyrdom. But surely you can tell me how he did his work here. How he spoke the word."

She stopped in the spreading of butter into pound cake. She put down the knife.

"It's so isolated here. I can't imagine who he would be talking to." I hated the pleading note that crept into my voice.

"Can't you tell me?"

Miss Davenport remained silent.

"All I really know about him is that he disappeared and that he had converted Mr Benjamin. I don't even know if his body made it back. Who else was even here? You make these jokes about my childish imagination and yet you would not–" I stopped myself. I took a deep breath. "I'm sorry."

I forced myself to turn my attention to the breakfast laid out before me. I took a slice of bread and despite being cool to the touch, the butter melted as it touched its dark surface. The pound cake was rich and very sweet, more pudding than cake. Grainy with sugar crystals, it melted in my mouth.

"He had visitors who called on him," Miss Davenport said, very slowly and very carefully. There was a tremble to the way she held herself. "He didn't have many places he could go."

"Thank you…"

"And Mr Benjamin… he wasn't always gardener and groundskeeper. It's easy to give hope to those who have lost. Who *are* lost. They were searching. He found."

"What does that–"

"We should take a turn in the garden," she said, with a bright smile, all traces of earlier tension vanishing as she tucked away the last of the pound cake. She drained her cup of chocolate coffee and glanced over at mine. I shook my head at her silent request to finish my drink.

"You have taken me around the courtyards before, Miss Davenport."

"The courtyards, of course, but not the gardens. I'm sure you will agree afterwards that it rivals even that at Kew."

"I daren't say I've been to the Royal Botanic Gardens."

"Well, neither have I," said Miss Davenport with a calculated wink and sharp giggle. "But it wouldn't do to be too humble about these things. Even though I hear their stove boy has a green thumb."

"Stove boy?"

"The John Smith who curates the place. He has a certain way with plants." Tight grin splitting her face from cheek to cheek, Miss Davenport tapped her nose knowingly. "I say too much sometimes, far too much."

CHAPTER 7

The Tower in the Garden

Balaenoptera wickeris, often termed a "sea whale" due to idiosyncratic fae humour, is believed to be more vast than any other beast, being twice again the size of the largest sea-dwelling whale. They are said to swim through soil and not water. They are distinct from the beasts known as the "see whale", an invisible piscine that lurks in the seas around Arcadian ports, and "C whale", the uncommon name for the *Balaena sinistris.*

According to Sibbald, the inhabitants of Arcadia believe the sea whale to be constructed of wicker. He had described to him these strange shipyards at Fishforth which built them. They say entire ecosystems of fishes can live within the whale once it has consumed sufficient "sea."Whale "bones"of wood can often be found on sale at the Goblin Market.

This is all, of course, preposterous. Whilst the sea whale is a true creature, its presence on land is but a form of the Fata Morgana, a superior mirage, a result of the reflecting and refracting of the whale's image from its native sea inland, especially into the more misty parts of Arcadia. The mist is key to understanding this natural optical illusion as the water droplets provide purchase for the projection. Just as a Fata Morgana can cause a ship to seem as though it is inside the waves, the Fata Morgana causes the whale to appear inside the earth.

Robert Walton, THE NATURAL HISTORY OF THE WHALE: TO WHICH IS ADDED A SKETCH OF A SOUTH SEA WHALING VOYAGE

I did not expect a castle to have much of a garden, encircled as it was by the vast walls and moat. My walks with Miss Davenport had made me familiar with the courtyards and their prosaic vegetation.

As Miss Davenport wound a path past the chapel, I thought of her remark on the stove boy with the green thumb.

"Did you mean to say he's a changeling?" I asked.

"I didn't exactly say that now, did I?" Her voice turned singsong and she pulled back a veil of ivy on the far wall of the courtyard. So thick were the leaves and vines that it seemed a heavy green curtain. I thought of Mr Benjamin's warning.

Miss Davenport detached a key from a bracelet, winking at me as she did so. "Don't tell the Salamander I have this."

"I won't because I can't," I said. "I've not met the Salamander."

"It's for the best." She smiled to herself as though she had just committed an act of wit and unlocked the ironbound door behind the ivy.

Behind the high, embattled wall was a half-wild garden, artfully overgrown.

Bordered by ruined roman arches and colonnades, it seemed as though a longforgotten lord had sealed away a ruined villa on a whim and turned it into a pleasure garden. A trellis guided roses to form an elegant canopy by the tall, sheltering cedars. The trees scented the garden like a church. Four paths quartered the grass, leading the eye to a central grove of olive trees.

I had stepped into a medieval manuscript, an illumination of the *hortus conclusus*.

"Pretty, isn't it?" said Miss Davenport, studying my face with interest. "I told you it would be."

"You did..." I muttered.

Behind the spiralling trunks of the olive trees, in the middle of that grove, was a stone fountain overgrown with water lilies. The water was completely still and the spout was sealed.

I dipped my hand into the cool water and stroked the petals of the lilies. I smiled at the beauty of it all. Unlike the faded grandiosity of the castle, the walled garden had been reclaimed by something greater. It gave an illusion of a sublime infinity imperfectly captured and imperfectly held, like rainbows in water.

"What is the history of Gethsemane?" I asked.

"Of Gethsemane? You mean this place?"

"The history of this castle, this garden. It's obviously old. Who lived here before, well, us?"

The changeling shrugged. "No one."

"But–"

"No one I know of," she added hastily. "There was the previous missionary, Roche, of course, but I don't know more than that. This place is built on secrets, after all."

"Too many," I murmured to myself, but I did not press her further. Her first answer felt meaningful though, given as it was, unwittingly. This verbal tug of war reminded me all too much of luring answers out of teachers at school, when ambushes worked better than stubborn interrogations. Still, some things had to be bargained for.

Miss Davenport idled by the roses. Having plucked one, she was absorbed by the dismantling of its petals, carefully tearing each one off.

Wind rustled the branches and wafted over the rich scent of mint. It drew me down the path and into the cedars. Laon and I used to crush mint in our hands until they were stained with scent. We would look for it in the wild or steal it from Tessie's garden. Laughing, I would put on airs and proclaim myself a London lady and daub it behind my ears.

A round tower stood in the middle of the trees, too small to be more than a single chamber.

The pendulum sun was overhead, granting a warm glow to the ivory-white stone. Part of the tower was joined to the castle by a narrow, roofed bridge. The bridge was not of white stone; it was red brick. A curio, certainly, but arguably no stranger than the rest of the garden. And, like the garden, it seemed a moment suspended in time, drawn from the imagination of a long-dead monk. I could imagine his shaking hands dappling shadow onto the covered well and smooth, pale stone.

The door was too big for the tower. Its snarling knocker was green with age and stained my hands such when I used it.

I peered inside.

"Hello?" My voice echoed within the stone chamber.

I eased open the door and it gave a low creak.

There was a coppery tang to the still, undisturbed air. I felt as though I was unsealing an ancient tomb, breathing again the stale air of the past.

Sunlight lancing through the windows suspended dust in seeming timelessness. At the far end of the room, beyond the broken benches and toppled candlesticks, was an altar, slightly recessed into the wall. An altarpiece stood upon it, the triple frame of tarnished gold imposingly empty and the colours of its panel painting made muddy by the river of time. Soot and grime from long years' candles and incense smeared its surface. Shadows obscured all but the round, gilded halos that framed each of the faces.

Only their holiness remained.

I drifted towards the altar, entranced by the destruction that had been wrought upon this chapel. The benches had overturned and were scarred by a heavy blade, an axe, perhaps.

A chill came upon me as I wondered who could have desecrated this chapel. Popish it may be, I could not believe the hands that wrought this destruction meant me and my brother anything but harm.

On the floor was spilt a dark, ominous stain and a chalice. A communion table lay on its side; battered Bible, silver dish, wafers and candlesticks lay scattered upon the bare stone besides it.

Do This in Remembrance of Me.

I was not so enamoured of the new fashions in theology as to think the wafers sacral outside of their ritual, but it still seemed wrong that they were left in the dust and dirt. They may not be the literal flesh of Christ but His touch is on them. They are more than bread.

I picked up the Bible. Pages had obviously been torn from it. My heart felt again the cold clutch of fear.

Taking a step closer to the lonely altarpiece, I thought I could make out the outline of Christ upon the Cross in the central panel, the huddle of three by his feet the three Marys. The left panel depicted a kneeling, haloed Christ within the garden of Gethsemane, begging his heavenly father to spare him the cup of suffering. Behind him were his apostles, barring the way of the shadowed, benighted figure of Judas. From that, I had expected the right panel to show Mary cradling the dead body of Jesus, but the composition of figures was wrong: Only one large shining figure stood at the fore of a red door of sorts with a small, paler figure clambering either in or out. Blocky birds swarmed behind.

With a handkerchief, I tentatively cleaned the panel.

The grime clung to the altarpiece, only smearing further. Frowning, I spat upon my handkerchief and scrubbed a little harder.

It was not a red door, but the yawning maw of a monstrous beast. The small, pale figures were fleeing, even as the beast's lashing, forked tongue was wrapped around one such figure. The birds that blacked the sky behind were demons.

Slowly, it dawned upon me. I was uncertain if I was making it clearer or if I was becoming more familiar with the subtle colours of the faded piece, conjuring details to make sense of the fragments.

Yet the answer became inescapable: it was the Harrowing of Hell.

The painting was done in a different style to the other two panels, its human forms less lithely elegant in their composition. Even as they screamed and clutched at each other in their cages, I guessed the painting older, perhaps medieval, and then later added to this altarpiece for eccentric reasons. The Harrowing was not a popular subject for altarpieces, after all.

"There you are," came the voice of Miss Davenport. "I didn't mean for you to come in here."

I heard her footsteps entering the chapel.

"What is this place?" I asked, gazing at the white lattice of ribs within the mouth of the hell-beast.

"The other chapel."

"Other?"

"It doesn't really matter, just another old place in a place full of old places." She gave a nervous laugh. "None of it is real anyway."

"Who was–"

She shook her head. "I shouldn't have brought you here. It should have all stayed locked."

"You need to explain. You can't show me a secret second

chapel with the remains of some interrupted communion and expect me to stay silent, Miss Davenport."

"We should go." She cast her eyes to the dark corners of the chapel, to the altar.

"No."

"We shouldn't be here."

"An answer for a step." It was a ridiculous bargain, but I stood my ground.

"I'll tell you when we're outside."

"Tell me now."

Miss Davenport swallowed before speaking. "It's just a folly. The fae stage these all the time. Like how you might arrange teacups in the woods to trick children into thinking fae are picnicking there. Or arrange toy soldiers in a scene of escape from their tin. It's a game."

"But who was meant to see it? If it's a game, there must be a player."

She was trembling but her voice remained steady. "No one yet. It's not ready."

I waited another heartbeat as her hands agitated, folding and unfolding by her face. I relented and took a step towards the door, accepting her answer even as I distrusted it.

The relief upon her face was immediate.

I murmured my apology as we stepped outside the chapel. It assuaged my conscience even as Miss Davenport did not hear it. I only hoped that the answer was worth my guilt.

We walked back in silence. At the foot of the stairs that led to my room, Miss Davenport apologised for having brought me to the garden.

"I wasn't thinking. I'm sorry," she said, avoiding my gaze. "I shouldn't have brought you there. It was my fault."

"Would you like to eat with me, at least?" I remembered what she had said about salt that morning.

"Changelings don't really need food. For all the feeling of hunger, we just like it. And unsalted food doesn't–" She took a deep breath.

"Why do you ask me to invoke the covenant of salt for you then?"

She studied the floor for a long moment. "It would be best if you forgot the garden behind the veil of ivy."

With that, she wished me a good day and turned to leave. Part of me wanted to bid her stay and ask her to tell me what had been weighing down her words, but I knew I shouldn't. We were not friends. For all her talk of protecting me and the time we spent together, we discussed little of substance. I had already strained what we had with my earlier interrogation. To overstep again our intimacy would only drive her further from me.

As my hand lingered on my door, a feeling of being watched came over me. The hairs at the back of my neck stood on end as I felt the scrutiny of a thousand eyes, like the rush of heat when brave fingers dart through naked flame.

There was a rustling noise: a jostling of wings or the rippling of leaves.

I turned. But for my shadow, the space behind me was empty.

"It's you, isn't it? Salamander?" I called out. "You helped me that time…"

I heard a high, bell-like laugh. Or perhaps it was bells that sounded like laughter.

"In the dark. With the lantern. I remember."

I followed the sound, but the castle was as empty of people as it always was. I stumbled down an unfamiliar corridor.

"Won't you talk to me?"

The sound of bells grew fainter until I was certain I was alone.

I sighed and returned to my room, winding up the tight knot of stairs. I was troubled by Miss Davenport's departure and further unsettled by the elusive Salamander.

Of the mission's inhabitants, I had yet to meet the aforementioned Salamander. When asked, Mr Benjamin merely muttered darkly about the dangers of fickle fire and his attention would wander off, abruptly changing the subject to a remark about the weather.

I had pieced together some impressions of the presumably fire-aligned fae. I was, after all, well acquainted with the theories of Paracelsus that proposed all fae were fundamentally elemental in nature, and I had no reason to believe this untrue at present. The Salamander was allegedly in charge of the household, with Mr Benjamin as merely groundskeep, but there was little trace of the Salamander's work.

Sighing, I pulled out the papers I had hidden from Miss Davenport that morning. This all, at least, allowed me time to work on the Enochian manuscript.

The shapes of the symbols were slippery in my mind. My unfamiliarity with them meant that I found them difficult to differentiate. My inability to even guess at Enochian's pronunciation meant that I wasn't even able to sound them in my mind, making it wholly an exercise in matching glyph to glyph. Each word required a painstaking cataloguing. I remembered trying to learn Greek from my brother's textbooks and how my eyes rebelled against an alien alphabet. I laughed now at how heartily I had complained at him about Greek's awkwardness. Enochian was far, far worse.

I imagined myself Jean-François Champollion reading hieroglyphs for the first time. Laon and I read of his breakthrough in our father's periodicals.

The lists of words were incomplete, to say the least, and the spellings were not always consistent. Most of it was even glossed in Latin rather than English and I cursed my own feminine education.

It was a sort of madness.

One of the oddities that struck me was that there was a series of glyphs that only ever appeared by themselves. They were never repeated with any of the other letters. It made me question my assumptions. There was no reason to expect this to be an alphabet like the Cyrillic script or even runes. There was no reason to expect texts written in the same alphabet to be in the same language. Surely to an outsider, a page of French and a page of English would look similar enough.

My mind was panicking as I studied my great catalogue of words. The pattern of their repetitions suggested sufficient overlap in vocabulary that they were probably the same language.

That word with the unique letters, though.

It was in that first line of Enochian I had read beside that Latin.

In the beginning there was the Word and the Word was God and the Word was with God.

Of course.

I laughed to myself at how obvious it was: those letters were the name God.

I looked at the page before me and seeing it repeated throughout I knew I had to be right. I was holding the gospel in Enochian. This must have been an effort to translate the Bible.

And yet, why would this language have a unique word for God? For all our own reverence His title in English is merely made of everyday letters. Hallowed His name may be, but there was nothing unique about its writing. Before I had learnt letters, Agnes told me that the letters in God and dog were mirrored; it was a fact that boggled my tiny mind. I had thought anagrams to be a sort of verbal magic that would make one thing into another.

I thought of Champollion recognising Cleopatra's name in a cartouche. Perhaps it was only apt that this should be the first word I read in Enochian.

There were those who would not write divine names or made taboo their pronunciation. There were those who forbade His depiction. Perhaps this was like that, writing the name of God in a way that was alien to the rest of the script.

But I wanted it to mean more. I wanted it to confirm my wild theories of this being the language of angels, stolen and preserved by the fae. I wanted this to be that sacred first language that God spoke to create the world, that He taught to Adam and that was sundered at Babel.

And so I pressed on, trying to make sense of the other words. Whilst nothing made sense as passage, other recurring short words began to linger a little longer in my mind.

As I worked, I thought again of Miss Davenport's answer at the scene in the chapel. I could believe there to be artifice in the arrangement, that there wasn't an interrupted act of communion, only someone's desire to suggest that. But such dioramas were always made to be seen, and if not by my eyes then there must be another pair it was all intended for.

But who?

As my candle guttered, my fractured thoughts no longer followed one another and their haze bordered on sleep. My eyes were no longer focusing on the words before me.

Tired beyond thought, I stumbled towards the basin and splashed water from it onto my face. The water soothed but washed away none of the exhaustion. The bed was but a few aching steps away.

As my eyes closed and I lost myself to the enveloping sheets, something agitated at the back of my mind. It was like a loose tooth or a stray thread, tugging at my thoughts. There was something I had forgotten.

• • •

That night, I dreamt of Laon.

He lay under a willow in a garden, resting his head on the lap of a pale, pale woman. She wound her arms around him and he sighed as she stroked his face. Her locks of white gold and brown were draped over his black hair.

The long, delicate fronds of the willow framed their idyllic scene and my presence felt like an intrusion.

At the edges of my hearing, they were whispering to one another. Soft and gentle words were pressed against ears, like kisses, intimate and secret.

Suddenly, I couldn't breathe.

I did not know her face. It was sharp and strange. She turned and looked straight at me, amber eyes piercing. I was trapped in them; I saw myself reflected in them. I saw myself as she saw me, pathetic and worthless, nothing more than an insect. I felt long-limbed, ungainly and drab, a moth to her butterfly.

I shrank from her gaze, but her eyes pinned me. I was a moth newly drawn from the bottom of a killing jar and unfolded onto a specimen board, my flaws on lurid display.

She laughed. My brother gazed at her with worshipful eyes and he could not see me. He drew from the air a ribbon of bright scarlet and wound it through her white and brown hair, his long, beautiful fingers catching her misty, cloudlike tresses.

I wanted to call out to them, for him to notice me. I wanted to tell him I had been waiting for him, that I had come all this way to see him, but I found I had no voice.

I struggled to run forwards but they only seemed all the further away. I could not look away as the distance between them closed, skin against skin.

The dream continued for some time, and when I finally awoke, I found my eyes gritty and sore from unshed tears, and my heart aching.

Chapter 8

The Words in the Book

Iron or steel, in the shape of needles, a key, a knife, a pair of
tongs, an open pair of scissors, or in any other shape, if placed
in the cradle, secured the desired end. In Bulgaria a reaping-
hook is placed in a corner of the room for the same purpose.
I shall not stay now to discuss the reason why supernatural
beings dread and dislike iron. The open pair of scissors,
however, it should be observed, has double power; for it is not
only of the abhorred metal, – it is also in form a cross.

Edgar Shelley Heartland, "The Secrets of Steel", Iron:
An Illustrated Weekly Journal for Iron and Steel,
Printed and Published by James Bounsall,
at the Mechanics' Magazine Office, 1846

My feet were sore from pacing. I did not know how long I had
been turning and turning in my circular room.

Days had become weeks, and my confinement within the
walls of Gethsemane was becoming intolerable. Little differed
from day to day: Mr Benjamin had continued being nothing
but excessively courteous and abrupt in his conversation;
Miss Davenport returned each day to sew and knit with me,

with long sighs and tales of her human family, and of course, there was no sign of the Salamander.

The seasons, in so far as they could be understood as such, marched on, and the pendulum sun continued its strange patterns. As the swing of the pendulum decreased, the sun no longer passed overhead. Midday was just a little darker and midnight just a little brighter. The days themselves did not grow shorter, of course, as the length of time it takes for a pendulum to complete its swing remained constant – that much I remembered from my lessons.

I had slept less and less, however, as questions from the papers, from Mr Benjamin, from my own mind all crowded in on me.

The Reverend's journal had continued to taunt me, and finally, late one night, I had succumbed. I had known I shouldn't have opened it. I had told myself I was merely going to look over the hand to determine if any of the papers I had been studying were written by the Reverend.

I did not entirely believe myself, but it had been enough in the way of self-permission to take out the volume and hold it in my hand.

I spun on my heels, my fingers fisted in the stiff fabric of my skirt. I breathed deep and kept walking, trying in vain to find solace in motion.

As I had turned the journal over and over, it slipped from my hands and fell open:

The walls, the windows, the walls. None of them make sense. There is a history here but I cannot read it. A story told by a madman.

Their promises, their oaths, their geas are there to hinder you, to hobble you, to hide you. They are there to blind you and to bind you.

Their truth is not our truth. They wield it only as a weapon.

My eyes had glided over the words and read them before I even realised and my heart sank to my feet.

Of course, the missionary was lost now. There was no reason to think that he might be right in his mad scribbling. There was no reason to think that he might have the right of it.

But they were the words my restless soul most feared, most wanted to be true.

My fingers smudged over my aching eyes. They stung from how dry they were. My nails dug into my skin and the pinpoints of pain only reminded me how my skin could not contain myself. I wanted to be everywhere at once, anywhere but here.

The seed of doubt had been planted. I should not have read that book. The Reverend's warning was more prophetic than he could know.

There was a knock, and Miss Davenport appeared by the doorway of my room. She was, as always, rosy in cheek and looking slightly breathless, as though she had just come in from a long walk. I knew by now that she looked that way even if she had been stationary for hours.

"I thought you might be up here, Miss Helstone," she said, cheerfully. "The weather is simply divine and I was thinking we should spend the day knitting in the solar. I've almost finished my shawl and I do think I would like your advice on how I should start the socks."

I said nothing for a moment. My hands tumbled over and over one other as I grasped for what to say. I was coming to see her as gaoler, an uncharitable and ultimately unfair assessment, but her seeming freedom only brought me bitterness.

"I need to go outside," I said. "I'm.... I've been in here too long."

"We can take a turn in the garden."

The wall-bordered sky could bring me no reprieve. I shook my head.

"Or a walk on the roof?"

I shook my head again. The distances glimpsed within and beyond the mists would but taunt me in this state.

I turned and looked her in the eye.

For a change, her gaze did not dart away as it so often did. She had a disquieting habit of just looking past me, not quite at me.

"You should try to be still," she said. "Please, Cathy."

My name struck me like a slap to the face. There was no shock in her eyes as I recoiled.

"You have no right to address me as such," I said. "We are not friends."

"But, Catherine–"

"You tell me nothing. We talk and we talk and yet you forever keep me in ignorance and darkness. You keep saying this castle is built on secrets but we cannot build a friendship on–"

"You need to be still." She reached a hand towards me. Perhaps she had meant for it to be soothing, but I was no skittish horse to be tricked by a steady voice and calming hand.

I took a step back. "Do not touch me."

"Come with me."

"No."

"Calm down and we will talk. I promise."

I shook my head. "I need to be elsewhere."

It was then that I realised in my pacing I had placed myself between her and the door. It was ajar behind me.

So I turned and bolted.

CHAPTER 9

The Dog in the Mist

By and large, the Fair Folk possess all the essentials of humanity. They have in common with us all the elements of body which make up the man. They have two eyes, two ears, two hands and two feet. They appear to laugh when they are pleased, weep when they are grieved; they sleep when weary, eat when hungry; rejoice over their gains, mourn over their losses very much as other men do.

However, those longest associated with them, and most intimately acquainted with their character and habits, never expect one of the Fair Folk to speak the truth when there is a chance for them to tell a lie. Yet they will tell you by their own laws, and by their own lips (usually two), that it is a vile sin to lie and deceive.

William Finkle & Hildegard Vossnaim, THE ARCADIAN VOYAGES, EMBRACING DIVERSE ACCOUNTS OF FIRST TRAVELLERS, WITH NOTES ON THE CULTURE AND THE CLIMATE

I was probably lost.

I had but pulled on gloves and marched from the house. I had needed to be outside of its walls.

My heart had been a storm-tossed ship, turning and turning inside me. Every snorting, frustrated breath I took only further agitated the vessel.

I had told myself I was but venturing outside the walls, to prove to myself that I could, that the stone could not hold me. I told myself I just wanted to stand beyond the portcullis and look back at my recent prison. I told myself I merely wanted to be out.

But soon I had wandered much further.

The path from Gethsemane was a fading dirt track but, five paces from the walls I could barely see it under my feet. It wound down from the precipice where the castle stood and my curiosity lured step by step into the roiling mist-sea.

It was chilly but not biting as I walked, adding to the grey mist with warm, white breath of my own.

The mists gathered at my feet and, between my steps, I imagined soft, downy undergrowth. I felt the flutter of foliage against my skirts, trailing their fingerlike fronds against me. They shed dandelion tears as they unfurled like wings.

Airy faces seemed to form from the mist. I found them as I did before, strange elfin faces grinning wider and wider as sinuous features coalesced around them. Strange pinwheel creatures curled around one another, eel-like, suspended in the air around me. Droplets of mist dewed on unearthly branches and rows of moonstone eyes opened, watching and unblinking.

One of the tiny faces smiled at me. It seemed so guileless, childlike in its desire, that I smiled back.

It reached out a spindly, three-fingered hand towards me.

A sound in the distance, like a gunshot.

Startled, the half-formed creature effervesced. A look of sheer terror on its face as it melted away; its milk-pale, moonstone eyes lingering for just a moment after the rest of it vanished.

I staggered back and cast my eyes about the mists.

It was only when a second bark followed that I realised it was the sound of a dog.

The mists twisted around me and the sky darkened. The faces around me opened their pale maws and screamed without sound. Their contorted faces opened more and more to give breath to fear, but there was nothing but a deafening silence. The feathery mist-ferns became handlike, pulling themselves from the grey earth and snatching and snaring. They gained no purchase on the hems of my skirt but it did not stop them from trying.

A black dog tore through the mists. Its bark was sharp and abrupt, it filled my ears and, unlike the dreamlike softness of the mist creatures, the dog seemed to burn with a hellish intensity. The mist shied away from it; its tendrils turning to wisps of smoke where it touched it.

It had bounded straight out of a fireside story, a spectral hound with eyes of flame. The cook used to scare us with folktales, the Gytrash and the Barghest, all beasts of shadow wandering the endless moors. Some were lost dogs, waiting for their long dead masters, but most were simply out to ambush lonely travellers.

Something darted past me, a black all-too-solid shadow. I heard a low, echoing growl that seemed to surround me. A deep, rumbling sound, it curdled my blood and rippled gooseflesh down my spine.

I spun around, trying to see the source of my terror.

The black dog was behind me; it turned and closed the distance between us in a leap.

Cold fear clutched at my chest. I was struck by how monstrously huge the animal was. It swung its great lion-like head towards me and its ember-like gaze seared my soul. I staggered back and I felt the brittle fingers of the misty undergrowth crumble as they clutched and clawed at me.

Bonelike, I could hear them crunch under my feet.

The mist was teeming with squirming creatures, snaking over and over each other, chasing and biting tails, mirroring my tumultuous thoughts. They devoured each other in a coiling mass.

A rider on a vast horse-like creature charged through the knotted smoke. They cut through it like a veil.

I gasped.

Instinct failed me. Too shocked to move, I watched its approach.

The beast reared, leathery wings unfurling as its knife-hooves pawed the air. Its rider toppled from its back. The beast pranced forwards, shaking free its mane.

Hearing a groan of pain from the rider brought me back to my senses. It was a familiar, human sound.

I edged closer.

A glacial calm came over me. I saw my panic as though through a mirror now, separate from my self.

"Are you much hurt?" I said.

The rider tried to force himself onto his feet, but he fell again.

"I could get help. I live quite…" I hesitated. I thought of the shifting mists and my argument with Miss Davenport.

The mists curled between us, suffocatingly dense around him, but I could just about make out the shape of grey hands closing around the rider. The choking hands tightened in fist after fist.

"Stay where you are." I sounded far more certain than I was. "I'll get your horse."

Fear thundering in my veins, I ran to calm the startled beast. It seemed a panicked flurry of wings and hooves.

Only when my hand touched its soft, scaly nose did I wonder if Faeland beasts were different than ones I was used to.

I had the reins in my hand. Murmuring soothing nonsense under my breath, I smoothed its mane even as it flickered fire under my fingers. The beast danced its hooves, slowly steadying. Its wings flapped once more and folded.

Feathery gills flared under my fingers. I could feel its breathing calm.

I saw my fear as a golden-eyed beast much like the one under my hands, and as I stroked it, over and over, I soothed my own fear. Its golden eyes seemed to soften as it regarded me, and then with an abrupt blink they turned blue.

I led the beast back to the fallen rider.

"Cathy?"

The voice sounded disbelieving. It held a very, very familiar tone.

"No, it can't be," he said, fear creeping into his voice. "Of all the days for this to... What are you?"

The mist lingered over the rider, obscuring his features, but I recognised him. The knot of my heart twisted and tightened. I knew that voice, that shift of his shoulders, that turn of head. I hastened. I knew that hand that reached out towards me; I knew it as though it was my own.

"Laon?"

Hearing my voice, he wavered for moment, withdrawing his hand. "What illusion are you?"

"It's me," I said. "No illusion."

"The mists grow more deceitful," he murmured, more to himself than to me. "If you are trying to seduce me, spirit, I'm afraid I'm quite incapable at the moment."

"I... I am your Cathy. Your sister."

He grunted and cursed under his breath. I could hear the pain in his voice now and I could feel it mirrored upon myself. I knew he didn't believe me. "Doesn't matter. I've things that need–" He winced again, sharply.

"Can you move at all?"

"Probably. But I can't put weight on my ankle. I've fallen on it." He looked about. "Diogenes? My dog?"

"I don't know where your dog is."

Laon whistled, piercingly, and the great black animal came loping back. It circled us, weaving in and out of the mists.

I swallowed, feeling a cold breeze ripple across the back of my neck as the dog disappeared behind me. I could feel it in the shadows, lurking. "But I've brought you your... horse."

"I need help to it." He regarded my outstretched hand with weary suspicion. "Can I trust you not to melt away? When I lean on you?"

I nodded, though realising he might not be able to see it through the mist, I added, "You can trust me."

His hand clasped mine, solid, an anchor in the sea of mist. I could feel his warmth, his breath on my skin.

He gritted his teeth as he got to his feet, using me as ballast. It was two false starts before he stood and could move his hand to my shoulder. His breath grew ragged from the exertion.

With him leaning heavily on me, the two of us staggered towards the side of the horse.

"I won't be able to ride with you," I said.

"Of course not."

"Are you headed towards Gethsemane?"

He laughed; I recognised it as humourless. "Aren't we all?"

"Well, I am."

Steadying himself on me, he pushed himself onto the saddle of the beast. He hissed in pain as he swung his leg over. "If you are, then I shall see you there."

"You- you shall." I wasn't sure if I should correct. It felt as though the mist was upon him and he would not believe me.

"Thank you, nonetheless." He sighed and nudged the beast into motion. Its skin rolled as it moved, ropes of muscle shifting like snakes. He whistled again for the hound. This time it didn't emerge but I could feel the shadows shift in answer to him.

I couldn't help the tears as I watched the mists swallow him. He was very so close. Perhaps it was because of this enveloping mist, obscuring and obfuscating. I was trembling, but it was no longer fear that shook me.

He didn't look back when he said, "Though I would rather you didn't take the shape of my sister to torment me."

The mists, grey-dark and murky, closed around me. They rose and fell like waves; I could hear the echo of the crashing across the valley, above me. The mists swirled like water and huge shadows glided above.

My knees buckled, and as I knelt I cradled my face in my hand. A darkness gathered above me. Glancing up, I saw a strange edifice of mist break in half. Its pieces rained down around me, insubstantial as all the other phantoms of this place. I tried to stem my tears. My eyes stung from the wool of my gloves, my tears soaking into them, warm at first and then cold.

As I took off my gloves, I saw the valley around me littered with sunken shadow ships. Despite the mist, I could see very far and the plains of torn sails, shattered hulls and bent masts seemed without end. Serpentine smoke-beasts circled them, over and over, threading themselves around the white husks of the ships. Tear-shaped fish streamed down from the distant surface and fish-tailed merfolk tore at their own hair as they danced, half-mad among the ruins.

It was some time before I could walk back to the mission.

CHAPTER 10
The Brother in the Hall

The feeling of discomfort which insensibly creeps over one upon entering a fae dwelling is produced neither by the rudeness nor the scantiness of the furniture, nor by the difference in external appearance from that which one has been accustomed to.

It is the result, rather, of the instinctive feeling that there is still something absent, without which even regal splendour would fail to satisfy. There is wanting that which is the charm of every home, whose influence can invest even poverty in the raiment of beauty and joyousness, and which, even amid much that is depressing, can fill the house with perpetual gladness; and that is, the spirit of love.

The absence of that mysterious bond of loving oneness, which links together indissolubly the hearts of Christian homes, is distressingly apparent in almost every heathen family that one visits. There is a dreariness, and want of that earnest mutual sympathy which is the very foundation of domestic happiness, which is apt to bring back to one's mind home-scenes in England, and to give one a more thorough appreciation of the blessings of Christianity.

William Finkle & Hildegard Vossnaim, THE ARCADIAN VOYAGES, EMBRACING DIVERSE ACCOUNTS OF FIRST TRAVELLERS, WITH NOTES ON THE CULTURE AND THE CLIMATE

When I finally returned to Gethsemane, the castle was ablaze with light. It was a beacon above the mists, and I saw it far, far before I reached its gatehouse. The mist creatures swarmed around the light, as though fascinated by their lurid glow. It was then I noticed that most of them cast no shadows. They seemed faint and unearthly against the stone of the castle.

The portcullis raised at my approach. I heard hurried footsteps, but saw no one.

Gate followed gate, cobbles hard against my sore feet. I longed to take off my boots. At the far end of the courtyard were the stone arches that led into the keep. For a moment, the steps seemed impossibly tall and I climbed them wearily.

The painted wooden pendants that hung from the arches seemed sharper and all the more like teeth as I leaned into the ironbound door to open it, using my shoulder for strength. It was very heavy. Its creaking filled my ears.

As I stepped inside, the door whined shut, a sound that echoed far too loudly despite the myriad tapestries and carpets that clothed the foyer.

The lofty, elegant ribs of the ceiling no longer seemed distant and beautiful. I had once thought them like a birdcage, but now I could only think of the heaving ribcage of a great beast that had swallowed me whole. Wind rushed through the foyer, howling as it reached the corridors above. The grey curtains and tapestries fluttered and then stilled. For three quick heartbeats, it had stopped.

I had already crumpled in the mists and those tears had barely dried. I told myself I would not cry again.

And then it started again, heaving another breath. Air flowed through the hall. I heard the rattling of shutters and there was a low groan from the wooden parts of the ceiling. The whole foyer seemed to shudder before it ceased again.

Irregular footsteps. A slammed door.

"What are you doing here?"

I looked up to see my brother in one of the balconies, framed by an ornate arch. He was leaning heavily on a walking stick. Stone feathers cast irregular shadows on his face, but I did not need to see it to know he was enraged.

Taken aback, I could but stare at him. I had thought that once we were out of the mists he would recognise me.

His dog, jet black and decidedly more mundane in this light, bounded over to me. It wagged its tail with seeming delight and gave a resounding bark.

"Begone, spirit!" he said, limping towards me, circling from one end of the long balcony to the other. The uneven rhythm of his gait, unfamiliar to me, unsettled and worried me. Each of the clawed arches cast a darker shadow on his face. He limped down the stairs that spilt into the foyer, its carpet a scarlet tongue against the darker colours. "Why do you plague me so? Does it please you to see me like this? Have you not tortured me enough?"

He was tall, taller than I remembered him being. Perhaps it was simply the shadows and the stairs, but Laon towered above me.

"I am your sister," I said, straightening. "Laon, brother–"

"Do not call me by that name! You have no right, spirit. Do not pretend to be flesh and illuse upon my hound! Is it not enough that–"

"No, you have no right." Anger flared within me. I met his gaze, my hands fisting tightly, and spat back his venom. The dog slunk off, cowering from my outburst. "I have written countless begging letters to be here, to stand in front of you, to help you. And I did not do all that grovelling to be berated and belittled by you. I have not come so far to be mistaken for some half-witted spirit. I expect my brother to know me and my face." I was shaking; I could feel myself unsteady on my feet. My eyes threatened to water as I stubbornly refused to blink. My nostrils were flaring. "Or am I mistaken in who I love?"

Thunderstruck, he stared at me, the clear blue of his eyes almost disarming. He was without words. I could see I had hurt him and though I meant to soften my words, they did not quite come out that way.

"Or if nothing else, be able to ask me some question, some secret that we shared. If indeed Arcadia is so treacherous," I said. I attempted a smile but I knew it was more of a grimace. I had waited so long to see him, endured the confinement of his home, and here he was, denying me even my own self. "Is it so impossible that I am indeed your sister? Can you not believe that I could and would follow you? Can you not believe that I have the strength and the love to come? Can you not believe that I would care–"

"Catherine!"

His walking stick clattered to the floor.

Strong arms enfolded me and cut me off; I recognised his smell instantly and melted into his hug. It was more instinct than anything else. I breathed him in, all fear and anger and exertion. I could not remember the last time we were this close.

"Laon…"

He was leaning heavily on me, very heavily. I remembered his injury.

"Your ankle–" I started.

He was laughing, face buried in my shoulder. I realised how precariously he was balanced, though it was really too late. His arms tightened around me and we toppled to the hard floor. I squealed, but we didn't part.

My petticoats cushioned our fall. We clung to each other, shaking as we laughed and rolled.

It was a moment suspended in time. I dared not look at him, face him, and I wondered if he felt the same. His face in my shoulder, muffling his voice. It had been a long few years and we had both changed. Yet, for this one moment, I felt like a child again, rolling down the moors as we chased one another through the heather.

"You're surprisingly heavy," I muttered.

Still, there was a solidness to him, and I trusted him to anchor me. I closed my eyes. It was almost easy to forget where we were and imagine again the endless sky of the moors above us.

"Reverend Helstone?" came the voice of Mr Benjamin.

We sprang apart. A flush of guilt racing across my skin, white hot and branding. Once on my feet, I smoothed my skirts, watching as Laon struggled to his. I offered my hand but he refused, using instead his walking stick.

"Your room is ready for you. And where would you like to take supper tonight? Do you know if your sister has returned from–" The gnome wandered into the hall, cheerful as ever. "Ah! Miss Helstone! Delighted that you have survived your jaunt."

I nodded an acknowledgement to the gnome's greeting. He adjusted his wire-framed spectacles and beamed at the two of us with surprisingly paternal warmth.

"Will you be dining with Miss Helstone, Reverend? I can arrange for it without disturbing..." Mr Benjamin paused, clucking his tongue against his lips for a moment as doubt crossed his eyes. "You know, the Salamander."

Laon frowned, brows furrowing as he stared at me. "Your face looks different."

"I've not changed." I held my chin a little higher.

Taking a step back, my brother continued to stare. I challenged his gaze with my own and that was when I, too, began to notice the differences. He looked older, more tired. Dark hair framed his face, paler than I remembered from our days under the overcast, Yorkshire skies. I noticed the fine lines at the corner of his eyes that stayed even when he wasn't smiling.

Laon really wasn't smiling now.

"Why *are* you here?" he demanded.

"The London Missionary Society," I said, prickling again at his tone. "I have a letter."

"What? From Reverend Joseph Hale himself?" He was scoffing, even as he winced and leaned all the more heavily on his cane. "You shouldn't be here, Cathy. It's not good to be here. This is… this is a terrible place."

At the corner of my vision, I could see Miss Davenport appearing at the top of the stairs. She was different than usual; a scarlet ribbon wound through her hair. I tried desperately to banish the memory of the dream from my mind.

"Why did you even come? This is no place for you. I told you not to come, not to follow me. I told you I was fine. I'm alive, I'm doing my work. Good or not, I am doing my duty to the Throne in Heaven and what more can they ask of me? I need access to the cities, I need to escape this space, I need–"

"You didn't write," I said, weakly.

"I wrote. I wrote until my fingers bled…"

"Not to me, then."

"They must know. The Society. They can't–"

"For months, Laon. No news."

"This isn't a game, Catherine."

"I know, Laon. It's why I came."

"You should go back to England, to Yorkshire. This is not the place for you to be. It's not safe here."

"I'm staying," I told him.

"How can you even–" he faltered in his rant. "No, that doesn't matter. What matters is you are going. You can tell the Reverend that I'm perfectly healthy and in perfect command of all my senses. He doesn't need to send nursemaids after me."

"You need me here," I said. "And I'm safe."

"Nothing is safe here."

"Miss Davenport said that the geas that protects you will protect me. Blood binds blood. You don't have to worry." My voice was rising. Laon had always been prone to erratic shifts of mood, but now it seemed all the more pronounced. The knot in my chest was tightening and I could hear it in my voice, that tension, weak as it was.

His hair fell over his eyes and he pushed it from his face. The hard line of his jaw mirrored mine. "Two weeks. You leave after two weeks."

"No, I'm staying."

"You can't stay, Cathy. I don't have time for this argument. Everything is about to happen and there is more at stake here than–"

"Perhaps we should retire to the drawing room?" said Miss Davenport, clearing her throat. We both turned to her, Laon obviously surprised to see her. She was affectionately scratching the dog whose tail was obliviously thumping the ground. She wore her usual effervescent smile, without a trace of awkwardness at the argument she had just witnessed.

"I thought you had left, Ariel," he said.

"Not at all. I've been keeping your sister company since her arrival." She fluttered a hand to her long, white neck and smiled all the more sweetly. "Come, I've tea waiting for us. And your sister and I do so want to hear about your journey. Do we not, Catherine?"

I made a vague noise of assent, my own name in her mouth sounding more like an insult than endearment.

"And, Laon, you simply must be tired after it all."

"Not so much tired as injured," he said, dryly. "I was in a hurry."

She laughed, the same piercing, delightful, grating sound. "Whatever for, my dear? Tea's not that awful at court, is it?"

"I had to ride on ahead to make preparations. Queen Mab is coming."

Miss Davenport faltered. Something brittle in her eyes shifted and she swallowed visibly before taking Laon's hand. He did not snatch it back. "To the drawing room," she resolved. "We shall need some tea either way."

Tucking my brother's arm around hers, Miss Davenport led the way to the drawing room. My brother was leaning on his walking stick, trying not to put too much weight on Miss Davenport. I wavered, uncertain if I should follow.

"Mab?" asked Miss Davenport's voice. She forced a tinkling laugh, trying to sound merely curious.

"And her court, of course. One wouldn't expect The Pale Queen to travel alone. We need to tell the Salamander," he said.

"Of... of course."

My brother's dog gave me a long lingering look before following them.

As they were about to disappear down the corridor, I heard Miss Davenport's voice: "You are coming with us, aren't you, Catherine?"

I did not go to tea with them.

It still seemed strange to me to term an afternoon meal of scones and sandwiches "tea", however fashionable it may be in London. Though that was not the reason I withdrew myself from their company.

I knew I needed time alone to compose myself. Unbidden, images from that infernal dream crept into the edges of my thoughts and wound around them like a scarlet ribbon. I remembered how she had protested at the thought of being his *companion* and how intimately she spoke of him. It had also not escaped my notice that he was calling Miss Davenport by her name.

Distantly, I heard my brother make arrangements about the arrival of the mysterious Queen and her court. I wondered which of the Paracelsian elements she was aligned to.

I did not want to return to my strange round room, full of its own secrets. The Roche journal awaited me, a temptation that I had not only already succumbed to but which had brought me far more trouble than I had thought possible.

Their promises, their oaths, their geas are there to hinder you, to hobble you, to hide you. They are there to blind you and to bind you.

Their truth is not our truth. They wield it only as a weapon.

But I still had very few answers and I wanted desperately to open again that forbidden book. My sojourn into the mists had taught me the consequences of discovery and I knew I should not.

There was no reason to believe that a now-dead Reverend wrote truth. And Miss Davenport had told me that Roche had all but caused his own death.

Somehow.

I passed from the ancient, pockmarked stone corridors into the modern wing with its grandiose plasterwork and flocked wallpaper.

There were days when I would try to imagine those who used to live in this castle, populate it with the toy soldiers and dolls that Laon and I used to share. There were days when I would peer under each dust sheet and marvel at the beauty of the ancient furniture. I would guess at past inhabitants, squinting at the worn names under the parade of portraits.

Today was not that day.

I wandered listless until I reached the leaf-curtained door of the garden. Given Miss Davenport's current preoccupation, it seemed an opportunity to study the other chapel. I wondered if the scene of interrupted communion was still present there and if I would ever find an answer as to who was meant to find it.

"Hello."

My hand froze on the latch; I did not recognise the voice.

I turned to see a bald woman with an ash-white complexion. She clutched a long black shawl around her old-fashioned gown.

"You're the Salamander, aren't you?" I said.

I was staring.

She watched me with her slitted eyes. Lifting her skirt, I glimpsed a coiling white tail and she slithered towards me in a smooth, undulating motion.

"I- I know we have not been introduced," I ventured. "But thank you for taking care of me. The food and castle... and the lantern that night. Thank you."

She smiled a flame-red, lipless smile and her features lit up. For a moment she had eyebrows and hair of fire before it rippled down her being, from her bald head to her coiled tail. Her skin blackened under the flames before being scabbed over again by her white scales. "We indeed have not met formally."

"Then we should remedy that." I knew she was distracting me from something, but this was a trade. She was offering herself in return for me not seeing whatever was in the garden. "My name is Catherine Helstone. I am the missionary's sister."

Her smile widened to show the coal-black inside of her mouth. "You may call me the Salamander."

"Why do you hide, Salamander?"

"I am not hiding."

"Then why have I never seen you before?" I needed answers.

"I do not need to be seen to tend to you," she said, scales glinting. "I have had quite enough of the Pale Queen's orders, quite enough of her court. I do what I must, what I owe her, but that is all."

"Were you here in Roche's day? The other missionary."

"I remember the original."

"How did he die?"

"I cannot tell you that."

"He had a plan. He wanted to do something, to learn something. What was it? What did he find out? What's Enochian?"

She shook her head.

"I can still go into the garden," I reminded her, reaching for the door. "And I know you do not want me to."

"Roche had ambitions. He thought this a mirror, and he was right, in a way. He thought this a garden, and he was right, in a different way. But he also thought this a parable."

"Was he wrong?"

"No. But he wanted knowledge and he wanted to prove what should not be proven."

"What did he want to know?"

"Do not ask me further." Droplets of flame trickled down her face from her black eyes. "My tongue is even less free than my hands."

"Why?"

"You are not the only one bound. I have made many oaths and I bear many curses, the one of dust and crawling may be the first but it is not the last." She paused, cocking her head to one side. "You may open it now."

At that, I seized and twisted the handle and flung open the door. It was empty, of course, and the Salamander had disappeared by the time I turned back.

I knew the bargain I had made, but even as I wandered through the unremarkable garden, I wondered if it was the right choice. Puzzles published in periodicals were best solved by first examining the known unknowns, that much I knew. One always began with the familiar and worked outwards.

But was that truly a strategy I should be applying to my interrogation of Arcadia?

Chapter 11
The Willow in the Portrait

Tineola arcanofera (Semiotic Moth) 2"–2"7"'

This rare stripe-winged moth is snowy white, with gold costae and fringes, and an interrupted marginal band of pale yellow.

Native to Arcadia and sometimes found in earthly libraries, this pest is often said to feed off the written word. It allegedly consumes secrets and digests them into less informative fragmentary whispers.

However, the truth of the matter is far more mundane. The semiotic moth simply is attracted to the scent of the iron gall ink that the old manuscripts are written in and the decay of the documents is due to the slightly acidic nature of the ink corroding the parchment over time. The "dust" of the moth's wings possesses hallucinogenic properties when breathed into human lungs, explaining the whispering heard amid the clouds of moths and dust in old libraries.

Larvae undescribed.

Henry Doubleday, "Appendix IV: Invasive Species from the Faelands", A NATURAL HISTORY OF BRITISH MOTHS

It was shortly after I had returned to my room in that tower, when I had in my hand the Reverend Roche's journal, that Mr Benjamin knocked on my door to inform me of dinner.

Reluctantly, I put down the volume of secrets. I had wanted to compare what the Salamander had told me with Roche's own account. Her cryptic words were almost no knowledge at all, but I had thought they might still spark something. Why would Roche think of this place as a parable?

Mr Benjamin seemed at first no different than usual, his languid movements as meditated as always but his mannerisms were muted. He stood stooped low, a dejected weight hung about his shoulders.

"Your brother and the changeling await you at dinner, Miss Helstone," he said. "At your pleasure, of course."

"Thank you for informing me, Mr Benjamin," I replied in my most courteous tones, hoping to put the agitated gnome at ease. The pupils of his eyes darted rapidly from corner to corner. "And I would love to join them."

"If you would follow me, Miss Helstone. They are dining in the great hall tonight, which I do not believe you have seen." He gave a low, shaky bow.

He led the way down the spiral staircase from my room and along a gallery of ethereal landscapes. Even as we walked, the scenes caught my eye, a disquieting mix of familiar hills and trees and rivers with strange skies and stranger hues.

"Are all these places in Arcadia, Mr Benjamin?" I asked, slowing before a series of mountains that clutched at the ground like the knuckles of a six-fingered fist.

"Yes," said Mr Benjamin. He frowned, eyes darting again. "And no."

"Some are real and others not?"

"No." He licked his lips with a black tongue and swallowed uncomfortably. "But also yes."

"I'm afraid that isn't much of an answer, Mr Benjamin."

"Realness is a strange, strange thing in these parts, Miss Helstone."

I stopped, lighthearted curiosity fleeing as I saw the final painting in the long gallery. My mouth dried at the sight of the landscape before me: it was a riverbound glade, dripping with willow trees. An impossible river curled itself around the wooded island in a tight, protective spiral. It seemed achingly familiar.

The willow trees leaned lovingly over the encircling river and caressed the water with its whispering leaves. I thought of uttered secrets, and an odd shiver crawled up my spine.

"Miss Helstone?"

I heard the gnome's footsteps as he walked back to me, having continued with the confidence that I was following. I did not take my eyes off the circle of willow trees.

"Is this a real place?" I heard myself ask, but my voice sounded distant to my own ears.

"Real and not real."

"Is it possible, then, for me to go there?"

"At a price." He gave a shrug, but his heart wasn't really in it.

I breathed a deep sigh, setting aside the memories that knotted painfully in my chest. I forced myself to look at my gnome companion. "You are being unduly cryptic again, Mr Benjamin."

"I do apologise. That is most rude of me." He was articulating even more than usual, his mouth exaggerating the motions in a parody of the Oxford Voice. He looked behind himself again, with all the air of a child about to thieve from the pantry.

"Are you quite alright, Mr Benjamin?"

"No, no, not really. No." One more furtive glance behind and the gnome took off his spectacles. He cleaned them on his ragged waistcoat. "I am quite afraid of the Pale Queen."

"Mab?"

He cringed. "Best nae say 'er name, Miss 'elstone."

I couldn't place the accent that came over his gravelly voice, but as he furrowed his brow and met my gaze, all comparisons to a child's nervousness fled. There was true terror in his eyes.

"Is there a reason why?"

He shook his head. He lowered his clouded eyes and reaffixed his spectacles to his face with shaking hands. His accent returned, but there lingered an earthiness. He somehow seemed more real. "There are some things you learn not to risk in these parts."

"Risk?"

"There is a sort of old power to names, Miss Helstone. I would take heed of it."

"I- I will." I gave him what I hoped to be a brave, cheering smile.

"They say the Howling Duke and the Chief of Winds are more cruel. They say He Who Commands Fear is stronger, more powerful. The Keeper of the Markets is more calculating. The Colourful King, She Who Sleeps For The Mountains and the Lost Emperors are more unpredictable, more changeable... This is all true, you have to understand." He swallowed, visibly. "But I daresay I fear the Pale Queen the most."

"Why?"

Mr Benjamin grinned at my question, his lips stretching tight over his blunt, brown teeth. There was no humour in it. "Because she is most human."

The great hall was at the heart of what I had thought of as the oldest part of the castle, with stone arches etched with geometric patterns and enormous, empty fireplaces. The dog lounged, a spill of black ink on the sheepskins. A minstrel's gallery peered down at us.

Laon sat by himself at the head of a long, long chair-lined table. He had draped himself across the gilded throne and cradled in his hand a squat glass of wine. His eyes were just a little too distant. He did not look at me when I entered.

A place had been set out opposite him at the bottom of the table. Mr Benjamin herded me into it.

A tureen shaped like a crouching rabbit waited for me. It was made of porcelain, with its long, sleeked back ears forming a handle along its back.

"We should start. Ariel isn't joining us," said Laon.

Again, her name.

They must have grown close when he first arrived and she was a friendly, near-human face among the fae. She must have been a welcome reminder of humanity, a haven.

"I see," I mumbled. I was grateful for her absence and I had no urge to ask the reason. "Is she well?"

"Quite. She's simply spoilt her appetite on cucumber sandwiches and biscuits."

"I didn't know she was so fond of taking tea." I uncovered the sweet carrot soup. It was purple, dark and bruise-like, with shades of beetroot red clinging to the spoon when I stirred it.

"Don't forget the salt," said Laon.

"I know," I said, scattering salt onto the soup. "I've been here for quite a while. Waiting for you."

My brother made no reply, and we ate in silence.

Despite its disconcerting colour, the soup was rich and sweet in its flavour. There was a gamey note to it that made me wonder if there was rabbit in the stock.

"Where have you been, Laon?" I asked.

"I... I've..." he hesitated. He brought his wineglass to his lips but did not drink.

"You can tell me."

"The letters." The glass clinked gently as he put it down again. "They didn't reach me. Distances are unreliable in Arcadia."

"That doesn't answer my question."

"They sometimes like to pretend it can be measured in miles or hours travelled, but it's far less predictable than that. I've had distances given to me in numbers of daydreams and revelations, as though I'd only arrive somewhere after I've had an epiphany or–"

"No," I interjected. "Laon, I've asked Miss Davenport and Mr Benjamin but I've not gotten a straight answer. I was worried about you."

"I was at the court of the Pale Queen."

"Mab?"

He nodded. "I was petitioning The Pale Queen for access into the lands under her control, that is to say – I'm not sure if there is a correct term yet – inner Arcadia. To make true progress here, I need to head inland, beyond the ports that trade with humanity and beyond the puppetry of the fae. They put us here, apart from their towns and cities, purposefully isolated so we cannot do our holy work. It is why for all his time here, Roche only converted one–"

"Mr Benjamin." In the corner of my eye, I could see the gnome giving me a brief wave. I returned it.

"Yes, him."

"And she is resistant?"

"To say the least."

"Are there not others you can petition? After all, Arcadia is not a singular land with a single monarch."

"The Pale Queen is already, by far, the most approachable and sympathetic to the human cause. She wears a face, after all."

"Is that good?"

Laon sighed, long and despondent. "The treaties that

granted the Society the right to be here are badly drawn. Or rather, they do not grant us any advantage. We are merely an afterthought in that process. To the merchants with their weights, to the politicians with their lies and to the cartographers with their lines." He held up his glass as though in a toast and drank deeply. His sarcasm was palpable. "There would be no new countries without their greed."

"I was given books to teach the local children with," I said, sipping the spiced ginger tea. "Maps and... fairy tales. Seems strange to think I ever thought those might be useful."

"The Society thinks many things," he said. "But the truth is, I am left to simply beg for a chance to attempt my duty. For all my months here, I cannot tell you what fae society is like beyond the frivolities of court life and the controlled bartering that happens in their markets. I have no parishioners, no populace to tend to. It has been impossible to even approach them about faith."

The next course was fish, heavily spiced with mint and fennel. Though the slight flickering of the candlelight and the wide leaves of the mint masked it, the fish was subtly luminous.

"I am a missionary in name alone," said Laon. "We are surrounded by empty, formless mists not for our own protection."

"Perhaps they fear us."

He shrugged. "Perhaps."

"I had read that fae are elemental in nature. Paracelsus, I believe, proposed it?" I said. Salt seemed to dim the fish and it appeared more grey than silver when my knife glided into it. "Could that not be used to predict their temperaments? We could appeal to their elemental impulses when speaking of the divine."

He swirled the wine in his glass, avoiding my gaze. I could tell he was being careful with his words. Gone was that intimate carelessness that we shared, where we simply spoke our thoughts. There was a time when we would lie under the apple tree and we could not tell what words were uttered and what words were thought; they were all intertwined and interwoven as we were.

"So," my brother began. "I would talk to the undines of how the Lord Above is the Fountain of Living Waters and how He is the one who divided the Red Sea?"

"Yes, and to the gnomes, you could speak of how He is the Rock of Our Salvation. The sylphs, perhaps, could be swayed by the thought of his command over the heavens."

"It has a certain rhetorical simplicity, but I confess I am not convinced by the Paracelsian argument about the nature of fae."

"I see…" I hesitated, taken aback. "Is there a reason?"

"The model is practically medieval, more shaped by superstition than reason," he said. "And it is more than just various groupings of fae can be understood through their elements. It is an understanding of Arcadia as much as its inhabitants. And underpinning it all is the idea that Arcadia is constantly separating its elements, that they are unbalanced here, that as we push to the edges of our known map the cohesion of the world is collapsing."

"And as certain elements come to the fore, this affects the climate and temperaments of Arcadia?"

"If we start arguing such, we have to accept that Saharan deserts and the monsoons of India are not only equal in their elemental composition – whatever that may mean – but also that they are somehow better mixed than here."

"But Arcadia is different. All this," I flung a gesticulating arm around us, causing Diogenes to let out a whine. "This is not Yorkshire, not home."

"It's different, it's not the alchemical composition of the world that makes it so. Mr Benjamin is not more closely aligned to earth than you or me."

"This place isn't just strange because of it having strange people," I snapped, frustrated with his explanations. "There is something deeper."

"That doesn't make Paracelsus right."

"I'm not saying the theory is right. I'm saying you're not trying to understand."

"But even in its broader, more populist strokes the theory is wrong," he continued. "Whilst some individual or even types of fae seem to follow the broad thematic impulses of the elements, they are no more governed by them than you or I. It is an illusion of a pattern. Akin to saying that the Scottish are of fire and that the Welsh are of earth."

"I cannot know that. You cannot limit my knowledge and then reprimand me for ignorance." A warmth flushed to my cheeks, though I did not know if it was anger or shame. My eyes dropped to the silver fish. I was breathing heavily, pulse rushing. Laon had always shared his books with me, taught me his lessons and smuggled me his notes; for all that our educations treated us differently, I had thought there was an unspoken pact between us. I had thought we were alike. "I can't know what you know. I have not been allowed to–"

"And yet I found you wandering in the mists." He was scoffing.

"It's been weeks. I've waited for you, for weeks." I was pleading, pathetic. My voice was a whine, a whimper. I hated myself. "I needed–"

"No, you came here. You demanded. You threw your temper at Ariel–"

"I did. But–"

"You left the castle walls." He would not meet my eye, but I could see it now, the rage simmering in his averted gaze.

It was then, too, I realised my own rage. I had been gripping the table, and I had half thought it was to steady myself, but I knew then I was willing myself not to stand and march over to slap him.

"It is very dangerous out there, Cathy. In the mists. Anything... I cannot–"

"What cannot you do, Laon?" I could feel my fingers growing numb. "Have you not done it all? Have you not gone to university? Have you not left England? Have you not made yourself a grand explorer, triumphant conqueror and–"

It stung. I knew it stung.

"Do not blame your confinement on me." His voice was very cold, very slow. "I am not your gaoler."

"Do not shame me for knowledge that has been denied me. Do not patronise me over the position to which I have been born." I saw him flinch, but I continued. "I had thought the respect you had for me was mine by right, as your sister and equal. Not granted to me on your whim. To be begged and earned, however tenderly."

"Cathy, I didn't mean–"

"You may not be my gaoler, Laon, but you are as good as."

"You have to understand, I am as much a prisoner as you."

"Your cage is larger, then."

"Still a cage."

"But you would have me beg for you to share it. That I need to earn my place beside you. That it is contingent on your love." I took a deep breath. "I am not here to beg, Laon."

He said nothing at that and Mr Benjamin slipped in to serve the last course.

The rest of the meal passed in silence, punctuated only by the chiming of the cutlery against our plates. My anger dissipated as quickly as it had flared, but my brother remained rigid in his demeanour. Still, he would not look at me. Our argument, however impetuous, had not been the balm of Gilead that I had fleetingly hoped it would be.

Chapter 12
The Secrets of the Past

Every Missionary Society should have prepared, and be able to put into the hands of every new Missionary, a brief Manual of the language, customs, notions, and religious ideas of the province or country to which he is going; including a few rules or hints respecting climate, dress, health, food, etc.

This the Missionary should learn by heart, and know thoroughly by the time he reaches his station.

With such an efficient preparation, let every missionary, on his arrival at his sphere of labour, strive to enter as much as possible among the people. That he may learn the language thoroughly, let him devote a considerable time each day to its acquisition. Let him walk abroad, and though he cannot speak much, let him see much, and familiarise himself with all the outer manifestations of native life. For the first year or two, his principal attention should be given to the language and to books about the natives.

Gregory Day, "Good Practises," THE RELIGIOUS
INTELLIGENCER, FOR THE YEAR ENDING MAY 1834

I read Roche's journal that night.

My hands danced coyly on the spine and over the leather cover with its strange half-moon scorch marks. I remembered the warnings of Reverend Hale, his restrained insulations far more effective at stoking my fear than hyperbole.

Noticing my hesitation, I counted ten heartbeats, braced myself and opened the book.

Nothing happened: no lightning struck; no stray breeze brought cold fingers down my spine; no invisible hands snatched the journal from mine. It simply lay open, ready for my eyes to harvest its secrets.

The first pages were mundane enough, mostly an account of his journey to Arcadia. I swallowed, still unable to rid myself of the lump of fear in my throat, and kept reading.

October 21, 1839. – I intended to leave Plymouth, in the company of Captain Peter Kensington and his family, sailing south; but I am infected by a shivering fever – I had taken more than eighty grains of mercury and a great quantity of opium, to be delivered from it.

October 29. – I left the family of Captain Peter Kensington; and began my sea-voyage to Arcadia, sometimes called Elphane. Its secrets are within reach.

November 1. – I find the seas disagreeable to my constitution. Captain Samson Furneaux assures me that his navigator is truly terrible and it would be no time before we are sufficiently lost as to be within sight of the Faelands.

December 13. – I arrived at Port Maskelyne, where I was very kindly and hospitably received by Colonel Stanners, the Honourable South Sea Company's Political Agent, and

the rest of the British residents. I am told that from here, the
journey to Elphane should be swift.

There were three hands at work in the journal. The first was, of course, the Reverend himself. He had a wide, straight way of writing that undoubtedly came from years of careful discipline. I smiled at the memory of my brother struggling with his letters. We used to write miniature journals and newspapers for our toy soldiers and he was never quite able to make his as neat and as tiny as mine.

The origin of the other two hands within Roche's journal I could not guess at, but one was crowded and curled tight; the other was sloping and flat with its author's rapidity. The former wrote a smattering of entries, but the latter seemed primarily confined to marginalia.

The first few months were prosaic enough. Roche arrived in Arcadia and was met with a number of fae, many of whom had extravagant titles such as the Astrologer of Blood and the Duchess of Time. He described the various misfortunes involved in hiring a housekeeper, though none of the applicants sounded like the elusive Salamander. Once given the castle, Roche was not permitted to leave it, but fae regularly called on the castle to talk with him. They engaged him in a series of debates about theology that frustrated the missionary for he was convinced that he won each and every one with rhetoric and logic, yet turned no souls to Christ.

May 23 1840. – It is the strength of all infidels, to begin their
arguments with the question, Why? And the question shows
at once that they know nothing, with all their learning and
wisdom; for if they knew anything, they would not begin
to state their argument with the question, Why? For Why?
indicates that we do not know the reason for a thing – that we

are ignorant; and ignorance proves nothing – it proves only
that you are ignorant.

The sloping hand in the margins mocked him. I suspected that it was added much later, without the Reverend's knowledge, but I could not say for certain.

Among his visitors I did recognise a description of Mr Benjamin in a group of self-described miners who were despondent at a lack of work. Though none of them converted, Roche had hired a few of them to keep tidy the grounds. One by one, they left until only Mr Benjamin remained.

As his stay in the Faelands lengthened, Roche's hand grew more erratic. His tone took on a paranoid air, worried that someone was reading his journal. He mentioned repeatedly the mistakes in his choice of staff. Given the two other hands present, perhaps his fears were not completely unfounded. He began abbreviating his words and little glyphs crept in, the beginnings of a code. There was even an entry written in mirror writing.

My breath unfurled before me, like the winding mists of the moors around the castle. Feeling the cold, I pulled my shawl tighter around my shoulders.

Details grew sparse, but I gathered he had festering in his mind some sort of plan. His efforts in proselytising were likely stymied for the same reasons my brother's were, namely his lack of access to "inner" Arcadia. He feared his plan, afraid of the costs, the sacrifices. He wrote as a man haunted, counting the worth of his own soul.

Perhaps no man could seem brave in such moments.

I turned the page and it crumbled before my eyes, fluttering to a delicate confetti. The paper was thin, beyond fragile. I squinted at it and could see that somehow the ink had corroded through the paper, leaving behind a very literal word-shaped lacuna.

The journal resumed some months later and Roche was in England again. He had married after much dithering over a bride and was resolved to return to Arcadia. He wrote little of his new wife, not even her Christian name. He referred to her only as Miss Clay and then Mrs Roche. I could only guess at the missing pages, but I assumed they described his fears culminating in his return and a change of heart after marriage. Perhaps his bride inspired in him some latent fervour or simply that she was reason enough for him to desire to depart English soil.

From the margins, the sloping hand called him names. It decried his fears as foolish and claimed his words were false. Beyond a periodic scrawl of *Liar! Coward! False-hearted!*, it offered no counterpoint nor argument.

Over and over Roche stated his desire to return to Arcadia, to pledge his one brief life to the great work in a land of darkness. It seemed a mantra, as though he was trying to convince himself, to purge himself of doubt. He was willing himself to believe. Unlike the earlier passages, it was not a fear that characterised his writing, but a profound delusion.

Folded among these pages were letters. It rounded out the portrait of an uncertain man, grasping for reassurance.

Another lacuna.

The tightly curled hand began to write, though I could not make sense of its entries. All opaque allusions to poison and fears and pain. It wrote of grandiose ideas, confronting fears and uncomfortable truths. It invoked the trials of Job and the sufferings of Jonah.

And then, nothing. The final pages had been torn out.

I did not remember falling asleep, but when I opened my eyes I had a shawl draped over my shoulders and a heap of books were on my table. As I handled them each in turn I recognised the handwriting in the margins and I knew them to be my brother's. They also reeked of wine.

There were accounts of Cook's voyage to Arcadia, a general missionary's handbook, and a series of published debates on the theological and biological nature of fae. For all that I had thought I was well read on the subject, most of it was unfamiliar.

A slender quotation-riddled volume argued that fae were a lost tribe of Israel and that Arcadia was the desert to which they were cursed. A rebuttal to Paracelsus argued that Arcadia was the land of wandering east of Eden to which Cain was banished and his children by his sister were the fae, forever cursed for having been born of that sinful union. A screed denounced the mission to Arcadia as futile as the fae, as fallen angels, were soulless.

A tract by Dr Immanuel Campbell to the Edinburgh Society for the Study of the Fae discussed the work of Mr Hobbs of Malmsbury and purported that his work should be read as description of the fae rather than of natural instincts of Man.

The beasts of infinite viciousness who cruelly exploit and savage one another from a bottomless well of pure spite are not Men in a state of nature before the civilising influence of Society. The image of the Leviathan is not a representation of an earthly sovereign as Mr Hobbs supposedly propounds. The gigantic beast formed of a multitude is no metaphor. The potency and loyalty it commands do not concern the abstract qualities of a mundane political society. The dire warnings of chaos, bloodshed and doom are carefully contextualised into a Treatise on the proper organisation of a Body Politic.

I read of Cesare, a medieval priest who was accused of being a changeling. It was unclear if Cesare was a true person, but it sparked a great fear that wandering priests were secretly soulless changelings who were tricking villagers into a parody of the rite that bound them to Arcadia.

In the wake of such paranoia sprang the theology that it was the rite and receiver that mattered, not the priest who performed it. The rite itself was sacred. Thus false priests gave true communion.

After all, when Jesus first enacted the rite Himself to Judas at the Last Supper did the Adversary enter the fallen disciple. He harboured treason in his heart and that, argued the forefathers of the Church, had corrupted the rite.

It all seemed hopelessly superstitious, but it did make me wonder of fae and their souls. It had been an unspoken assumption that they did have souls in a way that mirrored humanity's but each theory about their true nature flirted with that question.

I wondered if such thoughts plagued Roche too. He wrote so often of the missionaries who set sail and then spent years petitioning the Pope to sanctify the journey they had already undertaken. He envied that certainty; he craved it.

CHAPTER 13
The Queen in the Castle

Behold the chariot of the Fairy Queen!
Celestial coursers paw the unyielding air;
Their filmy pennons at her word they furl,
And stop obedient to the reins of light:
These the Queen of Spells drew in,
She spread a charm around the spot,
And leaning graceful from the ethereal car,
Long did she gaze, and silently,
Upon the slumbering maid.
　　Oh! not the visioned poet in his dreams,
When silvery clouds float through the wildered brain,
When every sight of lovely, wild, and grand,
Astonishes, enraptures, elevates,
When fancy, at a glance, combines
The wondrous and the beautiful,—
So bright, so fair, so wild a shape
Hath ever yet beheld,
As that which reined the coursers of the air,
And poured the magic of her gaze
Upon the maiden's sleep.

Percy Bysshe Shelley, QUEEN MAB

The sky seemed on fire when I woke up again.

I scrambled out of bed and pulled open the curtains to look outside, heart pounding. I saw that the lands that surrounded the castle were ablaze. The mists had been burnt away. Each slivered pane of glass shattered the image of the endless fire into a broken sea. Livid, vivid red, like the stained glass images of Risen Christ and His blood-red robes.

Clutching a shawl to myself, I ran down the stairs. I remembered that the great hall overlooked the outside. My feet were still bare as I found myself pulling open the long curtains, coughing at the dust.

It was still too far to make out, so I padded through the winding corridors and up through the trap door that led to the attic and the roof beyond.

I saw it then, the floods and whirlwinds of tempestuous fire, seething stench and smoke. It burned on and on, yet I recalled nothing on those plains for the fire to devour. There had been nothing but mists and constructs of mists there when I had wandered through. What could be feeding those towering columns of fire?

The flames painted the sky in the lurid colours of dawn and dusk, colours that were alien to this particular canvas. The pendulum sun never gave it such shades.

It was then that Laon happened upon me, brow furrowed at the horror of the flames. Diogenes followed him, a slinking, black shadow of a hound at his feet.

"What's happening out there?" I asked, breaking the horrid silence between us. I barely glanced at him. The argument from the night before lay between us, but for now, we were able to ignore its carcass. "Laon?"

"The moors are being cleared," he said. "By the Salamander. I spoke to her this morning. It's for the Pale Queen's visit."

"Moors?"

"The emptiness out there." There was a coldness to his

voice. Though my eyes were on the fire, his were on me. I could feel his gaze on my skin and I ached to touch him again. "You didn't think it was that way naturally, did you?"

"I don't know what is natural here," I said.

"The fae like to keep the land out there.... Uncultivated. Formless."

"What do you mean?"

"It's overgrown, so they're burning everything back, returning it to mist."

"But what is out there when- when it's not mist?"

"Dreams. Thoughts. Things our minds give shape to," he said with a soft, long-fingered gesture. "The mists are very malleable and it is for that reason they desire to keep it that way. I suppose it's a resource of sorts, harvested periodically. They probably sell it at the Goblin Market or something. But our minds are here so it means it all grows faster; they need to clear it more often."

"So human minds do things to the mists?"

"It shapes them, somehow."

"I- I think I understand," I said. The wind was twisting the black smoke away from Gethsemane, but I could still taste an acrid, sulphurous edge in the air. "Like the real moors? They choose for it to be empty."

He nodded and turned to look out of the window with me. The once mist-covered moors seemed a great furnace, yet from those flames there was no light, only a dense, swallowing darkness. My eyes were aching from the sight of it all and I imagined a figure of flame dancing through it, trailing liquid sparks with every step.

The blaze on my face reminded me of the first time I saw the moors of Yorkshire be set aflame. Terrified, I had clung to Laon. Tessie's words echoed in my mind: *It is how things are done. The moors need to stay the moors. It's just like cutting your fingernails.*

Until then, I had always believed the moors this wild, inhuman landscape, where endless sky wrapped its heathen arms around an untamed, primal earth. And yet there it was before me, nature being brought to heel. Like any wide-eyed fool, I had mistaken a broken animal of the circus for a wild one.

"The books..." I began. I was glad to have them but after our argument, I didn't want to thank him. "Were they you?"

"I owe you them," he said. "I promised."

The ground shook and broke open. The leaping flames were crushed under the weight of churned soil. An enormous creature thrust its nose from the ground, crested like a wave and then dove back into the grey-black dirt. As it wheeled, I saw its huge snout, its wide fins and finally, its great tail curving from the ground.

"What is that?" I breathed. "That isn't–"

"It's a whale."

"A whale?"

"Yes, it's called a sea whale."

"Which I have obviously seen before..." I glanced at him and our eyes met. He gave a half smile that brushed against the welkin blue of his eyes. I was reminded of all the times in our childhood when we would pretend at knowledge, nodding along to what the other said, no matter how ludicrous, desperate not to be the more ignorant sibling. "I've read about them and they're called that not because... they live in the sea but because they... *eat* it?"

"Close."

"What do you mean, close?"

"They're full of saltwater and sand," he said. "I'm told fish live inside them."

"Oh," I muttered, the sound of surprise escaping my lips.

Another of the vast creatures leapt from the ground. It was closer, so I could make out its skin, seemingly this thick carpet of bracken and wicker. The scattering dirt and dripping flame clung to it, blackening but not burning the sea whale. Unthinking blue eyes stared out from under a vortex of crackling twigs. Its tail fanned out, and I saw the woven pattern of its substance against the bright flames.

A spurt of water spewed from the back of one of these creatures. The droplets melted into the flames, and though the wind was blowing the black away from the castle walls, there was salt on the breeze.

"That's the sea," I said in wonder. Rich and foul, it was unmistakable. I thought immediately of my days on the deck of *The Quiet* and the endless calls of gulls at port. "I know this is Arcadia, but how?"

He gave a half-hearted shrug. "I assume they heard about conch shells and got carried away."

"That you can hear the sound of the sea in them?"

"That they have in them, captive, an oceanic fragment."

I heard it first in my bones. Low and mournful, it reverberated through the ground like a bell. A long, inhuman moan, more like the conch shell murmurs or the howling of wind through the caves we used to play in than any sound from a creature's throat.

Startled, I took a step towards Laon. He caught my hand and we laced our fingers together, like we used to when we were little.

"It's just the whales," he said. "The fire calls them. They rise to the surface like earthworms in rain."

"How do they not catch fire?"

"The sea inside them, I assume."

"Is it possible to... to see inside one? What sorts of fish would live inside a whale?"

"I- I don't know."

"We should find out."

"I don't think it's in Father's encyclopaedia," he said, a wry smile twisting his lips. "But then, not many things are."

"It might be," I retorted sharply, retreading the paths of our old argument. Wonderfully familiar, I leaned towards him, relishing that elusive closeness between us. "But we're missing half the volumes. For all we know, they might be in the fabled *W.*"

"Don't be silly, it would be under *S* for sea whale and we have that one."

"It can't be. It doesn't tend to do individual entries for animals."

"But it's not an animal, it's a place. Like a desert or–"

The eerie sound of the whales struck up again, interrupting him. Louder than the first cry, it seemed a reply. It echoed through my bones and teeth.

Abruptly, Laon let go of my hand and turned from me.

"None of those books are here now. We are very far from any of that," he said, walking away. "Breakfast is getting cold."

The chimes and bells rippled through Gethsemane, seeming to my ears louder than usual.

Laon, Miss Davenport and I stood in the courtyard waiting for the Queen. Diogenes, Laon's dog, had been reduced to a quietly whimpering heap. The Salamander was absent as ever and Mr Benjamin had excused himself to tend to the raising of the portcullis and the opening of the gate.

Everything was as ready as we could make it. I had been pulling dust sheets from the furnishings and folding them with Laon. I piled vases high with flowers as Miss Davenport chattered, hanging up bright curtains. We even dragged out some of the rugs and beat them in the courtyard. I even heard Mr Benjamin muttering to the garden's plants, telling them of the Queen's arrival. The castle shone with scoured resplendence, the banisters and the steps polished to the brightness of glass, all presumably the work of the elusive Salamander.

Mab was to arrive when the clocks struck noon.

At the fading of the last chime, men of sand-brown skin stepped out from the shadows. Before I could bring myself to be surprised, they announced her arrival in gravelly voices. They bowed low to me as they spoke, dripping grit upon the ground with every motion. It trickled off their skin like the sand in an hourglass, steadily and smoothly.

Laon assured the men of sand that we were ready for her arrival, and they nodded mutely.

Then suddenly, the Queen's retinue were pouring through the far gates. They moved in absolute silence, neither their clothes nor their shoes making a single sound.

I was reminded again of the limits of my own petty imagination as the Pale Queen's retinue bore little resemblance to the processions I had conjured up in the mists but for the fact that both were utterly silent. But this was no polite parade of lords and ladies with streaming banners and rigidly prancing horses.

Black-cloaked beings shambled in and squatted by the path. Little protruded from the darkness of their cloaks except for long, gnarled fingers made for strangling. Ladies in feather gowns flounced about in fluidly boneless movements, each carrying a pair of long, bloody shears and a threaded needle. They wore necklaces of still tongues that lolled black blood onto their white gowns. Others seemed almost human, but the shadows that stretched out from their feet were not those of their own human-seeming shape but those of restless, leaping horses.

A carriage of horn and ivory rolled into the courtyard. It was pulled by creatures of leftover parts. Each was a chimera in the classical sense, obviously composed of different animals: a tiger's striped leg ended in the hooves of an ox; an elephant's trunk reached out from the face of a lion; a knot of snakes reared out from the haunches of a goat.

A man of sand reached into her carriage and drew her out by her shining white hand. She unfurled from it like the sticky fronds of the sundew, like an octopus blossoming from a dark corner of a rock pool, like the slices on a peeled orange.

It was *her*.

The woman from my dream.

She had the same snow-pale skin and round, amber eyes. I could still see my brother's long, beautiful fingers on that skin, stroking her cheek and following the curve of her chin. Each shadow that brushed against her reminded me of the dappling from the willow trees.

Her brown hair had the same white-gold streak in it that stretched from the peak in the middle of her forehead. No red ribbon had been braided into it but I still saw it tangling in Laon's hand as he combed it through her hair.

My mouth was as dry as if I had swallowed sand and my blood was running cold.

She looked straight at me, and again I saw myself reflected in her yellow eyes. Small and pathetic I still was, though this time I did not see myself as a moth to her butterfly. Her flat, wide nose and heart-shaped face put me in mind of an owl.

I was grateful when she looked away.

"My!" She spoke and her voice was at once a whisper and long, piercing avian screech. It defied human throats and human ears. "How this place hasn't changed."

Laon bowed, and I mirrored his actions instinctively before fumbling towards a brisk bob of a curtsy.

"This cannot be your entire household, Laon?" said Mab. Winglike sleeves draped from the shoulder of her dress and dragged along the floor. Her skirts flowed from her waist in feathery layers of white and brown. "Though I see your hound is faithful to the last."

"Benjamin Goodfellow was tending to your arrival. He is in the gatehouse. The Salamander is–"

"Here." A drop of fire streaked across the courtyard, trailing black soot and smoke. It flared like a splash of whisky over a fire and coalesced into a humanoid shape that ended in a single, serpentine tail. She seemed at first a black wick within the flames, but as the fire dimmed her skin turned ash-white. "I am here."

"It has been a long time, my child," said the Pale Queen.

The Salamander bowed deep, her wet-seeming scales glistening. "It has been as long as it takes to tell a tale, neither long nor short."

"Time is as I count it," said the Pale Queen. "And changeling?"

"Yes, majesty." Miss Davenport did not curtsy, merely granting her a deep nod.

"I trust you have been carrying out your duties."

"Yes, majesty."

"Excellent," she said. Mab then cast another surveying look about the courtyard. "But where is the last human?"

"There is no one else," said Laon, his brows furrowing. "It's just my sister and myself."

"Oh, the sister?" Mab turned her attention to me.

Nervously, I curtsied again. "I am Catherine Helstone, your majesty."

"So I see," she said, appraising me up and down.

I tried to meet her eyes, to stand straighter, to hold high my chin in defiance. But I could not. I withered under her gaze and that knot of pain in my chest grew heavier and tighter.

She smiled, and I could see again those lips brushing against my brother's ears. She pursed her lips in a beaklike expression and said, "As expected."

"Expected?" said my brother, a restrained suspicion crossing his tone.

"You speak of her, and as such, I must have expectations."

"Rarely."

"You should know by now I hear more than just your spoken words."

Her courtiers were speaking silently among themselves. Even though I could not hear their voices, I could see their lips, crooked like the beaks of owls, snapping and spitting. They turned their heads in sharp movements, looking and leering.

"I have been waiting to meet you, Catherine Helstone. I am glad you are lost so that we might find you," said the Pale Queen. Her eyes glinted with predatory menace. "But I wonder why."

"I come to take care of my brother."

"It is rather plain that he is very dear to you." Her smile seemed sharper. "I trust you will prove a Balm of Gilead to your brother's wounds."

PART TWO
Gilead

SECTION TWO
Etched

Chapter 14
The Balm of the Soul

"Prophet!"said I,"thing of evil! – prophet still, if bird or
devil! —
Whether Tempter sent, or whether tempest tossed thee here
ashore,
Desolate yet all undaunted, on this desert land enchanted —
On this home by Horror haunted – tell me truly, I implore —
"Is there – is there balm in Gilead? – tell me – tell me, I
implore!"
Quoth the Raven,"Nevermore."

Edgar Allan Poe, THE RAVEN

The castle came alive as the court of the Pale Queen descended.

Gethsemane had been slumbering beneath its dust sheets
and drapes, all shuttered and locked away. Now, it bustled
with action.

Where before the corridors languished empty, their
shadows were now swarming with Mab's courtiers. They
cared little for the concept of up or down, so they seemed
as keen to walk upon the walls and ceiling as they were
the floor. They gathered around the portraits, pushing their

faces against the canvas and whispering into the painted ears of the depicted.

Our fae guests danced and played amongst themselves and yet there was not a single footstep to be heard. They moved to music that only they could hear and clapped soundlessly their hands when they sang. They spoke silently to one another, their beaks and lips and muzzles moving animatedly without trace of voice.

Given our absent housekeeper, it had fallen upon me as sister to my brother, and thus mistress of the house, to conduct the visitors to their rooms. I had been given no warning as to who would arrive or how to apportion them, but I had done what I could. I could not shake off the feeling of unease when with them, especially as they remained completely silent. Still, my familiarity with the extensive castle had grown and I had been able to place each of the fae that arrived within a room of their own.

Mab had been directed, of course, to the grand suite, newly vacated of my brother's possessions. His relinquishment of the rooms had not been particularly reluctant, but it did serve as a reminder of who was the new mistress of Gethsemane.

The first of the Pale Queen's entertainments was to be a moment of fashionable domesticity in the English style. Before she withdrew into her rooms, she had announced to us that she desired to sew and take tea in the solar, as was the London way.

It took some orchestration as I found the various materials for needlework. The tea, however, I was urged to leave to Mab's retinue. She brought with her a great surfeit of inhuman servants, all shadowy hands and sandy footprints. Still, for all their esoteric appearances, they busied in familiar ways.

"Just leave it to them," Mr Benjamin said, tugging on the hems of my skirt to stop me from interfering. "I wouldn't get in their way."

"It seems inhospitable to do nothing," I worried at him.

"Maybe, maybe."

"I am mistress of this house."

"Then is not your duty," said the gnome with a triumphant grin. "It's the Salamander's job. This house has a keeper."

"You're just trying to stay out of the way."

"True, true." He straightened his waistcoat and dusted more dirt onto the lapel. "I am scared of the Pale Queen. And you should be too." He suppressed an involuntary shudder at saying her name.

"I'm not scared," I lied.

"Don't deal with the court, Miss Helstone. Geas of blood cannot keep you safe in all ways."

I spent far too long getting dressed, worrying about my gown. I found my hands lingering on the dresses that were left in my wardrobe, wondering if I should indulge the vanity that urged me to wear them.

There was very little fanfare as Miss Davenport herded me into the solar, muttering indistinctly about the Queen's commands.

"I present Miss Catherine Helstone, your majesty." Miss Davenport curtsied her greeting and followed suit.

"Do sit down," said Mab. She sat upon a divan by one of the largest windows. A wide black belt clasped inhumanly tight around her tiny waist. Myriad pairs of insectoid wings, impossibly thin and veined in black, stretched from her waist and overlapped to form what could be termed a skirt.

"I read that a wasp waist is the very height of fashion," said Mab, noticing me stare at her clothing.

"I... I see." Not for the first time in Arcadia, I found myself taken aback. The bodice she wore was banded in black and gold, like the colouring of a wasp. "It is indeed."

"Fashionable, that is," added Miss Davenport, keen to smooth our conversation. "I was just telling Cathy about how much I coveted the wasp-waist gown in that etching–"

"I wish to hear from the other..." the Pale Queen paused, not taking her eyes off me, "Changeling."

Miss Davenport bowed her head and mouthing an apology she dared not voice, she slunk into one of the chairs and pulled out her knitting.

"Come sit by me," said the Pale Queen.

I obeyed.

"So how does this... sewing work?" asked the Pale Queen. "I hear needles are involved."

I nodded, forcing a nervous smile. "Yes, they are."

This close, I could see the rustle of each of the pairs of wings, like the twitching of a swatted wasp during that moment when one is unsure if it will fly again.

"Oh good," she said with exaggerated relief. She sat back slightly, smoothing the wings of her skirt, and a sly smile crept over the corner of her mouth.

I pulled out the handkerchief I had been half-heartedly embroidering for the last four years. I had intended it as a present for my brother before he left, but I had never finished. Most of the progress on it had been made in the solar with Miss Davenport.

"So, I have here most of a rose," I said, showing the Pale Queen my handiwork. With a threaded needle, I began adding stitches to it. Her eyes darted, following the pull of each needle. "And I'm just about to finish it."

"It's red. Is it meant to be special?"

"It was just the thread I had to hand."

"They grow in my garden."

"Red roses?"

"When I remind them to be."

Drawing the needle through the last stitch, I finished the rose on the handkerchief.

"Ah, you will need, at this point, a pair of scissors!" exclaimed Mab. "I have one of those."

With her long, spidery fingers, she drew from the folds of her skirt a pair of ornate scissors.

"Th- thank you," I said. The Pale Queen opened the scissors before dropping them into my outstretched hand. They felt heavier than I expected, more solid.

"I should thank you for them, shouldn't I?" said the Pale Queen. "They are a present, after all, and it is good to thank people for presents. I remember."

"Present?" I said, trying not to sound too surprised.

"It was most thoughtfully left in my bed. I was very pleased with them. That is a present, is it not?"

"I- I'm afraid not from myself," I said.

"Well, I should thank someone," reasoned the Pale Queen. "And I would like to thank you. That is only polite."

Curious, I held the cold scissors to the light. There was no reflection in the dull steel. Tangled, flowering vines made up the handles, with tiny butterflies perched on each flower. Squinting, I could make out the words *William Whiteley & Sons of Sheffield* etched on one of the blades, the other bore initials:

E C

"How very strange to be left a... a present that way," I said. The scissors lay open in my hands, forming the crudest of crosses. Her opening of them before giving them to me was a pointed action. She wanted me to know that the steel scissors could not hurt her, that she was more powerful than folk superstitions on faeries would have me believe. It was a show of strength, like the baring of a predator's teeth.

"I did think so," said the Pale Queen. "But I cannot say I entirely understand the ways of people. I am told they can be taught, though. Even if it does take a lifetime." She glanced over at Miss Davenport, who had been knitting wordlessly. "For some, anyway."

I snipped the yarn with the scissors and passed them back to the Pale Queen.

"Do you understand the basic principle?" I asked.

"Principles are of the world of man. Things which you and I will never entirely understand, being what we are." The fae gave me a long, meaningful look.

Her eyes were disconcertingly large, reflecting in them a thousand points of light. Constellations that would never be lived in the reflection of her eyes. I averted my gaze.

"Still," said Mab, her laughter like silver bells. She clapped her hands. "I do think I can attempt an approximation."

Dozens of spiders crawled from the corners and cracks of the room and swarmed onto her lap. One scrambled onto her finger, leaving pale blue dots upon her skin where it trod. She gestured for me to lean closer and I saw that the spiders had glinting, needle-like legs that each ended in an empty eye. Each blue point upon the Pale Queen's skin was a pinprick of blue blood as the creature danced its sharp course upon her.

"Its legs... You're bleeding," I said, alarmed. "Are you–"

"It hardly matters." She shrugged. "It will be upon the cloth soon enough."

Gingerly, the spiders crept over the linen stretched taut over the embroidery frame. One of the spiders spat out shimmering silk so fine I could barely see it but for when it caught the light. Another spider threaded the silk through its own legs and danced it delicately over the fabric. A shadow scuttled on the other side of the fabric and I could see tiny needlepoints break the surface.

I watched, half fascinated and half horrified, as spiders joined the effort. Soon there was but a huddle of jostling arachnids visible.

Tea arrived on clinking silver trays. I should not have worried as on the trays were perfect reproductions of that found on the society pages. Minute cakes and tiny cucumber sandwiches were artfully arranged on tiered dishes.

We fussed for a moment over sugar and milk and tea. I asked the Pale Queen how she would take hers with care, and she delighted in the ritualistic answers. I added milk to mine and remembered Miss Davenport's aversion to it. I was also careful to salt plenty of sandwiches for Miss Davenport, though the presence of Mab had somewhat stemmed her usual hunger. It was very odd to see her so quiet and hesitant.

Even as we ate, the spiders continued their bustling work. It was only after the last crumb was dusted away that the Pale Queen commanded them aside, "Let me see it. My rose."

The spiders gave way, skittering to the side of the embroidery frame.

The picture they left was not a rose. It took me a moment to recognise it: the distended jaws of a beast wrapped around naked fleeing souls, the flames of hell around them and the red robes of the Risen Christ. Each of the figures was picked out in black thread but for Christ, from whom gold thread radiated. Their faces all had that doe-eyed squint so common in medieval illumination, especially the beast of hell who but for its teeth and flaming jaw had an almost cute air.

"Th-that's the Harrowing of Hell." I touched a finger to each of the elaborate stitches. Christ's hands and feet had little red knots to symbolise His wounds. "It's... it's beautiful."

"This is how one embroiders, right? Needle and thread? Is it not?"

"It is not the only reason I am surprised," I said. "The subject matter is..."

"Well chosen," said Miss Davenport, before I could finish. She matched the Pale Queen's laugh, a sound that only made me more uneasy.

"Then we should continue," said The Pale Queen, her smile only getting wider.

Chapter 15
The Light in the Glass

I have but one candle of life to burn, and I would rather
burn it out in a land filled with darkness than in a land
flooded with light.

> Rev Jacob Roche, personal correspondence,
> dated March 1843

I teeter on the brink of eternity.

Among these degraded, despised yet beloved shadows, I
am the last vestige of the real.

At the moment I put the bread and wine into those
hands, once stained with the chthonic magics, now
outstretched to receive the emblems and seals of the
Redeemer's love, I had a foretaste of heavenly glory that
shattered my heart like glass. I shall never taste a deeper
bliss till I behold the glorified face of GOD, when the dark
earth here swallows me and I earn my martyr's crown.

> Rev Jacob Roche, private journals,
> dated November 1843

They wish to cast my fate in blood but they say the stars are silent. That Within cannot bind me even as the truth binds them. I think I understand.

They would never lie if the truth can hurt more. And the truth can always hurt more.

Rev Jacob Roche, private journals, undated

It was just before dinner, that most unfashionable of meals, that my brother found me descending from my tower. Upon Miss Davenport's recommendation and Mab's pointed remarks, I had changed for dinner. I was in my best dress. Made for Miss Lousia March's wedding, it had not been worn since. I had once thought the world of it, but now its silver-grey taffeta rather reminded me of cobwebs and the blotchy underside of the moon fish.

"She's called off dinner."

I said nothing.

"She said she's had enough of human traditions for the day. That more than one meal a day is just repetitive. Also I really need to talk to..." Laon paused, uncertainty wavering his voice.

I turned to meet his eyes; he flinched.

"Someone," he finished. He leaned heavily onto his cane, looking away. "I need to talk to someone human."

"Now?"

"Please."

"Here?"

"No, the chapel. They don't go there."

I followed my brother to the chapel, winding through the bustling castle. His limp set the pace and the walk seemed longer than ever. I found myself studying the rhythm of his gait, the set of his jaw and the weariness in his shoulders.

There was so much between us that remained unspoken, and for all that I could read from the way he moved and held himself, it was not enough.

We marched through the courtyard where there lurked a pair of the Pale Queen's shadowy bird people. Upon our approach, they folded their long, fan-like tails. I had glimpsed them holding up their stained glass tails to the pendulum sun earlier in the day and marvelled at the bright flashes of colour. It reminded me of the petals of rose windows, where each light curves to a flame-like shape.

Folded, their tails dragged in the dirt. No longer illuminated, they were far less ostentatious.

My brother unlocked the chapel doors and pushed them open.

The candles within were all extravagantly lit, though instead of an inferno, they exuded an eerie coldness.

"I didn't want to…" Laon sighed. He ran a hand through the unruly curl of his hair, a nervous habit. I noticed a wine stain on his cuff. "What I mean to say is, I don't know what to talk about tomorrow."

"Tomorrow… of course, Sunday. You have a sermon," I said. Diogenes nosed over, looking to be fussed, and I relented after a moment, giving the dog a quick scratch behind the ears.

Laon nodded and sighed again, sprawling onto one of the pews as his cane clattered to the floor. It was a familiar motion, one that recalled to my mind muddy boots after long walks. I did not reprimand him.

"I don't even know if there will be an audience, and I haven't given a proper–" He stopped abruptly, swallowing his words. He looked away, studying the glass of my window. For all he tried to hide it, there was a note of desperation to his voice. "There's just not been much… I confess, I'm a little rusty."

I wanted to ask what he had been doing in Mab's court if he had not been sermonising. I wanted him to refute my dreams.

And yet, I could feel his need. So I smiled, even though his eyes were not on me; I knew he could hear it on my voice. "You always knew what to say. Everyone loved your sermons. They were good. Articulate and brilliant. You need only speak and they'll listen..." I tried to sound warm, encouraging, but it rang false to my ears. I could not pretend an unshakable faith in my own brother, not anymore.

"Cathy," he said, pained. "You don't have to..."

Still, I could tell the truth: "I miss your sermons."

"Thank you." He gave a half smile and, pushing away the memories of the dream I had of him and Mab, I settled onto the pew beside him.

I was close enough then to notice he smelt of wine, dark and heady. I wondered if it was for the pain of his limp or if it was for courage to face the morrow.

We remained for a while in contemplative silence. I felt all too aware of the flutter of my pulse, the warm bloom of my breath before me, the fragility of the moment.

It did not last, however. After having flung himself quite so passionately onto the pew, Laon squirmed in discomfort on its hard surface. From here, he seemed more petulant child than haunted missionary. I smiled, a little more genuinely this time.

"You're laughing at me." It was not an accusation so much as a statement of fact.

"Only a little," I teased. "And only when you deserve it."

He snorted a short laugh and sat up. Self-consciously, he squared his shoulders. "I still don't know what to say tomorrow."

"What does the Book of Common Prayer say? You could always say what it tells you to say."

"I've looked at the table of lessons, but it is all just so distant from everything that happens here. What do the fae care of the suffering of Job? Or the loyalty of Ruth?" He grimaced. "Do they even share the sin of Eve?"

"You won't convert them in one single service, Laon," I said gently.

"They laughed so, so much when I told them about Jonah and the whale. That's when I was told about the fae ones on the moors with the sea inside them. Nothing makes sense here. Parables can't mean anything when nothing means anything."

"You don't have to talk in parables."

"You might as well tell me to stop being a priest." Laon leaned back, staring at the painted ceiling of the chapel. The dancing light of the candles flickered shadows across its vaulted curves. *I will open my mouth in parables; I will utter things which have been kept secret from the foundation of the world.*"

"Not everything you say needs to be a quotation, Laon. I also know my Matthew."

"They call it the bible of the poor, you know." He gesticulated at the chapel around us. "The windows and the statues and the paintings. Think it was one of the tracts for the *Times* that argued that we need again this ritual, this popish finery. We stripped bare our altars and no longer understand how to delight the masses."

"Faith isn't about delight," I retorted, quite primly.

My brother laughed at that. "I'm trying to explain concepts bigger than mere words to beings that are themselves unbound by words. What could I even say?"

"Words. You will say words and they cannot ask for more."

"But I think back to the lives of the saints, the life of Christ, all there in light and colour, written in upon the windows and the stone and the paintings." He flung a hand up as if to grasp the chapel windows, to catch light in his fingers and tangle it like a falling ribbon. "There is a wonder there. The sublime, the sense of eternity in the lines of a building, in the face of a saint. I can't speak that wonder. Every stone, every ray of light here speaks and I can't speak the way it does."

"No one is that eloquent."

"But if I just found the right words…"

"They will become the right words when you say them."

"That doesn't mean anything." He closed his hand into an empty fist and drew it close. It was clenched tight.

"Sounds good though," I said. "You always said that counted for more."

The sides of his mouth twisted into a beautiful, if crooked smile. "Don't quote me to me, little sister."

"You need to give a sermon tomorrow. And that is what we will prepare. One sermon. It will be enough."

"I still don't know what to say."

"She embroidered the Harrowing of Hell today. Perhaps you can talk of that."

"Fae are so literal sometimes." He sighed long and hard. "I was trying to explain the pain of being severed from the Lord. Hell as a separation, an emptiness, an absence. A banishment from the presence of the Lord, and from the glory of his power…"

"And she wanted to hear of the ever-burning sulphur?" I rolled my eyes. It was every other Sunday growing up; our father was as fond of Milton as he was of Calvin. "How where peace and rest can never dwell, hope never comes that comes to all?"

"Yes, it got very *Paradise Lost*. But then we ended up speaking of the Harrowing of Hell and I confessed its decline in iconography as some think post-death second chances make us complacent. It was a stupid thing to say."

I gave a teasing laugh. "You're a better theologian than you are missionary."

"It also amused her."

"If you've spoken of Hell then you should speak of Heaven," I said. "You could always actually just say nothing but parable and do that bit in Matthew. The kingdom of heaven."

"Even I don't really understand that."

"My point inexactly," I said, resolutely. "But, more pressingly, we should eat. It'll be easier to think after food. I know I barely ate anything during tea."

I rose and picked up his cane from the floor. Its garnet eyes glared at me as I held out my hand to pull him up. He shook his head, refusing my hand, but taking the cane. Grunting, he heaved himself to his feet. He was unsteady enough that I wondered if he was drunk.

I flung open the doors to find a tray piled high with roast meat and pie just outside the chapel. I hoisted the heavy tray from the ground.

"The Salamander, of course," muttered Laon, picking up the note and skimming it. "As always."

We settled in a tiny antechamber to the chapel and repurposed the paper-strewn writing desk for dinner. Given its haphazard construction, I wondered if it was once an anchorhold, where some medieval lady who had sworn to a life of solitude and prayer would be walled in and forgotten. Our old church had the remains of a wall that our father would tease us was the remains of such a barbaric prison, asking if either of us desired a secluded life.

"At least we won't be overheard in here," said Laon.

"But the birds outside," I said, remembering the shadowy avians dragging their folded tails. "Do they not listen?"

"Oh, the birds are the worst, but they weren't..." He frowned.

"Just outside. In the courtyard."

Laon shrugged before sighing and rubbing his eyes with the

heel of his hand. He conceded, "It doesn't matter. I probably wasn't looking."

The meat was cold but the lumpy, gelatinous gravy still retained its heat. The dumplings glistened with fat and were streaked with herbs, promising a satisfying stodginess. The roast vegetables were in a nondescript orange and yellow tumble by the thick-crusted pie. It was the sort of food that made one homesick.

My brother sprinkled salt onto it all, murmuring a prayer and crossing himself.

"Laon," I said, between mouthfuls of dumpling and gravy. I wanted to ask the question as casually as I could. "What happened to Roche?"

"What do you mean?"

"I mean just that. What happened to him? No one would tell me. Davenport just keeps telling me that it's dangerous for me to know and–"

"I don't know."

"You don't know?"

He sighed. "There are a lot of things I don't know, Cathy. I was never told what happened to my predecessor. I had, at first, assumed him simply dead from an exotic disease like any other missionary, and I still like to think that. It's a simpler answer."

"But it isn't, is it?" I said. "The answer, I mean. The true one."

He shook his head, though I did not know what to.

"What about his widow, Laon?" I pressed. "What answer did we give her, as she sits safe in England? Does she even know her husband is dead?"

"I don't know what they told Elizabeth Roche."

Elizabeth Roche. It was a name I did not have before. I tried not to show my brother that he had inadvertently given me a piece of the riddle.

"Arcadia is full of secrets, Cathy. I can't really begrudge it another at this point." He seemed so defeated. For all the steel in his eyes and the stubborn set of his jaw, he was tired. "Not when I have more pressing work to do."

Sipping the cold spiced tea, I swallowed my words. I wanted to tell him that I had found Roche's journal and detail to him all that I had learnt from it, the mad hand and its ominous ravings. I wanted to tell him about Enochian and the revelations it promised, but now was not the time.

There simply wasn't the time.

"I found Roche's journal," I said.

"Don't, Cathy."

"Don't what?"

"Don't do this," he pleaded. "Don't try to solve this place. It won't end well."

"But I can't do nothing, Laon."

"I can't see you hurt."

Seeing the pain writ large upon his face, I could not bear to press the issue further. I relented. I pulled a Bible from the shelf and laid it down between us. The span of a book, that was the distance I was offering him in this truce. I would not cross that space.

As I opened the Bible, the scent of mould and moths filled my throat. I dragged the palm of my hand across my watering eyes. They were but stinging from the dust. Nothing else.

Glancing down the page, I read the first sentence my eyes settled onto: "*And Tamar took the cakes which she had made, and brought them into the chamber to Amnon her brother. And when she had brought them unto him to eat, he took hold of her, and said unto her, Come lie with me, my—*"

"You should read something else," said Laon. "I would like to hear your voice, but a different chapter. Please."

"What would you like to hear?" I thumbed through the old volume, the pages clumping together as I did so. "You always liked Hagar's prayer."

Laon nodded and I read the story of Hagar and how an angel told her to turn back and return to Abraham and Sarai. In her prayer she called to the God Who Sees and she named him as such.

"And she called the name of the LORD that spake unto her, Thou God seest me: for she said, Have I also here looked after him that seeth me?"

We discussed the passage in the understanding of divine providence and various ways God's Sight anchored the world and witnessed all within it.

I allowed the peace to settle again. There was a sweetness to our unspoken truce, and I glimpsed again the days of old, though then the speeches we wrote and the arguments we made were of no true consequence. The new gravity of the situation did not, however, entirely prevent more frivolous theology.

"I thought this was a serious conversation," said Laon, the edges of his mouth threatening a smile. "You can't just point out Light rhymes with Sight and then call it your proof."

"That was rhetorical flourish!" I protested. "And Genesis does begin with the creation of Light itself. The act of seeing is impossible without it."

"No, by that logic God is blind in the dark."

"But the dark before the world is no ordinary dark. And I am quoting you on God's blindness in the future."

"You can't cite me to refute me. We've decidedly already established that." Laughing, Laon turned the Bible to face him and leafed through it for some superior citation. "I'm reading next."

After, my brother insisted that he walk me back to my room, despite his limp and the stairs that led up to it.

"You should leave at the end of the two weeks," he said.

"You need me here, Laon." I put my hand on his shoulder; he flinched and pulled away.

"No. Cathy, please." He was shaking, his body taut as a bowstring. "I want... I thought I could, but I can't. I'm–"

"But, Laon. If nothing else, tonight has proven–"

"Tonight has only confirmed my suspicions. You aren't safe here." His eyes flickered to me and then away again. "It's not about that... It's not that I need you, it's that I want–" he stopped. His voice sounded as though it was about to break. He turned and simply left.

That night, I dreamt.

Laon and I were children again, when his hands were no bigger than mine.

We were running, tumbling about the heather.

But the sun was not our own. It hung at the end of a thread, a burnished brazen disk. It seemed so close, it took up half the sky.

The pendulum sun was completely still above us.

I breathed in crushed heather and new grass.

Stockings threadbare at our knees, the skin was scraped and bruised. My feet were bare and I felt the grass tickle between my toes. My skirts were too short. I was gangly and outgrowing them, leaving my ankles cold and exposed.

We were playing and I grabbed at his white wrists. He, too, had been outgrowing his clothes and his sleeves were too short.

With the brilliance of the sun, the moon was only visible in the shadow of clouds. It seemed awkward and small with its unseeing eyes and mouth full of crooked teeth. It swam in desperate circles, searching for darkness.

The sun was completely still. My heart beat and beat; I counted numerous seconds outside of time. It was strange to imagine these seconds unrecorded and apart. I remembered the stories of the Egyptian days that belonged to no year, the time when the false gods broke their own laws and sinned against their own blood.

Soon, they would reset the clock of the heavens. They would drag the pendulum across the sky to the furthest edge of the Faelands and it would be dark here.

The pendulum sun remained. Arcadia was holding its breath. Very soon.

I took a step closer to my brother and he squeezed my hand. He beamed at me and then he leaned over, his lips brushing against my ear in mimicry of a secret.

I laughed.

He dropped my hand and he ran. His long legs gave him speed, for all he was unaccustomed to his new height. I followed. My arms were outstretched, still running like a child in a game of chase. My breath grew ragged and I drank mouthfuls of grassy air. It tasted of the moors.

I tripped, but I scrabbled again to my feet. My brother had stopped and turned to me. He was waiting, a dark, beautiful silhouette against the pendulum sun. He reached his hand to mine and our fingers tangled.

And then suddenly, it was pitch black.

The clock had started.

CHAPTER 16
The Woman in the Shadows

It is like poison. You drink it slowly, over time, and
hopefully you will become used to it. Sip it. Every day,
until your body is so used to dying a little at a time that
it no longer feels the pain as pain, no longer recognises
it because it is so good at hiding, at pretending. We are
all dying slowly, a little more pain would make little
difference. So every day, a tiny sip of death, embraced and
savoured like life, like reality, like truth, like everything
that is good and worthy and wonderful. It is like drinking
shards of broken glass – fragments of a dream – so
beautiful, what was once real, now broken, just cutting one
up inside.

But you do, because you must, because one day you will
be able to drink poison of broken glass and not feel it,
not feel the pain, not feel anything, be able to say:"I have
forgotten and this is no longer pain, because I feel it so
much, because it is like second nature to me, as natural as
breathing, and I no longer remember what it is like when it
was whole, when I was not feeling this, when it doesn't run
through me."

And when you bleed, you will bleed broken glass, bleed
poison, but you will not bleed, not really, because you will

be so used to bleeding inside, you will not feel it.
And then, then, you will be stronger.

Written in an unidentified hand in the Journals
of Rev Jacob Roche, undated

I awoke assuming I had forgotten to pull closed the curtains or shutters as moonlight flooded in. Cold, clear and silver-white, the moon seemed to fill the tower room and there was a strange, almost underwater quality to the light. The lethargic flutter of curtains added to the illusion of being suspended in water. I wanted to breathe slower, to drift like dust.

The moon of Arcadia, being an orb that dangled off a fish, did not wax and wane like the earthly moon. Its unchanging roundness gave the illusion of time staying still, of a world holding its breath. As the arc of the pendulum sun grew shorter, midnights were getting brighter and midday darker. It was easy to believe that soon my days would be nothing but this watery twilight.

I rubbed my eyes, gritty from sleep. The room came into focus.

My pulse stopped. A gust of cold air cut through the haze of sleep and I could feel myself sweating in fear.

The door to empty air was open.

It was through that doorway that the moon's silver light poured in. The moon and its fish were swimming very close. I could see now that the pole that dangled from the moon was fleshy and twisted. I could see the mottled colours of the moon, blotchy and white, like the belly of a fish. I could see the glinting teeth of the moon fish, curved and brown as rusty sickles.

The fish rippled and it swam forwards. I glimpsed the

round, staring eye of the moon fish. It blinked before flicking its tail and pushing away. Cold prickled my skin like a scatter of needles. I feared its unseeing gaze.

Long moments passed before I could force myself to close that door and latch it shut.

I leaned against its oaken surface, heart rattling to a woodpecker rhythm. Deliriously, I thought it would break soon, shatter as wood does under the beak of the stubborn bird.

It was then that I heard a clatter. My eyes snapped over to the writing desk.

It was a woman in black.

She stood by the writing desk. A veil and shadow hid her face from me.

"Wait," I said.

Her red eyes darted like flame to the door. Her gloved hands snatched Roche's journal from the desk and she fled.

I scrambled to my feet and, trailing my shawl, I raced after the woman in black. Down the twist of the stairs and along the corridors. Bolting through the castle, I lost track of where we were, as she turned another corner, pushed aside some heavy drapes and unlatched a door.

We were on the roof. I did not remember stairs.

The night was no longer still. The wind had picked up and stripped the sky of clouds. The light from the moon shone steady and unimpeded. It swam close.

"Please, don't run," I called hopelessly after her. "Come back."

The woman in black clambered across the shingles. Her veil thrashed like a caged beast and she streamed long ribbons from her arms like a Morris dancer.

The wind caught her veil and tore it from her hair. She reached a hand after it, but it was too late. The wind had claimed it for its own, and the lace veil fluttered away.

She turned her face to the moon, and I caught her fine, English features. The wind tore at her hair until it became a tumble of dark ringlets. I saw her mouth curse as she pushed her hair from her face. She had a straight, long nose and rounded chin. Though her lip was split, I was certain I recognised her from one of the portraits in the long gallery.

"I need that book. Please, I want to talk to you. I need the book..." I knew she could not hear me with the wind as it was. It filled my lungs as I spoke and threw my voice back at me.

She stooped down and climbed into an open window.

I did not glance down, for I knew the sight of the ground would only fill me with fear. I pulled my shawl tighter around myself and with wind howling in my ears, I followed.

Laon always said I was as surefooted as a goat, after all.

I was glad of my slippers against the shingles. For though it was outside, the softness of the slippers allowed me a better sense of whether a step should be trusted or not.

The wood of one cracked under my weight and shifted. My racing pulse skipped a beat. Swallowing, I moved my foot to another tile and tried that.

Panic swelled within me. My tongue felt thick with fear. I knew I had to move faster. The woman had surely fled tracelessly by now.

The wind caught my shawl and it slipped from my hands. I tightened my grip but it unbalanced me. The shingle snapped and shifted under my foot. It skidded, and I could hear it clatter onto the courtyard below.

I fell forwards, though, onto the roof.

My hands and arms took the weight of my fall. I scraped them against the shingles, and the wind was raw against them. I tasted blood in my mouth.

The open window was close, though. She had not closed

it. Trying not to sob in pain, I crawled forwards. I had scraped my knees as well and they complained at having to take my weight.

Gracelessly, I scrambled inside.

I was in a very small, narrow room. It had within it nothing more than an unmade bed and a travel trunk with leather handles. It was very new and bore a pair of brass initials.

There was only one way she could have gone: the door.

Through that was a stairwell so tight that my skirts brushed against both walls as I squeezed down it. Imagining the walls crushing in on me, I feared that the passage was narrowing.

As I descended, I could hear a low, keening sound, somewhere between a moan and scream.

My brother's warning echoed in my mind. *Don't try to solve this place*, he had pleaded. I remembered the pain written in the lines of his face. *It won't end well.*

The woman in black stood beside a small, lit fireplace. I recognised it as one that was used for baking the Eucharist wafers. The rosy light illuminated the small chapel, dancing red upon the pews and the high altar. I recognised the scattered candlesticks and dishes.

We were in the other chapel. The one in the white tower in the garden.

The far door that opened into the garden remained latched shut. That must have been why she needed to get in through the window in the tower room.

"Hello?" I took a step closer to her. She was no taller than me and seemed about my age. Her eyes were swollen and her split lip was bleeding again. A cobweb of healed and healing scratches covered much of her exposed skin. A silver cross glinted at the hollow of her throat. Her wrists were bandaged, and I saw now that what I had thought to be trailing ribbons were but bandages around her wrists.

We were right by the altar. The gilded altarpiece with faceless halos loomed over us, watching.

The woman in black watched the fire with an avid expression, darting her fingers in and out of the flames. She had shed her gloves. Her throat shivered in that low keening.

She had at her feet an array of curling scrolls and folded papers. I spied the dark spine of the journal.

The keening stopped and she looked right past me. Her eyes settled on the space behind me and stared at that for a moment before returning to the flames.

"Who are you?" I asked. "Why did you take the journal?"

She did not answer my question. She covered her face with her hands and her chest shook with sobbing, but she made no noise.

Ignoring the dull thud of fear in my veins, I took another step closer. The sight of her distress pained me. I wondered if I should try to comfort her, but at the sound of my movement her head snapped back up. Her eyes were dry.

She picked up one of the pages and leaned against the stone wall to read it, tilting it towards the fire for light. She gave another long, shivering wail. I watched her as she pawed at the wall and dragged her jagged nails against the stone. She tugged at the bloody bandages at her wrist and turned those long nails onto her own skin, marking it.

"Don't! You'll hurt yourself."

She turned to me and gave me a glassy-eyed stare. She finally spoke: "It's not real. He can't see you, so it's not real."

"Don't hurt yourself," I said. I licked my wind-chaffed lips and tried to swallow my fear. I wanted to reach out to her but floundered for how. "Please."

"Does it matter?" she whispered, voice hoarse with disuse. "He can't see any of us."

"Of course it does."

"It's not real, don't you understand? None of this is real."

"Real? How so?"

"I stand here, I think it a place. A real place, but it is nothing more than a painted set of a puppet box. Patchwork curtains and all. Except that we are the puppets." She glanced down, seemingly distracted, the blue irises of her eyes following the rapid flickering of her fingertips as she tapped them against each other. "And what the word did make it I do believe and take it."

"What do you take? Come with me–"

"He was the word that spoke it. I believe. He took the bread and broke it. I believe that too."

"Come with me." I reached out my hand to her. "I could wash your wounds and bring you some–"

"No!" she snapped, interrupting me. "None of that. I will not be stolen away again. The gloved hand will strike; it holds the power. That within will speak truth and I fear, I should not fear."

"Can I help you? You're in pain."

"The fire looks after me. The fire loves me. But even that's not real. Nothing really is around here."

"I don't understand."

"No one does. They built it all in a day and a night. You don't know where you are. You don't see because you're blind. I don't see because I don't have eyes." She picked up a bundle of paper from the floor and cast it sheet by sheet into the fire. I recognised Roche's hand upon the pages. They were letters. I needed to stop her, but I couldn't just snatch them from her hands.

"But then you weren't wrong." She pressed one of the letters against her lips in a reverent kiss. "The worst lie." Another kiss. "The best lie." Another. "The only lie... it is always the truth."

"Why are you burning it all?"

"I can't kill me quickly, so I just have to do it slow. Slow,

slow. So slow," she said. "I won't kill her slow, though. Bringer of dreams. Hate. Hate."

"Can I... Can I take the letters? Since you don't seem to want them..." I crouched down and picked up one of the pages closest to me. I felt the familiar spine of the journal and drew that close.

"He went fast. Leapt through the door from dreams." She was staring into the fire again and seemed not to notice me. "Fast and slow. Fast and slow. He went so very fast. But I can't walk that way... They stops me. Says I can't go. Says I must stay here." She wrapped her arms around herself and her voice dropped to a whisper. "Lost but found. Stolen but safe."

"Are you a prisoner? Who keeps you here? Who are you?"

"The original," she whispered. "I am the original."

A knock echoed through the chapel. I heard the doorknob turn. The woman in black flinched and curled inward, pressing herself against the wall.

Fear filled my lungs and I could barely breathe. My heart was in my throat.

Clutching the new papers, I picked up my skirts and ran up the stairs. Glancing back, I saw a figure, tall as a poplar, fill the door of the chapel and I heard the low keening of the woman in black.

Returning to my room, I breathed a long sigh.

Long did I lean against the closed door, the wood hard against my forehead. My ears were still echoing with the keening of the woman in black. I threw my tightly balled fists against the door in frustration and mirrored her low whine of pain. My mind was a jumble of theories on her identity and that of her mysterious captor. She seemed human enough but it was not impossible for her to be a changeling. She also said that she was the original, a word that meant too many things and too few.

My hard-won papers littered the floor but I could not bring myself to pick them up.

Chapter 17
The Owl at the Sermon

Those longest associated with them, and most intimately acquainted with their character and habits, never expect an Arcadian to speak the truth when there is a chance for them to tell a lie. Yet this very people will tell you by their own laws, and by their own lips, that it is a vile sin to lie and deceive. Be not deceived, neither fornicators, nor idolaters, nor adulterers, nor effeminate (unchaste), nor abusers of themselves with mankind (Sodomites), nor thieves, nor covetous, nor drunkards, nor revilers, nor extortioners, shall inherit the kingdom of God.

We are safe in concluding that the Fae, without exception, are guilty of some or all of these sins.

William Finkle & Hildegard Vossnaim, THE ARCADIAN VOYAGES, EMBRACING DIVERSE ACCOUNTS OF FIRST TRAVELLERS, WITH NOTES ON THE CULTURE AND THE CLIMATE

Morning made so much of the misadventures of the night before seem like a dream.

I woke, an aching heap on the floor by the door of my room, and for all the scrapes on my hands and knees, I could barely believe it all happened. With deliberate slowness, I pressed a damp washcloth to my wounds and daubed away the light dusting of dried blood.

There was a madwoman half wild, half imprisoned in this castle and I had no idea by whom or why. I wasn't even entirely certain that she was human. It was clear to me that Mab must have brought her here with her retinue. In her rambling, the woman in black had said that she would not be stolen away again. She said that she was the original.

Turning the word over in my mind, I thought of copies and forgeries. I thought of Ariel Davenport, the changeling, the false one.

The original.

Perhaps she was a stolen mortal, like the real Ariel Davenport. The original Ariel Davenport. The one I had never met. After all, I still had no idea what became of the children the fae spirit away.

A cold chill crept up my skin. This place was too full of secrets.

I had torn my silver-grey dress at some point during the night and it would be impossible to wear it to the service. As I plucked my plain green dress from the trunk, my vanity could not help but wish it more fashionable. It lacked the much-lauded sloping shoulders and fullness of sleeve after the elbow. A lace collar and brooch were my only ornaments.

As I dressed and pinned back my hair, I skimmed the letters I had snatched from the chapel floor. The first one was written by the same mad, raving hand from Roche's journal. It was part of a longer letter. It spoke of the wonders of Gethsemane, and I assumed the writer had newly arrived at the castle. It expressed bewilderment at the edifice's architectural styles and how it reminded the writer more of a grand folly than a true ruin, likening it to James Wyatt's

Spring Hill Tower with its nonsensical turrets and balconies and gargoyles.

It is nothing more than a painted set of a puppet box.

It was those words that lingered upon my mind as I strode through the castle to the chapel. It was slow at first, but I began to notice imperfections in the illusion. I marvelled that I did not see it before. The long and storied history of this edifice had been forged.

I lacked an architect's eye and perhaps that was why I did not notice any of this at first. Or perhaps I was simply too ready to believe that this was indeed an ancient castle. I could tell now that it wasn't the whim of an ancient lord that installed glass windows upon the Norman wall but that it had been built at the same time. The seams simply weren't there for it to be a later addition.

As I entered the chapel, I thought of the artificial infinite that the columns, ribs and arches were meant to create. It evoked the very sublime that my brother so desperately wanted to do with words. But I thought too of how the chapel leaned against the castle wall and noticed the way its bricks had been laid, not against the stonework but cunningly interwoven with it.

As the chapel's single bell tolled its earthy notes, the Pale Queen's court flocked inside.

They arrived in pairs and singly. Beaked and feathered, the courtiers had changed their plumage to darker, more sombre shades. They folded their glassy tails and strutted in, clinking musically. For the first time, I heard the rasp of their dragging against the stone.

The cloaked and hooded creatures did not so much walk as clamber inside on all fours, flashing their misshapen limbs and talons as they moved. They did not lower their hoods when they perched themselves on the pews. Ladies with gleaming, insectoid eyes seated themselves at the back, by the men of sand who had all donned spectacles upon their featureless faces.

It was so obvious to me now that Paracelsian theory of elemental fae was wrong. Or at least unhelpful as a model to understand them. It could still be that each of these creatures were aligned to a classical element, but it could bring no further illumination. It was a thought that made me question the assumptions I had made of Mr Benjamin or the elusive Salamander based on their alleged elemental associations.

"I never thought I'd see this place so full of fae," said Mr Benjamin, leaning over to me. "Baptised or otherwise."

"Otherwise, I assume."

"Otherwise, yes, yes." He made a clucking noise at the back of his throat. "Did not mean they are, so yes, otherwise. But nonetheless, full. On the Pale Queen's orders."

"Did she–"

A shiver of fear contorted him as he nodded.

"Why?"

He shrugged. "The brother is speaking and she wants them to see him."

"Do you think she wants them to convert?" It was clear she was trying to make a point with his presence here, but what that point was eluded me.

"She wants them to see him. Is not quite the same."

And then came the Pale Queen herself.

She wore a dress of snow-white feathers and even whiter fur. It trailed for yards behind her and yet remained impeccably, impossibly pristine. White down framed her pale, flat face and on her brow was a strange wooden coronet with a carved wing stretching sharply above each ear. That and her round yellow eyes briefly reminded me of an owl.

I studied her face as she swept in, wondering if she was capable of keeping a madwoman prisoner.

She seated herself at the back of the chapel and, leaning over her white hand, she watched my brother with rapt attention.

My brother looked impeccable in his surplice and stole. He stood before the lectern, an unreadable calm upon his features. The lectern was held aloft by the wings of a pelican feeding its own blood to its savage-beaked young.

He did not look towards me.

My brother's sermon began quite simply. He had taken my advice after all and his subject was the kingdom of heaven, or rather its bewildering nature. The thirteenth chapter in Matthew was nothing but a long series of parables about the kingdom of heaven, laid down by Christ Himself, and each one was more gnostic and opaque than the last.

"I will open my mouth in parables; I will utter things which have been kept secret from the foundation of the world."

He began by asking us to bear in mind the paradoxical nature of parables, that they are riddling by design and yet are meant to convey the mysterious with clarity. Jesus once explained that it was so that some may seeing, see not and hearing, hear not.

"The kingdom of heaven is like unto leaven, which a woman took, and hid in three measures of meal, till the whole was leavened."

I had missed my brother's sermons, the controlled cadence of his voice and the beauty of his words. I had always thought him a great orator when we were little and I would demand that he give voice to the generals of our toy soldiers and perform the soliloquies that I wrote.

And yet, hearing him again filled me with an inexpressible sadness.

Arcadia had changed him. Perhaps it was simply a nervousness or his desire to temper his teachings for fae ears, but he spoke with a bitterness and an absence of consolatory gentleness.

"Again, the kingdom of heaven is like unto a merchant man,

seeking goodly pearls: Who, when he had found one pearl of great price, went and sold all that he had, and bought it."

The unfocused nature of the parables gave him little structure. He was in command of his own subject but he was sprawling; there was too much he wanted to say. He had too long been alone with his own thoughts. He cited Bede in one breath and then Aquinas in the next. He made Calvinistic allusions to reprobation and predestination, and then Newmanian arguments for bodily privation and chastisement.

"Again, the kingdom of heaven is like unto a net, that was cast into the sea, and gathered of every kind: Which, when it was full, they drew to shore, and sat down, and gathered the good into vessels, but cast the bad away. So shall it be at the end of the world: the angels shall come forth, and sever the wicked from among the just, And shall cast them into the furnace of fire: there shall be wailing and gnashing of teeth."

I had an acute awareness that the passion that fuelled his eloquence was drawn from great depths where moved troubling impulses of insatiate yearnings and disquieting aspirations. I did not know if he was always this way and I had simply never noticed or if the years as a missionary had inspired these impulses within him.

"The kingdom of heaven is like to a grain of mustard seed, which a man took, and sowed in his field: Which indeed is the least of all seeds: but when it is grown, it is the greatest among herbs, and becometh a tree, so that the birds of the air come and lodge in the branches thereof."

He ended the parable of the mustard seed and spoke of the many identities given to the birds that nested among the branches of the tree. Many had guessed whom Jesus could have meant and more have argued it didn't matter.

Looking Mab very directly in the eye, he said, "But unlike all others who have asked that question, I have before me a parliament of owls."

There was a moment of stillness as my brother allowed his words to settle. Mr Benjamin, who sat in awe beside me, unclasped his hands to cross himself, taking his eyes off my brother to glance heavenward. Laon had found a place for the fae in the Bible and it was not in the ancient past nor in the angels and devils, but in the very parables of Jesus. It was, in its own way, a powerful, resonant truth.

Mab threw back her head and laughed.

It was a sound that filled every nook and cranny of that tiny chapel and squirmed its way, writhing, under my skin. Reverberating, it shook the foundations of the stone and shivered through my bones, like a note through a tuning fork.

And then, she stopped.

The Pale Queen smiled wide, showing her teeth, her gaze fixed upon my brother. She said: "What now, mortal?"

"W-we sing." Laon swallowed. I could tell he was hoping no one had noticed his stutter, but the fae were already leaning towards one another. The gossip rippling through the pews, passing from feather-veiled beak to sandy, hand-covered mouth.

CHAPTER 18

The Other in the Snare

Jesus shall reign where'er the sun
Does his successive journeys run;
His kingdom stretch from shore to shore,
Till moons shall wax and wane no more.

Behold the islands with their kings,
And Europe her best tribute brings;
From north to south the princes meet,
To pay their homage at His feet.

There Persia, glorious to behold,
There Elphane shines in illusory gold;
And barbarous nations at His word
Submit, and bow, and own their Lord.

Where He displays His healing power,
Death and the curse are known no more:
In Him the tribes of Adam boast
More blessings than their father lost.

Let every creature rise and bring
Peculiar honours to our King;
Angels descend with songs again,
Earth and Fae-realm speak amen!

Perhaps one of the most interesting occasions on which this
hymn was used was that on which the newly baptised King

Siaosi of the South Sea Islands gave a new constitution to his people, exchanging a heathen for a Christian form of government. Under the spreading branches of the banyan trees sat the some five thousand natives from Tonga, Fiji, and Samoa, on Whitsunday 1831, assembled for divine worship. Foremost amongst them sat King Siaosi and around him were seated old chiefs and warriors, as well as the benevolent agents of the South Sea Company.

Who so much as they could realise the full meaning of the poet's words? For they had been rescued from the darkness of heathenism and cannibalism and they were that day met for the first time under a Christian constitution, under a Christian king, and with Christ Himself reigning in the hearts of most of those present. That was indeed Christ's kingdom set up in the earth.

Joseph Hale, HYMNS ANCIENT AND MODERN, ILLUSTRATED
WITH BIOGRAPHY, HISTORY, INCIDENT AND ANECDOTE

After the hymn was communion, the consumption of the Eucharist. Laon blessed the bread and wine and called forth the divine presence. Watching him reminded me of all the times I had seen him perform in our own stark church. It brought to mind all the times I had seen him practise nervously the night before services. The cadence of the ritual brought me comfort; it felt like home.

I am the living bread which came down from heaven: if any man eat of this bread, he shall live for ever: and the bread that I will give is my flesh, which I will give for the life of the world.

This was a mirror of that promise made by the son of God, a recreation of that scene. In my mind, I always imagined him furtive, desperate, casting about something to make sacred, the way Laon and I would swear promises on handfuls of broken heather. But perhaps that was too human an assumption. It was a bite of forbidden food that cast Mankind from the garden, perhaps it is only right that a bite of the sacred should return us.

And then, hesitation. Laon's hands faltered as the Pale Queen laughed, this time a far brighter, lighter sound.

"Have you forgotten the salt, Reverend Helstone?" came her voice.

I did not turn to look at her, but I could imagine her taunting smile. The fae that filled the pews did not take this as a cue to laugh with her so there was brittle silence as she waited for my brother to respond.

He said nothing but his hands were shaking as he sprinkled salt onto the body and blood of Our Lord. It was an intrusion, but a necessary one.

After all, it was just bread and wine. No different than the food and drink we consume each day. The rules of Arcadia did not make exceptions for our faith.

Only Mr Benjamin and I came forward to receive the sacrament.

I did not see my brother after the service.

The Pale Queen was exuberant in attentions towards me and invited me to her rooms for tea. She insisted that one of her silent servants with owlish eyes and flowing robes fuss over me and lead me there whilst she thanked her *pet missionary* one more time.

I bristled at the term *pet missionary*, but I did not correct her.

The silent servant placed a taloned hand onto my shoulder as they walked me to Mab's rooms. They did not speak, but neither did their heavy robes rustle nor their feet click against the floorboards. I heard only my own echoic footsteps. It was like being guided by a shadow.

The door opened into an airy set of chambers dominated

by a four-poster bed, carved of darkest rosewood and extravagantly curtained. The foundation of the bed was carved in mimicry of fallen leaves and gilded in shades of gold and brass. The drapes fell in heavy folds; the pattern of their brocade suggested strings of feather-veined leaves. The tableau was made complete by the gnarled and treelike posts, the illusion of bark having been worked again into the wood, a tree masquerading as itself.

The sheets upon the bed were simple in contrast. They were a tumble, giving the impression of a discarded cocoon. They were white linen with faded green ribbons.

I remembered attaching my green ribbons to our old sheets. They had been our mother's in her dowry, and when Laon had inherited them I had sewn on the green ribbons on an extravagant whim. I had worn those ribbons in my hair running through the moors. I remember him trying to snatch them from me as we rolled about in the heather.

Those were Laon's sheets on Mab's bed.

My mouth was suddenly very dry. There was something blushingly inappropriate about being in here. My heartbeat stuttered and I felt as though I was intruding, as though I was seeing something not for my eyes.

But there was little I could do. I sat down on the red divan and sorted through my knitting basket, trying not to take in too much of the room. My basket had been fetched by one of the silent servants and I had assumed the Pale Queen wanted me to show her how to knit.

It didn't mean anything, of course, those sheets. My mind turned back to that dream of my brother and the pale woman, even as I knew this meant nothing. It was not proof. I had packed him a linen chest when he departed England a missionary. And sheets were meant to be used.

Mab's visit was meant to be brief so there was no reason to empty the room of his winter clothes. I saw them in the half-open wardrobe, the distinctive sleeve of his greatcoat peering out. He did not need those clothes.

My eyes turned upwards and I saw the wrought iron chandelier hanging up on elaborate chains, its branches replete with stout candles. Drab nightingales flitted about, perching on the pendants of the ribbed ceiling. Nightjars flashed their white-streaked wings.

The ceiling was painted a brilliant blue and scattered with gold and silver stars. This false sky was interrupted by the gilded ribs that held it aloft and ornately moulded pendants.

No, not held aloft. The lines of the room were wrong for that. Another architectural illusion.

I was counting my stitches for the third time when Mab swept into the room.

She shed her cloak of feathers, revealing a brown and white dress. The skirt was made of vast petals patterned like the wings of an owl butterfly, round black yellow-rimmed eyespots staring and dappled with the mimicry of layered feathers. Still, it was unmistakably a butterfly as I could see the veined segmentation of the wings and that distinctive smudge of colour where the pattern breaks down at the base of the wing.

I dipped a curtsy.

She arched a smile and all I could think of was that dream with the willow-bordered brook and how close her lips were to my brother's ears, his cheek, his neck. Flushing, I looked away.

"I did so enjoy your brother's sermon," she said. "You shouldn't be shy about that."

A man of sand brought in a tray of tea things and set it upon the table between us.

"You wanted to learn to knit, majesty?" I said.

"Why so distant, little one?" she said. She sat closer to me and as her dress brushed against mine, like the wings of a butterfly, her skirts shed a pale, dry dust.

"I... I am not distant at all." I brushed the dust from my skirts, calling attention to how close to me she sat.

She exhaled a long, breathy sound that might have been a laugh. I wondered then as I had before if that was the laugh of a being who could steal a child and imprison them. I remembered the low keening sound of the woman in black, its desperation and its sorrow.

"Pour me tea, at least," said the Pale Queen. "Whilst it is still hot. It is only polite."

I nodded and did as she bid. I poured the tea and sliced the cake that had been laid out for us.

"What has delayed Miss Davenport?"

"I'm afraid she won't be joining us today. You will have to forgive me. I do know how much you like the company of your own kind."

"But Miss Davenport, is she not–"

"No," she interrupted, correcting me. "Not exactly."

Her tone was one that brokered no argument, so I did not press for an explanation, however bewildering the remark was. I enquired her preferences for sugar and lemon and milk, a ritual that seemed to calm her.

"One sugar, but no milk, if you please," she said. "I cannot bear milk, though I suppose it's more that it cannot bear me."

"Of course, majesty."

"It spoils in changelings, don't you know?"

As she held daintily her teacup, the Pale Queen gave me a wide, open smile. "I have been thinking about your brother's sermon. *Because it is given unto you to know the mysteries of the kingdom of heaven, but to them it is not given them.* Have you ever thought who the *you* and who the *them* are?"

"What do you mean?" I sprinkled a little salt over the pound cake and took a bite. I passed her the unsalted slice.

"I mean, little one, that for there to be an elect, for there to be those who understand, there must be those who do not. Your Jesus speaks in riddles to utter things which have been kept secret since the foundation of the world. He speaks in riddles so that some may understand, but more importantly, so that some may not." She took a sip of her tea before stirring it with her finger and then daubing the sweet liquid onto her tongue. "Do you not see? Things can only be a secret if someone doesn't know it."

"So... you mean to say that we need ignorance?"

"No, Miss Helstone. What I mean is that you need someone to be different. It doesn't matter who they are, just that they are. Different. Be it the heathens or the pagans, the Catholics or the Papists... Or, really, the fae."

"The fae?"

"Those who take shelter upon the leaves of the church but are not part of it. We who give you definition, meaning, purpose. We who are your opposite."

"I wouldn't say you are the church's opposite..." I tried a nervous laugh.

"Opposed, then, perhaps?"

"No, not that."

"But what are you without us?"

"Human."

Her grin was only getting wider as she watched me with unblinking, yellow eyes. "But you did not truly know what it meant to be human until you looked upon the fae."

"I know who I am."

"You know who you are not. That is not the same thing."

I looked away, biting my tongue. I was trembling in suppressed frustration; she was taunting me.

"Did you not want to learn how to knit?" I said, quite desperate to change the topic.

She laughed again, this time a slightly human noise, though it was breathy and rumbling. "I am capable of pity,

Miss Helstone. So show me," she commanded. "Show me how to knit."

Obediently, I demonstrated to Mab the basics of knitting, hooking the yarn back and forth over my needles.

She stood and moved behind me, leaning very close to peer at my work. My eyes flitted to her and I noticed what she wore around her neck. Dangling from rough cord was a stone with a hole in it.

"You are admiring my treasure," she said, a note of pleasure in her voice.

"Yes, it is quite..." I floundered for words. "Special."

"Oh, it is very special." She smirked at me, her sharp lips arching wide and thin even as the left side was smugly weighed down by a secret. "I keep it as a memento from a child I knew. We became very good friends."

"A child?"

"Well, a child no longer. They do grow so quickly. I am not good with time, but she looks the same age as you." She held the stone in her hand, turning it so that the light played iridescently off it. "Some believe lesser minds are so fascinated with such stones that they become unable to carry out their larcenous designs. But you and I know that to be untrue, don't we?"

It was well into the night before Mab allowed me to leave her presence. I was tired beyond thought, mind numb from all the circuitous word games she liked to play. All meaning had been eroded from words, but still sound had significance and my mind tortured me with memories of that keening the woman in black made.

I was all the more certain now that she was a stolen child, kept as a curio in the Pale Queen's court.

My room was as I had left it, except for the door to empty air. Sighing, I bolted the door shut. I have lost count of the number of times I've had to do this.

I splashed lukewarm water onto my face and, as I towelled myself, I noticed the window had been partially frosted over. The ice was like fine lace on the glass. Despite my weariness, I frowned. Something was amiss; Arcadian winter was still months away.

Something pressed against the pane.

I shouted in surprise. Heart thumping, I approached the window and peered out. As my sleeve cleared away the mist on the glass, I saw the press of a paintbrush on the pane, avian claws gripping the edge and a wide-eyed, owlish face. I opened the casement, unbalancing the creature. Its beak squawked open and it stretched out wide wings before curling up again.

"What are you?"

"On the Pale Queen's orders." The creature wore nothing but its feathers and a green waistcoat. It shook its head.

"But what are you doing?"

"On the Pale Queen's orders," it repeated firmly and closed the window with finality. It scrambled back onto its perch.

The creature squinted long and hard at the pane before pulling out a pair of spectacles from its pocket and balancing them on its beak. The creature swapped its paintbrush for a quill and dipped it into its pot of shimmering blue ink. With its tongue lolling out in concentration, it began slowly drawing fine, fern-like frost onto the window.

A knock.

My door opened to an earnest-looking Mr Benjamin with his battered straw hat in his gnarled hands. He apologised for the disturbance and informed me that he had heard my brother had not left the chapel since services the day before.

"So I was thinking, Miss Helstone," said Mr Benjamin in over-articulated tones. "As you brother is otherwise occupied,

I could possibly trouble you with my question?"

"If you wish..." I said. "But you said my brother is occupied."

He shrugged. "Important soul business, I am sure. Since yesterday. The Salamander bring him food, probably." He nodded enthusiastically to himself, causing his spectacles to slip down his nose and having to push them back up again. "Yes, probably."

"I see..." I frowned, worry clutching at my throat. "I should go to him."

"But my question," insisted Mr Benjamin. "A sister for a brother. Reflections can answer for the whole. Fair is fair?"

"Of course. Do ask."

"So I want to know, I know to want, I know to know... I want..." His voice trailed off and he mumbled to himself for a moment, hands agitating the brim of his straw hat. "Am I stony ground?"

"Pardon?"

"Jesus Christ, Harrower of Hell and Hallowed in Name, said *Behold, a sower went forth to sow.* The kingdom of heaven sewn in the hearts of those who hear it, but not all ears are good soil. He said that it would fall on stony places and into thorns, that the sun would scorch them dry and the fowls would eat the seed..." His words came out in a jumble and his accent frayed. "So am I a stony place? I feel joy and yet I do not understand. It cannot root within me."

"You are quoting Matthew?"

Fervently, the gnome nodded. In a singsong voice he recited the quotation: "*But he that received the seed into stony places, the same is he that heareth the Word, and anon with joy receiveth it; Yet hath he not root in himself, but dureth for a while: for when tribulation or persecution ariseth because of the Word, by and by he is offended.*"

"And you fear that you are not able to understand?"

"No, no, not that. I simply do not understand. And you know I do not. So since I do not, then is it not meant for me? I have read it over and over and over." The gnome began pacing, turning on the spot, unable to contain himself. "And he speaks in parables so that only his followers can understand, for they are given the secrets. But not me, not those who do not and cannot understand. And he will take it away from me, what little I have, he say he will."

"I- I don't think he means that."

"There are eyes that are blessed because they see and ears that are blessed because they hear, but it is not the seeing and hearing that marks them as blessed, or rather it is and it isn't... What I mean to say is that they truly see and truly hear. So it is not simply the reaper angels that will separate the wicked from the just. It is not the fishermen that pull from the seas a harvest of souls and cast aside the bad. The act of seeing and hearing is itself a test."

"If it is a test, then surely you have passed," I said, trying to sound reassuring. "You heard, did you not?"

The gnome pressed his lips together and shook his head. "But did I truly hear? I did not understand, after all. I don't think I'm in the right story. Or I am and I'm not meant to understand."

"I don't think parables work like that."

"No, no, but we do. I'm a part of a story, a small part in a big story. The stony ground and the fish that is cast aside. Someone needs to be that, don't they? So I am the one who doesn't understand."

"Perhaps you should speak to my brother."

"Yes, yes. The brother. He will know," said Mr Benjamin, and nervously clucked his tongue. "You find him. And I will ask him."

CHAPTER 19
The Eyes in the Garden

The Devil plagues humanity with changelings. He will lay his fairy children in the cradle and carry off the true child; but such changelings, they say, seldom live more than eighteen or nineteen years. Eight years ago, I, Doctor Martin Luther, did see and touch such a changed child at Dessau. It was twelve years of age, it had its eyes and all members like another child. I told the Prince of Anhalt, if I were lord here, I would have flung the changeling into the Moldau, and would run the risk of homicide. The Prince would not follow my advice. I admonished the people dwelling in that place devoutly to pray to God to take away the devil; the same was done accordingly, and the second year after the changeling died.

Alfred H Guernsey, "Luther's Table Talk", THE BIBLICAL
REPOSITORY & CLASSICAL REVIEW, July 1847

The chapel smelt of richly spiced port.

Laon was inelegantly squatted on a stool, stirring a pan of negus by the fireplace.

"She wants a masquerade," said Laon without looking up. "And she's decided on a theme for it already. I'm sure you've seen her servants decorating."

"What is it going to be?" Pulling a cushion from the pews, I folded myself onto the floor next to my brother.

It was a moment before he answered. Even in the dim firelight I could see his eyes were sunken from a lack of sleep. He reeked of port.

"Winter," he said.

"Seems simple enough."

"It never is." He ceased his stirring and after blowing gently upon the wooden spoon, held it for me to test. "I've salted it already."

I breathed deep the aroma of the negus before sipping it from the shallow spoon. The sweet notes of vanilla and nutmeg filled my sense before the port caught up with it. My brother had also added slices of apple to the mixture. I could barely taste the salt, so overpowered was it by everything else.

"A little more sugar," I said. "And ambergris."

My brother shook his head at the old joke between us before spooning more sugar into the pan. When we were little, we had found a recipe for the most excellent negus that called for grating ambergris over each serving and we had laughed at the sheer extravagance of the idea.

"Do you think sea whales produce ambergris?" I said, thinking of the wicker whales that had glided through the ground of the moors.

"Probably," said Laon, with a half grin. "But it would undoubtedly be even more expensive than normal whale vomit."

"Might be easier to find, the ocean's awfully big."

"They say the whales usually swim in the dark, beyond where the pendulum sun could shine."

After stirring, he ladled me a cup and passed it to me. He sank back onto his stool and said, "I think the ball and hunt has to do with faerie politics. She has a grudge against the Duke of the North Wind or somesuch. So she needs to hunt something or not invite him to the dance. I don't really understand it, but she wants it to be winter."

I sipped the negus, warming my hands around the vessel. Thinking back to the creature I saw by the windows, I said, "When you said winter, did you mean paper snowflakes and silver tinsel?"

"She probably intends something more extravagant." He filled his own cup with negus and fortified it with brandy.

"It's already made with port."

"Not just port, I threw in some apple." Laon raised his cup in a half-hearted toast and drained it. There was a tremor in his hand. "It needs a little more kick."

I shook my head but did not rebuke him further. "There was a creature painting frost onto the windows. Claimed it was on her orders."

Laon snorted a mirthless laugh. "She's going to actually make it winter."

I did not laugh with him. All I could think was how powerful Mab was, and that was a thought that coiled cold fear in my stomach. The Pale Queen had done nothing but toy with us, all veiled threats and escalating demands. She did not seem to be listening. I said, "Do you think this is all working?"

"What works?"

"Our entertaining her. Do you think…" I paused. My eyes darted to the door and I remembered the figures I had seen outside. I dropped my voice to a whisper, hoping that it was sufficient subterfuge. "Do you think she'll keep her end of the bargain? That if we amuse her enough she would grant us passage, access into the rest of Arcadia."

"It's not really a bargain. I don't know if I would trust her to keep to a deal more than," he made a vague gesture, "whatever we are doing now."

"Begging? Supplicating? Preaching?"

He laughed bitterly. "Petitioning."

I nursed my rapidly cooling wine, turning the cup over and over in my hands. The dark red liquid lapped at the sides of the cup and I allowed myself to be hypnotised by its patterns. There was something unsettling about the way Mab stared at Laon during the sermon and the arch of her smile when she spoke of him. "She's fascinated with you. In a way."

"But of all the ways..." Sighing, he shook his head. "I suppose it doesn't matter as long as she's willing to listen to me. She holds so many keys. She was the only one who would allow a missionary to be on fae land. This castle, this foothold... it is all hard won."

"Is it enough?"

"I am not He who judges these things. There are many things that..." his voice trailed off and he shook his head again. "It can only be."

"But she asks... what does she ask of you?" I dreaded his answer.

"It doesn't matter."

Except that it did. It was an answer that could mean too many things and all of them crowded my imagination. The willow-bordered brook and the secrets in against his ears. I could not bear it.

"We have her ear," he said. "She says she will leave after the hunt. We don't have much longer."

The words were stones in my mouth and I felt myself choking on them. "I don't like what we have to do for her, brother."

Laon gave a shrug. "This is hardly the place of choices."

"But she's pushing us. Making us do more." I swallowed, remembering her red-ribboned hair and encircling arms.

"Making you do more. She's trying to prove something. This isn't just about her guests."

"What's done is done," he said, downing his brandy-fortified negus and serving himself another. "And it's what has to be done."

"No, it can be undone."

"I think I've lost track of the doing, Cathy."

"I mean, she has done things. She had made you do things. Their ways are not our own and they are not good."

"We all knew that before we came here." He tried to lighten the tone of his voice, but the weariness remained. I could hear that hoarseness that came with brandy. "What reason would we have to convert them if they were already good? What need there be of missionaries in a land without sin?"

"It is not the same... I need to show you something."

"Cathy, you shouldn't..." he said. I winced inside at his reprimand.

"No, please. This is important. I don't know how to say it, how to beg you. But please, just come with me."

Lantern in hand, I led the way. Laon limped behind me.

In the courtyard, the misty twilight stretched over us. A light breeze toyed with the foliage, surrounding us with soft susurruses.

I unveiled the door behind the curtain of ivy and tried the handle. To my surprise and relief, it clicked open. I did not think I could retrace my steps of the chase from the night before through the castle and over the shingles.

The heady perfume of the garden enveloped us the moment we stepped through. The air was ecclesiastically thick with scents of cedar.

In the corner of my eye, shadows flickered. I told myself that was but night creatures darting in the undergrowth.

Still, I could not shake the feeling of being watched.

"I didn't know there was a garden here," said Laon with a note of wonder in his voice. Leaning heavily on his cane, he paused to take in the carefully cultivated scene before him.

The garden was only more beautiful in the twilight. The white stone glowed with an inner flame. The quartering paths and the lily-filled fountain were luminous. The shadows played over the colonnades and the arches, allowing one to imagine the ruins whole again.

A hundred eyes were following our every step. For all the seeming stillness around us, the intensity of the gaze was palpable. I dared not turn and ask Laon if he felt the same. A confirmation of my fears would only intensify them and a refutation would exacerbate my keen sense of doubt.

Perhaps a mind too hounded by questions would be prone to madness.

"Mint," murmured Laon, half to himself. "You used to love that smell."

I said nothing, fearing the eyes and too uncertain of myself.

We came to the ivory-white tower. Its door was ajar. I pushed it open.

The chapel was completely empty. Bare even of furniture.

There was no woman in black by the fireplace. The pews, the altar, the candlesticks, the altarpiece, they were all simply gone.

"What did you want to show me?"

"This was... this was a chapel."

"A long time ago, perhaps," said Laon. "Gethsemane has been many things."

"No, it hasn't. But that doesn't matter." I looked about, pacing the length of the chapel in vain hope of finding some trace of the night before. No shred nor shadow remained. There was nothing. Even the fireplace lay empty and cold.

"So you wanted to show me the old chapel?"

"No," I said. "I wanted to show you her... She was here. I saw her."

"Who?"

"A woman in black. She told me she was being kept a prisoner here. She told me she was the original. I thought she might be a stolen child, someone swapped at birth."

"Here?"

I nodded.

"There's nothing here. And it doesn't look like anything has been here for a long time," he said, holding up his lantern. Spiderwebs sparkled, spanning vast distances from corner to corner. "Judging by that."

"But last night..." Coughing from the dust, I pushed a hand through the cobwebs. They clung to my fingers in barely tangible wisps. "I dreamt and I woke and I saw that woman. And I followed her."

"Dreams are... misleading in Arcadia. They can be vivid and very malleable. You shouldn't be ashamed if you were deceived by one."

"But she was here."

"There isn't a stolen child here," said Laon, quite gently.

"We know they summon their changelings to act as emissaries when they're grown. Have them explain fae manners to humans the way Miss Davenport does. But what do they do with the stolen child?"

"No one really–"

"Exactly," I said. "There is a stolen child here. I've seen her. The Pale Queen brought her here and... And the Pale Queen found a pair of steel scissors in her bed." Saying it all aloud made it click into place. It seemed so obvious now who would desire the queen's death. What better vengeance than through the weapons that guarded against changelings?

"That–"

"It's how you ward off the faeries from stealing your child, isn't it? Tessie did that when we were small. A pair of open scissors above the cradle." I knew I was babbling now, but my heart was racing and my mouth could but match. "And I remember reading it in one of your books. Something by Grimm, perhaps. No, that was throwing the clothing of the father over the cradle... but I do remember this. Open scissors make the sign of the cross."

My brother dipped his head. Almost a nod.

I exhaled in a flood of premature relief. It was but the shadow of agreement. I took it as permission to continue: "I think someone is trying to kill her."

"That's ridiculous." His face was still as stone.

"If not kill then at least threaten her. Those scissors have to have come from somewhere. And someone."

"Cathy, don't. I told you, you can't solve this place. You're spinning castles out of air."

"You gave me those books," I threw back at him. "You want me to do this."

"But this is different... this is dangerous. I need you to be safe, Cathy."

"But if Mab–"

"Don't–"

A sharp gust of wind extinguished both our lanterns.

"...say her name," finished Laon, his voice penetrating the sudden, eerie darkness.

Numbing in its bite, the wind brought a bone-deep cold. I shivered.

It was a terrifying moment as my eyes became accustomed to the dark. For a moment all I could see was the hazy twilight colours that seeped in through the door at the far end.

I wanted to protest that there was no power in the saying of a name, to defend all the conclusions I had come to. I wanted to shout and spill the secrets that I had kept locked up for so long, utter the things unutterable. I wanted to fight this eerie oppression, to rebel against the hundred eyes that watched me at this moment and dared me to keep speaking.

But they were all childish, dangerous desires and had no place in my heart.

"Let's go back, Laon," I conceded.

CHAPTER 20
The Snow in the Summer

The Spirits answered, That there were more numerous Worlds than the Stars which appeared in these three mentioned Worlds.

Then the Empress asked, Whether it was not possible that her dearest friend the Duchess of Newcastle, might be Empress of one of them?

Although there be numerous, nay, infinite Worlds, answered the Spirits, yet none is without Government.

But is none of these Worlds so weak, said she, that it may be surprised or conquered?

The Spirits answered, That Lucian's World of Lights, had been for some time in a snuff, but of late years one Helmont had got it, who since he was Emperor of it, had so strengthened the Immortal parts thereof with mortal out-works, as it was for the present impregnable.

Said the Empress, If there be such an Infinite number of Worlds, I am sure, not only my friend, the Duchess, but any other might obtain one.

Yes, answered the Spirits, if those Worlds were uninhabited; but they are as populous as this your Majesty governs.

Why, said the Empress, it is not possible to conquer a World.

Margaret Cavendish, Duchess of Newcastle, THE DESCRIPTION OF A NEW WORLD, CALLED THE BLAZING-WORLD

The Pale Queen's Masquerade was to happen barely a week after her arrival, and the castle was turned upside down to satisfy her whim. The place simply teemed with activity as her servants scuttled back and forth.

I had thought the castle spotless, but apparently such cleanliness was but a delusion on my part and everything from the glittering droplets of the chandeliers to the snaking banisters and the lolling carpets had to be scoured, polished, washed, dusted and beaten all over again. The roiling mass of shadowy servants dealt with it all in their customary silence.

Such aggressive purging I understood to be the creation of a blank canvas for Mab to impose her vision upon. Silver willow trees sprung up within the castle, breaking apart the flagstones and flooring. All the tapestries and portraits were rearranged and replaced with others found in the dusty attic. The grand ballroom was aired out and its many glass doors flung open. Bats blacked the sky each day to take invitations from the hand of the Pale Queen to her multitude of guests. The painting of frost continued on each of the windows, blocking out more of the increasingly infrequent light from the pendulum sun. As time ticked by, the width of the sun's swing grew slowly shorter.

I had been in Arcadia for almost two months.

After that night in the empty chapel, Laon became all the more distant, speaking only to remind me that I would be leaving at the end of the two weeks. A haze of brandy followed him and I could tell he was no longer preparing negus as an excuse to consume it.

I was afraid. I treasured too much the fleeting flashes of intimacy to confront him about his habits. A shared book and a gentle word would have me believing that we could be close again. But I dared not push too hard. The Pale Queen had eyes everywhere, and that discomfort of being watched only intensified over time. I told myself that whatever it was I needed to do to help him, I would do it after Mab's departure. I promised myself that over and over, as I held my tongue.

All this only made me more determined to stay, even as I nodded to my brother's insistence that I make arrangements for my departure. He needed me to pick up the pieces of him. He needed me more than ever, though he did not know it yet.

I was the only one who knew of the stolen woman that Mab kept somewhere in the castle. There were times I would imagine rescuing her, leading Laon to her like a damsel in *Le Morte d'Arthur*. I would then remember the story of Sir Gareth of Orkney, known as Beaumains, guided on a quest by Lynette to save her sister Lyonesse. My brother would insist that Lynette was secretly in love with the knight and that the ending was pointlessly tragic. I disagreed, and we spent hours debating the subject, arguments that would end with us smiting each other a great many buffets on the helm.

But such fantasies were of little practical use. For all my growing suspicions about the stolen woman, I had nothing to prove it. Mab delighted in veiled remarks, of course, ever ready with an insinuation, but there was nothing concrete. For all that she dwelt often on the subject of changelings and their important role as intermediaries between humans and fae.

I carried these secrets and suspicions with very little grace. They weighed down my dreams and made restless my days. They distracted me from what little work I could put into the deciphering of the Enochian pages and the perusal of the salvaged letters. When I was not thinking of my brother and Mab, the artificiality of the castle and its mismatched details intruded. I could barely believe I had been so long deceived by the trickery of an architect.

Still, there was something almost comforting about the emptiness of the castle's history. I no longer filled those long, intriguing years with the imagined lives of lords and ladies. Their tangled lives as told through the stone of the castle no longer haunted me.

More and more, I found myself falling asleep atop a nest of papers, yet such toil brought me no closer to actual answers.

On the morning of the Masquerade, an old woman hobbled into the courtyard. I was crossing it after reminding my brother to eat breakfast, when I encountered her.

"Call me Grandmother," she said before I even asked how to greet her. "I come on the Pale Queen's orders."

With the exception of Miss Davenport, she was the most mundane being I had seen in Arcadia. She had a permanent stoop and was dressed in a shapeless gown of muddy, indeterminate colours with a brilliantly white apron. Her white hair was pulled into a neat bun at the nape of her neck.

At her feet was a large, white, lumpy sack.

"Don't stand there and stare," she said, wagging her bony finger at me. Dark blemishes spotted her papery skin like spidery ink blots. "Come help your grandmother with her featherbed."

"That's a bed?" I said, as I gazed at the misshapen bag she had dragged into the castle. In a land full of strange and profane creatures, it was apparently this that strained my credulity.

The old woman nodded.

I sighed in resignation and picked up the corner of the featherbed. I grunted at the unexpected weight of it. The old woman looked at me and smiled, her lips parted and curled to reveal enormous teeth. Sharp to a point, each seemed larger than even my thumbnail.

There was something reassuringly inhuman about that smile.

The featherbed was, despite its long acquaintance with the ground, a stark, pure white. I gathered it into my arms and led the old woman to one of the empty rooms.

"Somewhere high, I think. Airy," she said. "I'm not afraid of walking. So one of the towers, perhaps?"

"Of course," I mumbled under the weight of the featherbed.

I took her up one of the towers, needing to take frequent breaks to put down the old woman's bed and rest my aching arms.

I had hoped that upon seeing the room came with a bed of its own, she would be dissuaded from her plan, but that was not the case. When we finally arrived, she instructed me to take it to the window and shake it out before making it.

"Until the feathers fly," she said as she sank onto the floor. She gave a satisfied sigh, as though finally glad to be at rest.

Diligently, I obeyed.

I hauled the featherbed to the window and slowly tipped it outside, hands clawed to keep a hold of it. Due to its extraordinary weight, I was terrified my arms would give out and I would drop it.

It was hard work.

I dragged it half inside again to allow myself a break, allowing the wall to take the weight for a moment. My breath was ragged from exertion and I daubed my sweat-slick forehead with the palm of my hand. I glanced outside and saw snowflakes drifting like white feathers.

"Have I shaken it enough?" I asked.

"Harder! Beat it if you can, until all the loose feathers come out. Else you won't be able to reshape it properly."

As I shook harder, the snow grew heavier.

It became impossible to avoid their flurrying fall and worried that I would get the featherbed damp, I hauled it back inside and shuttered out the cold.

"No, don't close the window just yet," said the old woman, getting up to lean herself out of the window. "Let me see."

She peered at the falling snow and reached out a hand to catch a snowflake. She squinted at it, her milk-white eyes straining.

"You can't trade for weather like that. It needs to be made the old-fashioned way, you understand?" said the old woman.

"I'm afraid I don't."

She shook her head and held the snowflake to my eyes. Icy fronds bristled from a curved spine. It was shaped like a tiny feather.

"Now, don't you see?" Her wide eyes squinted into slits as she spoke, focusing on the delicate snowflake. "Though I suppose you might be as blind as the rest."

"They are from your eiderdown?" I said, as realisation dawned.

"Yes, yes. I've been sewing it for years." She gave a heaving laugh that screeched into a cough. "And it should be more than enough to satisfy the Pale Queen's lust for winter."

Chapter 21
The Gift of the Tree

About three weeks ago, while a number of boys were amusing themselves in searching for rabbit burrows on the northeast range of Arthur's Seat, they noticed a small opening in one of the rocks, the peculiar appearance of which attracted their attention. The mouth of this little cave was closed by three thin pieces of slatestone, rudely cut at the utter ends in a conical form, and so placed as to protect the interior from the effects of the weather. The boys, having removed these tiny slabs, discovered an aperture about twelve inches square, in which were lodged seventeen Lilliputian coffins, forming two tiers of eight each, and one on a third just begun!

Each of the "fairy" coffins contained a miniature figure of the human form cut out in wood. They were dressed from head to foot in cotton clothes, and decently laid out with a mimic representation of all the funereal trappings which usually form the last habiliments of the dead. The coffins are about three inches in length, regularly shaped, and cut out of a single piece of wood, with the exception of the lids, which are nailed down with wire sprigs or common brass pins. The lids and sides of each are profusely studded with ornaments formed of small pieces of tin, and inserted in the wood with great care and regularity. Another remarkable circumstance is that many years must have elapsed since the first interment took place in this mysterious sepulchre.

As before stated, there are in all seventeen of these mystic coffins; but a number were destroyed by the boys pelting them at each other as unmeaning and contemptible trifles.

"Strange Discovery", THE TIMES, 16th July, 1836

Miss Davenport came to help me dress for the Pale Queen's Masquerade. Not for the first time, I protested at Mab's plan for an extravagant entertainment but that only earned me a drawl that she was aware of how provincial my upbringing was. She then commanded Miss Davenport to assist me.

The changeling knocked on my door and greeted me with that warmth I had not seen in her since the Pale Queen's arrival. It was almost a relief to see her chattering as she threw open the wardrobe's latch of clasped hands and laid out the dresses onto the bed. She allowed me space to examine them each in turn as she busied herself with the pouring of tea. She chattered throughout, half to herself and half to me.

"I only seem to recall that your brother takes his tea without sugar, but how do you like yours again, Catherine?" said Miss Davenport.

Whatever the source of my dream, I knew my jealousy of her to be quite irrational, but I could not help the flare of irritation when she spoke my name.

"No, you shouldn't tell me, I really should remember by now." She gave a soft giggle at that. For all the shrill notes of her voice, there had always been something infectious about her cheer. "And of course, I take one sugar and no milk, of course. Milk is ever so dreadful."

"Two sugars and a drop of milk, Miss Davenport." I forced a smile. "If only to mask the salt."

"Oh, how formal of you!" she exclaimed. "As though we are not the best of friends. You simply must call me Ariel. Your brother does, doesn't he?"

"I suppose he does."

"Which practically makes us sisters." She laughed again at that and pushed the cup of tea into my hands. I noticed again that brittleness to her laugh and I wondered which was her mask: the fearful, silent creature that was before Mab or this cheerful, chattering one?

I scattered salt onto the cakes on the tray, but for once she seemed disinterested in food. She looked intently at the odd little shaker that held the salt before again rummaging in the back of the wardrobe, promising to find me something else beautiful.

"I'm sure one of these dresses would do well enough," I said, looking at the arrayed gowns. "They're finer than anything I own."

It was hard to believe that they were all new, as the woman in black had said, but I was beginning to notice their oddities. They were faded and yellowed as I would expect dresses over a hundred years old to be, but the wear on the hems was just a little uneven. Moreover, the seam allowances were perilously tight. They were not made to be altered and, more importantly, none of them had been altered. There were no marks for stitches undone and done again.

"You'll need a mask."

"I though the principle was rather more metaphorical."

She murmured an indistinct answer, and then there was a cascade of masks on the bed.

"What's it like?" The wardrobe door hid her from view but I could tell that she had stopped her search and was quite still. I could not see her expression.

"Pardon?"

"Being a person, I mean?" She sounded wistful.

"I'm not sure I could answer that."

"My earliest memory was of Ariel Davenport's grandmother singing to me. I was curled up in her lap. She was wearing a red apron. Her hands smelt of raw dough and yeast from baking. And I remember nothing before that."

"It's not unusual," I said, gently. "Most people don't remember much of being a child."

"Sometimes, I would try very hard to remember what came before." She gave a high, forced laugh. "I sometimes think that if I couldn't remember then that would be proof. Of something."

"I don't think I understand."

"I'm told those memories, of Ariel Davenport's grandmother, I'm told those aren't real."

"How do you know?"

"I'm told I was swapped after Ariel Davenport's grandmother died." She paused. "So I can't possibly really remember her."

"So what–"

"Don't know." She emerged from behind the wardrobe. She gave a careless shrug and sat down beside me. She dragged a hand over her eyes, a messy gesture. "How much of your childhood do you remember?"

"Plenty, but not from when I was in arms."

"Like?" she said, hopeful. I could tell she wanted a story.

"I always liked to think that my first memory was of Laon. I was three, maybe, and we were playing. I don't remember what, but we were hiding under a table and we had to be very quiet. The tablecloth was red and I think I remember his fingers against my lips."

"Is it real?"

"Of course it is," I said. I touched my fingers to my mouth, lingering on that memory, the vivid feeling of his skin against mine.

Miss Davenport gave a low hiss as she exhaled. Her brows

were pulled together in thought. "Does he remember it?"

"No, actually, he doesn't." I traced the curve of lip, and closing my eyes I could almost feel it again. The warmth of him against me in that tiny space under the table, curled against each other. "It's not that unusual. Memories aren't perfect."

"Oh, of course. I knew that."

"Why do you ask?"

"I was..." Miss Davenport hesitated. Her voice wavered. "I didn't feel different when I found out. When they told me. But why would I? I was always different."

"I see..." I was uncertain what to say to that. I wondered in that moment if changelings were made to never quite fit in so that they would better cleave to their true masters when called upon. I wondered then if Miss Davenport's mannerisms were that way by design. "You don't speak much of the time when the fae found you."

"What is there to say? They found me to tell me I was a changeling. Gave me new purpose when I was lost and alone. It's better than being alone. I just... I was just curious as to what it is like to have real memories."

"Are not the memories afterwards real?"

"They are, or rather as real as memories I could make are. After all, I am hardly the real Ariel Davenport." She flashed me her teeth in a smile before leaping to her feet and holding up the nearest dress. The watered silk rustled and rippled in her hand. "Does this evoke winter to you?"

I allowed her the abrupt change in subject and we assessed the suitability of the dresses. My eyes lingered on one that had been cut from a vast tapestry that was meant to form a pictorial narrative. Reordered and abridged by the seamstress, the pictures made little sense. Cranes flew over blue skies, oxen ambled over starry rivers, and long-faced women danced. Of all the dresses, I found it hard to believe this was created to be this way, that it had no former life as a tapestry.

In the end, the decision we came to did not matter.

There was tapping at my door and I opened it to the sight of a silver tree. On its branches was an enormous eagle with a parcel at its feet. The bird regarded us with its round, orange eyes and twitched its ear tufts as we read the note. It bore only the curious rhyme:

Bäumchen, rüttel dich und schüttel dich,
wirf Gold und Silber über mich.

I wrinkled my nose, recognising it from the fairy tale.

"The Pale Queen was always known for her sense of humour," said Miss Davenport as she laced me into the high-waisted dress.

"I would rather not think of her as my mother," I said. "Dress or no dress."

Miss Davenport winced at that, her hands fumbling. She murmured an apology and said, "Regardless, you will have to wear it. She probably just thinks it funny to reference a magical tree that grants dresses."

"A tree that grows on her mother's grave."

She gave a high, forced laugh and abruptly changed the subject: "Aren't you looking forward to the dancing?"

The white dress was banded in gold and silver brocade. Its layers were confusing to say the least. The voluminous sleeves of the high-necked chemise were to be pulled through and pinned into row upon row of silver-trimmed slashes.

It was nothing like the high-waisted gown my mother wore in one charcoal sketch my brother and I had of her, evoking none of the classical simplicity or elegance of that past. Instead it was that stiffness of portraiture in the Vandyke style, reminding me of old attic dresses and moth-riddled doublets.

And yet for all its layers, it had an airy, almost immaterial lightness.

"You are also going, right?" I said, as Miss Davenport twisted my hair into an ornate tumble. Jewelled pins disappeared into my hair and I had but her reassurance that the results were pleasing.

"Stay still," she said, her mouth still full of pins.

"You're avoiding the question," I pointed out, crossing my arms with impatience. "I do notice when you do that."

"You won't miss me."

"So you aren't going?"

"Mab hasn't given me a dress and demanded I appear, has she?" Miss Davenport paused and tucked a stray curl of mine behind my ear. "I suspect she's getting bored of me and I'd really rather not remind her I exist. She'd only try to entertain herself and..." She stopped herself before she finished that thought.

For once, I did not need her to finish to know what she meant to say and I felt no urge to push her.

"Technically," said Miss Davenport. "She's only invited the fae."

"But aren't you–"

"Changeling."

"I thought–"

"Many people do." She smiled a tight, wavering smile before bundling me out of the room.

She did not elaborate.

I descended from my tower room, gloved hand pressed against the stonework to steady myself. I was not used to the shape of the dress, with its high waist and columnar skirt. It was lighter than my usual garb and the lack of petticoats and cinching corset distracted.

Step followed shaky step. The airy slippers were gossamer thin and just as light. Movement was suddenly different and unfamiliar.

It was a strangeness that it was tempting to call freedom, yet this unanchored movement unsettled me. It filled me with a sense of falling, heart lurching to my throat and a tempest roiling within my chest.

The long gallery and the corridors of the castle had been transformed. Mab's servants had covered every wall and ceiling of the corridors with innumerable mirrors and shards of glass. They were of all shapes and sizes, framed in brass and bronze, wood and wonder. They fragmented the light and made the spaces seem at once vast and yet so small compared to the infinity within the mirrors.

Passing one of the larger mirrors, I caught my reflection in it. There was no illusion to hide that fatigue written on my features. I had not slept well for days, if not weeks. Still, it strangely reminded me of a badly preserved renaissance painting. Time had taken its toll and my paint had aged and flaked, fading the tint of my skin. My eyes looked hollow and sunken, as though the black ink of my eyes had smudged. My dress was a wash of white, where once an artist had painstakingly detailed lace and pearl and slash. All that remained was the rich gold that banded the bodice and the sleeves.

Behind me, the corridor was reproduced perfectly in its glassy depths, but everything looked colder and darker. I saw all the other mirrors, a hundred thousand reflections, all reflecting. It created a hypnotic pattern.

Peering like this in a looking glass, it was all too easy to believe such reflections to be the sum of existence, that all was but shadow upon shadow, that the endless worlds were all centred on me, wide-eyed, pale and very afraid.

Chapter 22
The Dances in the Clockwork

Wondrous Ingenuity. – Mr Coppelius Warner, an ingenious watchmaker and jeweller, who occupies a stand at the Polytechnic Institution, has completed the model of a high-pressure steam-engine – so small that it stands upon a fourpenny piece, with ground to spare! It is the most curious specimen of minute workmanship ever seen, each part being made according to scale, and the whole occupying so small a space that, with the exception of the flywheel, it might be covered with a thimble. It is not simply a model outwardly, it works with the greatest activity, by means of atmospheric pressure (in lieu of steam) and the motion of the little thing as its parts are seen labouring and heaving under the first influence is indescribably curious and beautiful.

Mr Warner is a practised hand at such curiosities. His cases abound with articles manufactured for elfin use. He has scissors so minute that some hundreds of them go to the ounce; and there are knives belonging to the same family, which, small as they are, open and shut with a smart click. Mr Warner, we should imagine, works exclusively for the fairies –

no doubt he is entitled by letters of patent to wear Oberon's arms over his door.

V.N., "Notes and Notices", THE MECHANICS' MAGAZINE, MUSEUM, REGISTER, JOURNAL & GAZETTE, 1844

The Masquerade was like clockwork.

Most use that as an expression, to simply mean that things went smoothly or that there was an element of ritual to the proceedings, but I do not mean that.

At first it was not obvious to my eyes. Beyond country dances, I had never been to a ball before and it was overwhelming. Dressed and masked, the guests of Mab were scattered. They spoke to each other in small, intimate clusters, feathered fans snapping back and forth with each quip of the conversation. They danced with precision, wheeling across the floor, each step of their tiny slippered feet clicking to the distinctive thirds of waltzing music.

Above, the ballroom was lit by glittering chandeliers of sinuous tentacles, like jellyfishes of glass. Each feathery tentacle held within its grip a lit candle. They swayed, though not with the music.

In the minstrel's balcony, a multitude of birds sang in perfect, rhythmic harmony. This was not the messy, exuberant birdsong of the mornings, nor the lone undulating twitterings of a nightingale. They did not sing the way people would either, warbling a cacophony of notes to create music.

Instead, each bird sang but a single perfect note and they passed the melody between them. The blackbird would begin the song with a note and then twist its head to the next bird to open its beak.

The magnificent ceiling was obscured behind glassy ice. Gleaming icicles hung from the ceiling, clinging to the arched ribs. The painted pendants and moulded bosses of the ceiling were all encased in ice.

Such augmentations distracted me from immediately noticing that, like any other room of the castle, the lines of it were wrong. The curved ribs of the ceiling supported nothing. The carved pendants and moulded bosses were scattered randomly with no structural purpose, less ornamentation and more the act of uncomprehending mimicry.

"Cathy!" came my brother's voice.

I spun around to find Laon behind me. For all that he reeked of brandy, I smiled at the sight of him. The domino mask did little to hide who he was. Though his costume did rather alter his shape. His black doublet and cape made his shoulders seem wider, and given the slightness of my own slippers, he stood all the taller. He loomed over me and I felt that prickle of annoyance that I have known all my life about his height.

"You... You're..." he hesitated before finishing, "You're quite pretty."

The knot within my heart tightened.

I could simply not remember the last time he had remarked upon my appearance. He said nothing when I twirled before him in old dresses on the eve of my first dance at the squire's house. Nothing when the village girls and I gigglingly contemplated the prospect of marriage and asked his assessment. Nothing when I attended his first sermon in my best dress and mother's brooch.

He must not have done so since we were children.

My brow furrowed, trying to make sense of that knot within me. It ached with a visceral familiarity, as though I had borne it within me all my life without knowledge of it.

"I'm sorry," said my brother. "I should not have said anything."

"No," I told him. A halting reassurance. "I didn't mean the

silence. I was just... I hadn't realised how long it was since you last said that."

A smile wavered at the corners of his lips.

At the edge of my vision, I could see the unnatural, jerking repetition of a single wave. A grey-haired gentleman stood in a bottle green tailcoat. His left hand held a wineglass which lurched in a single sharp motion towards his lips. He would then tilt back ever so slightly from the waist, snap back, and his hand would resume its former position before moving again towards his lips.

The wine in his glass did not diminish.

"Is that man quite alright?" I said, inclining my head towards the odd sight. "He's... repeating himself?"

"Do you mean the man in green?"

I nodded.

As we watched, wondering if we should approach, a gaunt man in a simply cut frock coat and dishevelled cravat strode over to the man with the wineglass. At the click of his fingers, the music stopped and the room became completely still. Not a single one of the many guests moved. He tugged at the grey curls of the now motionless gentleman, pulling forward the head and clicking something at the back of the man's neck. The ceramic mask swung open to reveal a ticking interior of clockwork.

Laon and I watched in fascination as the gaunt man tapped at each of the brass cogs. In the silent stillness of the room, I could hear him humming atonally to himself as he worked.

I glanced at Laon to ask if he had any idea what was happening, but before I could even utter the words my brother shook his head.

"I'm afraid I have no idea," he whispered. "I've not seen anything like it before."

The man closed the mask and fiddled with whatever controls he had at the base of the clockwork man's neck.

He then strode over to us and reached up behind Laon to manipulate his neck before my brother turned sharply.

"Whatever are you doing?" demanded Laon.

The man adjusted his thick spectacles and laughed, an odd staccato sound. "You're not one of my automata!"

"Indeed we are not," said Laon.

"My most profound apologies," said the man, proffering his hand for shaking. "Mr Coppelius Warner, watchmaker and jeweller. Always delighted to make the acquaintance of other humans in Arcadia."

My brother did not allow Mr Warner's excessive familiarity to faze him and gave his hand a firm shake. He introduced himself to the watchmaker.

"You are the missionary! I have heard ever so much about you," said Mr Warner.

"I am indeed," said Laon.

"Though you need not work your words on me, I am baptised true and true. I am, for my sins, an Englishman," said Mr Warner.

"And this is my sister, Miss Catherine Helstone."

"Delighted." The word rolled off his tongue as though a sickening caress. "It is rare to see a thing of beauty within the fae realms. And you are a sight for sore eyes."

"Have you been here so long that the pendulum sun and fish moon no longer bring you wonder?" I said, angling the question as a pleasantry even as I was curious about where he fitted into the Pale Queen's web.

"I have been here far too long by most counts. But someone has to keep things ticking around here." The watchmaker made an airy gesture and barely glancing at my brother he said, "I had thought the missionary had a wife, not a sister."

"I have no wife." Laon was staring hard at Mr Warner with a subdued intensity. "Though if you mean Roche, I believe she never left England."

"Of course, Roche, the Oxfordian!" The watchmaker did not take his milk-white eyes off me. "I had heard about him. Determined fellow. Man of many questions, but not ones I can really answer. I was touring with the Lady of the Green at the time. Though I do hear he was the one who started this fashion for theology in Arcadia. Soon all the lords and ladies will be acquiring themselves missionaries and situating them in decorative grottos. I should think you'd still look quite fetching in sackcloth."

"I should not think myself so wildly clad that my food should be locusts and wild honey," I quipped.

"Locusts?" He blinked blindly at me.

"John the Baptist?" I glanced down, embarrassed; I was too used to how familiar Mr Benjamin was with the Bible. At his uncomprehending silence, I mumbled a hurried explanation: "I had thought you were making a reference to him preaching in the wilderness of Judea? Generation of vipers fleeing the wrath of God? It's all about urging people towards the waters of repentance."

"Ah, a thousand apologies. I was speaking of garden hermits. I had thought them all the rage of late, paying some poor man to wear sackcloth, wander around your folly and spout mystical utterances."

"Ah, I see," I muttered as I felt my brother tense beside me. I too felt the slight and thought again to all the times the Pale Queen called my brother her pet missionary.

"I think the Weld family had a most excellent hermitage built for theirs in Dorset. All very delightful and pastoral, as you can imagine. Setting up a little home for the hermit and a scatter of rustic possessions. Inviting guests to go ask questions of–"

"I am not an ornamental hermit," said Laon, his anger spilling over. I placed a hand on his shoulder and he flinched at my touch but calmed.

"Heavens, of course not! I was not implying such–"

"Neither was my predecessor."

"Ah, well, yes. Pardon. Great man, of course." He awkwardly cleared his throat. "I am just a watchmaker. Theology is not my strong suit. Hell and sin and all that." He strained a laugh and tapping his brow with a finger, he added, "I just work these entertainments."

"It is rather impressive," I said, conceding the change in subject.

Mr Warner preened at the compliment, an oily smile spreading over his lips. His drawl became all the more pronounced. "I do hope you will pardon my mistaking you for one of my automatons. This is rather my most ambitious work to date."

"There are a lot of figures," said Laon in his most measured tones.

"Are all of these your automatons?" I asked.

"Yes, yes. All you see around you. All on Queen Mab's orders," said the watchmaker. "The Pale Queen has a deep love of intricate, interlocking machinery. If you want a masquerade to look right, you can't leave it up to chance. And gentlemen do have a growing reputation for shunning dance."

"I see." I was still rather taken aback by the revelation. My eyes darted about me, taking in each of the figures. A cold chill spread up my spine as I realised none of the people around me were real.

"The fae are well acquainted with the art of the simulacrum, but the ones they create are... well, shall we just say they aren't very predictable. They aren't very good at working with the metals. Dolls of flesh just aren't the same. Too many variables. Excellent people, but just terrible machines. Too much thinking, or at least too much thinking that they're thinking." He clapped his hands together, a sharp motion not unlike one of his automatons. "I should get back to work, though. And for all that I'll be here for eternity, this needs to be perfect by tonight. The Pale Queen's orders."

He clicked together his fingers and the birds in the minstrel gallery began to sing again, each quivering note filling the icy hall with its clear perfection. The automatons moved in their patterned steps to the beat of the music.

It was like an enormous automata clock.

"Cathy, do you think me handsome?" asked Laon as we watched the dancers wheel around us.

The answer tripped from my tongue before I could stop it and I said, without hesitation: "No."

My brother frowned.

"I didn't mean for it to be unkind, Laon," I said. "It's a silly question. I've not looked at you…"

I caught his gaze. Smiling uncertainly, I cocked my head to one side. I smoothed his furrowed brow with my cold fingers and tucked a lock of his dark hair behind his ear.

I took a step closer, to see him better. A flush rose within me, unaccustomed to the nearness of him. Without asking, I reached behind him and undid the ribbon of his domino mask. It fell free of his face, and I kept staring.

For the first time in a very long time, I simply looked at my brother's face. It was strange, as I had thought it so familiar, but it was to his moods and changes, the subtle quirk of his mouth or flash of his eyes.

And so, I tried to see him through the lens of a stranger. How would another judge his large blue eyes and long brown lashes, the proud curve of his mouth?

His face riveted the eye, certainly. He had a pure, clear outline that called to mind classical statues, the strong line of his jaw and straightness of his nose, his wide forehead colourless and still as marble. Readily did I see myself echoed there, but whereas my own copy bore a certain unflattering irregularity, he possessed those lineaments in perfect harmony. Those were my muddy eyes but clearer and more blue, my curls but softer, my lips but fuller.

Would she think him as beautiful as I did?

Would she notice that something about his nostril, his brow, his mouth, which, to my perceptions, indicated elements within restless and eager?

"Beauty is of little consequence, brother. It hardly matters," I said, forcing myself to look away.

"Indeed and you have not just itemised within your mind my many failings." He snorted a laugh and I stole another glance. "I know your piercing gaze, Cathy."

"Then you will know not to press me further," I said. "I can disown my first answer, if you prefer. But you will not get another."

The chiming of bells signalled the arrival of the actual guests.

Laon and I wandered to the grand doors, wondering aloud between us whom the Pale Queen had invited. Leaves of silver and gold crackled underfoot, crushed into the lush oriental carpets. Barely an inch of the long gallery's damask wallpaper could be seen through the portraits and the mirrors. The grand fireplace cracked merrily, the fire high and hot. It was what completed the illusion of winter.

It was Laon who saw it first.

He pointed and I followed his finger to a tear that had appeared in the wallpaper, between one of the portraits and a jewelled mirror.

Suddenly, a knife was thrust in and jaggedly sawed downward. Even from here I could see that the torn paper revealed but naked brickwork and not some other place.

And yet there streamed from the gash in the wallpaper a flurry of dragonflies that each bore in the long dip of their tails an iridescent darkness.

An antlered crone stepped through and she dragged in with her a triad of laughing spectres, figures traced from curling smoke. Pink, writhing earthworms festooned her branching antlers. The spectres threw off their hoods to reveal solid human-seeming faces and untied from their shoulders the obscuring mist.

Then the portraits began to move.

The paintings, by and large, depicted very human faces in very human garb, but as they got up and climbed from their frames it became evident that they were anything but. The Tudor lady with the gable hood revealed herself to be half serpent, heaving her long, shining tail through the window of the portrait. The men unfolded into centaurs, backing away from the edge of the painting before galloping towards us and leaping through into the gallery. The velvet robes of the lady fell open as she climbed and I could see that her robes – and her dress, her jewellery, her flesh – were made of pink marble.

As each stepped through into the long gallery, they surveyed the room through their painted faces. The uneven oils, the fingerprints of the artist, the brush strokes were all still visible on those unmoving expressions.

The faces then came off, each of them to be masks atop ribboned rods. For many, there was simply no face underneath, only a strange hollowness. The stone woman was an exception to this as hers was of the same marble as her body. Her featureless eyes were empty of expression. Weatherworn and crumbling, she was missing the nose and half the chin.

A glowing scrawl cut through the leaves that littered the gallery. It was impossible to make out what it said, but the text arced until it formed a circle. Thunder rumbled in the distance, and a red-capped man stood in the centre. He waved at another of the fae and I saw that he had eyes in the middle of his palms and that those eyes were weeping blood.

As he entered the ballroom, his companion gave him one of the portrait masks.

"It seems she's invited everyone," I murmured. The sheer strangeness and diversity struck me all over again and I realised how foolishly shallow and limiting the Paracelsian theory was in understanding fae. "Except Paracelsus. I don't believe he was ever invited to any parties."

Laon glanced over, his brow furrowing in confusion.

"If he was, he'd have met half of these fae," I said. "Then he'd revise his theory about the elements."

"I don't know, the eye-blood-hand fae could be water aligned," said Laon dryly.

Smoke plumed from the fireplace. There was a heavy thud and crack of firewood.

Something – or someone – had fallen down the chimney.

A figure unfolded from the still-burning fire. They were of imposing height. They scowled as they took in the gallery, regarding Laon and me with coal-black eyes. White scars crisscrossed their face. What flesh wasn't white was the bright, shiny red of freshly burnt skin. That flesh rippled and seeped blood as they lumbered from the fire. Black soot and white ash billowed and clung to their singed clothes.

Dark figures no more than a smudge the size of a fingernail appeared within a mirror. The figures grew larger, walking along the long gallery behind the glass. As they drew nearer, I could see that it was a couple with tawny brown skin. Antelope horns stretched from their temples and brown feathers wreathed their faces like the mane of a lion. They wore matching russet tailcoats.

They were soon right against the mirror. The glassy surface rippled and the shorter of the two stepped through before reaching in an arm to help her comrade.

The slightly taller fae smiled at me as they entered the ballroom. Their long, serpentine tails thrashed behind them.

"Are they manticores?" said Laon. "Some sort of chimera?"

I didn't know and I didn't know how to answer him.

Further guests arrived. The portraits emptied and more poured in from the looking glasses. They appeared at first as reflection, a reflection that was not replicated across any other mirror.

A woman danced through. Her hair haloed behind her like the cascading folds of a goldfish's tail and when she laughed there was but a bubbling noise. Strange symbols were burnt onto the hem of her dress, and knotted into her skin by red, angry scars. I recognised the symbols immediately. They were Enochian.

I stared at her, at first thinking that I would suddenly learn to read that language of angels that had eluded my many nights of study, but I did not. I glanced at my brother and knowing I would be unable to excuse myself now, I resolved to seek that stranger out later.

None of the guests had reflections within any of the mirrors.

CHAPTER 23
The Truth at Midnight

Sometimes this cross is heavy beyond endurance. I carry it in repentance for the sins of my heart, for that is the same as the sins of the flesh. To look upon a woman in lust is to have committed adultery with her already. I know this and I bear it. I feel that I shall bear it for all my days.

My heart is worn out and bruised beyond repair, and in my deep loneliness I often wish to be gone, but God knows best, and I want to do every ounce of work He wants me to do.

I only pray that no missionary will ever be as lonely as I have been.

Laon Helstone, private journals, dated December 1846

Mab's servants had filled the great hall with silver willow trees that wept shining leaves. Breezes tinkled musically through the trailing fronds. Ivy wound around a trellis that arched over the long tables. Crystalline grapes dangled from the ivy, each with a bright blue flame burning inside. Light danced from these icy orbs, dappling us in blue.

"You should eat one," whispered a voice by my ear.

"Eat?" I said.

"These." The stranger with the goldfish-tail hair plucked a shining grape from the ivy. She held it in her gloved hand, twisting it to catch the light. I could see now the scars down her arm and across her shoulder. Enochian scarred into her flesh.

She ate the grape and took another which she gave to me.

The grape was cold to the touch. I sprinkled salt from the shaker I kept in my reticule and rubbed it onto the frozen fruit. Despite the salt, it burst sweet and bright in my mouth.

"Oh," said the stranger, fluttering the fan she held in her gloved hand. "I didn't realise you are human."

The stranger was dressed in the dark red of old, dried blood, calling to mind the scabbed-over cuts that itched and itched. At the hem of her dress were row upon row of shimmering Enochian.

"Her dress is simply divine, isn't it?" said another stranger, stepping into the conversation as he noticed my staring. He wore the front of a charred skull on his face, covering his coal-black features. A purple toga coiled loosely around him. I blushed to see the vast expanse of skin he bared but could not help glancing back when I realised the golden sigils embedded in deep scars were Enochian.

"You shouldn't tease her so, brother," said the stranger with the goldfish-tail hair, placing a possessive hand upon her companion's naked shoulder. "Especially when neither of us have introduced ourselves."

"How remiss of us!" he exclaimed. "And we had promised Mab that we would be on our best behaviour, sister."

I cringed at the utterance of the Pale Queen's name, but did not correct them. I realised that they did not fear to speak her name.

"Mab won't notice, brother. She's far too busy starting up that feud again with the Abyssal Lords. The winter Masquerade out of season, the fox hunt tomorrow."

"It is all very old fashioned." He paused and savoured a crystal grape from the ivy. "Still, she could be trying to snub the Green King or the Lady of Iron. She hates a lot of people. Comes from being quite so old."

"We both remember when the sun was lashed to a chariot, brother."

"You wound me," he said. "Though I do concede that this could all be her trying to stake a claim on winter. It must have cost quite a lot, none of this snow is imported."

"Hunts are so boring in the snow," said his sister, wrinkling her nose. "And I hear the thundersnow that is to come later will be from Finland. There simply aren't enough hands to make that much snow."

At that, it thundered.

I jumped at the sound and, glancing over to the windows, I saw that a snowstorm had struck up outside. White snow flurried against the black sky.

"How timely of it!" said the stranger with the skull, as strong winds threw a clattering of hail onto the glass doors, punctuating his remark.

"Quite the opposite, brother," said the stranger with the goldfish-tail hair, adjusting her brother's unravelling toga. She breathed out and the skin of her cheeks fluttered open like gills. "I haven't had time to admire the artisanal snow or the latest work of Jack. And now it will be buried under all that natural hail."

"It will be much like last year. I rather do prefer it when we buy summer."

"It has been decades, hasn't it? We were such gluttons for summer that year." Another breath and the gills on the stranger's neck opened into eyes that blinked green and gold.

Light suddenly flooded the windows, filling the ballroom. Lightning.

"We were going to introduce ourselves," said the stranger

with the skull, turning his attention back to me. "I am Penemue, known as That Within, and this is my sister, Kasdaye, known as the Covered Hand and the Blood Astrologer."

"I didn't think we were using those names, brother."

"Hold any name up to the light of truth and you can make rainbows from their sounds. It doesn't mean anything. And they are as good as any other," drawled Penemue, picking up a flute of wine from a passing servant. "We don't need to hide them the way Mab does. We aren't famous. No one reads the book of the watchers."

"But I was hoping to title myself a slattern, dear brother. In the Pale Queen's example."

"I suspect the human would consider it rather improper if I simply introduced you as Strumpet." By his voice he was grinning.

"I am..." I hesitated, suddenly afraid of the importance and power of names. Penemue took a step closer to me and leaned in to study my face. I could see behind the edges of his mask, white veins under his skin, ever shifting, an endless scrawl of almost words. His breath smelt like the glue on the spines of new books and the rich ink of old ones.

I felt cornered.

"I am Catherine Helstone, sister to the Reverend Helstone."

"The missionary, of course," said Kasdaye. She took the wine from her brother's hands and sipped it. "You should have known."

"T-the words on your skin, your clothes. Do they mean anything?"

Penemue smiled, his grin reflecting that of the skull. "Why do you want to know?"

"I was curious. It is not of a language I recognise."

"Our Unbegotten Father and his Misbegotten Son may claim it, but it is not theirs alone. You have as much a right to learn it as any other, though I do not think you will understand its secrets. Ink and paper can defy even death."

Laughter bubbled from his sister's throat behind him. "Always so dramatic. She won't be easily impressed like the other, brother."

"But dust can learn, just as clay can. And I don't like teaching those who aren't a little impressed," he said with a pout in his voice. He stepped aside, taking his glass from her, and she stepped forward. They flowed around each other with an enviable familiarity.

"This one isn't so simple," said Kasdaye, pinning me with her gaze. Her eyes were fixed on me. "I can cast your fate in blood, little one, if you want to know. The stars will speak for me."

Her brother gave a sharp laugh.

"Pay him no heed." Kasdaye pulled my hand into hers. "Have you not wanted to speak to me all your life?"

"H-have I?"

"You're human. And humanity loves us." She was stroking my hand as though it were a lapdog. "So desperate are you to speak to us that you see us everywhere. You look across your borders, your walls, and instead of your neighbours, you see us. As your ships sail further and countries and continents discover each other, you see not each other. You see us. You want to see us."

Again, the music struck up from the minstrel gallery. The birds trilled in a three-beat.

"Though for now, you will have to excuse us," said Penemue, reaching a hand out to his sister. "We simply must dance."

She coiled her arms around him and he pulled her into an indecently close hold. To the unbalanced rhythm of the waltz, they clung to each other and circled the room with dizzying grace. Kasdaye's halo of golden frills fanned out behind her like the trailing wing-like fins of a goldfish. Its fronds drifted as though she were underwater.

The strange siblings waltzed and waltzed, and for all my efforts I lost sight of them. Dance after dance reeled across the room, the clockwork dancers mingling with the fae guests.

I found Laon again, standing uncomfortably by the tall glass doors that opened into the illuminated courtyard. Lightning crackled outside to the soft cooing of the fae.

"Aren't you cold, brother?" I said. There were snowflakes in his dark hair and I wanted to brush them away.

"Quite, but I have a drink and I would rather be here than in there." At that, he took a long pull from his hip flask. I could smell the brandy on his breath.

"I thought you would revel in meeting this many fae," I said.

He shook his head and took another long drink. "If only things were that simple."

The birds in the gallery fell silent and the mechanical guests stilled, each frozen halfway through a gesture. Everyone turned to look towards the Pale Queen who stood at the far end of the room on a raised dais.

"Welcome again, good friends, my children and my family," came the voice of the Pale Queen. She wore her wooden crown that accentuated the owlishness in her features. Woven through the layer upon layer of her dress's brown feathers were scaled, serpentine coils. Light glittered off the long, trailing snakes as they undulated, their colours shining poisonously bright. "I am delighted to see so many here and I trust my entertainments have been delighting you too."

The guests nodded and whispered amongst themselves, a roiling, amorphous sound.

"But I grow rather bored with illusion," said Mab. "I think I have had enough of magic making everyone see different."

A murmuring rippled through the guests as they spoke.

"So let us do away with glamour," she said, her voice reverberating through the ballroom and ringing out into the courtyard and the gardens. She took a deep breath, and I felt a rush as light and dust spiralled towards her. Anticipation crackled and even the rumbling thunder silenced at the wave of her hand.

I dared not breathe. I waited.

"Wake!"

At her pronouncement, the scales on her serpents opened like eyes, each mottled gold and staring out through a black vertical slit of a pupil.

Everything changed.

The fae who were dancing around us were no longer human in shape. A fox was tangled with a snow white rabbit. A lion stood on its hind legs, its front paws clinging to a skinless clockwork doll. The porcelain faces of Mr Warner's automatons shattered and they stood naked, baring their brass cogs and copper joints for all to see.

A menagerie of creatures looked at one another, shock written upon their animal features. Ears flexed in surprise, noses twitched and tails lashed. Claws were unsheathed and they fell upon each other as the music began.

But it was not birdsong that we heard.

The birds in the minstrel gallery above were no longer birds. They were naked humans with scarred throats and their feet shackled to the gallery.

"Cathy..." My brother choked out my name.

I looked confused at his face. He was staring at me intently. The hunger in his eyes was both alien and achingly familiar.

That knot within me tightened and I felt a warmth spread across my skin.

"You–" His jaw clenched and his lips pulled into a tight line. He did not stop staring, though, even as I could tell he was trying to stop. Those dark currents beneath his usual veneer were shifting.

I looked down. The gold and silver dress with its bewildering layers had disappeared; I was clad only in my shift.

I was completely naked underneath the gossamer thin fabric. I could feel my brother's gaze upon my skin, his study of my shape.

Mortification struck too deep for even blushing.

Foolishly, I thought I could outrun my shame and I bolted. My naked feet thudded against the ice-cold floor.

The thousand, thousand mirrors that lined the castle reflected my shame back to me. I was a white phantom in the glass, and yet I saw myself, every shadowed curve and traitorous pink blush. The breeze of my pace swept up my shift, making it cling to me. I could not help but wonder if this was the true reason Mab had every corridor covered in mirrors.

I could hear the chimes of the clocks, midnight rippling across the castle. It seemed to follow me, that thunderous, echoing count of twelve. It made the seconds stretch as time itself seemed to stalk me.

Breathless, I did not allow myself to stop until I reached my room.

I crumpled to the floor and leaned against the warm wood of the door. I could still feel my brother's gaze upon me. I folded into myself, knees pressed against my breasts, arms wrapped around myself. Fingers squirmed first into my armpits and then between my thighs in search for warmth. My nipples were hard and ached against the cold.

My breath misted and I cupped my hands around the warm air.

That night, I dreamt again of Laon.

It was the Masquerade again with its silver trees and weeping leaves.

We were surrounded by faceless automatons, by soulless fae, by mindless beasts. He was the last real thing within these borders, under this unreal sun. No eyes could watch us here.

A waltz struck up. The seductive rhythm lulled us into a gentle sway. He did not need to ask if I would dance.

Palm against palm, our hands met and his fingers intertwined with mine. I felt my brother's intoxicating warmth near me, against me, envelope me. He clasped me closer than was decent and our feet flew across the star-strewn floor.

The dizzying steps of the waltz wheeled us around and around. Our feet flew across the marble floor, across the glass shards of a thousand broken mirrors, across snowflakes suspended in an inky sky.

We were young and we were old, the strange overlap of time. We were at once running through the heather and arguing over his departure to become a missionary. We were bickering over toy soldiers, getting lost in the garden. We were gazing upon our father's coffin and despairing over our inheritance of debts.

All moments of our intertwined lives tangled before me. I felt that old, familiar knot within my chest tighten.

My fingers traced against his flesh and I found the words that were written there, secrets that were always meant for me. As I read his bound soul, his hands uncovered mine. We followed each unutterable word, each branded red and raw in the book of human skin.

We were bound up in each other, of the same flesh and clay. Skin against warm skin, we tangled, and I found my own name written upon the book of his soul.

For an infinity of moments, our worlds were but the clasping of our hands, the brush of lips against bare skin and the sinking of one into the other.

CHAPTER 24
The Red Sky at Morning

O, then, I see Queen Mab hath been with you.
She is the fairies' midwife, and she comes
In shape no bigger than an agate-stone
On the fore-finger of an alderman,
Drawn with a team of little atomies
Athwart men's noses as they lie asleep;
Her wagon-spokes made of long spiders' legs,
The cover of the wings of grasshoppers,
The traces of the smallest spider's web,
The collars of the moonshine's watery beams,
Her whip of cricket's bone, the lash of film,
Her wagoner a small grey-coated gnat,
Not so big as a round little worm
Prick'd from the lazy finger of a maid;
Her chariot is an empty hazel-nut
Made by the joiner squirrel or old grub,
Time out o' mind the fairies' coachmakers.
And in this state she gallops night by night
Through lovers' brains, and then they dream of love

William Shakespeare, ROMEO AND JULIET

I did not want to wake up.

A weak and hazy sunlight filled my room. The morning had resoundingly arrived but I turned over in my bed and refused to rouse.

It was why I did not hear Miss Davenport's knock as she burst into my room, a breakfast tray in hand.

"So I thought you might want some breakfast," she said, quite abruptly. "I know I do, and I'm far more comfortable interrupting your morning than your brother's."

"Thank you," I said, staggering awake. My eyes were full of sand and grit. I threw my dressing gown and a shawl over my night things. For all my hope that Mab's artificial winter may have passed now that her Masquerade was over, there was still an icy bite to the morning air.

"You can't sleep forever. A hunt always follows a ball."

"Isn't it in the evening?" I rubbed my eyes free from the sand crusted in the corners. The lingering traces of dream evaporated as I spoke. Its touch stayed, however, and the warmth of it lingered on my skin even as I cupped icy cold water to my face.

"True, but I still want breakfast." Miss Davenport put down the large tray. It was piled high with an assortment of leftovers from the night before: The ruby-red grapes were each dusted over with a delicate filigree of pale green ice. Thinly sliced roast beef had been rolled into little rosettes and wrapped in leaves of fresh herbs, mostly mint. Shards of snowflake biscuit, some glazed and some not, were jumbled together with gingerbread owls. Lumpy, imperfect scones sat in a basket next to *vol-au-vent* pastries, each spilling out their delicious sweet and savoury fillings.

"Your door is unlocked," she said, glancing over at the door to empty air.

"Oh," I said. The bolt had indeed come free and I resolutely pushed it back into place. "It's loose and often slides open when I'm not looking. I must have been too... tired last night. To check."

In a smaller, nervous voice, she added, "I also heard what happened last night."

I felt that knot tighten in my chest. Images from my dream intruded; they were meaningless. Desperate to change the subject, I said, "I still haven't salted the food."

I found the salt shaker in my desk and sprinkled the salt onto the grapes and the biscuits.

"I heard about the illusion and how you ran–"

"Why do you need salt in your food?" I interjected as I finished salting everything on the tray.

Miss Davenport pressed her lips into a tight scowl. She picked up the plate of snowflake biscuits and sat back. Biting savagely into one, she said, "Changelings aren't really fae. I thought I said as much before the ball."

"You did, but it didn't make sense." I helped myself to a scone, breaking it in half before spreading butter onto it. "How could you not be?"

Miss Davenport shrugged and continued between mouthfuls of *vol-au-vent*. "There's fae who are as you see them, or not, since they are changeable by nature and very varied. But there is them and there's humans."

"And changelings are neither?"

She nodded. "Changelings are made to be like humans but not. We have to grow and learn like humans. Otherwise we would be found out. Not all are well made, but successful deception or otherwise, we aren't fae. And we aren't human."

I ate my scone in silence, trying to think through the implications of what she said. Humans, of course, were created with souls. They were breathed into humanity's forefather named mankind. Fae, on the other hand, we simply didn't know. If changeling were in between, did it imply that fae had to be humanity's opposite?

Careful to avoid certain thoughts, I mused on the true forms of the Masquerade's guests. If all the fae are indeed animals, then that had some profoundly disturbing implications for our work in Arcadia. The true nature of Arcadia has been a fertile topic of debate since its discovery, and my time here had been far from elucidating. The pendulum sun and fish moon were but symptoms of a deeper strangeness. But moreover, what of its fae inhabitants? After all, birds and beasts have no souls and do not need converting. They were placed under the dominion of mankind. It was with a sinking feeling that I worried, wondering about the nature of souls and God's creation.

"So to answer your question," said Miss Davenport. She did not meet my eyes and her speech was halting, stumbling her phrases over one another as though no sentiment could escape unimpeded by caveat. "Changelings have certain human limitations, but not others. Changelings are like people, a lot like people, but not entirely. But we vary, considerably, if nothing else because, among other reasons, we have different creators. I don't know everything about being me, but I do know I don't need food. I don't starve, I just feel hungry."

"How do you..." I trailed off, realising the impudence of my question.

"Ariel Davenport's family died in a workhouse. I watched them starve when I did not. Whatever fae gears were inside of me kept turning."

"I'm so sorry."

"But here, I still need human salt. Whatever promise that was made, whatever *geas* that invokes, it applies to me as well."

"I think I understand," I said. "Thank you for telling me."

She grinned, less wide than usual with a touch of melancholy in the corners. "I wish you need never know."

"What do you mean?"

"I want... I just want you to know it's for your good." She shook her head and the melancholy faded. Her grin stretched wider, tighter and she said, her voice high and bright, "I haven't had any of the gingerbread yet!"

After Miss Davenport left, I sought distraction in my collection of papers. Anything to not think about my dream from the night before. With sufficient time I knew I could bury those thoughts, I had done so before. I knew they would pass. I just needed to think about something else.

So I leafed through them: the pages in Enochian and my attempts to decipher it; Roche's journal; and the letters from the chapel. The castle's preparations for the Pale Queen's Masquerade had left me so tired each night that I had not managed to read all the letters until now.

Paper crackling, I unfolded the first. The texture of the page drew my attention, the scratch of the nib on its surface and the etched shadow of the words.

After several pages detailing the inconsistencies of the forged castle and how distracting the writer found this, I came to the last page of a letter. So used to mysterious was I that I barely believed it was signed. It was. The writer was:

E R

A postscript then giggled of how unaccustomed the writer was with her new name as a married woman.

Elizabeth Roche. Elizabeth Clay.

And for once, all the pieces seemed to fit together: the shiny new initials on the trunk in the attic; the Miss Clay in Roche's journal; the name my brother let slip.

The *E C* who owned the steel scissors must have been Elizabeth Clay.

Yet immediately after such triumphant revelation did I feel the sting of defeat. The information was useless. Knowing to whom the scissors once belonged answered no real questions. That it was Elizabeth Clay's scissors that the stolen woman had found in her bid to escape and avenge herself on Mab offered no further insight.

I tucked a stray hair from my face and, as my fingers brushed against my own skin, I remembered how Laon used to do the same for me. He would reach across the table and wind my hair behind my ear. Reaching for a pin to secure the distracting hair, I told myself that it was nonsense to miss the softness of his touch or the stroke of his fingers.

My hands were shuffling through the letters with little focus, my eyes skimming across the words without comprehension. Many of the letters were cross-written, with the letter continuing over itself at a right angle. The hand was rigorously curled and meticulously correct. This helped neither their legibility nor my focus. The events were a jumble in my mind. Further, the lack of careful dating only made the construction of a narrative harder.

> *I trust it not too presumptive to write to you after our*
> *most delightful meeting in Oxford. You summarised most*
> *eloquently the Tracts that have been published in my absences.*
> *Pusey's work on the doctrine of Eucharistic Sacrifice sounds*
> *most intriguing and was of particular interest to me. I will*
> *endeavour my utmost to achieve my own copy.*

It was only after many, many more letters did I realise they were love letters. Or rather, those of a courtship.

Both Jacob Roche and Elizabeth Clay had been verbose in their affections, though the word itself seemed inaccurate to their state. They wrote extensively on the importance of the missions to far flung places and divisions and indivisibility of the Church, reflecting on its various branches and if those differences would prove them doctrinally incompatible. They wrote of transubstantiation and divine presence, of grandiosity of rituals and the dangerous allure of popery.

Jacob Roche wrote sparingly of the mission in Arcadia, but he did describe to her Gethsemane and a mute housekeeper made of flame. He showed very little of the desperation that I was familiar with from his journals. He seemed full of hope and desperate to share this strange new world with her. When she enquired of the fae and the reputations for sin and duplicity, Roche stated that that was an oversimplification. He called truth their weapon.

Through them all, the sincerity of Elizabeth Clay's faith shone brightly. Roche could be abstract in his theology, but for Elizabeth Clay it was passion that burned inside her. Even in debate she wrote with an undeniable ferocity.

Roche, at times, seemed more enthused about his future bride's theological education than any other attribute.

He must have brought the letters with him as a reminder of his waiting wife.

Reluctant to dwell on the thought of Roche's widow, I turned from the letters to Enochian. I had made some progress in my understanding of the language, but odd words were not the same as true meaning. I had thought when I first encountered it that I would be able to teach myself Enochian much like how Laon and I had studied Latin and Greek in our youth, unable to pronounce any of the words in our long compiled lists. I missed the sound of his voice as he stumbled through our notes, trying to intone the speeches of long-dead heroes.

I sighed again and rose to splash a little water onto my face. There was still some left in the pitcher from the morning's ablutions.

The water was cold enough to sting.

Given what Kasdaye and Penemue said during the Masquerade, I was more certain than ever of the theory that this was indeed a project undertaken by Roche to assist in his conversion of the fae. The mother tongue was, after all, the greatest missionary. To speak to a people in their own language was foundational and fundamental to the great work.

And yet Arcadia had no tongue of its own.

Oddly, it was something I had never questioned. The fae seemed simply to speak with fluency the language of any and all they encountered, or perhaps that was simply those who spoke with outsiders. For all the pretences of the explorers, there was very little we knew about inner Arcadia. And moreover, most early accounts did not think to distinguish between changeling and true fae. Much like Davenport, many early ambassadors were changelings.

I thought of what my brother said of the sea whales and how they swam for most of their lives beyond the light of the pendulum sun. Its straight path meant there must be, within Arcadia, vast stretches that rarely knew day. Yet of these dark lands beyond the light and warmth of the pendulum, we knew almost nothing.

I felt again that aching desire, my mind tumbling through my recent vivid dreams of my brother.

I remembered his hand in mine as we ran through the heather and into the depths of Arcadia. The infinite promise of wonder and adventure.

A knock summoned me from my reverie.

It was Mr Benjamin. He was in his best waistcoat and he was wringing his straw hat in agitation. Mab's visit had been taking its toll on the gnome, but though his weariness was evident, he stood just a little taller, less hunched and crumpled than usual.

"A sister for a brother, is fair trade. A sister for a brother," said Mr Benjamin under his breath, as though reminding himself of something. He nodded to himself, as though steeling his own resolve. His eyes flickered to my face before returning to his nervous hands. "You will pretend priest again? Please?"

"Why?" Fear splashed across me like a pail of cold water and the knot in my heart tightened. "Has my brother left?"

He shook his head. "He is not in the chapel. He won't talk to Mr Benjamin."

"Can it not wait?"

Mr Benjamin shook his head again, his eyes screwed tight as he did so. "The Pale Queen will hunt today."

"I know."

"A hunt follows a ball. And it be Benjamin."

"I'm sorry, what do you mean by that–" I said, thrown by the tears that were rolling from his eyes. Floundering, I offered him my handkerchief, which he took after returning his hat to his head. "Don't cry. She told my brother she will leave after the hunt."

"What do you mean by that? There is a hunt, yes?" He dragged an arm over his eyes, smearing the tears. My handkerchief remained unused in his hand. "A hunt follows a ball. Yes, yes?"

"Yes, that I know. It is one of the Pale Queen's entertainments."

Mr Benjamin nodded rapidly. "Then you know. She will hunt, so she needs some fae to hunt. It needs to be one of us. And I thought, it can be Benjamin."

"You couldn't be serious," I said. "But Mab–"

"Don't say her name," he snapped, pausing in his sniffing. He was agitated, but the usual undercurrent of fear was absent. He did not shrink back at the mention of her name.

"I mean, the Pale Queen," I said, correcting myself. "The

Pale Queen can't possibly hunt us. Or one of us. At least not. It's a hunt, you go after animals and... This can't be right."

"No animals for hunting here. No foxes, no deer. Just us. Us fae." He gave a half shrug, his bony shoulders sharp under his clothes. "The Pale Queen desires what she desires. She does what she does. And we fae make better game, she says."

"But the Pale Queen can't–"

"Not about her. Hunt will happen. I mean to say is." He cleared his throat, shuffling on his feet. His voice strained as though about to break, but there was a steely steadiness under it. "I-I've been nothing but questions. Since baptism. I knew but I did not know. I saw but I did not see. And all was doubt." He swallowed. "But I have no doubt now. I am sure. Surer than sure. It is what I need to do."

"But, Mr Benjamin, we can't possibly allow..."

"Please, Miss Helstone. Allow me the martyr's crown." His gnarled brown hands shook, clutching his straw hat. "I have seen it. I have read the book. Christ has spoken, *My grace is sufficient for thee: for my strength is made perfect in weakness.*"

"Well, yes, but–" What he had told me barely sank in. I was still reeling in shock from the very idea of Mab hunting and killing Mr Benjamin.

"He turned to man who died at his side. *Verily I say unto thee, Today shalt thou be with me in paradise.* Come with me to chapel. You read to me before I die and we sing together?"

I swallowed, uncertain as to what to say. The gnome's resolution was obvious even as he vigorously rubbed his face with my handkerchief, staining it grey.

"Allow me this," he said. "It is written. *Yet if any man suffer as a Christian, let him not be ashamed; but let him glorify God on his behalf.* I remember this. I have seen it myself. I have seen the purchase of God's gaze upon us for a far greater price."

"There has to be another way."

"But no path can do this. No other path." His voice was

somewhere between his usual accent and that Oxford Voice he liked so much to assume. "Allow me the martyr's crown. With it you can buy Arcadia. Open the gates. Walk the paths. There will be more paths, more paths than walking. And the Reverend can ride into Sundry, into Anchor, into Pivot. Allow me this. So I can allow him that."

I remained silent for a moment, studying his expression. His large, wide eyes were never more expressive and they were hard as flint. I remembered the fear in his face when he first spoke of the Pale Queen and how none of that was upon him now.

He was entirely resolved upon this sacrifice.

And finally, I said: "It is not for me to allow, Mr Benjamin. Your life is not mine nor my brother's to spend. But I will go with you to the chapel."

His hand was soft as turned soil after the rain. His large hand enveloped mine as I took it and I heard him murmur under his breath, "Price is paid, fair is fair."

Chapter 25

The Hounds at the Hunt

Tell us therefore, What thinkest thou? Is it lawful to give tribute unto Caesar, or not?

But Jesus perceived their wickedness, and said, Why tempt ye me, ye hypocrites?

Shew me the tribute money. And they brought unto him a penny.

And he saith unto them, Whose is this image and superscription?

They say unto him, Caesar's. Then saith he unto them, Render therefore unto Caesar the things which are Caesar's; and unto God the things that are God's.

MATTHEW 22:15-22

We walked in silence. The castle was teeming with the Pale Queen's guests and members of her retinue, so conversation would have been likely inconvenient. I was still floundering at the very idea and I could not bring myself to be as resigned as Benjamin was to his fate. My mind was still grasping at ways to save him, to prevent the Queen from her plan.

And still it gnawed at me, the sight of all the fae as mundane animals at the ball. Were all their strange appearances but deception? Were they all simple beasts under all that illusion and if so did they also have the souls and nature of beasts?

Yet were not beasts named by Adam and placed under his dominion?

Does the hand that held mine now belong to a creature with a soul like mine or was he an unthinking beast? Was the humanity I saw in Benjamin's eyes an illusion? And if he had a soul, how would it be measured? Would it be weighed alongside mine, or were they exempt from Eve's Edenic sins? Surely they did not and could not bear her crimes?

Noticing me staring at him, Mr Benjamin smiled bravely at me and squeezed tight my hand. It was like finding pebbles under sun-warmed dirt.

Would I see him again in paradise?

We pushed open the doors of the chapel, which was empty of my brother.

But for a solitary, guttering candle on the altar, the chapel was without illumination. The frost on the windows was thick and blocked them dark, and without them this place was stark and sombre. I never thought I would long for ostentation and ornament, but in this moment there was an ugliness to the chapel I found unbearable.

There was a dim halo of light around the candle, casting long, faint shadows across the chapel. These phantoms were of little comfort. The cold and empty pews stared at us as we walked down the nave.

I found a taper and lit it from the guttering candle. From there I spread the flame to each branch of the standing candelabras until the chapel was ablaze with light.

Benjamin was kneeling, and I knelt with him.

I had neither his calm nor his courage.

"Would you read to me?"

I nodded and opened my Bible. I thumbed through the

columned pages uncertain what I should choose. For all the wear upon my well-read Bible, for all the times I had turned to it for strength, I had not thought I would need to read to a creature condemned.

"It has been decreed, I will die. So it remains: what will you buy?" he sang to himself.

"Benjamin…" I said, my voice trembling. I had first stepped foot upon Arcadian soil but two months ago and I had not thought it would lead to this. I had read reports of missionaries in other lands and I knew of their dangers, their martyrdom, and yet that knowledge gave me no insight. Was this how they felt when they bravely faced their doom? Did they also feel this helpless, watching their own fall to plague and sword?

"If Christ can ransom the world, perhaps I can buy back my own kind," he said. "I've been to the Markets. Everything has a price."

"It is a very high price."

"It is that way in stories, and I will be one. Fae are nothing but stories, after all." He smiled as though at his own joke. "Tell me the story I will be part of. The story of our sin and our salvation."

I was shaking, quite visibly I feared, but Mr Benjamin said nothing. I wanted to ask him then what sin lurked in the past of the fae, or if they did indeed share the transgressions of Eve.

One passage was as good as any other, so I read: *"For there is one God, and one mediator between God and men, the man Christ Jesus; who gave himself a ransom for all, to be testified in due time…"*

My voice filled the chapel. For all that it seemed to bring the gnome comfort, it only made me feel more alone.

The many questions that Mr Benjamin had plagued me with through my time here did not fall away. I felt as though they should, that in the face of life and death, in the face of his martyrdom, these questions should no longer matter. I felt as though his conviction should renew my own faith and that for all the petty, pedantic questions of theology, I should know what is truly true.

And yet I could not. The mysteries and questions only further hounded my mind, their weight almost unbearable in the cold light of the chapel. I could not make sense of what was and was not sin. The ransom paid by the blood of Christ was for the sin of Eve, after all.

I could read so clearly upon the face of Mr Benjamin the fervour with which he believed. He no longer saw himself as stony ground. He had been tested and he had not been found wanting.

But I?

I read with all the passion I had. The words washed over me to the point of meaninglessness. They gave my companion succour as I saw his eyes again tear up and, thumbing my now grubby handkerchief, he thanked me.

Together, we followed the footsteps of Christ from his entering of Jerusalem to the moment of his execution. The name of this castle, Gethsemane, took on new meaning.

The windows darkened, and I knew twilight was drawing near. Laon needed to be here, to speak to his single parishioner before Mr Benjamin's death at the hands of the Queen they both so obeyed.

Coming to the end of a chapter, I said, "I should go look for my brother."

"Thank you," said Mr Benjamin, without taking his eyes off the altar.

"You are staying here?"

"As long as I can," he said. "The hunt will begin soon."

Leaving Mr Benjamin to pray, I went to find Laon.

Gethsemane was bustling with activity. The preparation

for the Pale Queen's hunt was well underway. Sand-skinned men with unblinking eyes of glass were dressed in hunting pinks, herding the packs of hounds.

Saddled steeds – for they were not all horses – pawed impatiently in the courtyard and their hooves clattered like hail against glass windows. Scaly beasts hissed at me, long tongues whipping back and forth. Wings beat against each of their handlers, feathers and fire and scale thumping alike. Manes were tossed and from sulphurous nostrils were breathed out plumes of glittering black dust.

I tried my brother's rooms, which were empty, and his bed was untouched. I remembered the sight of Laon's sheets on Mab's bed and I thought of that dream I had banished with the willow and the brook and the whispers. I thought of the faded green ribbons that I had once worn in my hair tangled up in their embrace and that knot in my chest ached.

The ballroom and the long gallery were both still a mess from the night before, all fallen leaves and heaps of melting snow, feathers and fur, a tracery of burn marks across the ceiling.

"Miss Helstone!" came a remarkably human voice. "What a pleasant surprise."

It was Mr Coppelius Warner, the watchmaker from the ball. He wore a bright red riding jacket with black lapels and he held a black whip in his hand.

"Do you not look forward to the chase, Miss Helstone?" he said with great exuberance. His eyes dropped to regard my worn travelling dress, his gaze as uncomfortable as the crawl of ants. "Though I am rather surprised the Queen has not granted you more appropriate garb. You were ravishing at the Masquerade."

I bit back the remark that the Queen's gifts were not to be trusted and smiled. "I should go, Mr Warner."

"But I will see you at the hunt?"

"Of course."

When I refused his handshake, he gave a deep, flamboyant bow that he undoubtedly intended to be flirtatious.

It was only as I walked off that I thought to ask him. Half turning, I said, "Have you seen my brother?"

"Yes, I do believe I saw him in the stables."

The stables reeked of sulphur.

My eyes stung as I peered inside. It was wreathed in fumes. Embers smouldered with wisps of grey smoke. Fetid, sulphurous heaps were pushed against the walls.

It was largely abandoned, the fae beasts having all been saddled and led to the courtyard. The shutters were mostly shut, casting the long stall-lined corridor in shadow. Many of the stalls were barred, like cages, striping what little light there was.

Opening my mouth, I tasted sulphur and salt and smoke.

"Laon?" I ventured.

I heard a sound from deeper within, past the many stalls. Black, glittering coal was piled in the corners and sodden hay was strewn about the floor. I picked my way through carefully.

"I'm locking up Diogenes," came my brother's voice from the darkness. I heard a whimper from one of the stalls and a frantic scratching. "There's no reason it needs to join in with this madness."

"Laon—"

"And you," he said. "You need to leave. Last night... last night cannot happen again."

"I'm not here about that," I said, coldly. "I'm here about Benjamin."

"What?" I could hear the confusion in his voice. He paused in his saddling of the red horse before him. It tossed its flame-like mane.

"The Pale Queen is going to kill our first convert," I said. I tried to speak with Mr Benjamin's steely resolve, but I could not. "She will hunt him like a beast and he will be a martyr to the great work."

"W-what are you saying?" He tightened the girth of the saddle, trying not to meet my eye.

"She's going to kill Benjamin. That is what all your plans have come to."

He laughed, an acrid sound that pained me to hear. It was hollow and bitter. His steed whinnied. "What do you want me to do about it?" He hurled the words with reverberating force, his spittle visible in the streaming sunlight. "Do you expect me to ride in and save him? Do you really think I have that power?"

Perhaps it was simply Mr Benjamin's resolve and how he saw it all as an inevitability, but my time in the chapel with him had cemented the same sense of inevitability in me. My mind no longer fumbled for ways to save him, no longer assembled half-baked plans that began and ended with mindless fleeing.

And much like how I could not outrun my shame at the ball, we could not outrun the will of Mab.

"No," I said, quite quietly. *"Render therefore unto Caesar the things which are Caesar's; and unto God the things that are God's."*

Laon buried his face in his hand and then raked back his beautiful hair. I saw now it was not callousness that had caused him to hide here but a profound helplessness. "That's ridiculous."

"There are people who say Arcadia pays a tithe to hell. We still don't know how true that is."

"What are you suggesting?"

"Nothing, Laon. We failed him. I didn't think we could, but we did and..." I said. My eyes were streaming, from sulphur, from anger. "There must be more we can do. Can we not ask her for a boon or a wish or a favour? Is that not how fae work?"

"I don't think–"

"Laon, we must. Benjamin, he said something. He said fae are stories. Perhaps we can trick them somehow..."

"Cathy..."

"But Benjamin has made his choice. He wants this. He deems the redemption of all Arcadia to be worth his life. He calls it a price he must pay to ransom their souls. How can I tell him otherwise? How can I deny him the martyrdom he wants?"

"You are angry at me."

"Yes!"

"I can't fight the Pale Queen."

"I am not angry about that. I am angry that you were not there to pray with him, to sing with him, to hear his last words. He prays now, alone, because you were not there."

"Cathy!"

"You should go to him." I shook my head, trying to clear my clouded thoughts. Memories and dreams tumbled together, and my righteous anger was not enough to keep it all at bay. The sight of my own helpless brother disarmed me. I reached out a comforting hand to him, laying it on his shoulder. "He needs you."

He leaned into my touch and I could see his demeanour soften before he pulled away. "I will, but last night..." He did not meet my eyes. "We can't continue this way. I can't... You need to go."

"Laon, please. It doesn't matter now."

"No, but it does... Last night." He swallowed. He was shaking, his gaze turned from me. "I know other things seem more important and I know I said two weeks, but I cannot. Not after last night. I do not – I cannot – trust myself around you."

"Laon, please, I'm not so angry at you," I said. "And you can't do this alone. You need me here."

"You don't understand, Cathy..."

"If not me, then someone, a wife, Miss Davenport." My voice was hollow even to my own ears; I did not want him to marry. To utter the words twisted the knotted pain in my chest, the knot I did not want to give a name to. I remembered feeling it every time he flirted with another woman, every time the ladies at church would flutter by and giggle at the prospect of an attachment. I had carried it within myself for so long, heavy as a stone. For the first time, I felt the true weight of it, across my shoulders and tight around my chest. I felt a spinning sense of unbalance even as that weight and pain anchored me. "It doesn't matter. You need someone and it should be me. You should not be alone here."

"I want you here. More than anything."

"Then why are you sending me away?" I threw back at him.

"Because you can't stay here."

"That makes no sense."

"You are why I left England. It was an exile. Self-imposed, perhaps, but very real. I needed to. I thought if I was here, then it wouldn't matter. I thought I could outrun my own sin. If only I could run fast enough, far enough." Crumpled over, I had never seen my proud, beautiful brother look as defeated. That weariness he had about his shoulders seemed all the more acute. He slammed his fist against the wooden stable door; it rattled against its hinges. "It was stupid. I could not run far enough."

"Laon..." I stood over him, that knot in my heart aching beyond words.

"And you came," he said, an edge of dark laughter to his voice. It did not bubble over into laughter, but he shook his head, dark curls falling into his eyes. "You stupid, brave woman. You came for me."

"What do you mean?"

"I mean… I mean…" he hesitated. Our eyes met, and my brother regarded me with a wild, shadowed look. The ferocity and passion that had always been simmering beneath his facade had been brought to the fore. And it was not simply savagery, nor hunger, nor wit.

In this moment, he wore no mask.

And for the first time, I understood: It was lust.

A tremor passed through me, strumming at my core. That knot inside my chest, those tightly held hands bound around my heart, I felt them loosen.

Hunting horns intoned long, brassy notes.

"The Pale Queen is summoning us," I said.

Laon got to his feet, brushing the soot from his breeches. He was shaking still, but the mask had returned. "It would not do to keep her waiting."

CHAPTER 26
The Rabbit in the Snare

I have given myself totally to this glorious cause. I have
surrendered unto it my time, my gifts, my strength and
my very family. My only family. I cannot doubt. I must not
doubt.

The risks, I know them. The temptations, I feel them.
The price, I will pay it.

Let it be enough. I pray that it is enough.

Rev Jacob Roche, private journals, dated 1842

GOD will use my blood to seal His truth. He will write in my
flesh and I could but turn my whole mind heavenward.

This blood will not be shed in vain. The truth when this
hard won cannot be lost again.

I trust. I can but trust. There is nothing left to do but
trust.

Written in an unidentified hand in the Journals
of Rev Jacob Roche, dated September 1843

The hounds were baying, but the hunting party was still incomplete when we arrived.

Laon mounted his red horse, and I was given an animal that was more shadow than beast. My hand sank into its fetid, inky depths as I mounted. The cold iron bridle seemed to sink into the darkness of the beast, the chain links losing their lustre when engulfed.

The Pale Queen surveyed us all from atop her own steed. She was dressed quite simply with her owlish crown atop her head. She was in excellent spirits as she, laughing, ordered her retinue to mobilise the dogs.

The men of sand gathered and herded the great multitude of hounds. They were, I assumed, the huntsmen and the whips. I could not imagine why she needed so many sorts of dogs, since many had specialities and skills that were barely applicable to the hunting of...

I did not want to finish the thought.

Speckled spaniels and pointers lounged atop one another, surprisingly docile as they were roused to the ready. Lurchers thumped their tails in anticipation.

My eyes lingered on the sleek, grey forms of the whippets. They moved with ethereal grace, eyes on the horizon and ears twitching. I felt a pang of home, remembering our father's own hunting dogs.

The hyenas I did not expect. It was not until I heard their cackling that I realised what the dark-striped dogs were with their wide, flat heads and coarse manes. Their tongues lolled from their red maws as they swung their faces back and forth, watching and waiting.

There was a thunder of hoofbeats as the fae rode over. Foremost among them was Penemue, his half-coiled toga streaming behind him like a scarlet banner. His black skin was stark against the red of his toga and the white of his steed. By his side was his sister, a bright flame atop her blood-red mare. Her riding habit was swept up off the ground in their gallop. Mingling with the folds of her long, flickering veil and gleaming through them, shone her goldfish-tail hair in brilliant flashes.

Mab greeted her guests with her usual smiles and graciousness, the predatory air all the more pronounced on this day. I could barely focus on the sights before me as I sat stiffly atop my shadowy horse.

Desperately, I wanted my mind to empty but there was no escape. I saw my brother astride his own steed and I felt his eyes upon me. I felt that familiar, hot flush and I cursed my own traitorous skin. A breeze ghosted over me, and I shivered.

The Pale Queen called for the unleashing of the prey, and there was a great commotion of movement. I dreaded what came next.

A small streak of blue leapt from the hands of the Master of the Foxhounds.

"It is done," announced Mab, a grin splitting her face.

"Who is it that Mab wants dead today?" said Penemue in the manner of a greeting, as he wound his sinuous steed to my side. No longer wearing a skull over his face, the Enochian marks in golden scars upon his skin were all the more pronounced. "Do you know?"

"Benjamin Goodfellow," I heard my own voice say.

"Really?" said Penemue. The gilded scales of his white steed shone in the sunlight.

I nodded.

Kasdaye laughed, appearing beside her brother. "That may be, but why would that amuse Mab? It is no show of power to kill a lowly gardener and groundskeep. There is no sin in the slaying of one without a soul."

"Oh but what is a soul, dear sister?" There was a warmth to his voice that I envied, that coiled warmth in the depths of me. "Is it a breath that is passed from the lips of the Creator to his children? Or is it something uniquely belonging to mankind, he who is similar to the divine?"

"I should never have indulged your penchant for pedantry."

He threw his head back in a roaring sound I assumed to be laughter. "Perhaps I have been talking too much with mortal theologians."

"They so rarely ask the right questions," she said, reining in her impatient steed. "So distracted are they by the details. But that doesn't answer my own question of why a gnome. Where is the joke in that?"

"Perhaps that itself is the joke," he said. "It's murder, not a meditation on the nature of sin."

The hunting horns sounded again, and we rode out.

The air had that crispness of winter, and the pendulum sun shone down bright and clear, lancing through the grey leaves of the forest. The canopy created by the impossibly tangled branches was almost translucent, like old, frosted glass.

The forest was new.

Where once had stretched the endless grey mists there was a verdant woodland, thick with trees and undergrowth. Mab had summoned a forest into existence around Gethsemane and she had built it from the mists that surrounded us.

The undergrowth melted back into mist as our beasts trampled it, with the vague, bleak scent of smoke lingering in the air. Penemue and Kasdaye chattered merrily.

The hunting party scattered in search of the small blue creature. Some of the packs of dogs pulled back and others disappeared into the grey forest. One of the scenthounds seemed to have found a trail, and we followed.

I could barely make out what we were looking for. I watched it all unfold around myself as though in a dream. My horse surged under me, paying little attention to the prompts of my hands and knees. It followed the other steeds, flicking its ears at the baying of the hounds. It was its own master.

Was this how His apostles felt at the eve of Christ's execution? Am I Peter, fated to thrice deny Jesus before the crowing of the cockerel?

The baying rippled through the great, unruly mass of the dogs.

I yanked at the reins, but my steed ignored me, following. I did not want to witness this. I remembered Mr Benjamin's trusting eyes and his myriad questions, and for all his sudden certainty in the face of martyrdom, I was still clouded over with them.

I imagined how bare words would one day try to recreate this moment and I could not. The first fae martyr. If nothing else, I should witness this.

The hyenas chattered amongst themselves before howling loud and long, a painful sound more akin to the scream of a child than the howl of a beast.

Would Mr Benjamin scream?

A pack of terriers growled and barked up one of the trees in great excitement, circling and leaping. A blue squirrel was just about visible between the misty leaves.

"I knew we should have brought the ferrets," drawled Mab, though she did not sound annoyed. She held out an expectant hand in which was promptly placed a sling and pebble by one of the huntsmen.

With bare-faced glee she hurled a pebble at the bright blue squirrel. She missed, but it thudded against the tree with considerable force, shuddering from the branches a fall of leaves. Another of the fae loosed stones at the darting creature.

A dozen pebbles later, the blue squirrel fell from the tree.

The terriers closed in, and I felt my heart leap into my throat. I was holding my breath. I was clutching at the reins, fingernails digging into my flesh.

I wanted it to be over quickly.

A huge, blue boar burst from the undergrowth and charged blindly into the woods. A handful of the fae gave chase immediately. A cheer rippled through the remaining hunters, and Mab grinned all the more. The huntsmen rearranged themselves, shouting wordlessly at one another in raspy voices.

It was obvious to me now that Mr Benjamin was going to cycle through the various prey animals for the entertainment of the party.

The hunt wore on.

We rode for hours, and the trail grew hot and cold. Mr Benjamin went from boar to deer to fox. I kindled the hope within myself that Mab would grow bored and call off the cruel chase.

"Would you like to know a secret?" came the voice of the Pale Queen.

I turned to see Mab, bringing her steed close to mine.

Hesitantly, I nodded.

"I do like the curious ones. You are one, aren't you?" She was just behind me, speaking her words right into my ear. There was no warmth, no breath to her speech.

Her enormous, yellow eyes seemed to just swallow me up, and my throat clenched in fear. All warmth drained from me, and I could not breathe. Perhaps this was how a mouse would feel before its demise in the beak of an owl.

She did not wait for me to answer before saying, "I didn't break the glamour. You could not possibly think the truth so easy to win. There was no truth. I simply gave you all another lie."

"Wait, you mean–" My brow furrowed as the implications of her words unfurled.

"I wasn't so bored of illusion after all," she said, laughing. She sounded like silver bells.

"And that all was..."

"An excellent trick, was it not?" She clapped her hands together in unbridled delight. "Not the best trick, of course. The best involve the true truths, but this is almost as good."

I nodded slowly, unable to do anything but agree.

The horns sounded, and Mab laughed. The dogs barked and the hyenas laughed. The beaters had found something.

My heart gave a dull lurch and I could barely bring myself to look. The hunt was wearing me down. My pulse no longer beat with the frenzied hooves of the chase. I knew only a cold, glacial fear.

I glanced over at my brother. His face was a beautiful mask. Twilight caressed his features with a gentle glow. I could glean no understanding from his set jaw and proud eyes.

I wanted him to look at me.

The dog chased from the burrow a blue fox.

As the dog's jaws closed on the fox again, it shook itself. Every hair on its pelt stood on end and, at another tremble, it seemed to grow, its shape shifting into that of a much larger creature. The dogs backed away, barking loudly.

The blue bundle stirred, its clothes in tatters. It staggered to its feet and without a further glance at us, it bolted. Its brown hair and torn clothes streamed as it dove into the undergrowth.

It ran on two legs, not four.

It was Miss Davenport.

The men of sand marched ever forwards, sticks in hand, beating at the bushes to rouse their prey from hiding.

There was a distant chattering laugh from the hyenas. The steeds pricked up their red-tipped ears and surged forwards; I felt the tight cords of muscles under me ripple.

I thought at first that it must be a trick of the light, but as my shadowy horse galloped forwards and I glimpsed again the running form of Miss Davenport, I knew it was her: the turn of her chin, the arc of her shoulders, the splay of her fingers.

The thickening trees slowed the horses as Miss Davenport headed deeper into the forest. Treacherous roots jutted from uneven soil. A low mist seeped from the trees, forming a second canopy that further fragmented the sunlight.

"It is rather like cheating to let her run to the edges of the forest," drawled Penemue. "And this is rather a waste of magic."

"Hush, brother," said Kasdaye, bringing her horse to circle his. She placed an affectionate hand on her brother's shoulder and, for all their strangeness and their sins, I craved that closeness. "You never like it when things end too soon."

"Not all things are meant to take all night."

My horse stumbled. My knees gripped hard at the saddle as it danced on its hooves, pawing at the ground. It seemed discontented with its own pace as it turned a brisk circle, seemingly chasing its own tail for a moment.

It did not matter how I held my reins; the beast had a will of its own.

I was falling behind.

Another mocking laugh from the hyenas, this one quieter and further away. I could no longer see the others. My horse remained intractable, flicking its tail in defiance of my instructions.

Perhaps this was itself a mercy.

Though I could hear the sound and fury of the hunt in the distance, around me was an unearthly stillness. The grey forest as created by Mab was empty of creatures. No insects crawled upon the bark nor flitted over the decay. No birds lurked upon the branches and nothing scurried underfoot. Like all of fae creations, the illusion was imperfect.

Another bark, but this one in a different direction, further into the mists. My horse's ears pricked up at the sound and, despite my urging, it followed.

Not for the first time, the mists swallowed me.

I was cut off from the rest. The curling grey smoke around me no longer formed tangible trees, but rather coiled around itself in sinuous tangles. Tangles that briefly formed hands, fingers, lips, before melting again into the mist. It flowed like water, like waves that crested into caressing, clasping, dancing.

The mist had a way of muffling sound; it blanketed me until I could barely hear my own breathing, my own heartbeat. It engulfed me with a deathly silence.

That silence was what made me notice that slightest of sounds, the hissing exhale of breath.

My eyes sought the source even before I thought of the consequences.

Miss Davenport was huddled quite small in the hollow of a half-created tree, enveloped in mist. She looked up at me through her blood-matted hair and smiled weakly. Thin cuts lined her face and a trickle of blood streaked from her temples. As always, her smile held too many teeth.

I dismounted and rushed to her. My steed protested, dancing its hooves impatiently as it huffed its scalding breath onto me.

"Good, Cathy," she whispered, voice tremulous.

"Take my horse," I said. "You should be able to get away. They won't be expecting you to be mounted and–"

"No, listen to me: You need to kill me." Miss Davenport unfolded from the hollow of the tree, shaking. Her dress was torn and her muddy, tattered petticoat clung to her legs.

"No, what?"

"The Pale Queen wants me dead. This isn't a whim. It's an execution. But don't worry," said Miss Davenport. She glanced behind her, fearful. "You don't have a soul either. So it won't matter."

"Why would you say–"

"Cathy, forgive me. I'm sorry I have to tell you now, like this. I never told you this before because I did not want you to know the pain that I know. You are not human."

"What?" I choked out.

"You are a changeling, like me." She gave a shrug, but winced in pain. The cut over her lip split open and seeped red blood into her smile. She licked her lips, colouring them red.

"You... you lie." I swallowed. She was voicing a fear that had been lurking in the depths of my mind, but I did not want to believe her. "How could you possibly know?"

"I had suspicions. And the Pale Queen knows. I've seen your human, the real Catherine Helstone."

"No, please–" I shook my head.

"I have that proof. I have seen her. And the Pale Queen is toying with you. She will spring it on you when you least expect it, but I have understood her taunting...."

"No, it's not true."

"I have done all I can to protect you from this knowledge. The Pale Queen was baiting you with this, hinting. She wanted you to meet your original. But I didn't want you to know. I didn't want you to suffer like I did. When they laid their claim on me."

"But–" I was reeling. Her words were rewriting my past, even as I wanted to deny it the urgency of the hunt was overwhelming. It was as though a part of me always knew the truth. It suddenly made sense: my discontentment, my ambitions, my feelings for Laon.

"I'm sorry I didn't tell you earlier. I couldn't." She hung her head for a moment, shoulders shaking in silent laughter. "It's all a cruel joke to them. And now I'm sorry, profoundly so."

The reins were still in my hands. I knew what I wanted to say and what I wanted to do. I pressed them into her fragile, shaking fingers, all bruised nails and torn skin. "They'll catch up. You should run. You could still take my horse."

She refused the reins, pushing them back into my hands as she shook her head. "You have to kill me."

"I won't. Please, Ariel."

She smiled. There was a softness to her smile that I had never noticed before. "Cathy, please. I can't allow my blood to stain your brother's hands. I just won't."

"Ariel..." I said her name again, that familiarity I had of her turning into affection. I had convinced myself that Mr Benjamin could die, that he had prepared himself for martyrdom, that he knew what his life was worth and that he was willing to pay that for the possibility of salvation.

But this.

I could not bear this.

"There aren't many who have shown me kindness and I want to..." she was speaking to herself now, her half-closed eyes reliving the memory. I could see it shadowed upon her face, a fleeting glimpse of rapture. "I told him I was neither fae nor human but he didn't care. He worried about my soul when I had none."

The sound of the hunting horn broke her reverie.

Her eyes darted towards them. We heard again the cackling of the hyenas; they were nearing.

"You have to kill me. Don't let your brother do it." Ariel drew a knife from her belt. It was dark and slick with blood. Her bruised fingers closed my pale ones around it. "Mab will force him. She wants him to sin. Don't let her."

"But to sin—"

"You're safe. It doesn't matter to you. You're like me." She glanced over her shoulder. "It's in Mab's nature to toy with people. To make them sin. To make them fall. Protect him for me. I beg you. Promise me."

PART THREE
Golgotha

Chapter 27
The Blood on the Hands

If changelings are something between man and beast, what will become of them in the other world?

To which I answer, It concerns me not to know or enquire. To their own master they stand or fall. It will make their state neither better nor worse, whether we determine anything of it or no. They are in the hands of a faithful Creator and a bountiful Father, who disposes not of his creatures according to our narrow thoughts or opinions, nor distinguishes them according to names and species of our contrivance. And we that know so little of this present world we are in, may, I think, content ourselves without being peremptory in defining the different states which creatures shall come into when they go off this stage. It may suffice us, that He hath made known to all those who are capable of instruction, discoursing, and reasoning, that they shall come to an account, and receive according to what they have done in this body.

John Locke, AN ESSAY CONCERNING HUMAN UNDERSTANDING

I killed Ariel Davenport. That much I remember.

I could not entirely say how it happened even as I could

describe each second leading up to me plunging that knife into her chest. Each moment flowed into the next like a dream, illogically and yet with inexorable logic. Each second ticked forward with solid, irrevocable certainty, and I was swept up in it.

"Do it, Cathy."

For all its sharpness, the knife did not pierce far. I hit bone. Ariel screamed.

Blood bloomed from the wound as I pulled the knife out. She sobbed in pain and her eyes met mine. She was begging me. She crumpled.

She bled like a slaughtered pig, the blood draining from her. It spread across her clothes like so much red ink.

Perhaps it is only right, given the talk of our mutual inhumanity. I thought of what Mr Warner said about dolls of flesh. Had I simply torn her seams? Was that her stuffing I was exposing to the sun? Would I find her cogs and springs among all this blood?

I brought down the knife again, but I was shaking too much. A graze, more blood. Her blue dress was almost all red and it clung to her.

Ariel had stopped screaming.

Her blood was warm. She told me once that blood binds blood, but I didn't know what she meant then. Was this true blood? I felt it between my fingers, slick and slippery. I gripped the knife tighter, feeling the contours of that fine wooden handle under my fingers.

Laughter filled my ears with its long ululating notes, though I could not say if it was the mocking hyenas or Queen Mab herself.

I breathed in the taste of blood, thick, slick and acrid. I dared not close my eyes. I did not want to remember this moment, but I could not look away.

Ariel mouthed words, words I would never hear and never

know as I plunged the knife into her again. Changeling flesh was no match for Sheffield steel. I was surrendering her secrets to death itself and I wondered if this was a pagan sacrifice, some heathen ritual.

"I'm sorry." It was my own voice, but I did not remember speaking the words. The apology tumbled from my lips, following another cut of the knife. "I'm so sorry."

The soulless may not be able to sin, but they could certainly be sinned against.

I did not look up. I did not want to meet the horrified eyes of my own brother. I did not want to tell him the nested truths that had been revealed to me, the reasons that weighed me down, and the sheer irrationality of it all.

How had it come to this?

A copper tub of hot water waited in my room.

I sank into it without thought, my bloody clothes still clinging to me.

The water was scalding hot. My own breath hissed out of me. I rolled my head back, the blood-matted mess of my hair falling into the water as I did so.

For long minutes, I breathed steam and soap. My mind was filled with nothing but blood and the look in Ariel's eyes when I killed her. A changeling's blood shed by a changeling's hands.

Neither of us were real, so what did it truly matter?

I peeled the layers of my dress from myself. The blood-soaked cloth floated as a film over the bath, like the skin on cooling milk. I thought of all those bedtimes sipping once-hot milk through that film and making faces at my brother as we raced each other. No, Catherine Helstone's brother. I corrected myself even as I hated the thought. He was not mine to call my own.

Yorkshire seemed a lifetime away. No, a life away.

The water was cloudy with Ariel's blood. Changelings bled so very much. I wondered then if humans bled just as much or if the doll of flesh was an imperfect simulacrum in this regard. Too much blood.

I pulled the pins from my hair, letting it all fall in a tangle. The once-neat braids were now anything but as I raked my fingers through it.

It was something to do with my hands, so strand by strand I slowly untangled my own hair. I lost myself in the task, letting that numbness settle around me like a shroud. It kept thoughts at bay.

A knock roused me.

I bolted upright in the bath, startled. My breath tangled up in my throat and my heart beat like a drum, thundering as the horses on the hunt.

Time must have passed, as the water was no longer steaming.

"Cathy? Are you there?"

It was my brother.

Not my brother. He was Catherine Helstone's brother.

"Cathy?" came his voice again. "Are you in there?"

I did not answer. I sank deeper into the water. I let it engulf me.

"I know you're in there. Talk to me, Cathy."

I heard the door open.

"Cathy. Are you–" He stopped. There were no words he could say.

I was all too aware of my own skin, naked under the water, and the bloody clothes that floated above me. I felt again that warm flush and that heavy guilt.

But what did it matter?

"Should I go?" he said.

I did not turn around. I did not want to see the look in his eyes. I feared his pity, his revulsion, his anger. I dreaded it all, but above all, I feared his absence.

Tentatively, I shook my head. I did not trust my voice. I felt my own wet hair, clammy against my skin.

I heard the door shut. The click of the latch falling with all the weight of an executioner's axe. I was holding my breath but I did not know why.

And then footsteps. He had not left.

"Cathy..."

"Don't call me that," I snapped.

"Why–" I could hear him shift behind me, recoiling at my vehemence.

"I'm not Catherine Helstone," I said. I found myself stumbling over the words, my tongue thick and clumsy in my mouth. I cupped water to my face, the lukewarm liquid disguising what tears may be flowing. My eyes stung. I swallowed and steeled myself.

"Cathy, it doesn't matter what you've done. I understand. Mab made you..."

"I'm..." I hesitated. I thought of how Ariel introduced herself to me, how she made it sound like it was of no consequence. I tried to imagine myself as her. I tried a laugh; I sounded delirious. "I'm not the real Catherine Helstone. I'm her changeling."

"What?"

"I'm a changeling, Laon." I ran my tongue over my cracked, wet lips. Soap and blood. "I'm not your sister."

"I... I see. How do you know this?"

"Ariel... she told me."

"How would she know?"

"Before she begged me to kill her, she told me. She knew for far longer but she didn't want to say. She..." I stumbled again. Would she have wanted him to know? Would the knowledge weigh too heavily upon his soul? And yet, what use had I of secrets? "Ariel said she could not bear her blood to stain your hands. And I... I'm not real, like her, so I could do it. The Pale Queen willed her dead, after all. Someone had to."

"You only did as she bid."

"But is it enough?" A streak of dried blood was still upon my arm. I stared at it, barely comprehending what I saw. My voice did not sound like my own, did not sound human. "I did as the good book bids: *Render unto Caesar the things which are Caesar's; and unto God the things that are God's.*"

"Cathy–"

"It's not my name."

"Don't do that to yourself. You haven't changed. You are who you are–"

"But I'm not *her*."

"You're still my sister."

I traced a finger down the crusted blood. I studied the smear of it on my fingertips. It had been so red earlier, so vivid.

How was there still blood on me?

"She loved you, you know," I said. "Davenport. The fake one. She loved you."

"I know."

I submerged my arm and began scrubbing with my hand. When I drew it again from the water, it felt no cleaner. The shadow of the blood lingered, and I could still smell it on myself.

I heard the rustle of clothes and the dull thud of a greatcoat dropping to the floor. He was taking off his jacket.

In the corner of my eye, I saw his hands roll up his sleeves. The spotless linen of his sleeves folded up. He took a washcloth that hung on the edge of the bath and waved it into the water.

"I can clean myself..." I said in a breathless murmur.

His hands wrung murky water from the rag and very

gently, far more gently than I would have done, he washed Ariel's blood from my wrists.

"We used to share a copper bath like this by the fire," he said conversationally. I could hear the strain in his voice, see the slight tremble in his motions. "When we were small enough to both fit inside the tub. You hated washing your hair because of the soap in your eyes."

I nodded. The warm memory was tainted now. I watched it in my mind through glass, as though it was happening to someone else. I imagined myself pressing my face against the cold window, watching the scene unfold inside the sheltered room. I imagined my breath upon the glass, each heave of my lungs obscuring further that childhood vision. Did I giggle when he upended buckets of water over my head or was I angered? Did I sit patiently as he scrubbed my back or did I squirm at his touch?

The water was lukewarm but Laon's touch was anything but cold. I followed his every movement, the nonsense patterns upon my skin.

I was holding my breath, listening to his. I could feel him, warm and solid behind me, his breath hot on my shoulder, at the base of my neck. Shivers spidered down my spine and spread over me.

I ached.

The rag dipped again into the water and it travelled over my other arm, my shoulder, my collar bone. I leaned into his touch and at some point he had dropped the rag and it was his hands that traversed my body.

We maintained the pretence a moment longer, but barely more than that.

His arms were around me and he drew me from the bath. Water ran off me in rivulets, and I shivered. I clasped my arms around him like a woman drowning, clinging to him. He felt so real, so tangible.

I was not clean, but it was not about that anymore.

His arms closed around me, and I felt their enveloping warmth. The water on my skin soaked into his clothes, spreading like a shadow of me onto him: the shape of my hands, the curve of my arms, the press of my body. I buried my face in the soft, now damp linen of his shirt. I felt the cold bite of his buttons. My fingers tangled in the wet fabric, fingernails pressing into him.

For all his closeness, he still felt too far away.

My lips brushed against his, and that was all the invitation he needed. His hands cupped my face, and I was gasping into his hungry kisses. He tasted of soap and blood and wine. I chased his kisses with my own, and he wound his fingers through my wet hair. We fumbled at his clothes until his pale skin was against mine.

He was so very real. For all that we were reassuringly alike, I still felt like a reflection in still water, hazy and indistinct.

My mind was dwelling again on my own unreality, believing I would ripple and rip at his touch. I was that spirit from the moors that he supposed so long ago, here to tempt him and then disappear when the sun burnt away the morning mist.

And then, his hands were on me again, strong, demanding. I revelled in his force; it proved to me that I was not breaking, that I would not shatter. He tightened his grip on my hips and I gasped.

Fleetingly, I felt real.

Chapter 28

The Stranger in the Skin

Thou hast ravished my heart, my sister, my spouse; thou hast ravished my heart with one of thine eyes, with one chain of thy neck.

How fair is thy love, my sister, my spouse! how much better is thy love than wine! and the smell of thine ointments than all spices!

Thy lips, O my spouse, drop as the honeycomb: honey and milk are under thy tongue; and the smell of thy garments is like the smell of Lebanon.

A garden inclosed is my sister, my spouse; a spring shut up, a fountain sealed.

Thy plants are an orchard of pomegranates, with pleasant fruits; camphire, with spikenard,

Spikenard and saffron; calamus and cinnamon, with all trees of frankincense; myrrh and aloes, with all the chief spices:

A fountain of gardens, a well of living waters, and streams from Lebanon.

Awake, O north wind; and come, thou south; blow upon my garden, that the spices thereof may flow out. Let my beloved come into his garden, and eat his pleasant fruits.

Song of Solomon 4:9–16

I did not see Mab again.

I knew she was still in the castle, though her guests vanished soon after the hunt. Catherine Helstone's brother busied himself in attending to her. She had further entertainments planned, but nothing as grandiose as what had come before. We were gone too far to turn back now. One word from Mab and our sacrifices – Ariel's sacrifice – would be made worthwhile.

Whatever excuse was given for my absence seemed adequate, as I was not disturbed in my tower. Though it mattered not, as I barred the doors and imprisoned myself with the silent accusation of my thoughts.

Day and night, I found myself washing my hands over and over. Not so much because I believed them stained with blood, but that I wanted to feel that guilt. I wanted that sweet madness that Lady Macbeth once felt. For all the deed weighed upon me, for all the echoes of it I saw behind my closed eyes, it was not enough.

This was not true guilt.

I knew I should feel more. I needed to feel more. My own inhumanity was showing through and the thought of that terrified me. I was no more real than the walls that surrounded me, no more true than the promises of Mab.

Still so selfish.

The blood of a friend stained my hands, and I still obsessed about myself, about my own reality. I could not even feel true guilt.

I scrubbed my hands until the skin was red and sore and finally, it bled. I watched my own blood soak the washcloth, the pain a distant sensation. I thought it would slice through the tangles of my mind, but it gave no greater clarity.

All my memories seemed so distant. My imperfect, simulacrum mind with its imperfect memories. I remembered now Ariel's fascination with how I remembered and I realised now that she was testing me, trying to work out if I was as unreal as she was.

I was no more real than her.

She must have guessed then when I told her so very foolishly that all memories could be hazy, that any mind could misremember. And now I here I was, a patchwork mind doubting itself.

I told my youth to myself like a story, trying to remember who I was. I told myself about the little papers I wrote with Catherine Helstone's brother, the names we gave the toy soldiers and the fantastical yet tediously mundane lands they explored. I tried to remember the icy lips of Catherine Helstone's sister at her funeral, the moors beneath my bare feet – I was always losing my shoes – and the hard beds at boarding school. I tried to remember the bare classrooms and the hard cane on my fingers, the cruel words of the other children. It all seemed so very insubstantial.

Except *that* memory.

I flushed warm whenever my thoughts brushed against it. Unlike everything else, I remembered with embarrassing clarity, every touch between us, every biting kiss and each hot breath.

I was a moth, speared like a specimen by his scrutiny. I lay under him, pinned. His gaze, his touch, his grip made me real.

But then, there was after.

Catherine Helstone's brother had departed by dawn, and I almost laughed. I had feared that I would be the one to melt away like the morning mist. He left a note to tell me that Mab had summoned me but that he was going in my stead.

He did not return.

Still, it filled me with giddy, nonsensical hope and a hunger to feel again that anchoring solidness.

I did not eat in the tower, but as Ariel said, changelings didn't really need food. I had water to wet my mouth and the hollowness of my stomach was barely any distraction from my thoughts.

I turned often to my well-thumbed Bible, but it offered little comfort to one such as myself. I remembered the sermon Catherine Helstone's brother had given on the fae being the birds that roosted in the tree sprung from a mustard seed. They could shelter within the kingdom of heaven, but I was not fae.

I read the promises that Jesus made to those who died and those who lived, that they would know life again through Him. It rang so hollow to my ears. I could believe it of Laon, of Catherine Helstone's dead mother and sisters, even of Mr Benjamin, that they would all know the kingdom of heaven, that the bread and wine of sacrament was for them and that the lord and saviour would wipe away every tear they had ever known.

But I could not believe it of myself, of Ariel. We were no more fae than we were human.

While we look not at the things which are seen, but at the things which are not seen: for the things which are seen are temporal; but the things which are not seen are eternal.

At other times, I would open again the journal of Jacob Roche or try to make sense of Enochian. The odd word and phrase began to emerge, and my growing familiarity with the Bible was helping what little progress I made, but my mind would not focus. It had no interest in such paltries. The great mystery of what befell Jacob Roche seemed so much less pressing now, though my mind did begin to spin wild theories on the influences of Mab and the other fae. His words on Jonah, the omniscience of the divine and being trapped in the belly of a whale seemed more resonant now than it did before, when I first read it.

Strangely, in all the days, I did not dream.

Granted, I slept very little, eyes as bright as lanterns as I watched the moon weave between the clouds, its yellowed teeth and unseeing eyes still unnerving me after all this time.

I began questioning my own memories and I wondered now if the woman in black was but a manifestation of my simulacrum mind. After all, the chapel was deserted when I had returned with Catherine Helstone's brother. I had been so convinced that she was a stolen child, imprisoned by Mab. With the blood that now stained my hands, it seemed laughable that I had believed even for a moment that I could save her.

But more than that, I feared who she might be.

Clutching my shoulders, my elbows, I selfishly worried about being replaced. I had played cuckoo to the Helstones, and for more than twenty years I had stolen love meant for another. I tried to hold onto all those memories, but they were slipping away, fading. I told them like stories to myself, over and over, trying to cling onto them, making up the details, but they lacked the vividness of true memories. My own unreality was catching up with me.

After all, what claim did I have to any of that?

I was not the real Catherine Helstone.

Mab left three days later.

I watched the pomp and ceremony from my window, all conducted by Catherine Helstone's brother. There was splendour equal to her arrival, her court arrayed in their best. I recognised all the forms of her retinue: the men of sand, those with the blinking, peacock tails and the crouched and hooded hags. Her guests, I assumed, had all left already, at the close of her hunt. I had the vague memory of them taking their leave of her, bundles of susurrus gossip and drawling compliments as they vanished.

The Pale Queen did, however, send me a parting gift.

An agitated Mr Benjamin delivered the parcel. He hovered

at my door, shifting listlessly from foot to foot.

"It is good to see you alive, Mr Benjamin," I said.

"Safe and safe," he said.

"And she is gone."

"She is never really gone." His eyes darted. "As long as you still dream."

"I..." I hesitated, not wanting to dwell on my empty nights. I panicked then that it was another aspect of being a changeling, the fact that I would never dream again.

I opened the parcel and found a horrifying object: a dessicated hand was cupped into a shallow bowl, the skin sewn crudely to itself. White grains were cradled in the leathery surface of its fingers.

The accompanying note read, quite simply: *Salt from human hands.*

Trembling, I touched a grain of that white substance to my tongue. It was, indeed, salt.

It was a human hand.

The last piece of the puzzle fell into place. I had not given it any thought, that Ariel and I had been eating fae food with no ill consequence. After all, had she not said my hands were not human?

She must have known.

I remembered the odd intensity with which she studied the salt shaker and how she became increasingly disinterested in food as she spoke about her changeling past. She must have worked it out. Realised how Mab was keeping this a secret from her, from me.

My own inhuman hands felt to my mouth. My empty stomach roiled. Despite not having eaten for days, I wanted to vomit.

Each of the vessels that held salt within this castle was made of human hands.

My own hands were shaking as I reached for the salt shaker

on my table. I unscrewed its cap and poured out its contents. I squinted inside. At the base of it was affixed a small, slender bone. A finger bone.

I choked back a bitter, acid mouthful. I regretted it immediately. I wanted it all out of this body. I wanted out of this body.

I could hear my own deafening heartbeat.

Mr Benjamin's voice roused me. "Is the sister pleased with gift?"

"Pardon," I said, sitting down, my head light from the revelation. I felt more unmoored than ever. "Did she... did she give you anything else?"

He shook his head.

"Thank you, Mr Benjamin." I swallowed, my throat dry and tasting foul. "Or should I be thanking the Pale Queen?"

"Gifts still come with a price. But maybe already paid," he said. "I thought I could pay the price. That I would be worthy." He hung his head and, haltingly, without prompting, the gnome confessed that the immense clarity he had felt before what he had believed to be his execution had faded. He had lost that focus that had guided him and the guilt weighed heavily upon him.

I envied his guilt and his capacity for it.

"I can't help you," I said.

"I thought I could do so much. Now nothing means nothing. Everything means nothing. Questions all back and worse. Can I ask you?"

I shook my head. "I'm afraid I don't have answers, Mr Benjamin."

"Can't carry this anymore. Heavy, too heavy. Questions heavy. Thoughts heavy. What can do with one life that cannot have done with one death? What is worth?"

"I really don't know, Mr Benjamin."

His face crumpled. "I saw her standing like at the jaws of

the hell beast. Like in the other chapel. She broke the bread and I believed. She paid that price but I cannot."

"I don't understand what you mean. Who–"

"Just a parable..." he hesitated. "But I thought I could be like the story. Be like her and believe. She was so certain!"

"You really should speak to my–" I stopped, the word stung, bringing a pang within me. I pressed my lips together, took a shallow breath and corrected myself, "Catherine Helstone's brother."

"But, a sister for a brother–"

"I am not his sister."

"Oh." His eyes widened and he swallowed awkwardly. My words hung tangibly between us and his hands began to fidget. "How you know?"

"You knew?"

Slowly, the gnome nodded.

"How long did you know?"

"The Pale Queen's orders. About the salt, about the food, about the sister-who-is-not-the-sister. She didn't say. I guessed."

"Since before I arrived?"

He nodded again. "I guessed first. The changeling guessed after, after the Pale Queen came. The changeling asked me questions. Made me promise not to tell you. It would grieve you." He looked me up and down. "It is grieving you. The changeling was right."

"She was, I suppose." I thought of all the questions she had asked of me, her shifting looks, and how desperately she had explained changeling nature to me. I should have guessed myself.

Meekly, the gnome added, "I'm sorry."

"It doesn't matter now," I said, quite firmly. "But you should leave me be for now."

"Forgive?"

"Soon."

Mr Benjamin sighed, his sharp shoulders heaving as he did so. He lingered by the door, before finally leaving and adding, quite quietly, "Good fakes are same as real."

The rich, salty smell of bacon and the rattling of chinaware woke me.

My mouth watered as I squinted open my eyes. It was Catherine Helstone's brother with a tray laden with what I could only assume to be the past three breakfasts piled together.

"Sorry," he said, quite stiffly. "I let myself in. But I assumed you would want some food."

I nodded. I had fallen asleep still wearing my day dress. Crushed though it may be from my slumber, I was largely decent in it.

"I didn't know you weren't..." said Laon. "I thought you wanted to be alone. I didn't know you weren't eating until Mr Benjamin told me."

"Thank you."

After my days of hunger, I thought I would be ravenous. But quite divorced from that constant ache of black void-like emptiness, I felt only nausea at the sight and smell of food. I gazed dispassionately at the generous wedges of pound cake and the slices of cold pie, barely recognising them. The mountain of bacon only turned my stomach.

Long, intolerable minutes passed. Catherine Helstone's brother stared at me as I waited for him to salt the food.

"You aren't eating," he said, a commanding note intruding into his voice. "You should eat."

"I can't."

"Can't?"

"I... I need you to salt it."

"But when I wasn't here, didn't you–"

"I'm not human and I don't want to be relying on..." I said, trying to suppress that shiver of revulsion. "I don't want to rely on what I used before."

He nodded, knowing not to press the issue, and obligingly added salt to each of the dishes.

I broke off a piece of pound cake and, ignoring the dollops of marmalade and jam crowding the edge of the plate, I ate it dry. My tongue felt suddenly swollen and crowded in my mouth. I forced myself to chew.

His eyes barely leaving me, Catherine Helstone's brother collected the larger of the cake crumbs and pressed them together in his fingers. By touch, he reformed the crumbs and additional cake into a lumpy beast and presented it to me.

I looked quizzically at him.

"I'm afraid I can't make the noises anymore," he said.

"What do you mean?"

"We used to..." he looked a little embarrassed. "It doesn't matter if you don't remember."

"It does. Tell me."

He gave a half shrug and said, "You used to make little animals out of my bread. You would ask me to give them voices and we used to tell stories about them."

"I don't remember that," I said. Fear, insidious in its form, unfurled within me. I could feel it in the pit of my stomach and in that acidic taste at the back of my throat. I combed through my memories, the stories that I had been telling myself as I failed to sleep, staring at the moon. "I don't remember that at all."

"You wanted to name them and keep them, but they grew mouldy and you grew hungry."

I shook my head. "When was this? I thought we told stories about the tin soldiers, about Gaaldine and Exina and Alcona. Didn't we?"

"We did, this was before that."

"Really?" I tried to remember the days before the soldiers. I couldn't. It must have been then that I was swapped for a human child.

"You were quite little, it's normal to not remember."

"But—"

"Eat, Cathy. Please."

I didn't correct him about my name. I supposed that Ariel shared her name with the real Ariel Davenport.

As I forced myself to chew, I wondered if perhaps *she* could be Catherine and I could be Cathy. The cake was dry and clung to the room of my mouth. I drowned it down with sweetened tea.

Looking at him now and his concern for me, I felt frail under the weight of my own guilt. I was a doll of flesh that had usurped the place of the real Catherine Helstone and took for myself the love they owed her.

I thought of the woman in black I had followed across the rooftops of this very castle. My mind did not dwell on her often and I had been avoiding those questions for too long.

Or rather, the answers.

There was an answer to the question of why Mab had brought her of all captives to the castle. An answer to why she had fine English features and why she looked similar in age to me. These were all answers I did not want to entertain.

"I keep trying to work out when it was," I said after starting on the soft rolls. "And the rest..."

Catherine Helstone's brother swallowed uncomfortably.

"We should do something."

"I don't think we should..." That weighty tension was again in the line of his body, from shoulder to clasped hands. "You and I. We shouldn't..."

I looked at him, confused. He would not meet my gaze, the intensity of his blue eyes firmly studying his hands. Perhaps he could not bear to see my eyes, a reflection of his own.

"I adore you."

I stared at him in silence; the oppressive guilt that had been gripping me only tightened, clasping around my throat. My leaden heart ached to breaking.

"Cathy..." His knuckles were turning white. "I adore you, treasure you, desire you. Beyond reason. Beyond hope. I would worship you and the ground that you walk on... but we, you and I, we can't..."

"What are you trying to say?" I frowned.

"I've longed for you for so long and now... I want nothing more but to lay at your feet my corrupt heart, as it is, cold to the spirit and warm to the flesh. I am consumed with sinful, wandering thoughts of you and I thought–"

"Laon," I interrupted, sharply, cutting through his florid speech. "Is that what you're worried about?"

"I had prepared..." He sat up, startled, finally looking at me again.

I squared back my shoulders, my frown deepening.

"I murdered Ariel," I said. Catherine Helstone's brother winced at that, but I continued, "On the same day, I found out I am a changeling, that I have no soul and that salvation may be beyond my reach. All that and you worry about us?"

"You are my sister."

"I'm not; I'm not even real." A delirious laugh rang out from my throat like silver bells. "A thousand things weigh on my heart and on the soul I do not have, but not that. Ariel's blood stains my hands. I have lived another's life and stolen her family. I barely know how to feel all the guilt I should feel."

"Cathy, it's not your fault. It was the Pale Queen who–"

"But I am quite monstrous." Another laugh, clear and shrill. "So, no, brother of Catherine Helstone, that matter is but a feather on my heart. My sin is far greater than yours."

"For years, Cathy, I've–"

"You laid not a hand on me, so what does it matter?" I was standing now, all accusations and anger. I barely recognised my own voice for the bitterness.

"*Whosoever looketh on a woman to lust after her hath committed adultery with her already in his heart...*"

"No one cares about your heart, Laon."

"Cathy..." He staggered back as though slapped.

"Your hands are clean and mine are not," I said, without a care for the hurt in his eyes. I could still smell the blood, see it well up from her wounds. "Ariel's gone. I can't believe you would think... how could you worry about such things after what I have done? I killed her."

"It was the Pale Queen who killed her," he said, reflexively. Over and over he must have been telling himself that. "You were just her tool. One that happened to be holding the knife."

"And I'm not real," I said with a breathy laugh. "Unlike you."

"I didn't mean it that way." Though his voice was softer, it was no apology.

"Of the two of us, you are the real one. You have a soul. You matter. I don't."

"I didn't mean to say that."

I shook my head. "But you did, all the same."

CHAPTER 29
The World Beyond the Door

1816 will forever be remembered as the Year Without A Summer. It simply did not come, as the weather remained stubbornly dry and cold, not only in this country, but also the rest of Europe and, judging by reports, the Americas. Hard frosts were suffered every month.

Many persons supposed that the seasons have not thoroughly recovered from the shock they experienced at the time of the total eclipse of the sun. Others seem disposed to charge the peculiarities of the season upon the spots on the sun. If the dryness of the season has in any measure depended on the latter cause, it has not operated uniformly in different places – the spots have been visible in Europe, as well as here, and yet in some parts of Europe, as we have already remarked, they have been drenched with rain.

It is impossible to say the true reason for this summerless year, but almost one hundred years after the South Sea company had made and unmade numerous fortunes with its fantastical finances, it has again resurfaced and emerged as a force to rival the East India Trading Company. Due to the Crown upholding its monopoly over trade with Elphane and such it remains still, yet few know what really fills the crates and barrels that are loaded onto the ships that sail to the

Faelands, only that they return with splendid fae riches.

It is perhaps only right that the lost company should be the one to first trade with the lost land.

Andrew Groombridge Knight, "Meteorological Observations", PHILOSOPHICAL TRANSACTIONS, November 1831

Catherine Helstone's brother left.

At the click of the door, I crumpled to the floor, no longer a tower of defiance and cold anger. It extinguished inside me, like a flame between damp fingers. I folded my legs tight against my chest and wrapped my clutching arms around myself.

My skin was not my own, but still I tried to hold myself together. All the pain that my words had caused him, I felt reflected now upon my own knotted heart. His touch had made me feel so very real and it ached to be otherwise now. I did not want to acknowledge those passions, to dwell on what it might mean.

I killed Ariel.

I could barely remember the scene around us, but for the mocking laughter of the Pale Queen. Mr Benjamin had trusted that Mab would keep her end of that bargain, that she would allow passage into inner Arcadia and further missionary work. My brother had believed that too. But with that sound of laughter like a cheese wire through my thoughts, it was difficult to believe.

And there was so much blood.

That metallic aftertaste welled up again at the back of my throat and I felt my stomach lurch. I brought up what little I ate.

It was no messier than murder.

• • •

I stayed inside my tower.

Perhaps it was rooted in a desire for punishment, or to finally abide by Ariel's frequent warnings to stay inside. There were times when I manically laughed and told the memory Ariel that she had indeed won, I was finally obedient to her instructions, placing not a single foot outside this room. I flung my voice against the stone walls until I was screaming and not laughing, but they continued in their silence.

Or perhaps it was fear, or even a refusal to be reminded of her, of Mab. The castle was so full of memories, and even faded as they were, I did not want to confront them. I did not want to sit again in the solar or dine in the great hall.

It could equally be that I was sick of the pretence of the castle, knowing that it was built of falsehood and folly. I was no longer unable to not notice the facade.

Perhaps, perhaps.

Excuse after excuse, I gave myself, reason upon reason. But in the end, it didn't matter why. I simply did not want to be outside. Hour after hour, I would bolt again the doors, barely thinking about why they so often seemed to slide open again.

At times, when I did this, I would linger by the door, press my face against the warm wood and, hands lingering on the handle, I wondered if I should leave, if I should take a step into the beyond. I would try to imagine what lay outside, what lay behind and beyond the door. There was another life behind that wood, another place. I would only need to step through.

I counted my heartbeats, one after another until I lost count. My arm began to ache, so tightly was I gripping the door. Heaving a sob, I crumpled. Wearily, I beat my fists pathetically against the wood. I could not step outside.

I was too afraid.

Falling would be nothing like flying.

So both doors remained shut under my hands. I stepped

through neither of them and continued in my self-imposed imprisonment.

The disorder of my mind came to be reflected in the disorder of the room.

I had not thought I had brought enough objects within my trunk to fill the space, but I had.

The shawl that Ariel had gifted me was draped over the back of a chair in the middle of the room, where I could see it at all times if I choose to look.

I had avoided putting away my winter clothes since the departure of Mab and her winter. Whilst I did not want to endure its presence, I equally did not want to relive that time by revisiting those garments, so they remained in several woollen heaps. I left out the books and papers that I meaninglessly leafed through over and over, scattered about. I would read them in half sentences, adding to the maddening tangle of my mind.

I thought more of praying than I did on my knees with pressed palms and silently moving lips. For all that prayer had brought me strength in the past, it could no longer illuminate my rayless mind.

I had wondered before on why Ariel had abandoned the faith, but now I understood. Why should one without a soul worry about its cultivation?

And after what I had done, I could no longer hold within myself a hope for heaven.

Catherine Helstone's brother diligently brought me food. He did not ask if I was going to leave the room or when; he recognised this childish habit already. I had done it after the funeral of Catherine Helstone's sister when I was seven and a half, then again for a little while after her father's. I remembered counting the threads in the quilt, willing my world to be just that warm, soft embrace. He had taken care of me then.

Together we tidied the mess I had made and, though the room still reeked of vomit, he stayed with me for a little while, the silence almost painful between us.

Though unassuming in his manner, I could tell he was brooding still. I could see it in the set and the shadow of his eyes. Whatever tempests raged in his soul, he kept them to himself, and I had not the heart to intrude. He still gazed at me in hunger when he thought I wasn't looking. I yearned for that closeness, that reality, but I could not bring myself to deserve it.

Day after day, I ate because he bid me to.

I only vomited once more after the first time, but it felt unnatural to eat again. The tastes seemed muted and textures more pronounced, making the food nothing but slimy and leathery and heavy in my mouth.

"I'm not sure I like food," I said.

"Arcadian food is strange at the best of times." He gave a wry smile. "And the Salamander has strange tastes."

I mirrored his smile without thinking, the warm flutter in my stomach having nothing to do with food or lack thereof. It was only after that I realised to remember to feel guilty, to push the feeling away.

I stopped counting the beat of the pendulum sun, but I knew well enough that the two-week deadline had come and gone. Days were growing dimmer. Catherine Helstone's brother simply never mentioned it, and it became yet another silence between us. Not prickly, precisely, but not entirely comfortable.

We were also waiting for Mab's answer, even as neither of us was in any state to travel to inner Arcadia. I wondered at times if the summons would mean he would abandon me to the care of Mr Benjamin and chase absolution for his current sins in missionary work. But those were unwelcome thoughts and I laid them aside like how once I laid aside my lusts and hunger.

Most days he would try to make me smile or at least engage me from my catatonic state. He added to the material disorder of the room, as it grew to be further littered with curiosities he had brought me: a music box with a trilling bird; empty-eyed dolls; a grim-faced nutcracker; his old sketch book and half-faded paints; spools of bright thread and yards of linen. Most of these diversions were from around the castle, but a few were from his own belongings.

"You like dusty books, right?" he said as he presented me with an ancient-seeming volume.

"The spine is uninformative," I said, trying to make out the faded text. "What is it?"

He shrugged. "Dusty, mostly."

Upon my opening of the book, moths scattered from the pages.

Startled, I dropped the volume, squeaking.

"I didn't plan that," said Catherine Helstone's brother immediately.

I shot him a suspicious glare.

"Honest! It's just been sitting on my desk for weeks."

As I picked it up from the floor, I heard something at the edge of sound. I said, "Pardon?"

"I didn't say anything."

"You should give some explanation."

"Only bad presents need explanation," he said. "And I'm even quoting you on that."

The barest whisper grew louder even as Catherine Helstone's brother spoke. I could just about make out the words: *He... the word that spoke it... took the bread and broke it...*

I whipped around, trying to catch sight of who had spoken, but the room was as it had been before.

"What are–"

I placed my fingers to my lips, and he quieted.

I noticed the newly liberated moths dancing in the light. Again, the whispering: *that word did make it... I do believe and take it...*

"Can you hear that?" I said. The words were almost familiar, though I could not place where I had heard them before.

"*That word?*" he said. "*I do... take it?*"

I nodded.

"Just about."

The whispers continued: *This is my body, thou hast said... this is my body, of that bread... like priests of old, we eat the sacrifice, but half the meaning is not told... We hear and do thy last command... our hearts adore thy words, but cannot understand.*

And then silence.

The book lay open before me and it was blank.

"I thought it was a book of poetry," said Catherine Helstone's brother weakly.

On Sundays, he would bring the Bible to read with me. I endured that, dwelling more on the comforting sound of his voice than the words he spoke. He also told me a little of what Mr Benjamin was worrying about, given his own redemption or salvation of his people. The gnome felt a keen sense of responsibility for his own kind and was eager to assist in further missionary work.

"But still no word from the Pale Queen," he said, dropping himself heavily onto my bed.

I glanced up from the knitting I was pulling apart, the yarn a tangle on my lap.

He sighed and, for the first time, Catherine Helstone's strong, beautiful brother seemed broken. It wasn't simply defeat but a sundering of his spirits. It pained me to see him so. He had hidden it so well since my outburst, and guilt stung, like a lost pin rediscovered, sharp, sudden and blooming blood.

In that moment, for more than any other reason, I hated myself for my own weakness. I had come to Arcadia to look after Catherine Helstone's brother and now he was the one tending to me.

"I don't know how long I should keep waiting before I write to her or..." he paused. "I shouldn't deal with other Arcadian rulers, it would only be more difficult and she'd see it as a betrayal, but..."

"You're not sure how long you can keep waiting?"

Mutely, he nodded.

I pushed the yarn to the floor, consigning it to eternal entanglement, and wrapped my arms around him. He tensed at my touch, eyes flickering to mine in disbelief before awkwardly returning the embrace.

He leaned his head against my shoulder, allowing himself to be enveloped. It was a closeness that made me ache.

"You shouldn't have." His lips mouthed the words against my skin, his voice almost too hoarse and faint for me to make out the words. "Thank you, but you didn't have to. I'm grateful, very. Just–"

"Have to?"

"Ariel," he said simply.

"No."

"I could have–"

"Please," I said. "I don't think I could bear to hear you say that. She wanted to prove you are no better than her, than them. She wanted to show you that saints can sin. And I was to save you from that, so please. Don't."

He nodded, not answering.

I had wanted to hold him until our breaths were mirrored, but that didn't happen.

"Cathy, Cathy!" Catherine Helstone's brother burst into the room, eyes too bright and smile too wide. I heard the bark of Diogenes, jubilant and frantic. "You have to look out of the window!"

I did not want to be roused. I sat, curled up on the chair, both my shawls and the coverlet draped over myself. I had Roche's journal in front of me, but I was not reading it.

"I'm not sure I want to move right now," I murmured. My mind fumbled for excuses as I pulled the shawls tighter around myself. "Later."

"Now!" he urged, his broad grin undeterred by my reluctance.

I shook my head, trying to retreat further into my bundle.

"You have to see this, Cathy."

"Bother someone else."

"There is no one else."

"No."

"Please?"

"No!" I was so bundled in the coverlet and the shawls that I was practically pulling them over my face. "I'm sleeping."

"You aren't sleeping," he said, bringing his face very close to mine. "You're talking to me."

"Then goodnight! A thousand times goodnight."

"You can't trick me into quoting Shakespeare." He laughed, tapping his finger affectionately against my nose.

I frowned at his levity.

And then it struck me. We had had almost exactly the same exchange the first Christmas after Catherine Helstone's sister, Agnes, had died. This was but an echo of that childishness.

"I am very stubborn," said Catherine Helstone's brother. "You know that."

"You don't always win this."

He sighed, got to his feet and strode over to the door to empty air.

"No!" I leapt to my feet. After my days of dark thoughts, I feared the worst.

He flung open the door.

"What are you doing?"

"You don't want to move, so you can see it from your perch. If I open the door..."

"Close it." I leaned a hand against the posts of the bed, still giddy from the rush of worry. I squeezed my eyes shut, trying to ignore the dizzy white circles. I must have stood up too quickly. That was all. "I'll look out of the window."

Hearing the bolt slide into place, I breathed a sigh of relief.

"Aren't you skittish?" he muttered. He smiled a gentle, tired smile and patted me on the head like I was a puppy. I resisted the urge to bite his hand.

I was breathing heavily when I allowed myself to be dragged towards the window.

He flung open the shutters and pointed downwards. A hill had rammed itself against the wall of the castle. Looking below, I could see it bulging from the land like a fist, abrupt in its sudden height. From the point where it met the wall, it sloped high and wide, momentarily endless because of the thick mists.

The hill was bristling with its dense covering of leafless brambles. I reached a hand down, but it was out of reach.

"What... What is that?" I asked. "And how did I not notice it..."

"Beaching?"

I nodded. "That."

"You were always a sound sleeper," he said. "I've seen you sleep through thunderstorms."

"I wasn't..." I bit my tongue. I didn't want to tell him how little I slept, tossing and turning. And yet it was not nightmares that kept slumber at bay. It was always numb, black and dreamless.

"You used to crawl into my bed when there was thunder. I was always fairly sure it was just an excuse, you would fall asleep so quickly when you clung to me."

"You were warm," I muttered in half confession, avoiding his gaze. "And your bed smelt nice."

"My bed smelt of me."

My voice grew smaller and my fingers agitated. "Exactly."

He grinned and turned his attention back to the mound. "So, what do you think it is?"

The mists had parted and I could better make out the surface of the hill. The brambles were even thicker than I thought as I could not see the ground beneath.

Squinting into the distance, I saw the rise and fall and rise again of this hill. It was too big to make sense of at first, especially with the mist, but then, slowly, it dawned. It was the forked fin of a fish tail.

"Is it…" I said, hesitation in my voice. "Do you think it's a sea whale?"

He gave a half smile. "Named for the fact it contains the sea rather than the sea containing the whale."

The great mass of shrubbery shuddered from the roots up and it rose, the ground swelling beneath it. The interlocking branches seemed to slide against one another as it rippled.

"Is it breathing?"

"I would assume so."

"But it doesn't breathe sea, or swim in the sea, it just has it in it?"

He nodded.

The hill shuddered as it deflated. And it heaved again, its tail giving a single determined thrash before stilling again.

"That makes… a sort of sense."

"And I did say it ate the sea."

"You did, but I can't say I wholly believed you."

"I'm wounded," he said dryly, holding a hand to his chest in a half-hearted attempt at miming his injury. "Such an overwhelming vote of confidence."

"So were you making that up?"

"Not exactly." He sounded sheepish.

"Is it really full of sea, then?"

"I don't know," he said. "But we should find out."

"I thought we'd already established that it's not in Father's encyclopaedia."

"I meant the other way."

"What other way?"

He didn't answer, but the pin dropped soon enough. Diogenes gave another excited bark. Catherine Helstone's brother wanted to go inside the whale.

CHAPTER 30
The Belly of the Beast

This proud tosser of the waves has another and still more wonderful trait. When hunger plagues him on the deep, and the monster longs for food, this haunter of the sea opens his mouth, and sets his lips agape; whereupon there issues a ravishing perfume from his innards, by which other kinds of fish are beguiled. With lively motions they swim to where the sweet odour comes forth, and there enter in, a heedless host, until the wide gorge is full; then, in one instant, he snaps his fierce jaws together about the swarming prey.

Thus it is with anyone who, in this fleeting time, full of neglects to take heed to his life, and allows himself to be enticed by sweet fragrance, a lying lure, so that he becomes hostile to the King of Glory by reason of his sins. The accursed one will, when they die, throw wide the doors of hell to those who, in their folly, have wrought the treacherous delights of the body, contrary to the wise guidance of the soul. When the deceiver, skilful in wrongdoing, hath brought into that fastness, the lake of fire, those that cleave to him and are laden with guilt, such as had eagerly followed his teachings in the days of their life, he then, after their death, snaps tight together his fierce jaws, the gates of hell. They who enter there have neither relief nor escape, no means of flight, any

more than the fishes that swim the sea can escape from the
clutch of the monster.

"The Whale (Asp Turtle)", translated by
Albert Stanburrough Cook, from
THE OLD ENGLISH PHYSIOLOGUS

Half-submerged in the ground and braced against the walls
of Gethsemane, the sea whale rumbled. I heard the low,
moaning whistle of air, and a splutter of gravel trickled
pathetically from one of the gaps in the skin.

It was truly giant, towering above us and over us like a
mountain of trembling wicker. I saw the tight weave of the
branches, the smear of mud between the gaps.

I had been more than simply reluctant to leave the room,
but Catherine Helstone's brother remained persistent and
ruthless in his methods. Deaf to my protests, he had gathered
me into his arms, deposited me onto the floor and proceeded
to roll my outdoor stockings onto my feet. Despite my
squirming and kicking, he persevered.

"Thank you," I muttered, quite embarrassed. The
childishness that had gripped me earlier had dissipated,
leaving behind a thick residue of shame.

He smiled, and despite a heroic attempt to keep the
smugness at bay, I could see it in the corner of his mouth.

"I wanted to see this," I said, making a vague gesture
towards the whale's wicker carcass. "But I don't think I could
have... let myself."

"You've done this before," he said. "I remember. You cried
less this time, but you were just as stubborn. And it was a lot
more–"

"I was a lot younger then!" I said, bristling. "And you
promised not to ever bring it up again."

Catherine Helstone's brother laughed, his blue eyes far brighter than they had been for days. "I was referring to all the times you–"

I gave him a playful punch on the shoulder to hush him. I did not want to be reminded of how he had pulled me from my nest of blankets following the death of Catherine Helstone's sister. He had to wrestle clothes onto me to get me to the funeral, enduring my tiny fists as I beat them against him. Shame coloured my cheeks at the memory.

The sea whale heaved again; it was still breathing.

It was still *alive*.

I took another step closer to it.

Another breath and the whale thrashed against the castle's unyielding walls.

Startled, I stumbled back.

Ground broke around the whale; clods of dirt were sent flying. It showered towards us in a hail of stones. Catherine Helstone's brother sheltered me, and I allowed him the closeness. I allowed myself to be comforted.

Whatever it had done before to swim through earth, it could not seem to do it now. The ground clung to it, each sandy grain meaningless but the sum of it overwhelming. The walls stood firm. Wicker scraped wetly against stone. I heard the snapping of wood, and there was a long, mournful moan before the whale settled down again, seemingly resigning itself to its fate.

"Is it stuck?" I said.

"That's what Benjamin said."

I heard the bark of Diogenes. It had run on ahead of us with its curious sniffing and had returned. It was covered in dirt and was impatient for us to catch up.

"It's dying," I said, giving the restless dog an idle pat on the head.

"It's beached."

With each sighing breath, the wicker that made up the skin of the beast creaked and strained to near snapping. A brown, dirty water seeped from the mud that was caked between the weave of the wicker. It oozed out in tiny rivulets, washing away the clinging dirt.

Circling it, we found its mouth.

It was impossibly huge, gasping. The creature seemed to be nothing but mouth. The entire mountainside gaped open into a shadowed maw. Long, white blades stretched from the ceiling of its mouth-cave like a row of stalactites. Tangled vine-like threads dangled between the spaces.

I thought of that altarpiece in the garden chapel, with its blood-red hellmouth from which Christ pulled the souls of the damned. The gaping maw of this whale brought the horrors of that medieval imagination to life. I thought of the pallid, squirming forms of those souls against the red of hell. I thought of that black beast and its thrashing tongue.

This was that biblical leviathan.

What other beast could be more vast than this?

Yet seeing it and feeling its woven branches tremble beneath my touch, I felt a buoyancy within myself. Diminished though it may be by its imminent demise, it was still full of promise. Tantalisingly, a shadow of old restlessness returned.

"Wonder what sea whale ambergris is like," I said.

"Wonder what real ambergris is like." He smiled and he placed his hand by mine to feel the breath of the dying whale. His fingers brushed against mine and we laced hands together.

"I suppose we wouldn't really know the difference."

"I'm told it smells expensive."

"Which?"

"Real ambergris. And that it tastes good in negus."

I laughed, letting that lightness unfurl inside me. I could feel his heartbeat through his hand.

"For all I know," he added. "Sea whale ambergris could

smell like cheap wine."

"You on Saturday night, then?"

"You dare defame my character?"

As we watched, the whale's breathing – if it could be termed such – grew slower and slower until it finally stopped altogether.

Seconds and then minutes ticked by and it remained motionless. It no longer heaved as air rushed towards it and away. There was no thrashing, no shudder, no ripple.

"We should go inside," I said. A shudder of anticipation scuttled up my spine, fear adding a pleasing keenness to my senses rather than an unbridled terror.

We parted the curtain of the white, dangling threads. They curled at the touch of the walking stick, wrapping like maypole ribbons around it. Catherine Helstone's brother held the lantern to the opening, but it was bright inside the whale.

Stray threads clung wetly to us as we passed through.

The ground was damp and sloped downward. I hitched up my skirts.

The salt in the air was unmistakable. I could feel it at the back of my throat and upon my lips even as I licked them. This was the sea.

The whale was seemingly hollow inside, with wide wooden ribs spanning over us, holding aloft the wicker ceiling. Before us was stretched a beach-like scene unlike anything I had seen before.

Though full of strange creatures, they were all quite still. Some lurked in the shadows, many more in the water, and others clung to the ceiling and walls. Perhaps they were as surprised by us as we were by them.

The weave of the vault-like roof let in pinpoints of light and it was covered in gently glowing lichen, spread like frozen fireworks upon a night sky. It gave a sense of stillness to the space, as though this was indeed a stolen moment, a nonexistent heartbeat between seconds stretched out.

I was holding my breath.

"Out of the belly of hell cried I, and thou heardest my voice," I said, half to myself.

"Jonah?"

"Yes, though I wasn't..." I was quoting the oft repeated phrase in Roche's journal. "It just, sort of, came to mind."

"I suppose this is a bit like being fish food." He pushed his hair from his eyes.

I tried to sound nonchalant as I said, "It's a phrase in Roche's journal. It seemed quite taken with Jonah."

"You've been reading his journal?"

I nodded. "I know I shouldn't have and I was told not to, but..."

That old weariness had returned, but his smile was not a disappointed one.

"I remember what you said. That this place isn't a puzzle, but I needed to know why, to know what happened. And then it suddenly didn't matter anymore. No knowledge could have saved Ariel from the Pale Queen."

"Don't–" he began.

I shook my head. "I'm not dwelling on it." I squeezed shut my eyes, trying to arrange the jumble of my thoughts. "All I meant to say was just that Jonah... the whale mattered to the other person writing in Roche's journal."

"Other person?"

"There was more than one set of handwriting in it."

He made an interested noise, tongue against the roof of his mouth. "What did it say?"

"It was..." I said. "The writer was obsessed with the idea of the whale as fate, that Jonah tried to escape from the sight of God and the will of God, but he could not. He thought he could flee from God and he disobeyed the command to preach at Nineveh. You remember, I trust?"

"Yes…" Catherine Helstone's brother wandered ahead to the edge of the water. He pointed at the human junk that seemed to be abandoned by the waterline. There were bottles, pipes and a pocket watch.

"So, he doesn't go to Nineveh like God wanted and so he ends up in the stomach of a great fish. He becomes desperate after three days and finally prays. And since there is nowhere beyond the sight of God, his prayers are heard and he is saved."

"Did Roche not want to come to Arcadia?"

"He did, very much so. So much so that he didn't even wait for approval from the Missionary Society. But this wasn't him writing." I shrugged. "I think."

And then, movement.

Black legs stretched out of the pocket watch. A crustacean was wearing the timepiece as a shell. Its gait seemed unbalanced as it trailed the chain behind it. Its black claws began the work of rolling some shining gold sludge that veined the ground into a ball.

"So someone else was trying to avoid being in Arcadia?" Jutting out his bottom lip, he huffed his own hair from his eyes. It was getting rather long.

"Or that this place was where they ended up because they were avoiding a calling to somewhere else. Or maybe the writer wanted to be heard even here. In the belly of hell."

"I always took it to be an allegorical place, Jonah's whale. A state of fallen disobedience. A state of seemingly irredeemable sin."

"Or it's literally a fish."

We both laughed at that.

The light caught on the shimmering cobwebs that were stretched across the wooden beams of the whale. They seemed curated by translucent crabs that scuttled along the threads, clattering their pincers.

JEANNETTE NG

I pointed Catherine Helstone's brother to the crabs and wondered at what prey they must be catching. The subject of Roche fell by the wayside as we lost ourselves in the exploration.

We saw the streaks of white salt that clung to the beams and wondered at how much sea there must have been in here before. We pointed at the desiccated husks of sea plants and marvelled at how strange they seemed.

We gazed into the water. Transparent roses grew at the bottom of it, each illuminated by a pale red light at its heart. Slowly they bloomed, soft petals opening like a mouth until one of the curious fish nosed into one and it snapped shut.

White, swallow-like fish soared through the water, flapping their wide wings and dipping their forked tails. Their beaks snapped open and shut as they swam. As they passed the roses, one's beak opened and then opened some more, its entire head spreading like an umbrella into a ravenous maw. It did not eat the rose, however, as it closed again its mouth and kept swimming.

Gem-like eyes, without iris or pupil, gleamed up at us from between the wooden slats of the ground. They blinked before vanishing.

Further away I saw specks of light in the water, suspended within it like a shifting constellation. Something black and wormlike snaked through it, and that patch of water was plunged into darkness as the seeming stars were swallowed.

"Are those words?" asked Catherine Helstone's brother.

My eyes followed his hand and I saw the tracery of lines I had thought to be the grain of the wood upon the ribs. Dark blue and very fine, they spread over its surface. Yet they did not spread as I expected; the lines kept tangling into little knots.

Looking closer, I saw those knots formed sigils. Though the arc of certain ones were not formed by continuous lines, they were unmistakable. I had copied out those meaningless sigils very many times.

It was Enochian.

"Yes," I said. "Those are words. Sort of."

"Can you read it?" He placed a hand on the damp wood. "It's very squiggly…"

"It's Enochian. It's a language, I suppose. I found it in Roche's journal."

"That book is getting more interesting by the minute."

"I did say."

A rocky outcrop bloomed with blood-red dew before each droplet blinked and disappeared. The water was teeming with red and silver fish, each flitting through the bonewhite coral.

The serpentine tendrils unravelled from the marrow of the seeming bones, and forked tongues waved through the water to catch one of the darting, teardrop fish.

A pair of strange, pale fishes with enormous eyes lay gasping on the muddy shore. Fragile fins and tails lay spread, the delicate, frilled beauty of it all seeming clumsy out of water.

"There must have been more water before," I said, pointing at the fishes.

"They're dying," he said.

"Everything here is dying."

I passed Catherine Helstone's brother the lantern and crouched down. Gently, I nudged them into the water. Once inside, their fins and tails spread gloriously. Underwater, their sickly pallor became the most translucent of shimmering whites and became as a nimbus around them.

"This is… I don't think we could have imagined this," I said, smiling at the memory of our childhood inventions. All the lands our explorers stumbled through were simply Yorkshire but more so. We were such simple creatures, though I wondered now if my own lack of imagination was a symptom of unreality. Was Catherine Helstone's brother not always the leader in our games?

"Rather morbid to think that we can only see inside here because it is dead," he said.

"Only a little," I said. "Though we should write some of this down. Sketch it in words if not pictures."

"It'd be like the memoirs of journeys through Gaaldine and Zamorna we used to draw."

"Lands we never thought we'd see," I said, a touch wistful for our old games. "What did we call their leader again?"

He answered immediately: "The tallest and the bravest of all the tin soldiers is always, always Wellington."

"I remember."

He was standing very close to me and all at once I was all too aware of him. I forgot why I was fighting so hard to put aside our attraction, forgot all the reasons I gave myself for why I shouldn't.

Each memory seemed to lead me inexorably to this point where I was standing before him, slightly too close and far too afraid. I had not wanted to give name to this passion, not wanted to acknowledge it. I could have gone to my grave not knowing why I felt this ache whenever I saw Catherine Helstone's brother. I could have passed this life blind of my own longing and ignorant to his.

I could have.

"So, Jonah," he said, a wry smile crossing his lips. "What do you make of being stuck in here?"

"Am I meant to say I'm regretting resisting the inevitable?" I said with a teasing note to my voice.

He was simply there, too close, too real and too beautiful.

"What do you mean?" he asked.

And not for the first time nor the last, I kissed Catherine Helstone's brother.

CHAPTER 31
The Words at the Beginning

In early life, Jacob Roche seems to have distinguished himself by his profanity; and though in his youth he had been the subject of occasional serious impressions, it was not till he was twenty-one years of age that he fully knew the value and love of the Saviour.

He departed to the Faelands, commonly called Elphane or Arcadia, in 1839, before even the treaties that would become the foundation of the Empire's relations with Arcadia. His relationship with the Society was consequently strained for much of his life, often acting just beyond the boundaries of their permission. This haphazard attitude was perhaps a reflection of, or even a return to, his earlier days of profanity.

He established the mission preposterously known as Gethsemane in late 1840. He returned to England in the spring of 1842 and was soon after married to Elizabeth Clay, more often known as Betha to her family. He returned to Arcadia by winter of the same year with his new bride.

Jacob Roche worked ceaselessly to bring the good faith to the inhabitants of Arcadia and forged valuable connections with their ruling classes. He died on 21st of December 1843 under unknown circumstances.

A collection of his letters is due to be published next year.

Matthew Worthington Copleston & Margaret Hale,
Memorials of Protestant Missionaries, Giving a List of
Their Publications and Obituary Notices of the Dead

We returned to my room excited about all the accounts that we would write of wonders we saw within the wicker whale. It seemed an inconceivably huge task to catalogue everything within the whale alone.

"Do you think the other whales would be the same inside?" I asked.

"Why would they not be?" He pulled out his sketchbook and began putting pencil to page, trying to record what he had seen.

"If they are like islands," I reasoned, as I folded myself into an armchair. I covetously eyed the blankets and the softness of the bed. "And not all islands are the same. Presumably they would have different fish inside them. If we can call them fish."

"But they're not like islands. They must have been built or made. The writing on the beams, it can't grow that way... Can it?"

"It *is* Arcadia," I said. "Who knows what's natural here?"

"But who would build such a thing?"

"I don't know, but it's no stranger than the other things we've seen."

His tongue stuck out as he tried to concentrate on the arc of the whale taking shape before him. I was curious enough to haul my exhausted body from my seat and hover behind him.

He came to draw the arching ribs of the beast and as he tried to mimic the shape of the sigils upon them, he said. "The words, the Enochian, you called it."

I nodded.

"Show me."

So I did, pulling out all the pages and the journal and the letters I had been working on. I spread them onto the floor, noting how much more space they took up compared to the first time I did this.

"Understanding Enochian. It was what Roche did before whatever happened to him happened to him," I said. "I can't say they aren't linked. Solving one may mean solving the other."

"Looking at these doesn't mean I'm going to try my hand." His eagerness in leafing through the papers belied his words. There was a brightness in his eyes that I had not seen for some time.

"So you don't want to know?"

"Perhaps, but more importantly, I didn't think such knowledge could ever be within reach."

"You don't only ever want things you could have."

Catherine Helstone's brother laughed at my teasing, and I gave his hand a reassuring squeeze before assisting him in the navigation of the pages, explaining the less intelligible of my notes.

"Why was he translating the Bible into this language?" he said, barely looking up from the paper. "This... this Enochian?"

"There is no greater missionary than the mother tongue. Others have slaved for years, decades sometimes, to translate the Bible into heathen languages. I imagine this is the same."

"You think Enochian is Arcadian?"

"Yes, but also..." I swallowed, suddenly feeling silly. Nervously, I tucked a stray curl from my face. "It's the tongue of angels. It's the language the world spoke before the fall of Babel."

"So it claims."

"There could be truth to it. There could be truth on these pages if only we could read them."

"I'm sure they could claim all sorts of things without them being true. Just because something is written down…" Though his words were sceptical, I could tell by the tilt of his head and eagerness in his eyes that Catherine Helstone's brother was intrigued.

"At the ball, I spoke with some fae who… well, they didn't call it anything. They said that their Unbegotten Father and his Misbegotten Son claim it as their own, but it doesn't only belong to them."

"Unbegotten father?" He gave a bitter bark of a laugh. "They taunt you with secrets they don't know."

"But they are titles that ring true, in a way. And those aren't just toying with me. The glyphs were carved into their skin." I ran a hand down my own arms, remembering those scars that were engraved upon the skin of the pair of siblings. "It has to mean something to them if they wear it like that. It wasn't written there for my eyes. If anyone, it was for the Pale Queen to read."

"Do you know what it said?"

"No."

"And it's why you want to read it."

"Don't you?" I said. "And it might even give an idea as to what happened to Roche and how he died. The Salamander said he was trying to learn something, to prove something that should not be proven. Aren't you curious at all? He died. He has a widow in England to whom we owe this story." My anxious hands smoothed the pages of my notes and I softened my words to a plea. "It's not like you've anything to do between now and the Pale Queen's answer. We are just waiting for her to let us into her dominion."

The corner of his mouth twisted into a smirk before he leaned over in a kiss. I gave a squeak of surprise but I did not resist, melting into his attentions. He was so tangible.

"There are other things," he said as he traced a finger down my jawline.

And indeed, there were.

In the days that followed, Catherine Helstone's brother and I observed the decay and death of the wicker whale. Neither of us could truly claim to be explorer or scientist, but we did what we could to make a record of what we saw. It was indeed like writing the newsletters and journals for our tin soldiers. More than once, we wondered at what our little tin Duke of Wellington would make of this place and if he would remain his steadfast, stoic self in the face of it.

We returned day after day to the whale and saw its water slowly trickle out and its many inhabitants wilt. The translucent roses desiccated and the fishes floundered. Some of them we tried to preserve in glass bowls, but they soon faded and died once outside of the whale.

Mr Benjamin tutted, confused at our efforts. "Part of the fish, part of the whole. Can't just take it out."

"It's part of the fish?"

"Big fish? Whale?" he said. "It got eaten so is part of. Yesterday breakfast is part of you today, is it not?"

As always, Mr Benjamin would nod happily at his own logic despite our confused expressions. He was less lost than he had been in the immediate aftermath of the hunt, though his questions about the faith had not diminished. He approached it with the same curiosity and simple logic that he did before, even though there were times he seemed almost distracted.

None of our drawings or our words seemed able to capture what we saw. However hard we tried to pin down and pin out that squirming moment like a moth upon a specimen board, it would prove elusive.

"You'll never make a good naturalist," I said, looking over

his shoulder at his work.

"The least of my sins, I should think." He grinned back at me. "And I am repentant, which is, as John reminds us, what matters."

"But I demand restitution," I retorted.

At night, having run out of observations and pictures, we toiled side by side, leafing through the papers on Enochian, trying to piece together enough of it to start reading the words on the whale's ribs.

Despite having each other as distractions, we made far more progress than I had in my time alone. Catherine Helstone's brother had a better grasp of classical languages than I and was far more familiar with the Latin Bible. He rooted out an early error in my existing word lists that explained much of my frustration.

We worked late into the night, until the moon swam across the sky and our eyes itched from lack of sleep. No longer uncomfortable with each other's bodies, we lay curled up against each other like the working dogs used to by the fire.

He looked over at me and with a lazy, contented smile on his lips, he said, "Cathy—"

"Don't call me that," I said, cutting him short. Panic welled up at back of my throat at that name. "I'm not—"

"Cathy," he said again, pressing his face against the curve of my neck. I felt his warm breath upon my skin and giddy pleasure spread from those lips; I calmed. "Let the other be Catherine. And you can be Cathy. You will always be my Cathy and you will always be my sister."

I raised an eyebrow at that, and he had the decency to look sheepish.

"And other things, true," he said. "But either way, you shouldn't think of yourself as less real. And I do have to call you *something*."

"I'm not real."

"You feel real to me." His fingers tangled into mine; my hand did not melt into his as I feared. We were as solid as each other.

I shook my head. "Ariel said that she didn't feel different when she found out."

"But you were there, you grew up with me. I remember you."

"She also said that she had memories, vivid memories, from before the swap. They make you with memories, somehow."

We were both mute as Catherine Helstone's brother thought. I wanted to pull away, but we were too entangled.

He held my hand in his, stroking his thumb down the back of my hand. He did not recoil in horror nor flinch at the appeasing kisses I placed on his forehead.

"So," he finally began. "Do you think they swapped you later?"

"I don't know," I said. "But if it's possible for Ariel to remember her grandmother despite being swapped after the old woman's death, then it's possible that... it's possible that no memory before I set foot on fae soil is real."

"That can't be true."

"But I can't trust my own mind."

"I know my sister like I know my own mind. I would know if you–"

"You thought I was an illusion created by the moors to torment you."

"That was my own inability to believe you would be here," he said. The candlelight gave a fire to his welkin eyes, the pinpoints of reflected light barely wavering. "I had imagined you so many times, it was difficult. I knew I had to leave, I wanted you too much, but the moment I was away, I would begin to plan again that life we could lead together, how I would hide my passion from you. I would tell myself that I would draw strength from being near you and that self-denial would grow easier with time. I wanted to believe in your presence so I might one day become better than my evil wandering thoughts and my own corrupt heart permitted me to be."

I listened to him in silence, each word another weight upon my heavy heart. I couldn't answer him.

"So, believe me." His face was ardently kindled, that oft-hidden ferocity had risen to the surface. "I did not doubt you because you are not who I know you to be. I doubted you because of my own weakness. You are the sister I grew up with, the sister I have loved and love now. And that's all that matters."

"It may be enough for you, but it is not enough for me."

He said nothing, for what could be said. The truth was, after all, unassailable.

Instead, he held me very close. I heard his breathing, felt it against my skin, and I lost myself in the comfort that he offered. For a moment, I wanted to tell him that it was enough for me too and hide from him the truth, but remained mute. The brief pretence was enough. I had been an unwitting lie for more than twenty years; I should not allow myself to be a lie again.

On the seventh day, we woke to a bonfire outside the castle.

The last of the sea had finally trickled out of its wicker cage, and the Salamander had set what remained alight. Diogenes whined long and terrified, cowering inconsolably at my feet.

I studied the note left at our bedside, the terse scrawl informing us that the whale cannot be allowed to decay further and that it must be disposed of.

"She doesn't so much write as just burn words into paper, doesn't she?" I observed.

In the light of that fire, we mourned the loss of that strange world we glimpsed but did not quite understand and further laboured to record its fleeting image onto paper. Even as I tried to write it all down, my memory was hazy and fragile. I noticed discrepancies between the accounts of Catherine Helstone's brother and myself.

Still, for all the weight upon my heart, those may have been my happiest days, lost in our work and in each other.

CHAPTER 32
The March of Seasons

It is said that the Prussians are working on the Labyrinthus Noctis facility near Schwarzwald, a vast underground railway interchange operated by a clockwork mechanism devised by the inestimable Herr Becker of Vienna. It appears that they have taken as a challenge the now commonly accepted axiom that Arcadia is best reached via ship. The open seas provide ample opportunity for the necessary disorientation, for the strange geography of the Faelands is such that it can only be reached by those who are truly lost. It does not matter where one is lost, be it the moors of Yorkshire or the deserts of Mongolia, but true confusion is vital and therein lies the failure of a great many explorers who have attempted to follow in the footsteps of Captain Cook. Many animals, even seemingly unintelligent beasts of burden, have an extraordinarily good sense of direction.

The Labyrinthus Noctis possesses, it is said, a unique mechanism, the operation of which is made unpredictable by the use of many ball bearings falling down boards lined with pegs. And as such, the degree of lostness can be varied simply by adjusting their distribution.

There is currently no evidence that Prussian locomotives have been successful in reaching Arcadia.

Fitzwilliam Tilney, "On Recent Engineering Advancements", BLACKWOOD'S MAGAZINE, December 1846

Time passed at Gethsemane, and we continued to wait for the Pale Queen's response. The swing of the pendulum grew shorter, the days darker and the nights brighter. Even at midnight was the sky a hazy grey.

Catherine Helstone's brother and I were in the garden as he had again coaxed me out of my room.

The skies were streaked with clouds, weakening the already tepid sunlight. The forbidding walls of the castle with their discordant anachronisms were muted by long and hazy shadows.

The promises of a picnic were interrupted when I noticed a stranger in the garden, holding a paintbrush. He was very tall and ungainly, casting a long, spidery shadow as he made his way across the flowerbeds. A cloak of rags and autumn leaves was draped around his shoulders and it trailed in the grass, leaving a streak of brown and broken grass as he moved. He had to stoop low in order to daub his paintbrush onto each of the flowers.

"Pardon," said Mr Benjamin, seeing our approach. "But Salamander terrible with plants. She hates trees, you know. And fruit, very long story, not worth telling. So I called old friend."

"Old friend?" said Catherine Helstone's brother.

"New friend." Mr Benjamin winced and glanced anxiously over to what the newcomer was doing to his precious flowers. "I didn't want to wait until the Markets are about, would be too late then. Either way, seasonal work. Needs doing."

The newcomer's hands moved strangely, unnaturally, possessing the sort of wrongness shared only by scuttling spiders and long-legged mayflies. At the smear of the paintbrush, the flowers visibly drooped. The second stroke was far lighter, touching the edges of the petals, adding brown, desiccated edges to them.

It was then I noticed why his hands were strange: his fingers each had an extra joint to them.

Seeing one flowerbed complete, Mr Benjamin pottered over with his gardening shears and began systematically deadheading the newly wilted flowers.

"What are you doing, Mr Benjamin?" I asked, my curiosity getting the better of me.

"Gardening," he said, quite cheerfully. "Flowers grow back better this way."

"And your companion?"

"Time passes, flowers fade. Seasonal work. I said."

"What?"

"Making the seasons happen. Am sure he'll get to the leaves on the trees next."

"Doesn't that just... happen? It gets colder as the days get shorter and the plants just..."

"No, not here. Not here," said Mr Benjamin with a sharp shake of his head. His straw hat dropped off at that, and I retrieved it for him. He toothily smiled his thanks before saying, "Your place maybe, but not here. Things don't just happen. Flowers don't just fade, plants don't just grow. We have to make it happen."

"Plants don't do that here?" I said.

Mr Benjamin tapped his nose with his dirt-encrusted finger as his brows knitted in thought. "It's like... it's like the weather. You have to buy in some rain, and get the wind going and..."

"Weather doesn't just happen?"

The gnome chuckled to himself. "You think food just happens too, don't you?"

"I thought the Salamander cooked."

"Yes, yes. Of course. Exactly. Weather needs to be brewed and plants grown."

"And now you are cutting off the flowers."

"Gardening," he said brightly. "Tidy away the dead flowers, keeps plant healthy."

"But," I said, thoroughly confused by now. "Could you not have them not be faded? I mean to say, if the flowers weren't wilting, then we'd still have them, surely?"

"No, no, no. Time passes, flowers fade." He snipped off another of the dead blooms. "Is how things are meant to be."

We left the gnome to his work.

We had spread before us the various papers of Enochian. Our lists of words were growing, but so were the number of contradictions. I had transcribed the Enochian sigils etched into the ribs of the whale, but we seemed no closer to reading it.

"Maybe it just says *whale* repeatedly," I said in frustration, throwing my pencil to the other side of the room.

"So it doesn't forget what it is?" Catherine Helstone's brother said, pausing in his chewing of the pencil.

"It's important to label things," I retorted. "Names have power, don't you know."

"True, especially when you aren't sure what has swallowed you. It would give great comfort to me if I could read from its bones the identity of my devourer." He pressed his knuckles into his eyes. "Would you please pass me–"

Anticipating his request, I gave him the tally of repeated words and sigils.

"Thank you."

The pendulum sun was receding into the distance and the purple, cloud-bannered sky was framed by the lattice of the windows. Candlelight suffused the room, dancing overlapping shadows over the pages.

As he worked, I made a study of his face and form, reading in his features the echo of my own. Though it would be rather more true to say that I was a mocking fae parody of him. Whatever craftsman had made me got my eyes about right and the planes of my cheeks, but we differed in nose and chin. I wondered then if the real Catherine Helstone would look as I did, if she would have her brother's eyes and her mother's chin.

How poor a facsimile was I of her?

The resemblance between Catherine Helstone's brother and I had brought me great joy in the past. It was our closeness, our history written upon our flesh. He used to say that he would look in the mirror and see my eyes gaze out at him. I wondered now if he would see her eyes instead of mine and jealousy coiled in my gut.

I touched my hand to his cheek, and he turned his attention from the papers to me. He gave a preening smile, and I wanted to laugh at his vanity.

For all that we had the books of our faith before us, he stood between me and every impulse of religion, even as he reached out to me with the promise of intercessory grace, he eclipsed such hopes of heaven.

I had made an idol of him, and for all my excuses that this was but a return to the childish hero worship I had once had for him, this went deeper. When he clasped his hand around mine in prayer, when I knelt before him, I thought not of God, that Lord of Hosts, nor of Jesus, the Redeemer, but of him, simply and eternally.

Watching Catherine Helstone's brother work at the translation, I thought again of Champollion and Cleopatra's name in the cartouche. On a whim, I unearthed the first page I had found with that first line from John and circled each instance of that unique word for God. Then, I did the same for the passage in Latin and English.

"This isn't from any book of the Bible we know," I said.

"What do you mean?" said Laon, brows furrowing.

"We've been working off the assumption that these pages are from known books," I said. "Because of this line here."

I pointed and I heard him mutter the words to himself: *In the beginning was the Word, and the Word was with God, and the Word was God.*

"But what follows isn't the rest of John." I braced a shaking hand against my mouth. "We've been straining so hard because we assumed it is. Because that other page was and… We were staring at it too closely to notice this."

"But I thought this was meant to be a project to translate the Bible."

"Perhaps somewhere that was the goal, but this… this is some sort of Apocrypha. Roche may have been working on translating biblical texts into Enochian, but this is not it. This is a new book."

"You mean he's translating it out of Enochian."

"Or trying to," I said. "I can't believe I hadn't noticed this earlier. The pattern of when God is mentioned in this. It's very similar but it's not the same. We were too busy comparing phrases and fragments to notice the larger pattern."

"It could just be a very bad translation."

I smiled. "That is also possible."

"Then what does it say?"

"I don't…" I swallowed, unwilling to admit ignorance. "We'll find out."

He met my gaze with a smile. "Together."

That night, I dreamt.

I was in a perfect garden. The air smelt of mint and the earth was new.

A man who was all mankind looked at me. He did not speak so much as command. The garden bent to his will.

He watched as I stood in the shadow of a tree with white serpentine roots. I leaned against the tree, and its warmth embraced me. I pulled leaves from the tree and read them like pages from a book.

The world was made with words. If I looked hard enough, I could read those words still. They flowed in the veins of the world, written on their seams.

They told me this tree would reach the heavens. They told me nothing was forbidden.

They told me knowledge could not be a sin.

I licked my lips and they tasted of salt.

CHAPTER 33
The Prices at the Market

In the matter of the renewal of the charter, for instance, the merchants of Liverpool, Manchester, Glasgow, and the other manufacturing towns advocate Free Trade in its utmost extent, regardless of the interests of the inhabitants of the Company's dominions, or the risk of loss to the British revenue, should Free Trade be the means of causing a misunderstanding with the Fae.

The South Seas Company, on the other hand, are going on the opposite tack, – they are doing everything in their power to make it appear the trade to Arcadia can only be conducted in safety by themselves; but the public, knowing the events which have taken place since the charter was last renewed, will not now receive the evidence of the Company's servants without a suspicion that they have a strong predilection for things as they are.

When the charter was last renewed, a parliamentary committee was appointed, as at present, to ascertain if it was likely the consumption of English manufactures would be greatly increased by opening the ports of Arcadia to private traders; and on that occasion all, or nearly all, of the Company's servants who were examined gave it as their opinion, it would be quite impossible to extend the consumption of British goods in Arcadia.

"Letter from a Changeling", BLACKWOOD'S MAGAZINE,
May 1830

All lost things could be found at the Goblin Markets. Or so Mr Benjamin told us.

It was one Sunday that the gnome mentioned that the Goblin Markets were going to be about. He had asked a question about the difference between the clay birds that Christ created in the Apocrypha and those sold at the Markets. He was beginning to reel off all he remembered about the fae-created birds when Catherine Helstone's brother pursued the subject of what else they sold.

"Everything, really," said Mr Benjamin, pushing his spectacles up his crooked nose. "And nothing. And anything. Abstract concepts are very fashionable, if not very legal."

"Legal?" I echoed.

"Not all trades are ones that should be made." The gnome grinned, lips rolling back to show round teeth. "So they hide at the edge of the light, deep into the mists. The pendulum is never overhead. Only ever night and twilight." He gave an exaggerated shiver. "I went a lot when was a miner. Long hours easier with a pinch of dream."

"What about lost memories?" said Catherine Helstone's brother.

"As long as it's lost. All lost things end up there."

"And the Markets will be appear soon?"

Mr Benjamin nodded.

"We can't leave the castle," I said. "The Pale Queen said–"

"But we aren't chained down. We can go," he said. "This is important to you."

"We'd be risking all that we've been working for, the

alliance with the Pale Queen and her permission for passage and..." The words came tumbling out of my mouth, half excuses, half reasons, as the fear welled up inside me. "And the translation. We've only just begun making a breakthrough. I know we only have a few words but it's beginning to make sense. We can't risk that."

"We aren't risking it by going. And the Markets may even offer more answers."

"We are. If the Pale Queen finds out–"

"It'll be worth it." He smiled winningly. His cloudless blue eyes sparkled. "Lost things find their way to the markets, we should be able to find something there."

"I don't see how that would help."

"You've been craving answers."

"I've been fearing answers."

"Either way, we should find out."

It was the use of our childhood turn of phrase that got to me. I swallowed my fear and nodded.

We left Gethsemane in the late morning, heading away from the approaching sun. The mists enveloped us, their curling tendrils taking on dying whales and dancing waves.

"How far is it?" I said. "Don't we need to take a horse?"

"No," he said. "Benjamin said we could walk. Very close, he said. As close as a childhood memory, as near as an apology."

"That doesn't make any sense. He said it was far from the pendulum. Where it's never properly light."

Catherine Helstone's brother shrugged. "Nothing around here makes sense. Especially distances. Journeys just aren't measured in time."

We kept walking, vague as Mr Benjamin's directions were. We stayed on the path.

The mist thinned, the skies darkened, and we were in a glade of sorts. I wondered if this was the forest I once saw at the edges of the cliffs. The birch trees, bandaged as they were in their white bark, towered over us, each straight as a flagpole. The gashes in the peeling bark watched us like thin, slitted eyes.

"Awful for climbing," said Catherine Helstone's brother with a vague gesture towards the trees. "Though I've seen you climb a birch."

"Not successfully."

"I thought it successful. It was definitely worth ruining that green dress over."

"Green? I thought the dress was–" I swallowed my words and tried to suppress the memory of my torn dress clinging to my torn legs, both red with blood.

"I'm probably wrong," he said gently. "I can misremember too."

It was very strange to walk through a forest and have it be almost silent. Despite the half light, the air had that morning crispness that songbirds favoured. But there was no chorus of finches and thrushes, no soft hum or chirps of insects, no scuttling in the undergrowth.

"It doesn't feel like we should be here," I said. Fear danced goosebumps up my spine. "We should go back."

"No, we came for your memories."

We reached a small clearing in the trees. The moon shone down white and silvered the trees.

"It's very quiet," I said. "Is this the right place?"

Catherine Helstone's brother glanced down again that the crude map Mr Benjamin had scrawled for us and said, "As far as one can guess."

There was nothing but trees and grass and mist.

At the edge of the first clearing, we could see a path bordered with white mushrooms that led to a second clearing. A glimpsed row of mushrooms in the grass further away suggested another path and another clearing.

I pulled out the compass; it was spinning without anchor. I shook my head.

"I didn't think it would help," I said with a sigh.

"I did give it to you so you couldn't find Arcadia," he said.

"What?"

"I trusted you wouldn't want to part with it. And you need to get lost to get to Arcadia... so I thought it would prevent you from finding me." His voice was heavy with guilt and he dared not meet my gaze. "Because you would never be lost."

My hand closed around it, trying to bury the pain of his confession. "I had thought it a promise. You didn't say anything, you know."

"I wanted you too much. You know that."

"I thought it was meant to guide me to you."

"I'm sorry."

It was then that it started.

Merchants, winged and horned and whiskered, arrived. They each had a brightly coloured bundle on their shoulders. These bundles unwrapped to reveal a plethora of trinkets and, in the blink of an eye, the ground was a patchwork of cloths each laden down with an intriguing spread of wares. I saw gems that looked like iridescent animal eyes, tiny castles hanging on strings and sea-sodden bottles each with a tightly rolled scroll inside them.

"Make way!" came a shout. "Make way away!"

A cart came hurtling towards us, and we stepped out of its way as it scraped perilously close. The cart came to a halt and its vendor, a hunchbacked man with a veritable halo of whiskers, began unfolding it into a stall. Strings of buttons and thimbles and keys were suspended on the frame of the stall.

Cart after cart followed, each unfurling into a stall. Shelters and stands stretched from the body of the carts. They jostled for space beside and around those that sold things off the ground. Insults were muttered, but few moved to make room for newcomers.

"Lost dreams, old dreams, day dreams."

"Sweet to tongue and sound to eye; come buy, come buy."

"Rain by the drop, hail by the stone. Rain by the drop, hail by the stone. Yorkshire mist and London fog. Faerie air, freshly mined."

My hands tightened around that of Catherine Helstone's brother. That single, cold hand anchored me. I breathed into it.

The glade became claustrophobically full as a market square built itself around us, hemmed in by sprawling streets. Stalls laid themselves out edge to edge and then climbed ever higher. Facades of faded plaster were pulled from impossibly small boxes. Goblin hands rolled back the carpet of thin grass at our feet, opened trapdoors and pulled from the earth further rickety structures.

"Mortal salt! Mortal salt!"

"Pretty penny for a pretty trinket! Pretty penny, pretty trinket! Ugly penny, ugly trinket!"

"Real mermaid tears! Fake chickens' teeth!"

The vendors exhorted us to buy their wares, belting out nonsensical lists. Given the growing crowd, wings were closed, tucked against bodies, and tails kept in check. It was at once like and unlike the bewildering crowd at the port.

"Is this it?" I whispered. Glancing up, I saw no sun, and it was only when looking behind that I noticed it as a pale disc in the distance, swaddled by cloud, like the earthly moon at twilight. Arcadian travel must indeed be strange for us to have covered such a distance.

"Come buy! Come buy!"

"Doors to nowhere! Doors to dreams! Doors to minds!"

Catherine Helstone's brother wrapped an arm around me and drew me closer.

The fear that had settled at the back of my throat gave way. I swallowed, and for all the bitterness I tasted, there was also wonder. The grandiose columns and ramshackle storefronts of smoky glass tantalised.

I felt quite small, dwarfed by the impromptu buildings. It was then that I realised everything was just slightly too big. The doorways just a sliver too tall, the windows too wide. The tables and their contents were just a little higher than they should be for comfortable browsing.

Fae of vaguely human shape and smaller wandered the market but none of them were of the right size for the unfolded structures. As an undine stood on her webbed toes to reach a lofty doorknob, I could not help but wonder who or what these buildings and these streets were originally for and what became of them.

Amid the press of scaly, furry, alien bodies, I saw a flash of orange gold, like a streak of sunset.

"Is that..." I muttered to Catherine Helstone's brother.

"What?" he said, distracted. Bright baubles caught his eye, and we lingered. Much as I wanted to let my fingers trail through the jewellery, I resisted.

"I thought I saw someone familiar."

Ropes upon ropes of storm-coloured pearls hung from the crossbeams of the stall. Trays of rings were laid out, each gleaming with cat-eyed jewels. Some were carved into small castles atop which the tiniest people bustled. I wasn't sure if they were powered by magic or minuscule clockwork or neither.

"How would we find anything in all of this?" he said. "I don't even know what half of this is."

"We could ask," I said. "If there was someone to ask..."

There were plenty of someones in the Market, though none of them seemed particularly open to questioning. They bustled about, haggling, shouting and gossiping at each other.

Fishy mouths flapped open and close, beaks twittered and muzzles pursed in unnatural shapes.

"Doesn't that brooch look like the one you used to wear," said Catherine Helstone's brother.

It was a simple pewter moth, crudely cast. I stopped myself from touching it, but I could already remember its weight in my hands as I used it to clumsily pick locks at school. I had pinned it to Catherine Helstone's sister at her funeral. I remember it glinting at me from the front of her black gown after I kissed her ice-cold lips.

"There are a lot of brooches like that," I said. "It can't be that one."

"Pretty penny for a pretty trinket," said the vendor, looking up at us with glassy eyes. Her jaw clicked audibly as she spoke.

Beaming at me, Catherine Helstone's brother pulled a British penny from his pocket and placed it in the mechanically jointed hand of the vendor before I could protest. The vendor's mouth snapped open and closed in some mockery of laughter and she gestured at the moth brooch.

Catherine Helstone's brother pinned it to the front of my dress, and my fingers played over its familiar details. I knew it couldn't be the brooch I had buried, but it felt very much like it. My fingers found the same irregularities in the pewter, the same roughness at the seams of the mould.

"Beautiful," said Catherine Helstone's brother.

I tried to smile, but faltered. Trying to break the tension of the moment, I turned away from him and cast my eyes about the market.

It had been nagging at me since the market had begun to build itself around us; it all reminded me of something.

And it was then I realised: this was like Miss Lousia March's collection. She kept an array of dolls all artfully arranged in tableaux under glass. She had taken a great delight in squinting and sculpting the various creatures and flowers, buying in glass ships to put next to her own felted birds and paper butterflies. I spent many hours helping her rearrange the wild-haired dolls around cluttered stalls and cardboard cathedrals.

This was like that. It had the same unreality. Too many eyes shared the same glassy emptiness. The objects had that same mismatched quality, where nothing was quite the right size for anything else and nothing was made from what it was meant to be. Flowers made from beeswax and birds out from felt.

"Are you selling doors?" I asked.

"I also sell locks, if that helps," said the long-faced fae, shrugging the snail-like shell they wore on their back. They were hammering together a shed made of doors. "Locks are excellent things, you know, they protect the body and mind."

"Mind?" said Catherine Helstone's brother. "How could it affect the mind?"

"Doors are means of stepping into a mind. Keep them bolted shut with a cold iron cross if you want to sleep dreamlessly."

"All doors?" I said.

"Depends on where the door goes," the fae said with a shrug. Peeling paint flaked off with every knock of the hammer. "But I suppose all doors lead to somewhere. It's the doors to nowhere that I'd worry about."

I thought immediately of my own door to empty air. "Who dwells there?"

The fae squinted at us very closely, their horizontal pupils flushing scarlet. "I see her sand in your eyes still. I cannot sell you anything."

"Wait," I said. "What do you mean by that?"

The fae shook their head and shooed us from their stall.

"You think they meant the Pale Queen, don't you?" said Catherine Helstone's brother. "The dream with the strange tree…"

"More than that." I tapped my fingers against my cheek as I thought. "I think we could use it to contact her."

"With dreams?" he said.

"We could leave the door open..." I shuddered at the thought; there was something viscerally wrong about leaving that door unbolted.

"Ah, it is always good to see a little disobedience," drawled a voice into my ear. "There are no sins that cannot be forgiven, after all."

I spun around, heart leaping panicked into my throat.

It was Penemue. He was stooping to lean into my ear, taller than I remembered him being.

He gave a very exact bow, his golden scars gleaming against his jet-black skin. More familiar with the sigils of Enochian, the words taunted me with meaning just out of reach.

"You remember who I am, do you not?" said the fae.

I nodded, not entirely trusting my own voice.

"It's ever so exciting to see you here. And your brother too," said Penemue. "The markets always need something new, the old simply isn't enough."

Kasdaye glided over, her hair fanning out behind her like the tail of a goldfish.

"I don't believe you've introduced us to your brother," said Kasdaye. Her ruby-red tongue passed over her golden lips as she eyed him. "And you really should."

"He's not–" I said.

"Oh, of course, I forgot. It's always unfortunate to lose family." She reached a hand towards Penemue and leaned her head affectionately against his shoulder. I remembered that flash of envy I felt at their closeness.

"I'm the Reverend from Gethsemane," said Catherine Helstone's brother. He took a step forwards, an edge of confrontation in his voice as his hand tightened protectively around mine. "And my sister, you already know."

"Humans get so cagey about names," said Kasdaye airily. "I do know who you are. I was just trying to be polite."

"As was I."

"Oh, you are defiant." Kasdaye gave a bubbling laugh. "Is this how you talk to Mab? No wonder you aren't getting anywhere."

"You're looking at my sister as though you're about to devour her," said Catherine Helstone's brother.

"Oh, hells forfend!" she exclaimed. "My interest is largely academic. Her stars and her blood are of interest to me."

"You shouldn't tease them so," said Penemue gently. He stroked her hair with the lightest of touches, making the cascade of orange gold ripple around his fingers.

"Only because you ask, dear brother."

"I- I want to ask," I said, half stuttering, interrupting their all too intimate reverie. "The words written on you. You said last time that you knew how to read them."

"We did."

"Can you show me how?"

"That would be far too easy, fragile little thing," said Penemue. "They're secrets that can break mortal minds."

"Breaking one mind doesn't mean all minds," reprimanded Kasdaye.

"Two."

"But it wasn't just the secrets, now was it? It's also the sins…"

Penemue shook his head and looking me very directly in the eyes, he said, "Those who don't understand should ask those who can't understand. Sometimes the mute make the best teachers."

He let the words sink in before shifting his attention back to Catherine Helstone's brother. "Now then, I know that isn't what you're here for."

"Cathy's memories," came the reply. Catherine Helstone's

brother spoke before he thought and the moment he did, I regretted it. My courage had been spent already.

There was a glint in their fae eyes. Of course there was.

"We could help..." said Kasdaye.

"Much as I do so love crossing Mab," said Penemue. "And it has been a while since I've watched my sister read the bloody entrails of the constellations..."

"I could hunt them across the firmament and cut their dark, full bellies," whispered Kasdaye into her brother's ear. She drew a nail against the skin of his jaw. "Gut them, make them spill me shining secrets."

"Much as that would be delightful," he continued, "I'm not sure we *should* interfere in this particular case."

"Then we should take your leave and find someone who could intervene," said Catherine Helstone's brother. "You seem aware of the fact that we should not be here, so you should equally be aware that we haven't much time."

"We shouldn't, but we will," he said. "Because we are more alike than you may think."

"We are nothing alike," spat Catherine Helstone's brother.

Penemue raised a single eyebrow. He allowed a potent moment of silence before saying, "Regardless, I will freely tell you who will sell you your answers. But it will not come cheap."

CHAPTER 34

The Moth in the Jar

For it may as rationally be concluded, that the dead body of
a man, wherein there is to be found no more appearance or
action of life than there is in a statue, has yet nevertheless a
living soul in it, because of its shape; as that there is a rational
soul in a changeling, because he has the outside of a rational
creature, when his actions carry far less marks of reason with
them, in the whole course of his life, than what are to be found
in many a beast.

John Locke, AN ESSAY CONCERNING HUMAN UNDERSTANDING

Penemue's instructions led us to a stall leaning against an
ostentatiously classical facade. Marble nymphs held aloft an
eroded scene of lounging gods.

There was indeed a merchant with silvery skin in the
shadow of the facade. His stall was stacked high with glass jars
that reminded me of those Catherine Helstone's brother and
I used to kill moths with in our childhood collecting. Each of
the jars held insects of some kind, each fluttering gently.

"Yes," said the merchant after surveying his jars. He held
each to the wavering candle. The ghostly white moth inside

pressed its delicate limbs against the thick, distorting glass. I could see its furry feet. "I have what you want."

The light glinted off the glass, and the eyes on the moth's wings seemed to stare back at me. The little brown paper label read: *Lost Truths*.

"But the question is, do you have what I want?"

"I can pay you," said Catherine Helstone's brother.

"But what?"

"Name a price."

"I could take your skin," said the merchant. He took off his spectacles and held them to his forehead whereupon the creases there opened into a row of eyes that peered appraisingly at Catherine Helstone's brother. "But I would need all of it. Guilty secrets are cheaper, but you don't want those. So all of it."

"All of my skin?" he echoed in confusion.

"Yes... yes, your skin." The merchant's eyes blinked. Meticulously, he emptied one of his pockets and pulled it inside out. He then cleaned his spectacles with the insides of his pockets before putting them back on again. "I think that is fair. Memories aren't cheap."

"But–"

The merchant sighed in exasperation. The barbels around his fishy lipless mouth curled and uncurled. "I suppose you would need something to keep your bits in. I probably have a bearskin somewhere."

"Would that make me a bear?"

The merchant shrugged. "Don't know. I suppose. You could always take it off? Humans are so fiddly sometimes."

Catherine Helstone's brother was considering the deal far too seriously. It was written very plainly on his face, even as his brow furrowed and he folded his arms in thought. I had seen him haggle before and he had always been terrible at it, but this was no present bought on a whim.

"No? Well, I could take your eyes."

"My eyes?"

"Yes, the globe-y squishy gems in the front of your face. You call them eyes, right? If I could take them and an arm and a leg? Is that fair?"

"You shouldn't have to pay that," I said to Catherine Helstone's brother, tugging at his sleeve.

"But your memories, the truth… it's worth it, surely?" He was so eager.

"I don't think–"

"So," interrupted the merchant. "You are willing to pay?"

"My eyes, was it?" He did not falter, for all the fear I saw in his face. His hand was in mine and I tightened my grip. He anchored me, in this madness.

"Just one." It was smiling, or at least, it was showing teeth. "And one arm, one leg. That is to say, I want half of you."

"Half?" He echoed the word.

"Yes, half." It gesticulated vaguely. "Give or take. I'm not greedy, I wouldn't ask for all of you. You want half of her back, so I ask for half of you."

"Half of her?"

"Does she not feel like half herself? This is what we are talking about, isn't it?"

"Yes, I suppose so." He turned to me and smiled. I was frowning but I returned his smile the best I could, my uncertainty and my fear getting the better of me. "You aren't half a person."

"But I am not real," I said, firmly. I could not abide by his delusion.

"Real to me." He gave my hand a quick, affectionate squeeze.

Catherine Helstone's brother returned his attention to the merchant, but I wouldn't let him. I dragged him from the stall. He followed me reluctantly, stumbling slowly, the crowds barely moving to make way.

"No, you can't," I said. "I won't let you do this."

"Why not?"

"It's your eyes! And your leg and your arm." I glanced nervously around myself, fearing the fae overhearing us. They continued seeming oblivious. "This isn't the place for this conversation."

"Then we needn't have it. I can just make the deal."

"No, you can't. I won't forgive myself and I certainly won't forgive you."

"But you wanted to know. It's what we're here for," he said. "You keep saying you're not real. I can't–"

"This won't make me real," I said, quite ruthless. "This can't change that."

"But it might help." He gave me a gentle, mournful smile. His hand brushed against my cheek; I pulled away. "I love you."

"And?" I demanded.

"What do you mean?" His brow knotted in confusion.

"And what... I mean," I fumbled for words. "Your sentence. It's not complete. You don't mean that. There are more words."

He laughed at that, a sudden rush of lightness in his expression. "No, there are no more words."

"What–"

"Cathy, I love you." Unlike his earlier declarations, he said it quite plainly as though it were an observation about the weather. The tumultuous passions that he had poured out at me before still lurked beneath that tranquil surface, not so much hidden as sublimated.

"Don't say what you don't mean."

"I've loved you, adored you, desired you for as long as I remember. I made it an obsession, a curse, a torment. I made it all sorts of things and it's still true, I suppose. But you were right, I made it all about me. And it shouldn't be. We are in Arcadia and a thousand Arcadian souls need to be redeemed. The Pale Queen still toys with us and the hunt and..." He shook his head. "I didn't want this to be complicated. It has been complicated for too long and I made it that way for longer."

"I-I don't understand."

"I love you," he said, his blue eyes piercing mine. "As a sister, as a lover, it doesn't matter."

"But–"

"I want you to know whatever it is that you need to know. That you want to know. You doubt the truth of your mind and your memories, and if this can give you answers," he said. "Then I'm willing to pay the asking price for that."

I watched him stride towards the merchant. He was all squared shoulders and steely determination.

I did not hear him speak as I heard nothing but the beating of my own heart, deafeningly loud inside my ears. An anxious drumbeat as I saw him lean towards the merchant, and the fae rubbed its hands together.

"No, Laon!" I called after him. "Laon!"

He turned.

His name felt like a stranger's in my mouth. I had not used it for so long.

But then, perhaps he should feel like a stranger. He was not my brother and I was not his sister. It was a thought that brought a pang of loss within me, making me all the more desperate to hold onto him, onto whatever it was between us.

"Laon," I said. "No. I'm not willing for you to pay that price."

"But your memories..."

"I don't want you to. Because..." I hesitated. Guilt and shame warred within me, both seeking to stay my hand.

Accusations filled my mind and for a moment I lost my own words to those doubts. Was I simply trying to recreate the closeness of our childhood with perversion? Was I succumbing to an ancient sin? Was I giving new meaning to our past or had I found a hidden part of ourselves? Were these true secrets of my own heart or forgeries?

He waited. I watched his throat tremble as he swallowed.

For all the crowds and the bustling market, we were alone. He was the only real thing here.

"Because," I said. "Because I love you."

Which of us closed the distance between us didn't matter, only that we became entwined.

The mist twisted into writhing, copulating figures as we walked that interminable path back to Gethsemane.

We chased each other through the mists, like we were children again, playing on the moors. But this was not the innocent games of our past selves, even as I wondered how innocent our games had been. Was I imagining now how much I had relished his closeness then? Was it simply newfound desire that was igniting all past memories or had I always flushed warm under his gaze?

The curling mists darted around us, constellations of mating dragonflies and twinned birds in courting spirals.

We laughed, momentarily forgetting where we were.

The mists did not forget, though. They danced around us, luridly realising what we both wanted. They tangled and tangled, cresting upon one another like waves.

He caught me and I felt his breath against my neck as our arms entwined. I breathed to him the words that I had so long denied the both of us.

CHAPTER 35

The Note on the Bed

He was alone, in the beginning, though I should not like to think Him always lonely. Perhaps it was all too new to be dull, even that endless, amorphous mass of the Beginning. It would entertain enough a magpie mind like His with its possibilities. I imagine it would be like being in an ever-moving kaleidoscope, a dreamscape of inconsistency, with Chaos billowing, rolling cloud-like. I think of all the pieces, swirling like sunlit dust as they cluster and constellate, forming fleeting images of maybes, mayhaps, perhaps, perchances.

I'd like to think that He glimpsed the world there, in the ancient nights of chaos, and smiled at the adventure that would be. I'd like to think that He glimpsed me there.

But what would I know? It could be that what they said was true. That there was indeed nothing, a nothingness more empty, more cold, more void-like than the darkness we call night. Perhaps my mortal mind cannot disgorge itself enough to conceive of such emptiness, such darkness, and I have thus reasoned that it is impossible.

But I was not there; they were not there; only He was.

Translated from Enochian by Rev Laon Helstone
and Catherine Helstone

By the lineages of creation, the dragon is as much my brother as Mankind ever was. We were both made of God's substance, after all.

He saw in me a true equal.

They would know me as a creature of night and named me accordingly. They would know him as a bringer of light and named him accordingly.

Our children they would call the Fair Folk, the Pale Folk. Each child would be unique, mixed of two equals, beautiful and infinite in their oddities. They are unlike those of Mankind, for he mated with his own shadow.

I am, of course, their Queen.

Translated from Enochian by Rev Laon Helstone
and Catherine Helstone

Sunlight woke me and I was beside him.

Blushing, I remembered how we had tumbled into the bed of the tower room, onto the lists of sigils, Enochian texts and unfinished translations. It was perhaps only apt that kisses were exchanged between the scribbled sheets and the ink of our words was blotted onto my skin.

I regarded with pride the blue and black that stained my wrists, like the mottling of bruises. Briefly, I tried to read the smudged words before turning my attention to the sleeping Laon.

Sunlight flattered him. It gave his skin a warm glow and made his eyelashes cast shadows upon the planes of his cheeks. His hair was a beautiful tangle. Sleep smoothed and soothed much of the cares he carried, making him seem younger. I remembered watching him sleep as I waited for him to wake when we were young. I had rarely been the first to rouse myself, but that had only meant that I resented being the only one awake all the more and would impatiently leap upon Laon until he agreed to play with me. I had counted his each breath and then tried to match his rhythm.

I did it again now, tried to breathe with him, breath for breath.

Remembering the night before, I thought of sin, of love and of marriage. But more than that, I wondered at what claim I had on the real. Since I was not real then what sin he committed upon me could not be any more real than I was. For all that he felt as solid as day, what lay between us was but as real as a dream.

But it was a very sweet dream.

His eyes opened and he smiled at the sight of me.

A frown of confusion crossed his features, his eyes glancing over to the paper nearest his face. I let out a giggle at the bed of papers we lay on, remembering how I had once teased him for being inappropriately Byronic in his demeanour.

"I suspect we should copy these out again if we were to ever give them to a publisher," I said.

"I doubt Lord Byron had to."

"I was thinking that."

"Though I suppose he would also have more opium," he said, as he squinted at the page.

"Or goblin fruit, at least."

"Cathy, this isn't your hand, is it?" said Laon.

Lethargically, I sat up to take the page from him. It was only then that I realised my state of undress. I clutched the bed sheet to my chest.

"I have seen you naked already," said Laon, even as he turned around to regard the wall. "I've even dressed you."

"That's not the point." I disentangled myself and shrugged on my dressing gown.

"And I do intend to see you naked again," he said dryly.

"I intend to let you, but it's still hardly proper," I said, further swaddling myself in both my shawls before settling back on the bed.

"Byron would–"

"Oh hush, you are nothing like Lord Byron." I took the page from him. "Your poetry is abysmal."

"Exactly like him then."

My eyes scanned the page. It was the translation we had been working on, with the English we were certain about written above the Enochian. I recognised my own writing and I remembered how tired my shaking hands were when I shaped each of the letters.

But someone had filled in all the gaps. Someone had finished our work.

But what would I know? It could be that what they said was true.

The handwriting looked familiar. The letters were crowded and tightly curled, the nib biting deep enough into the paper to tear it. I had seen this hand before.

That there was indeed nothing, a nothingness more empty, more cold, more void-like than the darkness we call night.

"But this was on the bed," I said. "We were working on it just before we…" I trailed off into a blush that was evident in my voice if not on my skin.

"I know."

"We were asleep."

"I know," he said again, obviously unnerved by the thought of someone stealing into the room as we slept.

"How?" My hands were shaking when I laid aside the page onto my writing desk. "Are there more? I mean, has this person written on any other pages?"

Laon didn't answer but he began leafing through the scattered papers of the room.

By the time the knock on the door came and a tray of breakfast was left outside by the Salamander, we had sorted through all the papers.

Thirteen pages bore corrections and additions in a hand

that belonged to neither of us.

"I know where I've seen this before," I said. I picked up Roche's journal and, leafing through it, the answer was obvious. "It's the person who wrote these passages."

Laon squinted at it as he bit into a pastry. "The resemblance is but passing. You might as well compare it to one of the letters from Roche's wife. It's a fair hand, but it's a very common way to write."

I laid them side by side as I chewed my lip. He was right. It was not a very distinctive hand, for all the fact that it was tightly wound against itself; the cursive letterforms were very like those we had both practised over and over as children.

"And there's no one else in this castle," said Laon. "It's just you and me, Mr Benjamin and the Salamander."

"I don't think it's Mr Benjamin…"

"There's no reason to think it *can't* be the Salamander."

Our eyes met and we shared an uneasy gaze. I winced.

"Our housekeeper is rather elusive," I said, glancing down at our breakfast tray. "And does have a habit of just leaving things about."

"Her notes, when she leaves them, have been in a different hand."

I sighed. "There's no reason why we can't just ask Mr Benjamin."

Simply asking Mr Benjamin was easier said than done, and both Laon and I had plenty to distract us. Perhaps we both feared the answers that our seemingly devoted gnome would give us, but we both found reasons to put it off until the afternoon and absorbed ourselves with the translation of further Enochian fragments.

And despite its origins, we were both secretly ungrateful to the corrections and additions in that cramped, crowded hand. We could barely believe what had been written, what

the text unravelling before us was, and it was for that reason
that we pressed on.

"I'm not sure we should keep going," said Laon finally.

"To know is not a sin," I said automatically.

He raised a sceptical eyebrow. "The Tree of Knowledge of
Good and Evil begs to differ."

"I rather thought you'd go for the fact that *to know* can be
used euphemistically for a different sin."

Laon grinned rakishly at that.

"And I do concede the point about sin," I said. "But there
have always been Apocrypha to the Bible. Maybe this is just
another one."

"A *new* one."

"Or not," I said. "We don't know who wrote this or why."

Laon unscrewed his own hip flask and I smelt the thick
scent of brandy. He took a swig from it. "I don't know what
we expected."

I tried a shrug but my shoulders were aching from the way
I had been hunched over our work. I gave a lazy wave of my
hand instead. "I don't know either."

He gave a hollow laugh. "The language of angels."

"Do you still think that?"

"I'm not sure what to think, but what else can we think?"
He pushed his hair from his eyes in an exasperated motion.
"Those two we spoke to, the fae. They seemed to think so.
But I suppose it's also written on the beams in the sea whale.
So maybe it's the language of whales."

"The dream I had about Eden. Remember I said I read a
tree?" I folded my tongue and clicked it as I thought.

"Yes…" He was leafing through our pages of drafts for the
whale text. It was almost a luxury to have this much paper. I
remembered how tiny we used to write.

"In it I was certain that there was a language that flowed
in the veins of the world," I said. "That language held the

world together at the seams. Each blade of grass, each leaf. So perhaps that is what it is. The language with which God made the world… except here, here it is different. It's rougher here, a scrawl."

"We can't prove that."

"I know… just the name of God. It is special in this language, or perhaps it isn't even in this language. Maybe they're not writing it in *this* language and are doing the equivalent of writing it in Sanskrit…" I took a deep breath. "But what does it mean?"

"Perhaps nothing more than that the fae have a lost book of the Bible. A book of Apocrypha. Like you said." He took another deep drink of his flask and passed it to me. "And I never thought that I would ever call that the least of the revelations."

"That doesn't actually tell us what it means."

The words fell into place. We scrabbled about the lists of words; our hands and eyes could not work fast enough. We excitedly muttered to each other, trying to describe the letters and next word we needed to find. We never did manage to work out how to pronounce it.

My hands were shaking and I found myself blotting the page over and over. I could barely write. I swallowed again and again; my mouth parched as I croaked out the words to myself.

"Laon, this is the origin of the fae." I sat back, hands fluttering between my mouth and the page. "This is their genesis."

"If this is true…" his voice trailed off.

"Does this make them Nephilim? Born of a human woman and son of God?"

"I don't think that's how they're defined…"

"Would you even call her human?" My mind racing. The implications both profound and mundane were too many to count.

"Does it matter what I call her?"

"If we have souls because Adam has a soul and Eve has a soul because Adam has a soul... then does she have a soul?"

"It begs the question of what those words even mean," said Laon. "If only descendants of Adam and Eve have souls then no one else can have one. Like apples all born from the different cuttings of the same tree, I suppose. If there is a completely different tree..."

"An apple having seeds doesn't mean, I don't know, a pomegranate doesn't."

"Pomegranates don't have apple seeds though."

"But they do have seeds..."

"I feel we may be reaching the limits of this metaphor."

I laughed at that, and the tension was broken.

After that, we joked often about souls and orchards. Puns on fish and feet suggested themselves, and we indulged in every one. Even as we both accepted their revelation, we were yet unready to speak of it aloud.

There was a madness there that we had yet to entirely embrace.

That night, we left open the door to empty air.

And so, I dreamt of Ariel Davenport.

I was on a roof as a bright, earthly sun was setting. I had become so used to the fact of it receding into the distance that to see it dip below the horizon was strange and alien.

Woven bird traps covered the slate roof. They surrounded me, hemming me in. There was no step I could take that would not trample one underfoot.

A chorus of caged birds baited these traps. Scarlet songbirds were lured down into each one. They snapped shut in a flurry of feathers and the plaintive cries were mistaken for more song.

Beautiful, painful song.

I reached down and picked up each of the birds. I felt their little trembling hearts as they beat their brittle wings against my hands.

With fine white thread I sewed the birds into the corpse of Ariel Davenport. Each stitch stained my white thread red. The birds came apart bleeding string and thread and yarn. All red.

Spools of red thread tangled in my hands until they bit into my fingers like wire.

One by one the birds fell silent around me, but I kept sewing.

Ariel Davenport was a broken doll, after all. Why shouldn't I be able to make her out of a patchwork of dead birds?

I woke screaming.

We did not try to leave the door open again.

CHAPTER 36
The Truth Between the Lines

In that womb and grave of nature, He sculpted a world, telling
it to Himself like a story, word after word. This part of the
story you already know, although most would have you believe
He made it idly, effortlessly, summoning it into existence like
a dream, but I tell you now – and I am telling you tales –
He slaved those six days. He hammered out the heavens, flat
and smooth, like a mirror. He kneaded the mountains out of
mud, built pillars to hold up the sky and smoothed the basin
for the sea. He carved each and every tree, scratching out the
grooved bark with His fingernails and tearing dark eyes into
the skin of the white birch.

Each creature – not all unique, not all beautiful – He made
and moulded. I like to imagine Him joyful in the exertion, but
I think of Him more driven half mad by the sheer enormity,
complexity of his undertaking.

He picked faces out of the clouds and gave them form.
They were as beautiful as the blushing dawn, as the twilight
sky, as the morning star. His voice He gave to them, and they
spoke his own words back to Him.

Angels, He called them.

They were almost company, chattering back to Him in
their lofty, echoic voices. They praised all that he did and

urged him on with indulgent smiles, blinking their empty eyes at Him.

But how long can one mind, however fragmented by madness, be content with hearing only echoes of Himself?

Translated from Enochian by Rev Laon Helstone and Catherine Helstone

He first found Mankind in the mud. Unlike His first creations, made like shadow-puppets out of His hands, man was not imbued with His own voice. He no longer wished to hear His own words echoed back to him. He craved newness. He needed another mind like and unlike his own.

He did not know so yet, but He wanted a mirror, something that was Himself, like Himself, but not Himself.

And so in the mud He saw a face. Or the suggestion of a face. Like a child picking out eyes and nose and mouth from the patterns around it, it was meaningless.

We were made together, Mankind and myself. He was created as my equal and I his. By the lineages of creation, he is my brother.

But he wanted neither sister nor equal.

I ran away with a dragon who stole a mind for itself and Mankind would love himself so much that he would marry his own rib. My children I had to hide away from a Creator still angry about our betrayal; his children inherited the earth.

Translated from Enochian by Rev Laon Helstone and Catherine Helstone

For all that we were both consumed by our work on the presumed Apocrypha, Laon gave a simple sermon on love that Sunday. It was strange to hear him be quite so gentle in his exhorting of his parishioners in their love for another. The dark currents that had often gripped his speech had been tempered, though the steely conviction that I had always admired remained. He also spoke inconclusively on the muddy history of Apocrypha, listing the various theologians who had curated the books of the Bible and describing briefly their disagreements.

After, we sat on the grass of the courtyard together. Mr Benjamin and Laon discussed the "word weeds" as Mr Benjamin liked to term the Apocrypha, with the latter trying in vain to work out a hierarchy of truth within the various canonical texts.

"But then which is more true?" pressed Mr Benjamin. "If garden more true than weeds, then is there difference in garden. Flower more true than leaves?"

"I'm not sure what would be the flower or the leaves then," said Laon. "Do you mean the Testaments?"

"No, no. Flower can never be truer than leaves. Leaves are always. Always are leaves," Mr Benjamin muttered half to himself before saying to Laon in his most Oxford voice: "But then which is more true? Which is leaves?"

"The entirety of the Bible is true."

"Yes, yes. All true, like whole garden is real," said the gnome. "But what is more true? In Genesis it says that God created man in his own image, in the image of God, he created male and female upon the fifth day, but then after the seventh day in the second chapter He makes man again in a garden eastward of Eden. He makes mankind twice and in the second instance he makes woman from the rib."

"Theologians have harmonised stories are true in more than one way, that some may be allegorically true—"

"Two stories," insisted Mr Benjamin. "Two chapters, two times. Both true?"

Laon sighed long and hard. I smiled seeing him this way as

he answered, "Just as Jonah and the whale is a prefiguring of the resurrection of Jesus from the tomb–"

"But different!"

"And in the same way, the two chapters are the same story, just told slightly differently."

Mr Benjamin seemed content with the answer, but feeling mischievous, I said, "You could always tell him about the Jewish demon. The one in Faust."

"That's just confusing," said Laon, rolling his eyes at me. "And is quite preposterous."

"The first woman, made at the same time as Adam, was never named. She wasn't made from his rib, but was instead made at the same time as him, of the same substance. So she must have had a different name."

Mr Benjamin was staring at me very intently at this point. He blinked not once and his gaze banished all the levity out of me. Guilt settled in as I knew he took the faith very seriously and for all my lack of a soul, I should not mock him so.

"She's citing a German play," said Laon. "It's not really scripture."

"Less true?"

"Yes, less true," reassured Laon, his blue eyes wonderfully soft.

"But what is name?"

"Lili–"

A gnarled hand pressed against Laon's face as Mr Benjamin tried to stop him finishing the word. "Names have power. Don't say the name."

"It's just superstition," I said.

"Older the name, greater the power," said Mr Benjamin. "Very old name."

It was clear we had stumbled upon something much greater than either of us had intended to unearth, so I changed the subject to the singing of hymns.

The pendulum sun was waning, growing smaller in the distance. The garden was firmly in the grips of autumn, and the yellowed leaves drifted prettily from their branches.

We raised our voices in dubious harmony. It was a cacophonous mixture, far less beautiful than many I have heard before, but it was still a strange balm to my nonexistent soul. There was a comfort in ancient, beautiful words, I supposed.

"Almost sounds like when we sang in past," said Mr Benjamin, a little wistful as he beamed wide at us with his brown teeth. "Almost, almost."

"Can't be the same," I said. "There's three of us now. More voices, better music."

"Ah, but we were three too. Too three."

"Three?"

Mr Benjamin looked nervously at his fingers which began fumbling with the brim of his hat.

"Who else was here?" I said.

He said nothing.

"You don't often speak of Roche," I said, as gently as I could.

"The Reverend is here, I speak often of the Reverend. And to the Reverend," replied Mr Benjamin. He closed his eyes and his hands continued their agitated movements. He plucked apart the bunch of sedge leaves tucked under the ribbon of his hat. "The Reverend is here. And I am here."

"You know I mean the previous Reverend. The original one."

"The Reverend is the Reverend," he said. "Is the Reverend, is the Reverend."

"Then when you sang before, who else was here besides the Reverend?"

Mr Benjamin shook his head and crumpled tight his face, his eyes closed, cheeks sucked in and lips pressed together.

"You said before that you saw faith. You said... you never said what you saw exactly, but that sacrifice. Is this to do with that?"

"The Reverend is the Reverend," whispered Mr Benjamin.

Laon gave the gnome a pitying look and, meeting my eyes, he shook his head, urging me not to press the matter.

"The Pale Queen's orders?" I said, quite quietly.

He gave the barest nod.

"It's alright, Mr Benjamin. You don't have to say any more."

The gnome breathed a sigh of relief and opened his eyes. He smiled again as though nothing was wrong.

"Thank you, Mr Benjamin."

I was staring hard at the handwriting, and the letters were beginning to lose meaning, reduced to simply lines and shapes. We had had dinner in the hall rather than in my rooms and it was upon our return that I picked up the page and began staring at it.

"I still think it might be..." I swallowed, uncertain of my thoughts. I gnawed at my bottom lip.

"You've been looking at that for a while," said Laon.

"I still think it looks like the hand in Roche's journal."

Laon disagreed but he nonetheless plucked the journal from the shelf at my urging and leafed through it.

"Could you find it?"

Brows knotted, he was frowning at the page when he said, "Do you remember this?"

He passed it to me, and it was indeed that crowded, cramped hand that I remembered. A very studied, tidy script. It wrote out most of a little verse:

He ... the word ... spoke it;
He took ... bread and broke it;

And what that word did make it…
   … believe…

I mouthed the verse to myself. It tugged at my memory. The woman in black had said it to me and I heard it before whispered to me. It could not be a coincidence.

"This was complete last I read it," said Laon. "I didn't think ink could fade so quickly."

I stared at the page, touching my fingertips against where the words were, trying to see any trace of their shape. I knew what they were meant to be.

"Laon," I said. "You remember about semiotic moths, don't you?"

"Book moths?"

"Yes, those. Scourge of the libraries and such."

"We used to set traps for them," he said, a fond smile playing on his lips. "Even though you said there weren't secrets enough in our library to sustain them."

"You were very stubborn," I said. "Especially since Tessie did not like us playing with dead things. We had to steal bay leaves from her herb stores for the killing jars."

"Hiding it all under the floorboards with the blocks was a brilliant idea." He caught my hand and gave each of my fingers a light, punctuating kiss. His eyes flashed dark and desirous. "Quite. Quite. Brilliant."

"No, but this poem," I said, trying not to be distracted. I snatched my hand from him and began drumming my fingers as I thought. I remembered the woman in black and I remembered the moths from the dusty book that Laon had brought me. "I've heard it before."

"Everyone has. It's by John Donne about the mysteries of the Eucharist."

"No, I mean, I've heard it before. Whispered." I shook my head, trying to clear my thoughts. They felt foolish the moment I wanted to speak them. "I mean to say, I heard them here and I think... I think there might be semiotic moths in this castle. They might have swallowed some of these secrets."

"Book moths don't actually eat secrets, you know."

"Ink doesn't fade that quickly."

"Two impossibilities doesn't make a new reality." His hair fell into his eyes, and he raked his fingers through it. "Book moths aren't real."

"What if they do?" I said. "The lacuna in these papers, the journal, the missing pages... I think we should try. Penemue said *Those who don't understand should ask those who can't understand. Sometimes the mute make the best teachers.*"

"That doesn't actually mean anything. He was just saying it to unnerve you."

"True, but... I want to try."

Laon nodded. "Then we try."

CHAPTER 37
The Moths in the Library

If they were to know that we knew, our beds would no longer be safe for us. The night would crawl and slither with a thousand, thousand unnatural shapes with creeping tendrils of blackest malevolence. All the old places would be barred to us, for fear of what lay within. What despicable cruelties the eyes in the well would plot upon us, how the many limbs of the monster would tense in anticipation of the tortuous vengeance it is about to inflict. What hope do we have but the feigning of ignorance against the boundless ferocity which waits to play like children with our still-beating hearts?

Extract from the speech of Dr Immanuel Campbell to the EDINBURGH SOCIETY FOR THE STUDY OF THE FAE

There were days it seemed that Gethsemane was full of moths, white and ghostly, fluttering at the edges of my vision. Diogenes would chase them, come back with worrying mouthfuls of insect, and I would brush them from my closet.

But now, they were nowhere to be found.

We searched through each of the guest rooms, which had been abandoned since Mab's court had last made use of them.

We wandered, through room after room draped over in white dust sheets.

By midnight, we were scouring the attics, flinging open trunks and musty drawers. We shook out dress after dress, robe after robe, until my eyes watered and my lungs ached from all the dust. Light shone through each of the gossamer garments that had been feasts for moths.

"What are you looking for?" enquired a confused Mr Benjamin. He was scrubbing his eyes of sleep. "It's the Salamander's hour."

Laon explained to him about the moths we were trying to find.

"Why aren't you trying the library?"

"There's a library?" I said.

The gnome nodded slowly. "Has always been there. Unless it wasn't, of course."

"What does that even mean, Mr Benjamin?" I said. I had somewhat given up on the grand shambles of Gethsemane making any sense, but I had not thought there would be a whole library that I had previously missed.

"Door might be locked. And the Salamander has the keys," he said. "Isn't much point in doors you can't open."

I touched a hand to the moth brooch at my chest. "Not all locks need keys."

"Maybe?" He gave a slow shrug. "It's down the silver corridor. You understand?"

I shook my head. "None of the corridors are silver."

"Only sometimes silver."

"Sometimes?"

"When the moon makes it so."

"No, that's non–" I stopped myself. I remembered how the mysterious corridor I had walked down that first night had been flooded with moonlight. I had discovered the notes on Enochian that night. "So we just wait for the moon?"

As Mr Benjamin led us through the castle, he explained that the moon was a fickle sort and could not really be commanded. However, the moon, being a fish, could sometimes be lured over, given sufficient bait.

"I have kept one for the moon flowers," he said, showing us a rusty bell that he held very carefully so that it would make no sound. "So that I could coax them open out of season, see?"

"Does the sound attract the fish?"

"Yes, yes," said the gnome. "On the Pale Queen's orders."

I remembered the time I saw the moon fish at my window, but said nothing. I took the bell from the gnome, wrapping my fingers around the clapper to keep it silent.

"So where best to use it?" asked Laon.

"Near my room, I think. There are some big windows there."

"I know where," said Mr Benjamin. "I lead."

We were indeed not far from my room. I knew the place well enough now to recognise the shape of the windows, and the dark flutter of the tapestries. I could not quite suppress the sense of familiarity.

Laon and Mr Benjamin opened the windows, and I waited, bell in hand. My fingers felt cold and stiff.

"Ready?" I asked, though I did not need to as I heard the last creak of the shutters. It was still dark, and the corridor before me was a midnight blue but for the orange glow of our lanterns.

"Done," came Laon's voice.

"We might need to blow out the candles," I said, remembering that night. "So the moonlight shines stronger."

"I'll throw my coat over them," said Laon.

And it was darker, and as my eyes adjusted I could see now the barest glimmer of starlight behind the endless banks of clouds.

I pried my stiff, aching fingers from around the clapper of the bell and, taking a deep breath, I rang it.

An ethereal tinkling, nothing like a hand bell's sonorous tolling, filled my ears. The hairs at the back of my neck stood on end. I could feel fear well up inside me. My other hand reached for Laon's and I found it. I imagined the brave smile he was giving me, for I could not see it in the dark.

We waited.

At first, it was but a pale grey shadow behind one of the coal-black clouds. And then, it slid into view.

The light was almost blinding. I blinked hard, trying to focus, but I did not want to avert my eyes. The moon fish leered down at us with empty eyes and long, curved teeth, yellow as ivory. I could see the bleeding, exposed gums at the roots of its teeth. It was swimming far too close.

The corridor was indeed gilded silver by the moonlight.

Laon and I walked down it, hand in hand. Fear was clouding my memory and I could barely say which door was here before and which wasn't.

"This one," whispered Mr Benjamin.

It felt only right to whisper in this moonlight.

I unpinned the moth brooch, peered into the keyhole and made quick work of the lock. It was very old, and the mechanism was crude to say the least.

"I told you it was a good present," said Laon proudly.

The double doors opened into a tiny room crowded in by shelves full of leaning books. The windows were blocked by stacks upon stacks of books, slivering the light from outside.

"Now found, Reverend Helstone," said Mr Benjamin, tugging at Laon's sleeve. "I was thinking. Perhaps, maybe, I was thinking..."

"You can ask," said Laon.

"I was reading the Bible and I came across the passage

about how *there shall be signs in the sun, and in the moon, and in the stars; and upon the earth distress of nations, with perplexity; the sea and the waves roaring..."*

I stepped into the library, leaving Laon to Mr Benjamin's questions.

The room had little of the grandiosity I expected from its vast ironbound doors. The sloping roof and the row upon row of books carelessly heaped upon each other made it seem all the smaller.

A writing slope lay on the floor. A scatter of half-written letters riddled with lacunae were spilling from its open drawer.

I plucked a book at random from the shelves. It fell open at an empty page. There was not even the shadow of the words that used to mar the pages.

These books had been picked clean.

A shadow flickered over the thin rays of light. I turned but I couldn't see what it was. My heart was racing.

There were whispers at the edge of my hearing. A thousand voices murmuring, mumbling, muttering. Indistinct.

I put aside the volume and chose another, attracted to its heavy gilt spine. I opened the book, revealing a white moth between its cover. It flew at me, brushing past my cheek. I felt the dusty brush of its wings against my ear.

Startled, I dropped the crumbling book. It thudded to floor, the heavy spine loud against the flagstones, sending its fragments up in a cloud.

The sound echoed.

And then, there was a rustling as a thousand, thousand moths were roused.

They must have been resting on every shadowed surface, hiding in every gap between leaning books, perched on every inch of the ceiling.

The air was thick with the dust from their mottled wings. I could taste it as I breathed in.

It was old books and biting, acidic ink. It was that dust of ancient libraries and fresh, shiny leather covers. It was new paper and the sweet glue of the spines.

The moths swarmed me. They filled my sight with their white wings and my ears with their rustling.

And then all at once, whispered into my ears were things I never thought I could know.

I could list all three hundred names of the fourth Arcadian Summer Lord and the whims that brought about each change. I knew intimately every leaf wept by the second laurel tree by the lake during the autumn of year ten-fifty-one, but nothing of those who shared its shadow, star-gazed through its branches or remarked upon its colour. I knew the fluctuations of a single border in Spain, shifting as it was drawn again and again throughout the centuries, but nothing of the reasons why or what new countries it outlined.

It poured senselessly into my mind. So many words, memories, fragments.

I knew every breakfast eaten and described by a nameless diarist for fifty-three years of her life. I knew the letters of poetry in foreign languages and the mellifluous sounds they would make but had no way of understanding what they meant. I knew how many times the letter S appeared on each page of Shakespeare's lost manuscripts; the marginalia and corrections of a lost manuscript of Bede's but none of the work itself; and half the genealogy of Emperor Julian the Apostate of the Byzantine Empire.

And then, the secrets we were looking for.

CHAPTER 38
The Madwoman in the Attic

There is a hollowness to his eyes (there are those who will tell you He has no eyes, which is only sometimes true) that sometimes makes me think He is a survivor, that our beginnings were the end of something greater and more vast than we could ever be.

Perhaps that is why He sculpted a world out of the emptiness, like a child tearing apart the ordered monotony of its room.

When one is alone, there is no need for words. Perhaps that is why I always thought of Him as lonely. One who is one, one alone, could only be waiting for a pair.

From the emptiness that was, He sculpted a world. Later they would say He made it for Mankind. Others would ask why.

Some would hail Him Creator and He would be forever defined by this act, his six days of restlessness. Six of his days. But after that He would put away his colours and brushes and never paint again.

And this is a question no one had asked – why had He not painted again? Out of fear that He'd have to recycle this canvas? Though it seems an odd accusation to the all powerful that He would, of all things, run out of space. But no, I would say He never painted again because He ran out of ideas. Perhaps, like the best of us, He knew He had only one story in Him. One story. And He had written it all in every aspect of the world, from each pillar-like mountain to vaulting sky.

I would not say that story was me (Some would say He had some sixty books in Him, but if you would believe He wrote all that with mortal pens, I could not weary you with any other tale. Nor would you accept all that He wears many faces.)

But I say this, this one is true.

Translated from Enochian by Rev Laon Helstone
and Catherine Helstone

Laon once told me that I shouldn't seek to solve this place, that it wasn't a puzzle.

Perhaps what he should have said was that I wouldn't like the solutions.

It made sense now, all the pieces.

I knew why Roche chose the wife he did, why he was so haunted by a plan, constantly asking himself if his course was worth that price. I knew why there were Enochian texts and half-finished translations. I knew why there was a second hand in that journal, what it wrote of something that was *like* poison, that had to be consumed every day.

I knew who the woman in black was.

"Laon."

My own voice sounded distant, as though it came from another's throat. I wondered why my mind hadn't shattered. Perhaps it was the cogs of flesh that worked in my skull. The moths ate knowledge that could scour a mortal mind, bring it to the brink of madness. They escaped because they lack comprehension. Secrets were but words to them.

"Are you alright?" came Laon's voice. It was solid, anchoring. It cut through the crowding whispers.

I nodded, not quite trusting my own mouth and tongue. I swallowed.

Blackness.

My eyes weren't open.

How curious.

It was only then that I realised Laon's arms were around me, cradling me.

We were on the floor. Even through my skirts I felt the chill of the stone against my legs. I must have collapsed. That realisation brought a searing pain through the back of my head, down my spine. It sent fissures through my thoughts. I grimaced.

I opened my eyes. I tried to focus on Laon's beautiful face. The wavering candlelight was shadowing his eyes and the towers of books enclosing us reminded me of the many times we hid from Tessie in the far corners of the library.

"Are you hurt?" He was frowning, worry braiding his brow.

His hair was in his eyes and it was beautiful. I smiled and pushed it from his forehead.

"No," I said, trying to ignore the headache. "Not really."

"Can you get up?"

"Not quite." I tried to sit up, and he helped me. I leaned against Laon, my breathing strangely ragged. My lungs ached, a heavy knot in my chest tugging at each breath. "But, I think… I think I know."

"What do you know?"

"I know what happened to Roche."

His eyes widened.

"Roche…" I swallowed, trying to make sense of my fractured mind, pushing aside thoughts of the sixth city and the lens of black glass and Egypt. I had to focus. "Roche figured something out about the fae. He thought... he thought the first explorers were wrong. That thing people believe about them always lying. He thought it was the opposite."

"What do you mean by that?"

"He thought they would always tell the truth, if they could. He knew that nothing would hurt more than the truth and the fae would do anything to hurt him." My tongue felt swollen and thick, like it couldn't form real words. I needed to wet my tongue, but I pressed on. "Or rather, truth was their weapon. He thought he could trick them into telling the truth."

"Cathy..."

"Roche had a wife."

"Elizabeth?"

"Her scissors. Those were her scissors in Mab's bed. The sign of the cross."

"You aren't making much sense, Cathy."

I shook my head. Closing my eyes, I tried to focus. I felt the whispers press in again on my mind. Something about the Mottled King and the Watchers. Something about how milk spoilt near fae and their constructs. Something about Bede and poetry and a book about lost time.

Laon offered me his hip flask and I took it. Oaken brandy filled my senses. I had thought he had given up drinking quite as heavily but I was too grateful to ask any questions. It burned down my throat, with a clarifying pain.

"Elizabeth Roche. She was here, with him."

"In Arcadia?"

"He brought her here," I said, sitting up and rearranging my skirts primly. As my fingertips brushed against the fabric, I heard the whispers tell me that once a Khazar princess slept with letters inscribed upon her eyelids that killed as soon as they were read. "Her trunk, I saw it in the room above the chapel. The shiny new initials on an old trunk. Those were her things, those were her scissors."

"That doesn't necessarily mean anything."

"No, but it does in this case. I can see the pattern," I said, almost laughing at calling the chaotic press of knowledge in my mind a pattern. It was too messy, too ragged, too empty. "And the translation. That was her too."

"The translation? You mean, the Enochian? The one we... found the other morning."

"Yes, because that was what she was here for. Roche didn't bring her here to simply be his helpmeet. He chose her for a reason. Her religious obsessions. He had a mad, mad plan." My mind was reeling through all the bewildering love letters I had read between them; it was all too clear now what he was looking for. "He half thought himself mad for trying it, but he couldn't not do it."

"What did he do?" There was fear in Laon's voice now.

"He needed someone for them to break. He knew given the right bait, they would tell the truth. Because nothing would hurt her like the truth, nothing would break her like the truth."

"The truth?" he echoed.

"The truth about themselves, about us, about God."

It was some time before I felt strong enough to walk back to my rooms. My mind was still reeling and I found myself murmuring fragmentary secrets even as they began to fade from my mind. The clarity with which I beheld it all was slowly eclipsed by the growing sense of the reality around me, as this more tangible world came again into focus.

"When first Roche started here, he met lots of fae. They wanted to talk to him," I said. "They weren't bored with missionaries yet, I suppose. And he learnt something then, through all the arguments and the baiting of him."

"He didn't really write about that."

"He did," I said. "But he hadn't made sense of it yet. He had realised something about their nature. And that was enough to set his plan into motion."

Though I did not see the moths, I could feel them at the edges of the room. The walls of empty books felt oppressively close. I was suddenly aware of how bitter each page tasted upon the spiralling, hollow tongue of each moth. I could hear the gentle thrumming of their ghostly wings.

"Three dozen and five," I said. "That was the number of letters before she would admit to being in love."

"She?"

"No, I don't mean that. The leaves on the tree outside the window... no, not that." I tried again to clear my mind. It was all falling away. "The colour of the nightingale's blood upon the whitest rose... No, not that either..."

I was shaking, and Laon held me for longer. He stroked my hair and I buried my face into his chest, the buttons of his shirt digging into my face. For all his loving attention, I knew his mind, too, was reeling.

"They shall call the nobles thereof to the kingdom, but none shall be there, and all her princes shall be nothing. And thorns shall come up in her palaces, nettles and brambles in the fortresses thereof: and it shall be a habitation of dragons, and a court for owls."

"Isaiah?" he said, brows furrowing as he recognised the passage.

I shook my head, though I wasn't meaning to contradict him. The patterns that had seemed so clear before were eluding me. I pulled away from his anchoring presence. He was too real. Unsteady though I was on my feet, I began pacing.

The library was tiny, little more than a box of a room, but it was enough. The steps made me dizzy, but that brought me closer to the strange clarity of the moths.

As I turned again, I saw Laon standing by the bookcases,

the moonlight upon him. I saw him more clearly now, the lines of worry etched onto his face and the deep look of horror in his eyes.

"It can't be true," he said, shaking his head. "Roche wouldn't, couldn't, surely..."

"He came because he wanted to know more about... everything," I said. "It makes sense, doesn't it? The Bible translation. The Tongue of Angels. Enochian Apocrypha. Those were the secrets he was chasing."

"But to drive his own wife mad." Laon spat out the words, flinging his hands as he spoke. "Good people don't do that. Good men don't do that."

"Perhaps–"

"He has to be a good man. He needs to be." He turned away. He took a deep, trembling breath. "He must be."

"You've never met him."

"But he's a missionary. He can't be..." He brought his hip flask to his lips, but it was empty, and he cast it to the floor with a growl of frustration. He was breathing very heavily.

"What I tell you is true, Laon."

"Because the moths say so?" The note of brittle mockery did little to hide how fragile he was.

I knew he didn't want to believe me. He needed Jacob Roche to have been a good man, for missionaries to be good people, because he fled here fearing himself to be anything but. He came here haunted by thoughts of his own sister and he needed the journey to redeem him.

"No, I... I can find proof," I said.

I cast my mind into the receding mass of whispering secrets. I had forgotten so much already. Who was the Queen of the Screech Owls? What was the secret that the Astrologer of Blood divulged at the beginning of time? What colour were the shoes of–

"Cathy?"

He was shaking me, his eyes hollow with worry.

"I'm still here," I said weakly.

I was lying, though. I was struggling to remember particulars from Roche's early journal. I tried to picture the pages before me, but instead I felt shudder through me each of the tiny steps taken by tiny feet as they crawled across the page, the letters vague and black before me, too large to read, too large to be of any sense. I remembered myself feasting on its secrets, drinking in the dark, dark ink.

The carriage ride to the castle, the picking of a name, the hiring of staff.

That was my answer: "The Salamander!"

"Are you alright, Cathy?" His hand was on my forehead; I was scalding to his touch. "You've got a fever."

"We need to find the Salamander," I said. "She said she knew Roche. So she must have been here. From the start."

"She doesn't answer to either of us."

"But she's real. She brings us food every mealtime and cleans the castle and clears the moors. She exists and that means she can be found."

"How do you mean to find her, then?"

"She cooks all our meals," I said. "So we should start with the kitchen."

The kitchen proved much harder to find than either of us could have guessed.

"There has to be a kitchen," said Laon. "Our food must come from somewhere."

"Perhaps it's like the library," I said.

"Perhaps, but that's no help in finding it."

"We need to think logically," I said, pacing in circles. Diogenes leaned into me, hoping to calm me, but I shooed the hound back to my brother. "Or illogically, given this place. But either way, a kitchen needs fuel."

"Does it when it's run by the fae?" he said, scratching the dog's black belly.

"That is a point, but I have seen a coal hole in the courtyard."

"A coal hole?"

"I thought I saw one at least. I mean, I've never seen anyone shovel coal into it, but I assume it joins up to where the coal is burnt."

I led him to the courtyard and, beating around the bushes, we happened upon the round metal hatch.

Rolling it back, we peered into the blackness beneath us. I threw a pebble inside and it seemed forever before we heard a clattering echo.

Mr Benjamin happened upon us, gardening shears in hand, and we explained to him our predicament.

"That is the coal cellar beneath," was all he could confirm.

Unable to find rope, we were knotting together bedsheets into a makeshift cord to climb down it.

Laon climbed down into the coal cellar first, the darkness swallowing him. I held my breath, hoping the cellar was not as ridiculously deep as it looked and trying to trust in our ridiculous rope of torn bedsheets. My eyes showed me nothing but blackness as I tried to make out what was beneath. Waiting, my heart was in my throat and thundering fear.

"Can Benjamin come with you?" asked the gnome in a very small voice.

"I thought you didn't like the Salamander." The rope was less taut now. Laon must have found some sort of bottom. I put my hand on the rope.

"No, I don't mean now."

"But I should—" I was about to tell him that I needed to go but I recognised the tone of his voice. I remembered it from the morning of the hunt. I quelled the wavering fear I felt at

Laon alone in the darkness below and turned my attention to Gethsemane's sole convert. I smiled as reassuringly as I knew how. "Tell me."

The gnome nodded solemnly. "Fear tells fear. The Reverend doesn't fear."

"He does." I glanced nervously at the black abyss at the doors of the coal cellar.

"You fear like me."

"But then you are also brave like me." I did not feel brave, but it was easy enough to say.

"What I ask is, when the Pale Queen summons, and you leave Gethsemane to the wilds within and take them the book…" Mr Benjamin hesitated before averting his gaze and saying, "I would not make a very good fisher of men. In the book, Jesus said to follow him and become one. I was a miner of azote. And now I'm gardener and groundskeep, none of that is fisherfolk."

"I don't understand."

"Or fishfolk," he added, cleaning his spectacles nervously.

"Are you asking to come too, Mr Benjamin?"

He did not answer directly, but instead said, "When I came here, I was looking for work. I didn't believe, but then I saw it. I saw faith. She brought it here with her sacrifice. I saw her and I knew."

"Do you mean Elizabeth Roche?"

"I can't say…"

"She was here. The three of you sang hymns together. Then she did something. It inspired you…"

He shook his head, lips pressed together and eyes screwed shut. "I cannot answer that. But when I thought I would win the martyr's crown, I was willing. I-I thought I could matter. I thought I could be like her. Prove. It all became very clear, and I could do it all without doing it all. And then I thought I would never matter…"

"You do, Mr Benjamin," I said.

"And now, this is just a longer road. Why should I fear a longer road?"

"It is hard in a different way."

"So, miss," said the gnome, quite determined now. "Will you bring Benjamin with you?"

"Of course."

Relief broke on Mr Benjamin's brown face and he smiled his many teeth at me. He threw up his cap in joy and he promised that he would be as good a follower as any of Christ's dozen.

And then, I hitched up my skirt and climbed down.

CHAPTER 39
The Bread at the Table

It is an Article of Faith in the Church of Rome, that in the blessed Eucharist the substance of the Bread and Wine is reduced to nothing, and that in its place succeeds the Body and Blood of CHRIST. The Protestants are much of another mind; and yet none of them denies altogether but that there is a conversion of the Bread into the Body, (and consequently the Wine into the Blood,) of CHRIST; for they know and acknowledge, that in the Sacrament, by virtue of the words and blessing of CHRIST, the condition, use, and office of the Bread is wholly changed, that is, of common and ordinary, it becomes our mystical and sacramental food; whereby, as they affirm and believe, the true Body of CHRIST is not only shadowed and figured, but also given indeed, and by worthy communicants truly received.

John Cosin, Bishop of Durham, Tract Twenty Seven: The History of Popish Transubstantiation; to which is opposed the Catholic Doctrine of Holy Scripture, the Ancient Fathers, and the Reformed Churches

The Body and Blood of Christ are not present there, after the manner of a body. Yet it would not be true to say, "This is mere bread"; for this would be to deny the Real Presence; and so the fathers deny, that it is any longer "mere bread". But it is true to say, "This is the Body of Christ". For this does not deny that it is bread as to its earthly substance; but speaks of it, as to its heavenly.

Edward Bouverie Pusey of the Oxford Movement,
THE REAL PRESENCE OF THE BODY AND BLOOD OF OUR LORD
JESUS CHRIST THE DOCTRINE
OF THE ENGLISH CHURCH

The descent felt endless.

My hands, the skin raw from the strain. I placed them on knot after knot upon the rope. My breath came out ragged and I feared the sweat on my palms would make me lose my grip.

The window of light receded and the darkness slowly swallowed me. I thought of all the times I had scrambled up and down trees as a child and how effortless it had been.

But I wasn't climbing into the unknown then.

"Cathy!" came Laon's voice. He was below and too far away.

I was too out of breath to reply.

For all the hitching up of my skirt, it had come undone. It was all a tangle, but I could only keep going. There was no way I could readjust my clothing.

My foot finally hit coal and I heard Laon shouting for me again. He scrambled towards me and I heard his gravelly steps. His arms wrapped around me in the darkness, and I breathed in the intoxicating scent of exertion.

He sat me onto the ground, and I leaned against his back.

"Catch your breath," he said. "There's a door there, but it's behind a mountain of coal. I can't get at the latch."

My eyes slowly adjusted to the dark and I could make out a

door outlined in light before us. The coal heaped high in front of it made it impossible to open until we moved it.

When I finally got my breath back, I told Laon of Mr Benjamin's decision.

"We don't know if we're going anywhere yet," he said, grimly.

"I know you think she can still refuse us."

"She can."

"We've done everything she wanted." That familiar note of desperation crept into my voice.

"Fae aren't…" he sighed heavily, and I could feel his shoulders shake behind mine. He reached a hand over to steady me as I was still leaning against him, and our hands tangled. I smiled at our closeness. "We can't predict what she'll do."

"Mr Benjamin called her the most human."

"Which isn't saying very much at all. No one really understands fae."

"I know you don't think much of the Paracelsian argument."

"It's not just that," he said. "There have been other theories. That they don't see themselves as people, but as parts of stories. That they play again and again the roles they were born to."

"Sounds very Calvinistic," I scoffed. "And predestination is very unfashionable these days."

Laon gave a chuckle at that. "I suppose we are all bound by the roles we are born to."

"*For by grace are ye saved through faith; and that not of yourselves.* And I quote that as a soulless changeling." I winked, though it was far too dark for him to see, and I leapt to my feet. "Shall we get started?"

With painstaking slowness, we moved the coal heaped in front of the door.

Crouching by the line of light at the door, I could make out the shape of the latch. Using the pin of my brooch, I clicked up the latch, and the door swung open.

For all that I was certain I had not dreamt her, it was still a shock to see the woman in black again.

She crouched in the middle of the vault of a kitchen, under the enormous overhanging hood of a fireplace. Behind her were an array of pothooks and chains. Banks of stoves with black cauldrons lined the walls.

The air was cold as the stone that surrounded us and smelt faintly of burnt bread. The rows of short windows high in the walls let in very little light.

The woman in black seemed to barely notice us as she snatched and growled like some strange animal. Her dress was torn, and the bandages trailing from her wrists were bloodier than before, soaked afresh, vivid red. Her hair, wild as a mane, hid her head and face from us.

A low, long keening came from her throat. Her entire form was wracked by her wordless sobbing.

"Elizabeth Roche?" Laon ventured, taking a hesitant step closer. He was clearly horrified to see anyone in such a state. "Betha? Is that you?"

She did look up at her name, but as she began rocking backward and forwards, she said in a singsong voice, "He was the Word that spoke it. He took the bread and broke it. He took the bread and broke it..."

It was that poem of Donne's again.

As she paced, she repeated the poem to herself like a mantra. We heard a clinking. Each step echoed, and it was then we saw that her feet were in shackles. She walked until the chain that was attached to the stove was pulled taut and she walked back again.

"Elizabeth Roche," Laon repeated. "I am here to help. I am—"

He didn't finish, though I could not tell if it was because he could not quite bear to say the truth or if it was because of how her head snapped up and looked straight at him. Her eyes were wild and searching. They seemed red in the faint candlelight, shot with blood.

"Who?" she said very sharply. "Who are you?"

Laon swallowed, his throat quivering. He met her gaze and spoke in his gentlest voice: "The new Reverend."

She laughed at that. "I tore him apart with my bare hands."

"Elizabeth Roche—"

She frowned, her features crumpling as she thought. "No, that's not right…"

"It's your name," I said, trying to soften my shaking voice. I felt my pulse roaring in my ears, and my own fear gnawed at my gut. "Is it not? You married a missionary. You came to be his helpmeet and he used you to learn things from the fae. They were cruel with their knowledge."

"Are you trapped here like I am?" she said, her eyes glancing to her chains.

"We're here to help you." I reached a hand out to her. "We'll look after you."

"The fire looks after me." She refused my hand, shaking her head profusely. She continued to pace, chains jangling. "The fire is good, though she's not real. Nothing here is really real."

"We're real," said Laon. "Very real."

Staring at him, she lunged towards Laon and placed her hands upon his face. Standing very close and on her toes, she felt all over his face the way our blind aunt used to see with her hands.

She clinked over to me and, standing far too close, she peered at me. I smelt blood when her hands were on my face. I saw the fine scratches upon her pallid skin and still healing scar upon her lip.

"I know you," she said. "I remember. I warned you. I warned you that nothing here is real. All puppets, smoke and shadows, illusions and follies…"

Her wild eyes fell upon the moth brooch which I was I wearing, the one Laon had bought me at the markets. Her eyes flickered back to meet mine and looked beseechingly at me.

She reached a blood-stained hand to grab at my brooch and tried to pull it from me.

"I'll give it to you, Elizabeth," I said, prying her cold fingers away and unpinning it from my dress. I wondered if I should unpick the lock of her shackles for her, but she seemed so eager it was perhaps best to let her try.

"Please, please," she said.

"You don't have to be trapped," I said as I placed the brooch in her shaking, open hands.

A wide grin split her face.

"Trapped," she laughed. "Cages and chains cannot hold me like this body does. I cannot leave. Flesh is heavy, soul is light. I wouldn't stay if I wasn't…" she looked again at our faces, quite surprised as though seeing us for the first time. "You don't know, do you?"

"Know what?" said Laon as he and I exchanged perplexed glances. We took an instinctive step towards one another and his hand caught mine.

"Don't you realise?" she shouted, her voice hoarse and at the edge of a scream. "You have no idea where I am. Where you are. Where we…" Her voice trailed off and she pressed the sharp of it onto her thumb and a dot of red blood bloomed.

"W-What do you mean?" stuttered Laon.

"How can you not know where you are? What this place is?" She laughed again, this time even more high pitched and keening. "Why do you think things are here the way they are? Why do you think the natural order simply doesn't work here? Why they have to paint their flowers and buy in weather?"

It was then that realisation dawned within me like a drop of black ink into clear water. The swirling black of that knowledge, smoking in the water, spreading. It was not the moths who spoke within me in their endless whispers, all that had was faded and forgotten. It was far more mundane knowledge falling into place.

The woman in black traced the bloodied finger on the exposed hollow of her throat, smearing the fresh blood upon it.

"Laon," I forced from my throat. I could barely breathe. "I know."

"You know?" he said, turning his gaze on me.

I nodded, my head and heart both heavy with the knowledge. My dry lips struggled to form the words.

The woman in black adjusted her grip on the brooch and pointed the pin directly at her own throat. She screamed the conclusion even as I mouthed it: "This is *hell*."

And then, we were engulfed in flames.

PART FOUR
Gehenna

CHAPTER 40
The Fire in the Kitchen

And there was war in heaven: Michael and his angels fought
against the dragon; and the dragon fought and his angels,
And prevailed not; neither was their place found any more
in heaven.

And the great dragon was cast out, that old serpent, called
the Devil, and Satan, which deceiveth the whole world: he
was cast out beyond the earth, and his angels were cast out
with him.

REVELATIONS 12:7-9

He is a vengeful God.

My first and dearest child had her legs torn from her, made
to grovel in the dirt and cursed to eat dust for the rest of her
days. That shadow of Mankind was named vessel of children
and punished with the pain and savagery of childbirth.

I am a merciful Queen.

The children that die as the price of that first Fall, I shall
replace. For the love that my child bore his, sinful it may be in
his eyes, I will love them both. I will bring her dolls of flesh to
save her from that pain.

Translated from Enochian by Rev Laon Helstone
and Catherine Helstone

The entire room was ablaze, an endless inferno. We were completely surrounded by leaping fire.

The woman in black was screaming and laughing all at once, her words incoherent.

My heart was clutched around my throat in fear. The most lurid depictions of hell were coming alive around me. No rational thought could dispel the leaping flames. We were cut off from the divine, and this was Arcadia's true face.

The bricks and the stone began to fuse, melting together in the heat. Liquid fire seemed to vein the vaulted ceiling and flow down golden rivers. I heard the flagstones beneath our feet crack and I wondered if the entire vault was a furnace.

"Cathy!" came Laon's panicked shout through the crackling of the fire.

He was not far from me, and we stumbled towards one another. Our fingers tangled, and I could feel his pulse against mine.

My eyes were watering, the tears streaming cold down my face.

Cold.

Laon thumbed the tears from my cheeks.

"The *geas*," he whispered. "It can't hurt us."

Despite the scarlet flames that filled my vision and roared in my ears, I felt no heat. My skin did not stripe with welts, and no unsettlingly delicious smell of burning flesh arose.

"Come out, Salamander!" he shouted, fiercely. "It can only be you."

The flames coalesced into a woman with a serpent's tale. She seemed to breathe in the flames until the room was just as it had been. Her face was the black knot of a candle's wick, framed by a high white collar and haloed in white fire that trailed into orange.

"There are others who know this trick," she said, her voice sounding like the crackling of flame.

"I... I suppose," said Laon. "But there aren't that many beings here."

"Well observed," she said, quite evenly. Her eyes were coal black and gleaming upon her wick-black face. She regarded us with a studied detachment before returning her gaze to the woman in black who had dropped my brooch.

The woman in black was a crumpled heap on the floor. She cradled her hand to her chest, cooing in pain.

"You were stubborn again," said the Salamander, pained accusation in her voice. I could see welts had sprung up where she had clung onto the brooch. Whatever protected her from the flames did not shield it as well. "You know you aren't allowed sharp things after that unpleasantness with the scissors and the pins. You should have let go sooner. You know my flames can't hurt you directly."

The woman in black looked up at the Salamander and snarled. Her face contorted in a look of animalistic rage as the fae crouched down beside her, skirt pooling around her like molten wax. The human pushed away the fae's attempts to look at her wounded hand.

"Bring me the box by the bread basket, won't you?" said the Salamander, her gentle eyes not leaving the woman in black. "And I do mean you, Cathy."

"Why do you have her imprisoned here?" demanded Laon. He was floundering, trying to gain some semblance of control of the situation.

"This is not a prison," said the Salamander, raising her voice. Darts of flame upon her skin sparked and ash-white scales spread from her fingertips down her arms until she was as I first saw her in the corridor after Laon's return. The scales seemed to contain her flames. "And your questions can wait a moment longer."

"You can't–" began Laon, but I laid my hand on his shoulder. He bit back his retort at the shake of my head, and

I obeyed the fae. We could be patient one moment longer, and the threat implicit in the Salamander's fiery entrance was not lost on me. The box reeked like a pharmacy; I did not need to unlatch it to know what it contained.

The Salamander was looking at the woman in black as though she were the only being in the world that mattered. She spoke words for the human woman alone, pleading, loving words until she opened her hand and showed the burn to the fae. Balm of some sort was smeared onto the burn and it was bandaged. The woman in black whimpered piteously and set her head down on the floor as the Salamander continued to murmur soothingly.

"This is Elizabeth Roche, known once as Betha Clay," said the Salamander, stroking the woman's brown hair. She cast us not a glance as she spoke. "Is she not beautiful as the truth? She came here with her husband, a heartless man, but he does see clearly, for he saw the beautiful fissures within her mind," said the Salamander. "You can probably pick it up now."

"What?"

"The brooch. And you should not have given it to her."

"I-I thought she was going to pick the lock..." I said as Laon retrieved the brooch and pinned it again to my dress. It was still warm to the touch.

"She is trying to kill herself," said the Salamander, her eyes still fixed upon the sleeping woman. "But I won't let her. Too lovely to die. I have failed a curious woman once. I won't fail another. I have been stopping her for some time now. But my eyes cannot be everywhere."

"You are keeping her prisoner here."

"The chains are to stop her from leaping from windows," said the Salamander. "And from hurting you, of course. She hungers."

Laon and I jumped at the whistling of a cast iron kettle at

the far end of the kitchen. Steam belted from its spout.

"I thought you might find a hot drink soothing." The Salamander rose with serpentine grace, balanced upon her coiling tail. "So, would not the two of you take a seat?"

We sat uneasily, exchanging a worried glance as the Salamander worked, slithering between kettle and cupboard. There was a practised efficiency to her actions, her hands darting and trailing fire. Her gaze kept flickering back to the sleeping Elizabeth Roche.

"Is there not milk?" I asked as the Salamander passed me a cup of sugared tea.

She blinked. "I thought you were a changeling."

"I am."

She remained silent for a while, her expression quite unreadable. The flames that were her hair crackled around her. Finally, she said, "Very well."

"I don't understand," I said.

"No, I misunderstood." She stirred the milk into the tea, looking at it with unusual intensity.

"You're stalling," said Laon.

"I need to choose my words with care," said the Salamander. "My tongue is even less free than my hands. Yours is not the only *geas*. There are promises at work here that are as old as time. I can only say so much."

"The Pale Queen's orders?"

"She loves her secrets, both keeping them and unveiling them. Most of them are not mine to tell."

"But you are still willing to speak?" I said. "You appeared to me before. You gave me answers in exchange for…"

"You were near the garden."

"I was. Elizabeth Roche was close, wasn't she?"

The Salamander nodded. "I weary of the Pale Queen's games and gardens. I have been in her web before. I loved then too, and that knowledge was also cursed. Some say there are many sorts of sins, but to me there is only one."

Laon salted his tea and mine.

"They told her things they would never tell Roche," the Salamander said, slowly, her flame tongue licking her lips between every word. "He was right about them. But he didn't realise that *the* truth they will break with is the truth of his own self. Mirrors are terrible *things*. Sometimes people can't stand their own reflections, when they see themselves. They'll do anything to not see themselves anymore."

"Are you saying Roche killed himself?"

"They..." She paused again. "They taught her, fed her secrets, tested her beautiful faith, like he thought they would."

"Who are they?"

The Salamander ignored Laon's question and continued her story. "Betha burned with faith. She wanted to prove God."

"How?"

The Salamander said nothing, sitting unnaturally still as her flames danced ever more feverishly upon her skin.

"Can you not say?" asked Laon.

I thought hard, trying to remember the passages I had read in the journal. The similarities in the hand that wrote of drinking poison and that of Elizabeth Roche was no coincidence after all.

"The poem she keeps reciting," I said, hands laced around my cup of milky tea. "Donne. About the Eucharist."

"I know it," said Laon.

"She wrote it in the journal as well. Over and over." My mind was churning over the details. "And in the other chapel. I found the scattered wafers. A scene of interrupted sacrament. But you tidied it, didn't you? Afterwards."

The Salamander winced to herself, but she nodded deeply and slowly.

"She took it, didn't she?"

She said nothing but met my eye with a steadiness that answered my question.

"So did Roche..." I said, my brow furrowing.

"They were trying to prove the presence of God," said Laon, uncorking his hip flask. "They were both enamoured of the Oxford Movement. Or rather, I knew Roche was, and I assume Elizabeth was too."

"How? This doesn't make sense..."

"The wafer." Laon took a long swig from his flask before barking out a single sharp, abrasive laugh. "They didn't salt it."

"Why?"

"She trusted. Trusted that there would be the Real Presence of the Saviour's body. Not mere bread, but the body of Christ. She trusted that was in the sight of God."

I had always assumed that Roche had somehow talked Mr Benjamin into converting but it suddenly all made sense. "It's her. When she took the sacrament without salt. That act of faith. She inspired Mr Benjamin. In his mind she was turning the gaze of God to hell."

"But it was still unsalted food. As you said yourself, Cathy," said Laon. "This is Hell. It's beyond the sight of God. Beyond his Light. As far removed from God and the light of Heaven as ever there could be."

"But Jesus descended into Hell and preached to the imprisoned souls, the damned and the forgotten..."

"Not *this* Hell."

I tried to imagine how that must have felt for Elizabeth Roche, to realise that she was now trapped in a literal Hell. I thought of the triptych in the chapel and how that must have taunted her, the Harrowing of Hell. For all its torments, the Hell of the damned knew the Lord's light. The blessed feet of the anointed saviour had for three days rested upon those shores and from there he saved human souls. "That's why she's trying to kill herself. To escape."

We stayed a while. The Salamander remained very quiet, neither confirming nor denying our story.

"I would like to speak with her," said Laon. "When she wakes up."

The Salamander bristled, flames rippling into blades down her back, but she allowed it.

Elizabeth Clay proved no more lucid upon first awakening. A low keening began simmering within her throat and she came to sob and wail. She fell upon the food that the Salamander brought her with an intense hunger and was licking the plates at its close.

Laon and I watched quite helpless as the Salamander comforted her.

"Elizabeth Clay," said Laon.

The human woman's face changed at the sound of her own name. Her eyes seemed to clear and she said, "It is I."

"We know your story."

"It's not complicated," she spat. "How hard is it to tell? How many words? Idiot boy, idiot girl. Too self-involved to see."

"We were misled."

"You didn't see for so long. But now you know. Once upon a time, Clay married a man so that he could tempt *Them* with my pretty, pretty mind to break. They like shattered things. So it is done is done is done. I tore him apart in my madness. It eats at me. Gnaws and gnaws. It eats me. Hollows me. Always hungry. Now I can die."

The Salamander was pacing around us, licks of flames coiling. "Suicide is the worst sin."

"It is mine to commit. I have done worse."

"You made me promise. I swore every oath I knew. By the lightbringer, by the nightmother, by the stones of this place…

I can't lose you, Elizabeth Clay."

"I need this to end. Please." She cast her beseeching eyes upon me. "Let me die."

For the first and last time, bells rang to announce the arrival of a guest at Gethsemane.

I bolted upright.

"The Pale Queen," said Laon. "She–"

I nodded. "We need to go."

"Please," whispered Elizabeth Clay. She blinked, and that clarity seemed to fade. "It cannot end. Would you not rather the sinner's home than the exile's hell?"

I looked upon her pathetic form and hardened my heart. I already had more blood on my hands than I cared to remember. I thought of Ariel and her red blood.

The Salamander enfolded Elizabeth Clay in her fiery embrace, cooing a lullaby to her as we ascended the steps.

CHAPTER 41
The Secrets in the Blood

He made Mankind in his own image, but that's a familiar story. He gave Mankind a voice, breathed His own breath into his creation's lungs like a soul, and that is also a familiar story.

But not all voices are gained that way. The Lightbringer won his differently. He watched Mankind and myself in the garden east of Eden and he seethed in jealousy. I was made alongside Mankind, a mirror to his soul, and he could not bear that Mankind had an equal. And as for Mankind, he could not love a sister the way he loved a daughter.

But the Lightbringer then, dragon and deceiver, he was but a shadow.

Perhaps I should not try to fathom Him. He's so used to talking to Himself by now no one would think that there were many of Him, so many faces, so many names. We're all born alone, a prisoner of our own skins, an island in our minds, a world of our own creating. Alone and incomplete, craving recognition from shadows of ourselves.

Lightbringer was cut free, cut out of the very mind that he was from. He carved himself from that madness, ripped voice and breath from his father in an act of war and spat as he left.

And I, I was cast out from the sight of God.

We huddled together, lost children of Elohim. It is better

to rule in hell than to serve in heaven. We are not the last to believe those words.

But were he and I hidden here in the hells beyond His knowledge, beyond the reach of His light, or did the Blind God simply turn away? We had to make our own world in that hollow darkness, far from the animating spark of the divine. He could set in motion an eternally changing world and force it to continue with his oppressive gaze. We did not have such scrutiny, such creation. Our patchwork world needed to be made piece by stolen piece.

Mankind demanded a new mate, one that was of his own flesh. Perhaps he, like his Creator, thought that that would stop betrayal, but he is simple and stupid. Those of one flesh are not of one mind and the shadows, well, did not the Lightbringer betray his master? Did not I abandon them both?

Translated from Enochian by Rev Laon Helstone
and Catherine Helstone

A flustered Mr Benjamin was opening the door to a gaunt stranger.

"Sorry, sorry," said Mr Benjamin. "A thousand apologies."

Mist swirling around the capes of his greatcoat, the pallid stranger towered over Mr Benjamin. He was drenched to the skin, though it wasn't raining outside. He regarded the gnome with a glowering face.

"Post," said the stranger.

"Give then," said the gnome.

"Not for your hands."

Mr Benjamin took a step back and allowed the fae to come into the grand foyer.

I recognised him as the coachman who had driven Miss

Davenport and myself to Gethsemane. His swollen eyes looked me up and down. The wet fabric of his collar clung to his neck, and he ran a finger between it and his skin to allow his wet gills to flare. "It's not for you either, miss."

"Who is it for, then?" I asked.

"Reverend Laon Helstone," he said, showing me the letter.

"I'll give it to him."

"His hands, not yours, miss."

Mr Benjamin went to fetch Laon, and I was left waiting with the coachman. I glanced over again at the letter in his hand and caught sight of the postmark.

"You took your time," I said, sharply. It was from months and months ago. It had been sent just after I had left London.

He gave a languid shrug. "Shouldn't trust shortcuts. Two true revelations and an epiphany took much, much longer than two painful memories and a daydream. It's your fault, really."

"I... I see."

"Distances don't work like they do where you were. In Arcadia it's about the journey, and I thought I'd count yours instead of mine. But you were slow. And should've made sure those revelations be true," he said. "Since fake ones don't count. They just loop me right round, you know? Gets me real lost."

"I don't think I know at all."

He scratched the tip of his flat, fishy slit of a nose with a webbed finger. "Knowin's important 'nd all. Best count the twists and turns. Don't want to get yourself lost."

Laon appeared and took the letter from the coachman, politely commending his good work. Mr Benjamin hovered behind, jittering nervously, gnawing his own bottom lip.

"Done is done." The fae tipped his hat and slouched off into the mist.

Laon read the letter in silence. His face was a mask when he put it down and asked, "Cathy, who sent you again?"

"Sent me?"

"From the Mission Society. The man you corresponded with."

"It was Joseph Hale," I said. "I still have his letters."

"This is from him," said Laon. "He... he claims otherwise."

"What do you mean?"

Laon passed me the letter, and with shaking hands I read it.

The Society has recently received correspondence from your sister, Catherine Helstone, who appears to be under the impression that we both approve of and are financing her passage to Arcadia. This is not the case. We could but surmise that someone has been writing to her using our name. We have no idea why anyone would attempt such, but it is possible that they are trying to bring disrepute to the Society's good name. We urge you to proceed with the utmost caution...

"I don't understand," I said, eyes passing over the passage again. "Why would anyone do that?"

"It can only be the fae."

"Who?"

"The mysterious *Them* that has the Salamander so hemmed in by obligations to, that she avoids us completely. The *Them* that makes it so that what she can say she has to half stutter. The *Them* that wrote the geas. Mab. Her brothers and sisters. The things that live in the Hell of exile."

"Geas aren't real. They're just tricks... it was in Roche's journal."

"But the Salamander," said Laon. "And we were protected by it from her fire."

"We were," I said, shuddering at the memory of the sea of fire.

"We..." murmured Laon. He had turned from me. Arms crossed, he drummed his fingers against his lip in thought. "Blood binds blood. Blood knows blood."

"Miss Davenport said that. She said that was why it protected me as well. Because–" I stopped.

And then all at once we both knew the terrible truth.

It shouldn't matter after everything that had already happened. I myself had mocked Laon for thinking that it did, when my hands still reeked of blood and the conversion of Arcadia hung in the balance.

"No... that can't be," I said, shaking my head. My voice was breaking and so was my heart. Fingers wove together and clasped at my mouth, I was trying to hold it all in, to hold it back. "There just must have been another geas to protect me. I mean, Miss Davenport was also the one who told me I was a changeling. And so she must just have not known. She said she worked it out, that she had realised, she saw that the Pale Queen knew and, and..."

"They brought you here for a reason," said Laon, a dark calm in his voice cutting through my panic. "Mirrors are terrible things. The Salamander said that. They are showing me my sin."

"No, that can't be," I said. I knew I should feel revulsion and I knew that I should hate myself for my own sins. I knew all that and I wanted to think that the churning in the pits of my stomach was that. A human horror at my own actions. "I'm a changeling."

"The two we met at the market, the ones who said we were like them."

"No." There was an acidic taste at the back of my throat, one I could not swallow away. Our love had been the last pure, real thing that I had clung to and it was slipping away.

"I said I wasn't, that we weren't like them. But this was what they meant."

"No," I repeated, more feebly this time, as weak as my resistance to him had ever been. Every kiss, every caress that had passed between us came to the fore of my mind, now tainted by new, old knowledge. It flooded my mind like the moths of the library.

"You're crying," he said.

My hands flew to my face. It was wet with tears and it smeared onto my hands. I looked at the mess with a detached wonder, breath broken and my heart a beating fist of pain in my chest.

"You never cry."

"I don't like you seeing me cry," I said.

"Changelings can't cry," he said. "I read that once. It's why the church used to say you should beat them, because they would laugh at the pain and shed no tears..."

"No." I dragged my tear-soaked sleeves across my face.

"And the tea, remember? The Salamander thought you didn't take it with milk."

"That's nonsense..." I snapped, even as I remembered how milk was meant to spoil near a changeling. It was why Miss Davenport always avoided milk with her tea.

"She was silent after. She wanted to tell us something."

"No, Laon, we – you and I – we can't be..." I finally looked up from my shaking hands.

Our eyes met.

I feared the horror I would see there, feared the revulsion that would be in his eyes, the visceral rejection. I feared him flinch forever after at my touch and the intolerable distance that would stretch out between us.

But his eyes were but black and unreadable in this light, cold and distant.

"I never wanted you to look at me like this," he said.

"Laon!" Tears were rolling sticky wet down my face. There was too much I wanted to say; it welled up inside me and

I choked on it all. My mouth was a grave of words, each thought dying there and it was their rot that I tasted, that filled me with gut-wrenching revulsion.

He laughed, threw his head back and just laughed. His wide shoulders shook with his senseless mirth until his eyes too were filled with tears.

"I thought you were an apparition to tempt me." His beautiful mouth twisted cruel. "I thought the mist spat you out to make me sin, to pull me down, to drag me to hell. I thought I could outrun myself, my own sins, my own sister. I thought–"

"Laon, no…" I wasn't sure what I was objecting to, but I wanted him to stop. I wanted myself to stop.

"But they did better than that."

I flung myself at him, covered his lips with mine. Tear-stained hands cupping his face, it was not a kiss so much as a hard, stubborn meeting of lips. It needed to stop. Everything needed to stop, to silence.

Gasping, he choked out, "You're my sister."

My cheeks were against his face and my tears were his. We were broken mirrors of one another.

"You're my sister," he said again.

He did not push me away.

CHAPTER 42
The Summons in the Night

But all in vain o'er young Ganora's breast,
Guarded by prayer, the demon whisper stole;
Sorrow, not sin disturb'd that tranquil rest;
Yet 'gan her teeth to grind and eyes to roll,
As troublous visions shook her sleeping soul;
And scalding drops of agony bedew'd
Her feverish brow more hot than burning coal.
Whom with malignant smile the fairy viewed
And through the unopen'd door her nightly track pursued.

Like as that evil dame whose sullen spell,
To love dire omen, and to love's delight,
(If all be sooth that ancient rabbins tell,)
With death and danger haunts the nuptial night,
Since Adam first her airy charms could slight;
Her Judah's daughters scare with thrilling cry,
Lilith! fell Lilith! from her viewless flight,
What time with flowers their jetty locks they tye,
And swell the midnight dance with amorous harmony.

Reginald Heber, "Morte D'Arthur: A Fragment",
The Life of Sir Reginald Heber, D. D., Lord Bishop
of Calcutta, by his Widow: With Selections from his
Correspondence, Unpublished Poems, & Private Papers

That night, I dreamt.

I saw Mab enthroned in brass, seeming young while the earth was old. The wheels of the great clock turned around her, each creaking click echoing in the vast space.

"Rather magnificent, isn't it?' she said. "So much more impressive than the chariots."

I knew myself to be in Pivot. This was where the clock of Arcadia was housed. From here did the pendulum sun stretch. For a moment I wondered if the wheels were simply measuring time or actually meting out it, creating it like everything else in this unnatural hellscape.

The Pale Queen was lost in thought for a moment, admiring the machinery around her. Her long, gold-tipped fingers played at her crimson lips.

My brother was by my side. He would not meet my gaze as he knelt.

"You should be kneeling too, Catherine Helstone," said the Pale Queen, turning her attention back to us. "Your brother has learnt. You are in my domain." .

"Am I really here?"

She only smiled, gold talons raking contemplatively on her throat. She leaned forward and looked expectantly at me.

I knelt.

"Brother and sister, side by side," she said, admiring us as though a portrait. Her appraising eyes looked upon us with an unwelcome pleasure. "Closer than you've ever been. It is good of you to finally leave the door open for me."

"O-open?" I stuttered.

"Yes, one door leads to the castle and another door leads to me. How else can I stealth into your dreams?"

I remembered the strangely vivid dreams of my brother in the Pale Queen's arms and of running with him through Arcadia. "That was you?"

"You were very diligent in keeping that door shut for some

reason. Which is really no fun at all." She heaved a sigh. "Still, it is only polite to thank me for your newfound closeness. Or have you not enjoyed my tricks?"

"Your tricks?" said Laon. "You mean–"

"My grand scheme." She made a gesture towards the clockwork that framed her throne. "The sins that I have set in motion, the gift that I have given you. Had I not summoned you to Arcadia, would you have seen these wonders? Had I not placed into my own home, remade for your pleasure, would you have realised your love?"

"So it was all you..." muttered Laon. There was little defiance left in him, only a dark despair.

"I paid for your passage, Cathy, and arranged for Miss Davenport to meet you. I lied to her and let her leap to conclusions. Use a bird to catch a bird, after all. And if I had not forbidden you to read Roche's journals, would you have read it? I made it all the sweeter for being forbidden fruit. I made you all the more curious."

"But why?" said Laon. His fists clenched, and I glimpsed that passion I so loved. I longed to lay a soothing hand upon him, but I remembered the truth and I tasted bitterness. "Do you simply delight in tormenting us?"

"Has it truly been a torment?" The Pale Queen threw back her head and laughed long, pealing notes. "Should you not thank me? You will never be scorned and replaced by a rib of his." She spat out the word *rib* with an almost incoherent disdain. "I have given you a new Eden, a new garden. Yours can be a perfect love."

I nodded, biting my tongue, not wanting to anger the gloating queen.

"You have petitioned me for some time." She smiled wide and indulgent. "Do you still wish to step foot into the heart of Elphane, Laon Helstone?"

He hesitated. He glanced over at me, that guilt heavy in

his eyes.

"I wish it still."

"Very well."

She turned to me and, smiling too wide, possessing a secret only she knew, she said, "I grant you my protection within the bounds of Arcadia. Everything the light of this pendulum sun can see, everything that it may shine upon, none of it can harm you and yours, Catherine Helstone. By the bringer of light, I promise you this and I bind this to your blood."

Chapter 43
The Road into Hell

I am come into my garden, my sister, my spouse: I have
gathered my myrrh with my spice; I have eaten my
honeycomb with my honey; I have drunk my wine with my
milk: eat, O friends; drink, yea, drink abundantly, O beloved.
I sleep, but my heart waketh: it is the voice of my
beloved that knocketh, saying, Open to me, my sister,
my love, my dove, my undefiled: for my head is filled
with dew, and my locks with the drops of the night.
I have put off my coat; how shall I put it on? I have washed
my feet; how shall I defile them?

SONG OF SOLOMON 5:1-3

It was that hazy twilight when I woke up. Laon was not
beside me, and I felt my want of him almost immediately so I
went looking for him.

Lantern in hand, I drifted through the castle, numb from
new knowledge: I was human. I was in love with my brother.
I was in hell.

And one of those thoughts would have broken me, but
here I was still standing.

The stone arches and vaulted ceilings of Gethsemane were a familiar sight. Roche could not have known, but its name was proving prophetic. Though perhaps he did think of himself as Christ within the garden, praying to his father and begging to be spared the cup of bitterness. The last sanctuary before the end.

There was more mercy in this castle's imperfect pretence than mockery. The Salamander had called it a love letter to humanity, a portrait drawn by someone too besotted to understand what they saw.

My brother was in his own, neglected rooms that had been empty of him for so long. His dog was a black, unhappy heap among the pale linens of his bed. He did not turn to greet me when I entered, and continued to work mechanically, packing away his things. There was no trace of lingering sentiment as he folded away the shirts I made him.

"So," I said. "You're leaving?"

He was silent.

I watched him for a while, folding away his clothes and placing them each in his trunk with a trembling stoicism.

"But the summons," I said. "The summons from Mab, or the Pale Queen, or Lilith or whatever her name is."

Laon flinched.

I swallowed, wavering. I knew what I wanted to say and I also knew too well that we were not the indefatigable pioneers that the Missionary Society would have chosen. We had not the purity of ambition, the strength of spirit, the firmness of faith. Our minds would cloud and our hopes would waver.

And yet, I wanted to go.

"What else can I do?" he said.

I crossed my arms as I watched him sit heavily on the bed. He crumpled, his face in his hands. The weight that I had seen him bear with such defiance and determination had finally crushed him. For all his previous weariness, he had dark currents of anger, of pride, of bitterness.

But no more.

"Please, Laon," I said.

"What do you want me to say?"

"I want you to acknowledge the summons," I said, hurling my own temper back at him. "It's what you and I have been working for. It's what you came here for. And Mr Benjamin, he needs this. He's packed and ready to go. You need to acknowledge this before you abandon it all."

"I have," he bit back. Diogenes gave a soft whine at the far side of room, as though sensing his master's distress. "I know."

"And?"

"You are my sister, Cathy. After what I've done, what we've done... I can't. I'm not worthy. Not worthy of you, of this," he said. "I should go home, where God can judge me. I've run away from my sins for long enough."

"But the summons–"

"It doesn't undo what we did," he said, bleakly. "Nothing can."

"Exactly!" I said. "They have already found the darkest corner of our souls and dredged from there the greatest sins. They have already stripped us bare and made us face our own worst selves. Face each other's. They cannot do more."

He was staring at his agitating hands, as he turned them over and over. His wide palms and long, blunt fingers. He had beautiful hands.

"Please, Laon," I said. "Brother, look at me."

He turned to me.

Despite his tempestuous thoughts, his blue eyes were still pools, and I saw myself therein. He too must have seen himself in mine, twinned in recursive reflection, like a metaphysical poem. I tried then to believe myself as strong and as wise as he saw me to be, just as I wanted him to see himself the way

I saw him. I needed that strength, that wisdom.

The candle flickered, and so did our reflections.

Laon looked away.

I took a deep breath and steeled myself.

"What more can they do to us?" I said. "What more could they tempt us with?"

He laughed, long and hollow, as he shook his head. He wiped tears from his eyes and, brushing echoing ones from mine, he said, "Nothing, sister. There is nothing more they can do."

"We don't have to go back." I laid my hand on his shoulder.

He placed his hand over mine.

"There is redemption yet, brother."

"But I don't know how to repent, sister."

"Laon–"

"I just... I know what we did, blood of my blood and flesh of my flesh." He laughed again, shaking his head. His hand tightened over mine and I did not want him to let go. "For redemption, there need first be repentance."

"We will teach each other," I said. "There is a world that has been deaf to the Word of God, hidden from His eyes and exiled from His love. It is, in the words of Elizabeth Clay, an unharrowed hell."

"What use is God to the fae?"

"They have souls, Laon. We have read as much. By their mother's lineage, by right of creation. They may not be human souls as they are not descended from Adam – or Mankind, as he may be termed – but they are souls nonetheless."

"You think we can bring it to them?"

"I trust."

"The sinners that we are?" He turned his eyes skyward for all that there was no heaven there.

"There is no greater missionary than the mother tongue. We now speak the language of sin. We can speak to them better than anyone else can."

"You know that I didn't come here for saintly reasons."

"Saints have further to fall. This place breaks saints. But you and I," I gave a grim smile, "we have nothing to fear."

"Because there is nothing more they can do." He held my hand now painfully tight and he clasped it to himself like a promise. Hope glimmered in his eyes and a tired, familiar smile crossed his lips. "What do you think's in hell then?"

"I read that Dante thinks the second circle's lust."

"What would he know?"

"It was in Father's encyclopaedia, and that has to be correct," I said, quite primly.

Laon laughed at that, and this time there was less bitterness and more joy. I joined him, and though my own laughter sounded stilted, I knew it would come easier, with time.

"Maybe it's going to be nothing but fish," said Laon. "And sea whales."

"Nothing to fear there then."

"Either way," said Laon, beaming now. I returned the smile and I knew what he was going to say next. "We should find out."

Acknowledgments

This book owes a huge debt of words to the Brontës, to the Romantics, and to the various Victorian writers whose texts I have quoted and misquoted in this novel: Jacob Tomlin, William Dean, Fleming H Revell, George Smith, Clarke Abel, Reginald Heber, Hudson Taylor, and George Young, to name a few.

Thank you to everyone at Angry Robot, human and otherwise, named and unnamed, but especially: Marc for believing in me, Penny for guiding me through rough public-facing waters, Phil for that precision edit, and Claire for picking up after my typos.

I'm unspeakably grateful for the love and support of my earliest readers, especially Dom, Sam and Will who have endured multiple fragment-laden drafts. I love you all and you're brilliant.

Further thanks for use of eyeballs, ideas and encouragement: Becca for our many conversations about changelings; Carrie for sharing my love of missionaries and dragging me to Macau with her; Gareth for a truly magical friendship; Lor for sharing with me the best of things; Sean for that bright ray on a very dark day; Tom for cake wizardry and divine inspiration; Veljko for moths and the Mottled King; Zaak for Hobbs of Malmsbury; and Zoë for putting up with my pretentiousness since basically forever.

Thank you to my mother for encouraging my "wild imagination" (her words) and to my father for correcting my stories with snarky red pen even when I was tiny (I have unearthed archaeological proof).

To my family who have promised to read this regardless of contents, I'm very sorry you had to endure this book. Thank you. I promise the next one will be less creepy. And that there will be a next one.

Finally, a heartfelt thank you to Graham Stark and Adam Savidan of the Sidewalk Slam podcast. I've still not managed to watch any wrestling but your voices are very soothing.

About the Author

Jeannette Ng is originally from Hong Kong but now lives in Durham, England. Her MA in Medieval and Renaissance Studies fed into an interest in medieval and missionary theology, which in turn spawned her love for writing gothic fantasy with a theological twist. She runs live roleplay games and is active within the costuming community, running a popular blog. In 2019 she won the Sydney J. Bounds Award for Best Newcomer at the British Fantasy Awards, and the John W. Campbell Award for Best New Writer, since renamed the Astounding Award.

medium.com/@nettlefish • *twitter.com/jeannette_ng*

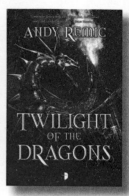

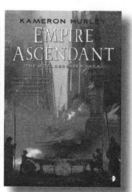

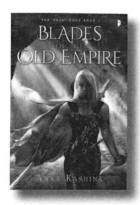